UpforHir

Christina Berry

Black Rose Writing | Texas

ISBN: 978-1-68433-632-6
PUBLISHED BY BLACK ROSE WRITING
www.blackrosewriting.com

Printed in the United States of America
Suggested Retail Price (SRP) $19.95

Up for Air is printed in Georgia Pro

*As a planet-friendly publisher, Black Rose Writing does its best to eliminate unnecessary waste to reduce paper usage and energy costs, while never compromising the reading experience. As a result, the final word count vs. page count may not meet common expectations.

To Errek,
I sure do love you.

Up for Air

The Fall

1—Wednesday October 13, 2004

Am I happy? How would I know? What is the measure of happiness?

Up until yesterday, the 365th day of my 28th year, I'd naively thought I was happy, or at least not *unhappy*. Like happiness were binary, a light switch you flip on or off—light, dark; happy, sad. Or like one of those creepy clowns who moves his hand across his face as he shifts his expression from one extreme to the other—psycho smile, freaky frown. As if anything in the human condition could be so simple.

Well, there's death, I guess. Death is pretty simple. You can't get much more binary than that—1, 0; alive, dead.

Regardless of what I used to think, my reality is now forever changed, a birthday present I can't return. Here I sit, on the dawn of my 29th year, at the end of the front row of pews in this quaint little church in this quaint little town, tears streaming down my cheeks, wondering how to quantify my happiness—or rather my unhappiness. It's making me miserable, this little epiphany of mine.

No, *little* is the wrong word. There is nothing little about my revelation. This isn't an idea illuminated by a single incandescent bulb flickering over my head. This dawning irradiates with the flash burn of a nuclear bomb.

I look up, half-expecting to see a mushroom cloud filling the chapel with the pulverized debris of my former notions. But there's nothing there, only a clear view of the honey-toned oak beams that hold up the roof, and the vaulted tops of the massive stained-glass windows which flank the parishioners with cheery, colorful mosaics forming various tableaus—Jesus, a lamb, a dove, a star.

At my side, Greg glances up, too, as if to catch a glimpse of whatever it is that's captured my attention. When he sees nothing special, he frowns at me and returns his attention to the pastor at the front of the church.

I sniffle again, and blow my nose into the handkerchief Greg's father gave me at the beginning of the service. The wet, snotty sound echoes up to the steeple and bounces against the towering windows, nearly drowning out the voice of Pastor Rick.

I glance at the pastor and catch a glimpse of Grandpa Chuck behind him, his face just visible above the edge of the casket. Speaking of death and its binary morbidity, there lies the reason we are all here today. Charles Elton Hendricks III is dead.

I quickly look away, down at the handkerchief fisted tightly in my lap, smears of black where my mascara has marred the white linen. I can't bear to see him like that. He looks so strange. The mortician has done a good job putting a bit of color in his cheeks to make him look almost alive, just resting. But with his hair combed over and dressed in a light blue suit, he looks like someone else. He looks like the 'used car salesman' version of himself.

Grandpa Chuck was a rough and rugged old man, whose entire wardrobe consisted of denim overalls and white t-shirts. He had a half-naked woman tattooed on his arm, and if you asked him to, he would make her wiggle while he sang an Elvis tune. He was missing the tips of two fingers on his left hand, but could still play a mean guitar; even played with Bill Monroe a few times. He was a moonshiner back in his youth, a train-hopping hobo for a time, and spent more than a few nights in jail. He had lived a full, long life—a life of bluster, moxy and gusto; a life filled with all the best stories. Grandpa Chuck was no used car salesman.

Of all Grandpa Chuck's stories, my favorites were the ones about Millie. His eyes would sparkle and his smile would stretch wide across his wrinkled face as he'd reminisce about the night he first laid eyes on her.

There was never any doubt in his mind; Millie was his love, his one and only for the seventy-one years they got to spend together. She took a little convincing, but soon she was just as smitten and their love never wavered. They were still in love three days ago when Millie sat beside Grandpa Chuck's hospice bed, squeezing his frail fingers and promising that she would see him again soon.

With that thought, tears start to well in my eyes...again. Shit. I'm crying...again.

Sniff.

At my left, Greg squeezes my hand and leans close to whisper in my ear. His tone is soothing yet vexed as he asks if I'm okay. It's a dumb question. Do I look okay? I nearly laugh. Jesus, who could laugh at a time like this?

Funny, asking Jesus dumb, rhetorical questions while sitting in a church. That thought nearly makes me giggle even more. I cover my mouth with my fist, swallowing the impulse.

Wanting to quell his concern, I try to cry more demurely, but it's impossible. I'm an ugly crier, always have been. As far back as I can remember, bawling over skinned knees and playground bullies, my face would puff up and my cheeks would stain with blotches of bright red, like a half-ripened tomato. It's never been a pretty sight. Without a mirror to check, I can only imagine what I look like right now in my neatly-pressed black dress, my long dark hair twisted into a knot at the nape of my neck, my makeup tidy and understated, except for the raccoon bandit mask of smeared mascara and drippy, bloodshot eyes.

The congregation is singing now, Amazing Grace, but I can't find my voice. I stare down at the pages of the Hymnal that Greg holds on his lap, my vision swimming in tears. I sniff again and blow my nose, then look up at my husband.

Greg isn't singing either. Sitting with his head lowered, he stares blankly at the song book's tablature. He's as handsome as ever, his classic-Hollywood looks complimented by the smooth lines of his gray suit, his jaw cleanly shaven and his honey-brown hair combed back. But his eyes, normally a warm whiskey color, look steel gray today.

He suppresses a yawn with the back of his hand, and I exhale with relief. That's all it is, exhaustion. Of course he's exhausted. When he received the call about his grandfather's stroke, we'd made the trip from Austin to this corner of Appalachia in one night. We'd wanted a chance to say our goodbyes before Grandpa Chuck quietly passed away three days later. The last week has taken a toll on us all, emotionally and physically.

I reach for Greg's hand and squeeze. He gives me a toothless smile before returning his attention to the song book.

I glance past him to Jake, our best friend, who looks even more dark and intimidating than usual, decked out in all black, his posture ramrod straight, his hands clasped tightly in his lap, and his long jet black hair plaited into two tight braids that hang down his chest. He sings the hymn lyrics from memory, and despite his imposing physical presence and perpetual scowl, his powerful baritone voice is a welcome, soothing comfort. I listen for a moment before looking back down at the hymnal in Greg's lap, only now noticing that it's open to the wrong song.

• • •

Outside, Greg, Jake, Greg's brother Matt, and a myriad of Hendricks cousins carry the cherry coffin to a spot beneath the wide branches of a hickory tree. The hole is already dug, and at the head of it sits a wide granite tombstone emblazoned with the name 'Hendricks' on the back. On the front, Grandma and Grandpa Hendricks's names and birthdates are already etched into the stone. Soon, Grandpa Chuck's death date will be added beside a void beneath Grandma Millie's information, a placeholder marking the time until she joins her husband in eternal slumber.

The morbid inevitability of it sends a cold shiver through me. I look away, distracting myself with the details of the blue pop-up tent set off to the side, three rows of plastic chairs laid out for family to sit. But no one is sitting except for Millie. Everyone else seems more interested in stretching their legs as they get in a smoke before the start of the graveside service.

In her black wool dress and wide-brimmed hat, Millie looks tiny, so frail and delicate. For a moment I think how odd it looks to see her sitting alone. If Grandpa Chuck were here, he would have his lanky arm draped over her shoulders, comforting her sorrow away. Then again, if Grandpa Chuck were here, she would feel no sorrow.

I can't stand the thought of her alone, so I join her. Leaving Greg and Jake behind, I make my way up the aisle along the edge of the tent and sit beside her. Millie flashes me a quick smile. Then we both stare at the cherry casket surrounded by sprays of fall floral arrangements.

After a moment, Millie quietly laments, "This morning, I read an article in the newspaper that he would have found interesting. I wanted to tell him about it, and then I remembered that he's not with me anymore." She pauses. "I miss him."

Fresh tears prick my eyes and I reach over to squeeze Millie's hand in mine. It seems like such a small gesture, given the wound she's just exposed to me, but she places her other palm over my fingers and squeezes in kind. I glance at her and she smiles at me.

"Ari, it's your birthday today, isn't it?" Millie asks.

I grin halfheartedly and nod, almost embarrassed to admit it.

"How old are you now?"

"I'm twenty-nine."

"Well, goodness. So young, and with so much time ahead of you." She leans in, as if to tell me a great secret. "Don't waste a moment of it, honey. It moves so fast, faster than you realize. Cherish the time you have and the people you love."

I force a grin for Millie's sake and try to swallow the lump in my throat. It takes everything in me not to start bawling again. I glance up at Greg, the man I've spent twelve years of my life with, and try to imagine the next sixty.

I furrow my brow with concentration just as Greg glances my way. He returns my anxious expression in kind, then focuses his attention past me, just over my shoulder. I watch him a moment longer before I too look past my husband to the valley beyond.

Fall leaves fill the landscape with fiery shades of orange, yellow, and red. Despite the cold of the day, the surrounding mountains are ablaze with ardent color, like an inferno stretching down the hillsides to the valley below, ready to engulf us all in flames.

I shiver.

• • •

In my old bathrobe, I curl up on the bed to look out the window. As I lazily stare, my eyes drift out of focus until the moving shapes of clouds and wavering colors of leaves blur into an abstraction.

Vaguely, I note the sound of the front door closing with a heavy bang. Greg's voice echoes as he calls to me and my parents. He's greeted with only silence. I clear my throat as if to answer, but there's no need.

Greg comes to find me in my old room. Closing the door behind him, he sits on the edge of the bed and stares down at his shoes for a long moment, alone with his thoughts.

The silence between us is unnerving, I speak just to fill the space. "My parents went to take a casserole to your grandma."

Greg nods, but doesn't speak; doesn't even look at me. I reach my hand over and lay it on his thigh.

"Greg, I'm sorry about your grandpa. And I'm sorry I was so weepy. I'm not sure what came over me."

Greg just shrugs, still staring down at the plush carpet at his feet. I watch him, urging him with a silent plea: *say something, say anything; please, just look at me.*

The telepathy works. Greg turns and looks down at me. He gives me no smile, nor a frown. He is blank, the lines of his face rigid and cold, like marble—a beautiful statue. With a tilt of his body, he leans closer to me, bracing his weight on one hand while he uses the other to play with a tendril of my hair, then tucks it behind my ear.

Slowly he leans down and kisses me. It's gentle at first, a delicate brush of his lips over mine, but soon his movements become harder, more urgent and insistent. He twists around until he's stretched out beside me, and then on top of me, his weight pressing me deep into the springy old mattress. I grunt as the air whooshes out of my lungs.

He moves fast. Tugging at my robe belt to try to free me from it, but his maneuvers only tighten the terry cloth rope. He settles for pushing the front flaps aside, and fixes his mouth to one of my breasts.

"What if my parents come home?" I can't remember the last time we had sex in my old bedroom. Probably before we were married. The idea excites me almost as much as it excited me the first time, on the night of my eighteenth birthday when I snuck him through my window and he took my virginity.

"We'll be quiet," he says with a rough edge to his words. "Please, Ari, I need you right now."

At my nod, he fumbles with the zipper on his pants, and enters me with a sharp thrust. I gasp at the sudden fullness, wince at the pinch of pain, but soon my body relaxes, excites. I arch my back as I brace one palm against the headboard and I use the other to grab at him, my nails pressing sharp through the fabric of his slacks, spurring him on. With each stride, his tempo increases until he's grunting as he moves hard and deep into me. I can't help but come. I'm easy like that. I freeze and spasm and bite his neck to quiet my cries, and my climax triggers his. He lets out a groan, then, spent, collapses on top of me.

Lying beneath my husband on my childhood bed, his weight pressing down on me, I can't help but cry. I'm easy like that. Greg pushes up onto an elbow, staring down at me in panic, worried he's hurt me in some way. The stricken look on his face saddens me even more. Tears slip from the corners of my eyes as I lean up and gently kiss him. Relieved, he drops to my side and gathers me in his arms, hugging me close to his chest.

Whatever dam existed within me washes away, and I am overcome with tears. I sob uncontrollably, sometimes moaning loudly, and other times, just heaving and shaking with silent convulsions. Greg tenderly strokes my hair and whispers soothing sounds into my ear, patiently letting me cry until I run dry. Then we lie together in silence.

I'm about to drift off to sleep when Greg curses. "It's the thirteenth. I forgot your birthday."

"Your grandpa died; you're excused."

"I didn't even get you flowers."

Trying to lighten the mood, I point to the assortment of funeral floral arrangements covering every inch of my old desk. Millie had insisted I take a few flowers with me, then loaded me up like a pack mule. "I have plenty of flowers."

Greg barks out a half-hearted laugh. "Well, I'm still sorry."

I give him a toothless grin before I close my eyes, lay my cheek on his chest, and drift off to sleep, finally drawing this birth and death day to a close.

2–Saturday November 13, 2004

I have never been a sad person. But have I ever truly been a happy person? If I am a happy person, wouldn't I know? But how do you know something like that? What are the signs, the symptoms of happiness?

These are the cold, cruel thoughts that ricochet through my head, leaving Swiss cheese holes and torn bits of gray matter in their wake. This is the fallout from my little epiphany bomb, dropped that sad day as I stared at the lifeless face of Greg's grandfather.

On the dawn of my 29th year, my eyes were opened to the revelation of my own eventual demise, my finite mortality reflected back at me from the grave. And those thoughts were not buried alongside Charles Elton Hendricks III. They infected me, they infect me still—growing, feeding, eating away at me like a necrotic wound.

Frustratingly, the thoughts that ping and pierce my mind like little bits of shrapnel, are neither helpful nor actionable. They come at me in the form of useless bumper sticker sentiments like:

Life is short. Live it.

Are you Carpeing your Diem?

Don't worry, be happy.

But I am happy, aren't I? I mean, I'm pretty sure I'm not *unhappy*. Doesn't that count for something?

I shake my head as I turn the corner and walk further through the neighborhood of mid-century ranch-style homes. On my left, I spot the remains of some poor, dead creature flattened in the middle of the road. I hold my breath, not wanting to breathe in the carrion scent that calls to the buzzards circling above. Thankful that I have my dreary thoughts to distract me from the morbid tableau, I quicken my pace until I'm far enough away not to smell the rot when I take a deep breath of the fresh air.

If happiness is not binary, not black and white but rather a spectrum of gray, then what shade of gray am I? Am I charcoal, gunmetal, slate? Maybe my happiness is taupe. Is taupe even a shade of gray, or is it more of a beige? Hell, maybe my shade of happiness is beige. *For fuck's sake, please don't let my happiness be beige.*

If I could choose, I'd opt for a heather-gray sort of happiness, flecks of light and dark blending together to form my own personal shade of middle of the road. But what is that emotion, the one in the middle? When you're neither overwhelmed with joy, nor drowning in sorrow, do you simply wallow in some muddy shade of numbness?

Talk about wallowing. I roll my eyes at my whiny inner monologue as I cross a footbridge over the creek and move deeper into the small city park nestled within the urban neighborhood.

Clearly, I'm in a funk. This is nothing new. It always happens when Greg goes away on business. I suck at being alone. It's a character flaw. Alone, I tend to retreat into my head, and that's only ever a good thing when I'm writing. This time, though, seems worse than usual. Just one week into Greg's two-week stint in Singapore, and I'm already going on daily hours-long walks so I don't suffocate as the walls close in on me.

I hug my jacket closed as I approach a bench near the edge of the water. It's Beatrice and Samuel Dickson's bench, dedicated in 2001, or so the little brass plaque screwed to the green metal slats reads. Settling onto Bea and Sam's bench, I let the quiet babble of the brook soothe my addled mind.

After a moment's repose, I pull my notebook out of my satchel, click my pen into action, and hover the tip over the page. Nothing comes. The black ballpoint leaves little tick marks on the paper, but no words make their way there. After too long waiting for inspiration to strike, I give up and stuff it all back into my bag, then hug my knees to my chest as I take in the scenery.

It's too late in the year for most of the birds, but the crisp breeze blowing through the naked branches of the trees is enough white noise to distract me from my dreary state of mind. And down on the leaf-strewn ground, a ginger-toned squirrel busies himself with the task of finding and burying pecans for foraging later in the season.

There's a shrill whistle, and the squirrel scurries up a tree. I yelp and cover my head as I twist around to identify the source of the sound.

Jake.

Shielding his eyes from the glare of the afternoon sun, He stares up the tree where the squirrel fled. With his long hair down past his shoulders and wearing his old leather jacket over a ratty Megadeth t-shirt, Jake looks much like he did when I first met him over a decade ago. Still tall, dark, and handsome, with a metalhead ensemble that makes him look mid-twenties rather than his actual age of 32.

"Did you see the testicles on that big, brassy son of a bitch?"

"Huh?"

Not waiting for an actual answer, Jake braces his hand on the bench, then swings his legs over the back and flops onto the seat beside me with a harrumph. He stretches his legs and lights a cigarette, offering me a drag, as he always does. I refuse, as I always do.

"That squirrel's balls were *huge*. Like, a third of his overall body weight. Can you imagine if humans lugged around *cajones* like that? It'd be like sporting a pair of watermelon in my Fruit of the Looms."

I blink and Jake chuckles, succeeding once more at his favorite pastime, the *Stun-Ari-Speechless* game.

"Well," Jake blows a puff of smoke into the wind, "how's it hangin'?"

The sound I make resembles "meh," which earns me a cockeyed scowl from Jake.

"I'm gonna need more words outta you, sis, unless you want me to do all the talking." He pauses to give me a window to speak, which he promptly closes. "Did you know that Brass Balls up the tree there has a bone in his penis. A legit 'boner,' the lucky little fucker." Another brief pause for a puff of smoke. "Actually, most mammals have a *baculum*—that's the Latin name for penis bone. Humans and spider monkeys are the only primates who don't—"

"Are you happy?"

"—have a boner bone."

Jake stares at me—this time he's the one who's stunned speechless—and I stare back at him, waiting for an answer.

"Happy?" He shrugs. "Sure."

"How do you know?"

Jake cocks his head to the side to give me a proper scowl. "The fuck are you talking about?"

"How do you know that you're happy? It's a simple question." I hug my legs tighter to my chest and rest my chin on my knees, watching him as he considers his answer.

And consider it, he does, furrowing his brow as he takes a long drag on his cigarette. After a moment, he offers, "I don't know, I mean, I've got great friends, a pretty decent band, I can pay my rent each month, I've got my health..." After a long exhale, he cocks an eyebrow and adds, "Plus, I'm ridiculously good looking, practically drowning in eager pussy, and I've got a girlfriend who can suck the chrome off a trailer hitch. Happy doesn't begin to cover it, darlin', I'm fuckin' ecstatic."

I roll my eyes. "Deep thoughts with Jake Sixkiller. I should have known better."

Jake extinguishes his smoke on the sole of his boot, and turns to face me, assuming the thoughtful pose of a therapist on the clock, "What's brought all this up, little sis?"

I stutter and stammer as I try to explain, "I don't think I'm very happy. But I don't think I'm unhappy either. I think I'm...neither...which is what scares me. It's like I'm just sort of existing without feeling, like I'm numb. Which seems like utter bullshit, right? I mean, I listen to your list and I nod and I say to myself, 'yep, yep, uh huh, me too.' I have a great family. I have Greg. I have you. I have a roof over my head and I don't have to work some shit job to pay for it. I have my health. I have...plenty. So why am I not, you know, more...happy?"

"Maybe it's PMS? You know, sometimes you get a tad bit emotional, and—"

"One more word and I swear I'll punch you in your goddamn squirrel sac, Jacob Mitchell Sixkiller. I mean it."

Jake just smirks.

"I think I'm going through a mid-life crisis."

"Twenty-nine is only mid-life if you plan to die by 60, little sis. Don't get ahead of yourself."

"Semantics. My point is, I'm going through a...thing. I've been taking stock, and while I have all these things in my life that should make me happy, all I can seem to focus on are the things that are missing."

Jake goes bug eyed and his posture snaps ramrod straight as he gawps at me. "Holy fucking shit, Ari, are you talking about babies? Is that what this is about?"

I shake my head decisively. No, this is not about babies. In fact, in the month since the funeral, as I've assessed my wants and needs, the thought of having a child didn't even occur to me. I've never once felt the tick of my biological clock. And I'm fairly certain that children are not the thing which is missing in my life. But, it's telling that this was the first conclusion Jake jumped to. At 29, I'm supposed to want kids, aren't I? That's the norm, that's the life path most taken, but here I go through the bramble and bushes off to the far left, wanting not babies, but—

"Then what is it that's missing? What are we talking about here?" Jake asks.

In that moment, I want to tell him everything. I look into his warm eyes and I see my best friend and closest confidant, the person I've shared just about everything with over the last decade. I want to stare him straight in the eyes, not flinching or stammering as I open my mouth and speak the truth of what I'm feeling: *I want to live. I want to breathe free. I want to explore my limits and try new things. I want to see and taste and smell and touch the world around me.* I catch my breath, the excitement bubbling through me, even though I'm only saying these words in my head. With new air in my lungs, I raise my imaginary voice even louder as I boldly declare: *I want to fuck and suck and scream and come. I want to travel the world and dance naked in the rain and howl at the moon. I want to love and lust and laugh, I want to hurt and scorn and cry. I want to feel...everything.*

Shit, I think I'm going to cry again. I look down at my boots and tug at the laces, tying them into double knots.

Jake clasps my fists in his. "What's going on? What aren't you saying?"

I panic. What can I say? I can't tell him any of this. Every time I open my mouth to speak the truth, I see a flash of images: Greg's face on the day we met, his smile on the day we married, the look he gives me when he makes love to me, the way he kisses me before he leaves for his long trips.

Everything I'm feeling now is a betrayal of him. Doesn't the mere fact that I want more than what I have suggest that what I have is insufficient, that Greg is not enough? I snap my lips shut like a child about to cross her heart and throw away the key which will unlock all her secrets. There is no way I can voice any of these thoughts or desires. In fact, I've already said too much. Jake isn't just my best friend, he's Greg's as well. The two of them have been practically inseparable since they were fourteen years old. What sort of nonsense was I thinking when I called Jake and asked him to meet me, explaining that I needed to talk. I can't talk to him about any of this.

"Ari Beth, babe, talk to me."

I can't bear the look in his eyes, such concern, so I open my mouth, stammering vaguely, "I don't know, I guess I just want...new experiences."

"Experiences?"

"Yeah." I want to end it there, but I know there is no way Jake will leave this alone. So I expound with ambiguity. "Don't you ever feel like you've missed out? Like you took a wrong turn somewhere and now you're miles away from where you want to be, and you've had your face stuck in a map the whole time, so you haven't even been watching the scenery as you've gone by."

Jake reaches his hand up to feel my forehead for a fever.

I chuckle at the gesture. "I sound crazy, don't I?"

Jake holds up his fingers a pinch apart to illustrate that, *yes, I do sound a little bit crazy.* But, back on topic, he gives me a shrug and admits, "I'm sorry, little sis, but I don't really know what you're talking about."

Of course he doesn't. I'm talking to a man who has never said "no thanks." Jake is a marvel to me, always has been. Fearing nothing, he will try anything at least once. We are opposites in that way: him guided by curiosity and a live-fast-die-young approach to life, and me ruled by fear. Since the death of his family when he was just a kid, Jake's thrown caution to the wind, living life in the moment, fully aware that it could end at any time.

I'm vaguely aware of the same thing, so why am I so reserved? Throw caution to the wind? What a joke. I wrap myself in caution, like it's a fuzzy blanket on a cold night. All my life, I've taken the safe road, the path of least resistance. And where has it gotten me—chafed and smothered by the boundaries of my small little life.

I scratch my too-tight skin until Jake grabs my hands to stop me. "Are you okay, Two Shoes?"

Two Shoes, Jake's nickname for me. It sounds like an Indian name, but actually it's a reference to an Adam Ant song he used to sing to me, "Goody Two Shoes."

It took exactly one week working at my first job at the bookstore in the mall—Jake the pothead assistant-manager and me the hardworking high schooler—for my name to transform from Ariana "Ari" Goody, to Goody Two Shoes, to just plain Two Shoes. The nickname stuck. Two Shoes is the name Greg knew me by when we first met. There are people in the various bands that Jake has performed with over the years who only ever knew me as Two Shoes. And I didn't mind. It never bothered me. It had always been accurate; I *was* a Goody Two Shoes.

But now, I do mind. Now, it does bother me. I don't want to be a *good* girl anymore. I don't want to live a cautious, safe life just to get to the end and look back with regret at every adventure I didn't take. I want to be more like Jake and Grandpa Chuck, to live a life of bluster, moxy, and gusto.

I clear the lump from my throat. "I'm fine, Jake. I'm just...fine."

Jake's jaw moves like he's chewing on the gristle of my lie and can't quite swallow it. With a shake of his head, Jake turns away from me and we both watch the squirrels go about their business.

This silence is a prison, a miserable punishment, to be here with my friend, yet sentenced to solitary confinement. I want to cry and scream and confess everything. Instead, I inspect my fingernails.

Jake reaches into his pocket and produces his pack of cigarettes and a lighter. This time, for the first time in as long as I can remember, he doesn't offer me a puff.

This time, I want one. "May I?" I ask, holding my hand out.

Jake frowns at me, clearly confused.

I point at his cigarette, my eyes imploring when I say, "I want to try it."

"Smoking?"

I nod.

"No."

"What?"

"No."

"But," I huff. "You always offer."

"And you always decline."

"Well, this time I'm not declining. Gimme."

"No."

"What the hell, Jake?" My voice ratchets up to a yell, full of righteous indignation. "Some friend you are."

"Is this what you're talking about? Is this the *new experience* you want to try? Nicotine addiction? That's just dumb, Ari."

"If *I'm* dumb for wanting to try *your* cigarette, then what does that make you? I mean, besides a giant asshole."

Jake smirks at me, but his breath hisses out of him like steam escaping a kettle. "I'm sorry. You're not dumb."

The last of my steam seeps out as well. "I'm sorry too. You're not a giant asshole, just medium-sized."

Jake tries to hide his grin as he extends the cigarette toward me. I squeal like a kid on Christmas as I awkwardly accept the small gift. Before he's even halfway through his instructions for how I'm supposed to work the thing, I stick the filter end between my lips and suck in a deep breath. Then I nearly cough up a lung...and breakfast...and last night's dinner. When I can finally breathe without dry heaving, I hear Jake chuckling at my side and raise my watery eyes to scowl at him.

"How's that new experience treatin' ya, Two Shoes?"

• • •

I catch the phone on the fourth ring, and pinch the receiver between my cheek and shoulder as I breathlessly answer.

"Everything okay? Sounds like you wrestled the phone from the jaws of a tiger." Greg's voice sounds distant, but 10,000 miles of separation will do that to a voice.

"Yeah, Austin's changed a lot since you left last week. Tigers everywhere."

That earns me a chuckle from the other end of the world.

"How's Singapore?" I ask as I make my way back to the kitchen, scrubbing the sauce pan I'd used to make dinner.

"I haven't had much time to explore, but so far my impression is that it's big and crowded. You'd hate it."

"Why do you say that? You never know, I might love it."

Greg scoffs, clearly skeptical, but wisely changes the subject. "So what are you doing, and more importantly, what are you wearing?"

In my sexiest voice, I inform him, "I'm in the kitchen, bent over the sink. I'm wet...dripping, wearing your Slayer t-shirt."

That earns me a low groan. "Which one?"

"South of Heaven, and I'm not wearing any underwear." That part's not true. I'm actually wearing my most comfortable granny panties, in addition to a pair of his old sweatpants rolled up three times at the ankles, and fluffy winter socks covered in little snowmen.

I can tell he appreciates my editorial decision by the hitch in his breath. "Keep talking. I need to hear your voice."

And so I do. I tell him about my last few days—grocery shopping, trying to write, lunch with Jake, trying to write again, renewing my driver's license, smoking my first cigarette—

"Wait. What?"

"Jake let me have a drag off one of his cigarettes."

"Why?"

"Because I asked."

"Why?"

"Because...I wanted to try it. It's this new thing I'm trying, where I try new things." Feeling an urgency to defend myself, I expound, "I've been thinking...the funeral got me thinking. I mean, you know, we've talked about this before—"

"Ari, he was 92." Math, Greg's pat response. We've had this conversation a couple of times before. It always ends here, with Greg explaining that his grandfather had lived a good long life and thus my tears were misplaced. What Greg has failed to grasp is that my tears are not for Grandpa Chuck.

The thing is, it's that very same math which Greg relies on as the basis for his logic that is the reason for my turmoil. On that day in

October, I'd turned 29 as I stared down at Grandpa Chuck in his cherry box, dead at 92. We were inverse, Grandpa Chuck and me.

It was then, the moment when I'd done the math, that my epiphany bomb exploded; a moment of clarity so bright it hurt my eyes, frying my retinas so that nothing would ever look the same again. Grandpa Chuck and me, we were inverse in every way. He'd lived a life filled with epic stories. Me? My life has been small and safe—all soft edges and sanitized surfaces. I have no stories, epic or otherwise.

Drying my hands on a dishrag, I walk the cordless from room to room, pacing as the walls close in. "I'm not talking about Grandpa Chuck. I'm talking about me."

"What do you mean?"

"I mean...life is short, I want to live it." Great, now I'm speaking in bumper sticker sentiments.

Greg says nothing and the silence between us is filled with static, a bad connection.

"Greg?"

"Yeah?"

I search for something to say, finally settling on a new subject, "When are you coming home?"

He clears his throat. "I have a meeting with the site engineers today. I'll know more then."

I nod, even though he can't see me.

"It's getting late there. I should let you get some sleep."

"Okay."

"Good night."

"Greg."

"Yeah?"

"I love you."

There's a pause, a hiccup of time between when I say it and when he says it back, but when he speaks there's a smile in his tone. "I love you too. Sweet dreams, sweet thing."

3–Sunday December 12, 2004

My eyes have drifted out of focus, but I'm pretty sure I can make out Vincent Van Gogh's self-portrait in the grain pattern of our wood floors. Behind me on the couch, Greg strokes his fingers through my hair, as he flips channels on the television. This is our ritual, our together time. When he's not traveling, we easily slip into a regular routine—dinner followed by couch cuddles, his feet on a pillow on the coffee table, my head on a pillow in his lap, his fingers gently stroking my scalp and trailing down my back as we watch old movies.

I remember this being the highlight of my day. The warmth of Greg's lap under my head instilled me with a sense of calm. The tender touch of his fingers twirling strands of my hair sent shivers down my spine. I'd moan at the sensation of his touch, and he'd grin as he'd keep petting me.

When did it stop meaning so much? When did the sweetness, tenderness, and need for constant connection abate? Now, it's just habit. Like a residual haunting; an endless, mindless repeating of a distant memory. It's as if Greg and I aren't here anymore, but our ghosts remain, continuing to pantomime the nuanced details of our daily lives together.

I wince when Greg's fingers reach a particularly stubborn tangle. He tries to be gentle as he works out the knot but the tugs and pulls send pricks of pain through my scalp and down my spine. I revel in the sensation. I need it. I need to feel *something*. Even if what I'm feeling is pain, it's better than feeling nothing.

"What's with you?" Greg asks as he turns off the television.

My eyes snap into focus. What I thought was Van Gogh's scruffy red beard and long, sharp nose are actually just knots in the floor's wood grain.

"Talk to me, Ari. It's like you're a million miles away."

I spring up to sit beside him, and watch him closely as I ask, "Do you love me, Greg?"

"Yeah, of course."

"Why?"

"What kind of question is that? You're my wife, Ari, of course I love you."

I frown. "Wife—that's a role, not a reason."

Greg grins, like he's laughing at some inside joke. "Come here."

I don't move, still waiting for an answer to my question. He clasps my ankle and gently tugs me onto his lap, my legs straddling his. I let him move me, embrace me. It feels good, being this close to him. I rest my head on his shoulder and breathe in his scent, fresh and clean, soapy.

"Look at me, Ari."

I lift my head.

He tucks a strand of hair behind my ear as he starts rattling off a list: "I love your big brown eyes. I love that little gap between your two front teeth. I love that you dip your pizza in ranch dressing and drown your tacos in salsa." He presses his lips to my neck and gives me a feathery kiss as he takes a deep breath. "I love the way you smell." His tongue darts out and tickles the spot just below my ear. "I love the way you taste." Greg pulls away to look me in the eyes again. With one hand, he strokes my temple, then he gives my head a little thump, thump, thump with his thumb. "But mostly I love all the crazy shit you've got going on up here."

I giggle.

"I love your laugh."

I sigh, a bit breathless, then yelp when he cups my ass in one of his palms.

"I love your ass."

His palm slides so far down my ass that his fingers splay between my thighs, and proceed to tease me. I gasp.

"I love that gasp."

Without another word, Greg kisses me. There is no hesitation, no awkwardness. Like a ballet, our kiss is perfect, practiced; a well-choreographed *pas de deux*. After twelve years together, I know his kiss intimately. I know to zig when he zags. I know that he starts gentle, the pressure in his lips soft and tender. I know that he likes to lick into my mouth with darting little dashes of tongue. Then he palms the back of my head, tangling his fingers in my hair, and groans into my mouth just before the kiss changes, grows deeper. I know to match his increased intensity stroke for stroke, nibble for nibble as our maneuvers grow more ardent and fervid.

We are proficient lovers of one another. Normally, there is a comfort in that. But today, the flawless kiss suffocates, the seasoned touch chafes, our studied embrace constricts.

I twist away from his mouth as I grab two fistfuls of his hair. It feels soft in my hands. I pause for a moment to stroke his head, then yank. Greg's head ratchets back, and I latch onto his neck like a vamp. Starting just above his collarbone, I bite, suck, and lick my way up to his jaw.

Nothing about the way I kiss Greg is studied or choreographed. I attack him, feral and ferocious, a cat pouncing on her prey. My teeth gnash against his as we each fight for control. His hands fist my hair, too, locked with me in a power struggle as we challenge one another with bites and licks, nibbles and tastes.

I feel Greg's excitement rigid against my thigh. He pulls his hands from the tangle of my hair, and slides them down my back to cup and squeeze my ass with bruising force.

I whisper a command. "Take me to bed."

His response rumbles in his chest. "No. I'm taking you right here."

We're like a couple of teenagers, all arms and elbows as we strip each other in a frenzy. I hear a tear of fabric when Greg pulls my shirt over my head. I paw at his jeans and he tugs at my bra, a tangle of fumbling fingers working to spring clasps, pop buttons and yank zippers.

When we're finally both naked, Greg gets me flat on my back, and hovers above in a stiff plank, not kissing me, not touching me; just watching. He's always liked the look of anticipation that dawns over my face right before he fucks me. He savors it now, a smug grin on his lips as I wiggle beneath him, my frustration an itch I need him to scratch. I open my legs wide, twisting them up on his back, as if to climb and mount him from below.

Catching me by surprise, he suddenly lets his weight fall. Greg is a lean man, tight with muscle, but not overly large, yet still he crushes me beneath him, forcing the air out of my lungs. Before I recover my breath, he spears into me, burying himself to the hilt.

The feeling sends a burst of energy through every synapse in my body, lighting me up like a Vegas sign. I love that about sex, it has the singular power to give me everything I need, right when I need it. Like being zapped with a pair of defibrillator paddles, I'm jolted out of arrest. My senses come alive with stunning acuity, suddenly able to taste and feel and hear and smell and touch *everything*.

I arch my back as he moves faster and deeper inside me. I curl my limbs around him, pressing up to meet his hips with each stroke. I come, hard, and holler up at him, holding his gaze when I'm able to keep my eyes open.

Greg loves to watch me come, and when I do, it usually brings him with me. It does now too. His eyes grow large as he presses deep and freezes, groaning with ecstasy before he collapses, spent.

We lay naked, wrapped in a knot of legs and arms, our faces cocooned in a tangle of my hair. He shifts to the side and gently arranges me above him so he's no longer crushing me. I rest my head on his chest and sigh at the sensation of his fingers tracing the curve of my lower back.

"Jesus Christ," Greg exhales a loud gust of breath. In a drowsy, sex-laden whisper he asks, "What's gotten into you? I think you've left marks."

I grin as I take a look at the hickey on his neck, feeling a strange sense of pride in leaving my brand on him.

"Is that what you meant by trying new things?"

The question surprises me. We haven't broached this subject since our brief conversation during his Singapore trip nearly a month ago. I can't believe he even remembers. Without thinking, I throw out a casual reply, "That...and other stuff."

"Other stuff, eh?" He gets a devilish glint in his eyes as he smooths his hand down my backside and gooses me. Of course, the final frontier *would* be Greg's first thought. He's asked to be my back door man more than once. My answer has always been a firm "no."

I squeal and squirm in his arms. "That hadn't made my list."

Greg chuckles and slides his hand back up to safe territory. I relax again. But as I start to think about it, I open my mind to the possibility. Why not say "yes" next time? The only thing to fear is fear itself, right? Well, there's the fear of pain, but it can't hurt *that* much, can it? Nothing ventured, nothing gained, and venturing into butt stuff would surely be a big leap—a bootylicious bounce if you will—toward living a life of bluster, moxy, and gusto.

"There's a list?" Greg asks with a yawn. "What's on it?"

There isn't actually a list in the strictest sense of the word, nothing has been committed to paper as yet. It's more like a Möbius strip of thoughts, ideas, and fantasies that has floated around in the back corners of my mind. But a few ideas do continue to surface, such as, "I want to get drunk. I'm 29 and I've never been drunk. That's kind of pathetic. So, yeah, I want to get drunk."

"*Mm hmmm.*" He mumbles drowsily.

"Also, I'd like to kiss a girl."

Greg's eyes rocket open. "What?"

I don't repeat myself. He heard me.

"Any specific girl in mind?"

I shake my head.

"Well, when you find this mystery girl you want to kiss, can I watch?"

I'm stunned by his nonchalant response. I've just told him I want to kiss another person, and he thinks it's hot? Then again, we are talking about a woman, and men so rarely feel threatened by women.

"What if I were to say that I wanted to kiss another guy?"

Greg's fingers stiffen on my hips and his eyes narrow as he asks, "Any specific guy in mind?"

I shake my head.

"Why do you want to kiss another guy?"

"I didn't say that I want to kiss another guy, I just asked what you would say if I did?"

"What are we talking about here, Ari?" Greg squints at me like he's trying to see through skin and bone and catch a glimpse of what's in my head.

Not sure how to answer him, I ask, "In all your travels, have you ever met a woman who you wanted to be with?"

"Are you asking me if I've ever cheated on you? Because I've never done that, Ari Beth."

"But surely you've been attracted to other women, right? You've thought about it?"

"There is a big difference between thinking about something and doing it." He answers without answering.

"What if we were to agree that it's okay to act on those desires?"

"Are we really having this conversation?" Greg shifts beneath me, gently detangling our limbs, then sits upright, "Because if we are, I, uh, I need a beer."

I nod.

With a fortifying breath, like he's about to dive underwater, Greg slides his boxers back on and walks into the kitchen.

I remain unmoved, alone and naked on the couch, staring up at the stilled ceiling fan overhead. Feeling too exposed, I jolt upright and search for my clothes. They're strewn about the room, my jeans inside-out in a pile on the floor. I wrestle the denim to extricate my underwear, then hurriedly pull them on. They're inside-out, too, but I don't care. I need cover for this conversation; any cover will do.

From afar, I hear Greg holler, "You want a beer?"

The words, "no, thanks," balance on the tip of my tongue, but when I open my mouth to answer, "yes, please," comes out.

Greg returns with two bottles of Shiner Bock, handing me one as he settles onto the far cushion of the couch, a gulf of leather between us. When he extends his beer toward me, I hesitate before clinking my bottle against his, surprised by the casual toast. He takes a sip and so do I. Curling my nose at the strange flavor, I set mine aside.

After another drink, Greg asks, "What's this all about?"

I take a deep breath, and before I can stop myself, I blurt it out, saying the words that once said cannot be unsaid, words that once voiced could change everything: "I want to open our marriage."

Greg considers, then, finally, he speaks. "Why?"

I begin to panic, babbling as my only defense. "It was the funeral that got me thinking about all the amazing things your grandpa had done in his life, all the crazy stories. By contrast I realized how small my life is." I backpedal when I see Greg flinch. "I don't mean *small*. I just mean..." I huff, frustrated that I can't seem to express myself coherently. I'd read an article about polyamory last month and it had set my imagination loose. Now I realize I should have done more research, learned the lexicon, because right now, when I need them most, the right words escape me. "I'm not putting any of this on you. My life isn't small because of you...I mean my life isn't *small*, it's just...limited."

Greg says nothing, and his frown seems to deepen.

So I talk more. "I love you, Greg. I've loved you since I was seventeen, and that hasn't changed. But sometimes I feel like we've limited ourselves by committing to each other so young. Or maybe it's just me; I've closed myself off to the world outside."

Pausing, I swallow hard, but I can't get the lump out of my throat. I pull my feet up onto the couch, and Greg does the same. We sit with our legs against our chests, as if our knees are armor and can provide an adequate defense for our hearts.

"I think I just want the space...the freedom to experience the world around me, on my terms, and I want to give you that freedom too."

"And you think opening our marriage will give you the freedom you need?"

"Us. It will give *us* that freedom. And yes, I think it will."

"Why can't you experience the world with me, with *just* me?"

My spirits sink. My fortitude collapses like a house of cards. "Yeah, you're right," I rest my cheek on my knees. "I've just been in a weird mood lately. Forget I said anything."

"No." Greg sets his beer aside and brushes his fingers across my feet to get my attention. "Ari, I'm not arguing with you. I'm just trying to understand where this is coming from. Because let's be clear, what you're asking for is permission to fuck other guys, right? That's the bottom line." Greg's tone isn't angry or harsh in any way. Even as he says the word 'fuck' he enunciates clearly, his tone phlegmatic. It's like we're entering a debate, and he's formulated his rebuttal.

I try to read him, to get some sense of where his emotions really lie. And that's when he surprises me with the hint of a smile. It's exactly what I need to regain my courage and continue this. I take a deep breath, and he does too. I steel my spine, and he adjusts as well. I stare straight at him as he levels those warm, whiskey-colored eyes at me. And I speak, finally sharing the thoughts I've stewed over for months.

"I'm almost thirty, and I feel like I've done so little. I skipped all the normal parts of being twenty-something. I've never been drunk, never been to a raging party, never had a one-night stand or a threesome, never gotten high... I've created this comfortable bubble, and existed within it for as long as I can remember. And in the meantime there are all these parts of life that have passed me by. I just want the chance to experience them, to experience all parts of life."

"Ari, for someone in their twenties, you've done a lot with your life. You know that, right? You're a published author, for Christ's sake. That's not nothing."

I don't know what to say, so I just shrug and then hate myself for shrugging. What a lazy expression a shrug is, and this is no time for lazy expressions.

"Okay." Greg chews the inside of his lip, deep in thought. "Let's say we agree to this, hypothetically. Would there be any ground rules?"

Ground rules? Holy shit, are we really talking about this? "Of course there would be ground rules," I answer before I've thought it through.

"Like what?"

I have no idea. "What do you have in mind?"

He hardly takes any time to think before he blurts out, "Not Jake."

Jake, as in my best friend who I think of as a brother?

"I don't think I can deal with you being with him. Also, we need to promise each other that any extra-marital activity will be safe. I know you're on the pill, but outside of us, it's different. We should always use condoms when we're with anyone else."

I'm stunned. I don't know where I thought this conversation would go, but I wasn't expecting it to go here. Though it does seem fitting that

Greg would completely gloss over my ethereal ideas of freedom and space, and focus entirely on practical matters like rubbers and safety. Afterall, Greg is an engineer, a scientist who approaches all aspects of his life with the objective detachment of an observer. To him, this open-marriage thing is really just a chemistry experiment—add part A to part B, get a reaction.

I finally squawk out a hoarse, "Okay."

"Do you have any ground rules for me?"

"I...I don't know. Can I think about it?"

Greg shrugs. *No shrugging,* maybe that should be a ground rule. After a moment, he speaks, and I'm not exactly sure what he means when he says, "Okay."

"Okay?"

"We can open the marriage. But if it starts to cause problems between us, we close it. You and me, Ari, that's what's important."

I never imagined we'd get this far in the conversation, so I'd never really given any of this serious thought. The longevity of our open marriage was not something I had even considered. How could I not have thought it through before bringing it up?

Jesus, I'm such a child. I'm a little girl playing dress up in a woman's body. I've managed to get older, without ever actually growing up. And now, here I am, negotiating the terms of an open-marriage with my husband as if I have the slightest notion what I'm talking about. But I guess I better grow up fast, because apparently this is happening.

"Okay," I respond.

"Okay," he repeats.

This is surreal. Should it hurt that he's not being jealous or possessive? His detachment is almost an affront, and it takes me a moment to remember: this was my goddamn idea.

"Okay," I say again.

Greg reaches for me, stroking the top of my foot with the back of his fingers. I link my pinky with his, and we sit like this for a moment, quiet, thoughtful, connected.

Then, completely in sync, we dive at each other and tangle together, a twisting mass of lips and limbs. As we kiss and touch and explore each other anew, I feel a growing and nearly overwhelming rush of nervous energy. It's euphoric, this promise of freedom. It fizzes and bubbles and explodes through me like uncorked champagne.

I climb on top of Greg as he tugs his boxers out of the way. With the sound of torn fabric, I push my underwear aside and we both moan when we connect. We move fast and hard, fucking like wild beasts.

I scream when I come. *Oh holy fuck*. More than just uncorked, my bottle of champagne is shattered into a million pieces, as if christening some new sea vessel.

This is going to be a wild ride.

4—Saturday December 18, 2004

Greg returns to me with all the quiet consideration of a tornado blowing the doors off the house. His arrival, just before 1:00 AM, is announced with the sound of the door swinging too wide and hitting the wall, then a series of whispered curses, then his heavy footfalls across the wood floor. I blink my eyes open as he trudges clumsily into the bedroom, suitcase in hand and a garment bag slung over his shoulder.

"Hey. Did I wake you?"

I rub my eyes in reply. He drops his luggage by the door and comes to me for a kiss. I consider protesting, late-night breath is surely as bad as morning breath, but he doesn't seem to care. And, anyway, he tastes like cigarettes.

When did he start smoking again? I open my mouth to complain, but stop myself. Is smoking allowed now? Can I nag him about the health of his lungs if I'm giving him *freedom*? We didn't cover that in the rules, and we haven't discussed 'The Talk' since that night.

That next day, Greg had been sent on a site review of a levee in Louisiana. As a result, we'd had little time to rehash our conversation or make plans for the future, we'd simply gone through our usual routine of goodbye kisses and hugs. Then a wave at the end of the driveway and he went off to New Orleans.

For the last few nights we'd been careful to stay on safe subjects when texting or talking - work, weather, and well-being. He'd bitch about the muggy weather and ask if it was cold here in Austin yet. I'd ask vague questions about his work and his off hours in the Big Easy, but nothing that could be answered with, "Well, I was fucking this chick, when..."

Finally face-to-face, I throw another softball question, "How was the flight home?"

"Uneventful." He shrugs as he unlaces his shoes and kicks them into the corner of the room. "You been up to anything interesting?"

I'm surprised by the question, not a softball. That question could most certainly be answered with, "Well, I was fucking this dude, when..."

But the truth is, I haven't been up to anything interesting, and I think Greg knows that. After twelve years together, no one knows my neuroses better than he does. He's well aware of my social anxiety, my awkward ineptitude at small talk, my fear of the unknown, the way that I will psychoanalyze a conversation for weeks after it's concluded. Strangers make me nervous, new places make me uncomfortable, and *faux pas* make me embarrassed. As a result, I've designed a life that limits the possibility for discomfort through avoidance. All my friends are Greg's friends, and all of my interactions are generally at his behest. If I were single, I'd probably be a shut in. And it's always been that way, so why would things suddenly change now?

I think he's convinced himself that for me the open-marriage is all talk, a hypothetical fantasy that will amount to nothing. And it pisses me off that, so far at least, he's right. For the last week, where the open-marriage is concerned, all I've done is take the insubstantial 'list' floating in my head, and commit it to paper:

- Drink whiskey
- Get drunk
- Threesome
- Smoke pot
- ~~Try cocaine?~~
- Kiss a stranger
- Volunteer
- Get a new hobby
- Explore

- Try anal
- Kiss a girl
- Smile more
- Dance more
- Make a fool of myself
- Howl at the moon
- Make mistakes
- Have a one-night stand

Well, "commit to paper" is an exaggeration, because the first thing I did when I finished was wad it up and throw it away. Soon after, though, I made another and another. Eventually, I started making my lists in spreadsheet form on my laptop. This way was better because I could sort them, and so I did: by order of most to least likely to happen, easiest to hardest to complete, high to low anxiety stressors, alphabetically. I would stare at the screen and the blinking cursor, considering what else to add. Then I would delete the whole list. Day after day, the same routine.

Lists.

Riveting.

"Ari?"

I realize Greg has asked me a question, but I don't remember what it is, so I just shrug. Greg smirks, but changes the subject. "I'm going to make something to eat. You hungry?"

I decline the offer of food, but hug Greg and tug him down into the bed with me for another welcome back kiss. He smiles against my lips and makes a vague promise of waking me up again once he's eaten. I grin, then drift back to sleep.

When next I open my eyes, I find the sun up, its rays streaming through the blinds in the bedroom window to form long white slashes across Greg's supine form. I stare at him while he sleeps. I can only see his lips, the tip of his narrow nose, and the fan of his dark lashes; the rest of his face enveloped by the cloudy puff of his pillow.

I've missed him while he was gone. It's been a week without him here to warm his half of the bed. A week without him winking at me in the bathroom mirror as we both brush our teeth. A week without cuddling on the couch to watch old movies. A week without sex.

I bite my lip, suddenly feeling frisky, and trace a finger along his shoulder. I half expect him to wake up and make good on his flirty promise from last night, but he just mumbles something in his sleep, smacks his lips, and turns away from me onto his side.

With a sigh, I stretch and climb out of bed. Half way across the hall to my home office, I yelp at the sound of a shrill whistle. Spinning in an awkward version of the Hamill Camel—my arms flailing like a dying bird, my socked feet slip sliding on the wood floors—I nearly fall on my ass as I look beyond the hallway to see Jake in my living room. One eye open, draped across the couch, shirtless as usual, his long hair hanging over the arm of the sofa.

"Nice shirt." He winks.

Shit. I'm wearing Greg's South of Heaven t-shirt and nothing else. I dive back into the bedroom to tug on Greg's sweatpants. Out in the living room I find Jake sitting up and finger combing his hair out of his face.

"What in the hell are you doing here, Jake? Last time I checked, you have your own couch and, better yet, your own bed."

Jake lets out a huff as he settles into the sofa. I'm reminded of the last time Greg and I had sex, right where he's sitting...twice. "I broke up with Rebecca. Now she keeps coming over to my apartment to yell at me."

"You're hiding from her?"

Jake shrugs.

"Real mature, jackass." I shuffle past him to the kitchen where I start a pot of coffee. Jake follows, retrieving a couple of mugs from the cabinet. When it's ready, we pour our drinks and settle at the table in a shared silence.

After a few sips, Jake speaks, "So, when were you going to tell me about you and Greg?"

I blink. "He told you?"

"Yeah, and I'd like to point out that *you* didn't. Is this what you were making all that noise about—oh, how long ago was it—a month? Smoking my cigarettes and blathering on about new experiences, and I'd just thought it was a spoke in your menstrual cycle."

I roll my eyes.

"So talk to me, Ari, what's going on?"

I don't know where to begin, I don't even know what to say. I try not to squirm beneath Jake's scrutiny, but it burns, like an ant under the lens of a magnifying glass.

Finally, I answer, "I read once that 'the worst sort of regret, is the regret for things you didn't do.' I don't want to get to the end of my life and look back at all the opportunities not taken, challenges not accepted, experiences unlived."

"Like what?"

"I don't know." With a huff, I start naming items from my copious lists, "Get drunk, smoke pot, kiss a girl—"

"Oh," Jake waggles his brow. "Can I watch?"

I roll my eyes again. "Point is, I just want the space to do what I want, and not worry that I'm hurting Greg."

"*Space.*" Jake says the word like it's the punchline to a joke.

His response bothers me. Jake is the last person who should be passing judgment about my relationship decisions. He's had countless sexual partners, and exactly one girlfriend in his life. And apparently he just broke up with her.

"So have you had any of these new *experiences*?" Jake asks.

I'm embarrassed to say, "No. Not yet."

"What are you waiting for?"

I shrug.

"I have an idea, come to my show tonight. Greg and I will get you drunk and watch you make out with girls. It'll be awesome."

I nearly spit out my coffee when I laugh. "Thanks for the offer of letting me satisfy your lesbian fantasy, but if I'm going to do this, then I've got to do it on my own."

The joviality in Jake's expression disappears, and his jaw goes rigid like he's clamped his teeth, trying to keep himself from saying something he'll regret. When he finally does talk, all he says is, "Be careful, okay?"

"Okay, Dad."

Jake smirks, but undeterred launches into a list of best practices for staying safe while out on my own. Part of me is annoyed that he's treating me like a child, but mostly it's endearing, and the information is helpful. So I listen.

• • •

"Ah, come on, Ari," Jake sticks out his bottom lip like an obstinate child.

I glance at him in the bathroom mirror as I twist a strand of hair around the curling iron, "We've been over this. I want to do this by myself."

"This is such bullshit. I've been trying to get you drunk since you were underage, and when you finally decide to jump off the wagon, I can't even be there to witness it? This sucks sweaty donkey balls, Two Shoes."

I scrunch my nose at the imagery. "I drank at your show back in November."

"Like, two beers, you weren't even trying." He actually seems mad about this. But it's hard to take him seriously when he pouts.

"Aren't you going to be late for load in and sound check?"

"Yes, he is," Greg chimes in from the bedroom where he's getting dressed. "Jake, leave my wife alone. If she wants to go out by herself, then that's what she's going to do. You know she's more stubborn than you are. Why do you even bother?"

Jake scowls in the direction of Greg's disembodied voice, then winks at me in the mirror before he bows out. "Fine. Remember what I told you?"

"Never leave my drink unattended."

"And?"

"Beer before liquor, never sicker."

"And?"

"Don't trust whitey."

"That's my girl."

Greg appears in the doorway, wearing the burgundy shirt I bought for him last Christmas. It perfectly complements his amber eyes, which sparkle when he smiles. He elbows Jake in the ribs. "Come on, brother, let's go."

Jake kisses my cheek. "Be safe tonight, Two Shoes, call if you need a ride home or if anyone gets aggressive with you."

Jake's departure makes room for Greg in the cramped bathroom. He kisses the same spot Jake had, mindful not to muss my lipstick. We hug, holding on a little longer than usual. Neither of us say the words, though I know we're both thinking the same thing. Tonight, we're entering a new frontier. The thought makes me giddy, excitement bubbling in my belly and leaving me a bit queasy.

Greg strokes his thumb across my cheek. "I love you, sweet thing."

I close my eyes and lean into him, resting my head on his shoulder as I whisper, "I love you too."

And then my boys leave and I'm on my own.

• • •

The bus is mostly empty. I take a seat near the back, claiming an entire bench for myself. We lurch forward and I settle in, watching the streets slide by. It doesn't seem to take long before we reach downtown. I pull the cord and disembark on Sixth Street, accompanied by a wide woman with a pronounced limp and a narrow man carrying an accordion and bedecked in full Mariachi garb.

Ah, the infamous 'Dirty Sixth,' a place known far and wide as one of America's sin streets. Like Bourbon Street in New Orleans or The Strip in Vegas, Dirty Sixth sings its siren song to college students and tourists, party-seekers and the curious, sinners and saints alike, to come, consume, copulate. Yet, after seven years living in Austin, this is my first real visit. Incredibly, despite having a best friend in a band, I've somehow managed to avoid this hedonistic paradise until now.

Like the bus, the street is almost completely empty. On either side, darkened neon signs plaster squatty brick buildings, their windows shuttered, the doors barred. Ice and beer trucks are double parked, making deliveries. Bands unload from a myriad of SUVs, vans, and hatchbacks.

As I walk up the sunny street, past closed door after closed door it becomes abundantly clear that I've screwed up. I'm early. Shit. What should I do? I could walk over to Red River Street, to the venue where

Jake is playing tonight. But if I do that, then I've failed. If I go to the boys, it will be in surrender, and it's far too soon for that.

I continue up the sidewalk at a march, a woman on a mission. Finally, when I'm less than a block from Red River—my point of surrender—I find my salvation, a bar that's open. Hesitating at the door, I take a deep breath and step inside.

It's dark. I have to pause and let my eyes adjust. When I can see again, I glance around with an "oh yeah, I've been in here dozens of times" air of nonchalance, trying not to look so new. I take a step toward the bar, but trip on a misaligned tile and stumble awkwardly into one of the tall red barstools.

Hello, world!

Fortunately, my embarrassing entrance goes largely unseen. The bar is completely empty, except for the bartender, who ambles my way. He holds his hand up in the shape of the letter "c." I stare at him, dumbfounded as I try to decipher his cryptic sign language. Finally, he grows impatient and gives me a hint. "I.D."

Oh. Why didn't he just say that? I hand him my driver's license and he scrutinizes it before handing it back.

"What can I get'cha, Ariana?"

Oh crap. A pop quiz. Beer, but which kind? The few beers I've had all tasted kind of gross, and more or less the same. I look at the taps in front of me and chirpily spit out the first name I recognize. "Shiner Bock, please."

He grabs a glass and starts to pour. I use the opportunity to take in the room: a long, skinny old repurposed store front with high ceilings and a second-floor balcony. Weird demonic gargoyles with glowing red eyes dot the walls and overhangs, and a naked female bust extends off the end of the upstairs balcony like the figurehead of a ship. Lined along one of the rough-hewn stone walls are black velvet portraits of naked women, and on the opposite side, a life-size mural of Betty Page is painted onto a piece of plywood.

I turn my attention to the man before me, holding my glass at an angle as he fills it with the dark suds. He's dressed for summer in December, wearing a pearl-snap shirt with the sleeves ripped off, cut-off jean shorts, and he's got a beat-up black cowboy hat to match his beat up black cowboy boots. He's covered in tattoos, full sleeves on both arms, and a few designs dot his legs and neck too. His nose and eyebrows are studded with silver, and there's a pair of large blue carabiners that dangle from the distended holes in his ears.

He mumbles something, too quiet to hear, as he slides the beer to me.

"What?" I inquire.

"Nothing. I'm Manic." For a moment, I think he's explaining his mental state until I realize that's his name.

"Nice to meet you, Manic."

"So what brings you in here, Ariana?"

It's weird to hear my full name. Only my grandma and Aunt Cece call me Ariana, but I don't correct him. "I'm just checking out the Sixth Street experience."

He grimaces and gestures at the empty bar. "This is not a typical Sixth Street experience."

"Usually more crowded?"

"There's that. Also, most Sixth Street bars are run for douchebags, by douchebags."

"And this bar is the exception?"

"Actually, no. We're douchebags too."

I smile. So does he. He has a nice face, like he used to be happy once, but time and life have worn their weary wrinkles into his skin. And his eyes, a moody blue, are too deep, oceanic, bottomless. He mumbles something to himself again, then enunciates when he asks me, "What are you shooting?"

Shooting? Shit, another quiz. While I panic, he grabs two shot glasses and sets them on the tile between us. I bluff, "Whatever you're having?"

Manic nods with approval, moves to the wall of liquor behind him and grasps the neck of a long, slender bottle. "Bushmills," he says as he pours.

Bushmills? I have no idea what that means.

Without a toast, Manic lifts his glass and swallows the entire drink in one gulp. I do too. It burns. It burns *a lot*. I gasp and my breath comes out like fire. Tears well up from the back of my throat and perch at the edges of my eyes. He chuckles, and I think he can tell I'm green, literally and figuratively.

With an alarming jolt, the door swings open, flooding the darkened space with the harsh light of the afternoon sun. Two women decked out in 80s goth garb step inside, laughing loudly. They remind me of the types of girls I emulated in high school, but it's a look I could never quite pull off. Their voices echo between the stone walls, and Manic flinches as the shrill sounds pierce his eardrums—probably the only parts of his body not yet pierced.

Manic pushes a portion of the bar surface up like the door of a DeLorean and comes out to stand at the jukebox. After a few clicks of the keys, a song starts. It's David Bowie, singing about a God-awful small affair and the girl with the mousy hair. When Manic returns behind the bar, he sings along as he tops off my beer, then goes to pour drinks for the newcomers.

The day grows dark, and the bar begins to fill. Manic is increasingly busy, and I watch the incoming tide of patrons fill seats and tables around me. It seems strange to be surrounded by people, yet alone. I don't know what to do with myself, so I try to look busy, tracing my finger along the grout lines of the tile bar top and thumbing through a copy of the Austin Chronicle.

"You alone?"

The deep rumble of those three syllables practically vibrates through me, interrupting my perusal of the Chronicle personal ads. I look up to find a pair of translucent blue eyes focused on me.

I mumble something incoherently.

A small array of fine lines fan out along the shores of those Caribbean eyes and the voice rumbles again. "I'm sorry, bad phrasing. I only meant, is anyone here?"

There are about forty people here. Why is he asking me that?

I blink and try to focus on something other than his eyes. He has a scar that cuts a jagged line through his left eyebrow, like a lightning bolt. I widen my focus. His dark auburn hair shimmers like fire in the candle light. There's a sharp-as-glass jawline beneath his five-o'clock shadow. And he's gesturing at the empty seat beside me.

Oh! My brain cycles back online. "No," I croak and have to clear the frog from my throat. "No one is sitting there. It's all yours."

He slides onto the stool and smiles at me, then he smiles at Manic and reaches across the bar to shake his hand. "Hey, man."

Manic looks to me. "Is this fuckwit bothering you?"

I shake my head, flushing red under the scrutiny of both sets of eyes.

"Alex," Manic says to him as he crooks a thumb in my direction, "Ariana here is *checking out the Sixth Street experience*." He uses finger quotes for that last part and I'm certain my cheeks flame three shades redder.

"No shit?" Alex raises his scarred brow. It gives his innocent grin a devilish quality. "So your plan is to get really trashed and fuck some stranger you met in a bar?"

"Is that why they call it 'Dirty Sixth'?"

Alex laughs. The sound is low and rumbly and tickles me all over.

I hardly notice when Manic sets a beer in front of Alex and moves on. Having introduced me to someone he clearly trusts, he's off to serve other customers.

"Visiting from out of town, or new to the city?" Alex asks.

"Neither. I've lived here for seven years."

"Seven years?" Alex's surprise borders on horror. "You've been in Austin for seven years and never been to Dirty Sixth? That's got to be some sort of city-wide record."

"Well, I don't really drink, so I never saw the point of going to bars."

Manic reappears and grabs my pint, topping it off again—I've lost count of how many beers I've had, as he's never let the drink get below the midway point before refilling it—then he lines up three shots from his bottle of Bushmills. Oh God, is he trying to kill me?

"To the Sixth Street experience," Manic winks at me as he toasts. Then we shoot the drinks. I die a little on the inside, but try to mask it on the outside. As I recover from the terrible flames in the walls of my throat, I look up to see Alex and Manic both watching me, amused.

"You don't really drink, but you shoot whiskey?" Alex asks once Manic has moved on to another customer.

"Actually, don't tell anyone, but that was only my second shot ever."

"Ever?"

"My first was about three hours ago when I walked in." My esophagus finally stops burning. "So Bushmills is whiskey?"

Drink whiskey: check.

Alex laughs and shakes his head with disbelief.

"Can I tell you something weird?" I hazard.

"Please do."

"I'm married."

"That is weird."

"That's not the weird part."

"Oh."

"My husband and I have agreed that we can sleep with other people."

Alex doesn't react as I thought he would, though it occurs to me that I have no idea what a normal reaction to that information would be—Alex is the first person I've told. His reaction is no reaction at all, as if he's still waiting for me to tell him the weird part. I consider continuing, but my train of thought derails.

"Oh neat," I giggle. "I can feel the whiskey in my thighs."

Alex quirks his scarred brow, and his mouth curls into a crooked smile.

I explain further, "I feel everything in my thighs first—menstrual cramps, orgasms, and I guess booze too."

Alex laughs again. "Are you for real?"

• • •

"He's a circus freak. Well, he's retired now," Alex explains, leaning in so close that I can smell his skin. It's a woodsy scent, like he's chopping logs for a fire, like it's winter and I'm home. He continues, "I saw his act once, many years ago when I was living in Seattle. He ate a lightbulb and hammered a nail into his nose. Also, he hangs stuff from his piercings, weights and household objects, stuff like that. The time I saw him, he hung an old metal windup robot from his dick piercing while shouting *Domo arigato, Mr. Roboto.*"

I glance over at Manic with wonderment. "Wow. I'd like to see that."

"Kinky." Alex waggles his brow. "Oh!" He exclaims and leans in close again like he's going to tell me a secret. "See the woman halfway down the bar with the black hair?"

I glance over, then turn back to Alex. "The one who looks like Siouxsie Sioux, or the one who looks like Morticia Addams?"

I don't realize I'm pointing until Alex clasps his hand over mine and presses my palm down onto my thigh. His hand is rough, his fingers callused; he has working-man's hands. He has working-man's arms too; they're big. Not big like those bodybuilders who can't put their arms down by their sides, but big enough that I can imagine him swinging an axe, chopping a whole winter's worth of firewood in an afternoon. I lean a little closer to sniff his woodsy mountain scent again.

"Don't point," he says.

The admonishment embarrasses me. I shrink into myself, just a little. But with a wink, Alex melts my anxiety away. Only then do I realize he's still holding my hand, resting our clasped fists on my thigh. He has the same momentary revelation and snaps his grip away, giving me a sheepish grin.

It's been like this all night: banter that borders on flirting, touching more often than seems prudent. I've lost track of time as we talk and drink and laugh. He hasn't asked about my marital situation once since my initial admission, and I'm grateful. Instead of heavy talk about relationships and social-norms and mores, we've been playing *Fact or Fiction.*

"Anyway," Alex brings us back on point. He nods toward the woman with long black hair, and a dress that looks like a collection of glittery spiderwebs strategically clustered at her boobs and hips. "Morticia Addams over there is Austin's Second Best Tarot Card Reader."

"Oh? Who's the first best?"

"That's the thing. No one knows. It's not like there was a contest. She just started calling herself that. It's her title. She has it on her business cards and everything."

"I call bullshit, that's a fiction."

"Fact!" Alex announces, puffing out his chest and looking rather proud of himself.

"How do I know you're not making all of this up?"

"Well, I could say you'll just have to trust me, but..." Alex shifts on his stool and yanks his wallet out of his back pocket. He digs for a moment and then pulls out a glossy black business card with thick red letters in a font meant to simulate dripping blood. It reads: Carmilla Westenra - Austin's Second Best Tarot Card Reader.

"No way!" I clutch the card to my chest as I bowl over with laughter.

Alex smiles and his eyes twinkle in the red flicker of the candlelight. "You have the most beautiful laugh I've ever heard."

His words, so stunningly sweet, serve as a cold shower. The compliment reminds me of Greg. My husband is just a few blocks away, and here I sit, shamelessly flirting with another man.

Despite my arrangement with Greg, I feel uneasy with how easy it is to be with Alex. We have an uncomplicated rapport, which is oddly sexy, but feels like an affront to my marriage. And, God, what time is it? How many hours have I spent with this man, flirting and joking and smelling his crisp, winter-fresh scent?

"Shit." I mumble as I frantically dig my phone out of my purse to check the time. The busses stop running at eleven. "I've got to go."

"How are you getting home? You aren't driving, are you?"

I frown at him. "No. Bus." Checking my phone again, I do the math in my head. I have just enough time to reach the bus stop before the last run north.

Alex looks to Manic, giving him a nod and slicing his fingers across his throat to indicate we're tabbing out. Within a moment we're paid up, and, incredibly, my tab is just ten dollars. I leave the money and a fat tip and push away from the bar, settling my bag over my shoulder.

"Let me walk you," Alex insists as he stuffs his wallet back in his pocket.

I start to protest, to assert that I'll be fine, that I'm a big girl and can find the bus all by myself, but when I move toward the door I wobble, then giggle, then wobble more.

Get drunk: check.

Manic interrupts my thoughts with a wave of his hand, beckoning me to come around the corner of the bar. He slides up his DeLorean door again and steps out to sweep me into a smothering hug. Planting a firm kiss on my cheek, he says, "Come visit me again sometime, sweetheart."

I nod and open my mouth to speak, but he's gone back on the other side of the bar before I can respond. I turn back toward the exit. Alex waits there, offering his elbow like an old-world gentleman. After a moment's hesitation, I take it.

"You ready?" Alex asks with a crooked grin.

"For what?"

The doorguy pushes the door open for us and the cool night air rushes over my skin. I blink, stunned by what I see. It's as if I've walked into an alternate reality. Gone is the city traffic and the bright sunshine of the afternoon, replaced by what can only be described as a Sodom-and-Gomorrah themed amusement park.

"Welcome to the Sixth Street experience." Alex sweeps his hand across the scene like a game show host.

The street is blocked off to traffic, and there are people everywhere. To my left, a gaggle of girls wearing mile-high stiletto heels stumble over the cobblestones. They yank down the hems of their miniscule skirts and complain about the cold. They're followed closely by a pack of hungry wolves wearing sideways ball caps and polo shirts with popped collars. On my right, a couple dry-humps on the hood of a car, the only car left parked on this stretch of road. The curb beside the happy couple is lined with half-asleep rainbow-haired punks, shoveling large slices of pizza into their mouths. In the middle of the road, a dozen or so women, all wearing matching wedding veils covered in plastic penises, are posing for a photo with an old bearded man in a white thong covered in cherries, a Hooter's t-shirt, and a rhinestone tiara. He has his back to the camera, with his head cocked around to grin at the lens, one hand resting on his ass like a pinup model.

"Is that—?"

"Yep." Alex nods.

"Didn't he run for mayor?"

"Yep."

"Awesome."

Alex cocks a grin at me, watching as I take it all in. He steps across the sidewalk to a lamp post where he retrieves his bicycle. It's attached to the post with a massive chain, which he loops across his chest like an industrial-strength beauty pageant sash. He rests a hand on the small of my back, and the intimacy of his touch makes me nervous. A rabble of butterflies flutter in my stomach with each step, as he leads me against the current of people toward the Brazos Street bus stop.

I can't seem to stop gawking. It's total sensory overload. The air smells like some strange combination of pizza and pot, with just a hint of piss. Music blares from the open doors of the bars and clubs we pass. It blends with the noise of the loitering crowd in the street to create a spirited and discordant cacophony. But it's what I see that fascinates me most.

We pass yet another scantily-clad old man, this one with a long gray wizard beard, who is wearing a red bikini and juggling. Across the street, a man with a plastic bucket cradled in one arm is drumming a beat, dancing to his own rhythm. A drunk girl is trying to dance to his rhythm as well, but she only manages to stumble and awkwardly flail her arms in the air. In the middle of the road, four police officers sit astride giant horses. They clop along the length of the street, parting the strange sea of people, and leaving piles of horse shit in their wake.

"Wow. I can't believe I've missed out on this all these years."

"Trust me; it gets real old real fast. Which bus are you taking?"

"The number five," I answer distractedly as I pry my eyes away from a preacher standing on a soap box with a bible in one hand and a hand written sign in the other. It reads: God sees you. I grin at Alex. "You know, you really don't have to do this. I don't need a chaperone. I can take care of myself."

"Chaperone?" Alex scrunches his nose in distaste. "Chaperones are dads and teachers. I'm neither. Think of me more as your escort."

"Isn't that just another word for 'prostitute'?"

"Good point." He laughs. "Anyway, I want to make sure you get to your bus safely. Not to be sexist, but this part of town can be a little sketchy for a beautiful woman on her own, especially a beautiful *drunk* woman."

He thinks I'm beautiful? I trip on a loose cobblestone and nearly faceplant on the gum-stained sidewalk. But Alex saves me, looping one of his axe-wielding arms around my waist to steady me against his chest.

He's very solid, and the impact hurts a little. The lumpy loops of his bike chain bruise, and I bite the tip of my tongue when my chin hits his collar bone. But none of that matters, because there's the smell of him. I breathe deeply and the butterflies in my stomach migrate south.

"You okay?"

I blink my eyes back into focus and look up to find him smiling at me. His lips look like the softest part of him. I wonder what it would feel like to kiss him. Do I want to kiss him? Maybe. Do I want him to kiss me? Definitely.

But he doesn't. He sets his hands on my shoulders, to steady me, like I might fall over again. The street lamp over our heads glimmers against the steely metal of his bike chain and captures my attention.

"You're my knight in shining armor," I pronounce.

"What?"

I run my finger along the heavy metal chain links. "You're not my chaperone or my prostitute, you're my knight in shining armor."

He bursts into laughter. "Come on, you'll miss your bus."

It's not much further before we reach the bus stop, which is mostly empty, a surprisingly quiet corner of the block. It's just us and a man stretched out and snoring loudly.

I slide down onto the empty bench. Alex stands his bike up, then sits beside me, leaning back and stretching his legs. It's the first time I've really taken a good look at him, top to bottom.

He's one of those guys who's accidentally attractive. Like he doesn't even try to be hot, but he succeeds at it anyways. He's not dressed for a night out on the town. His leather boots are worn down to the steel-toes. His jeans are threadbare at the knees, and his plain white tee is frayed at the neck and fits a little too tight on his biceps. He's like a greaser from *The Outsiders*, looking for a brawl. But which Outsider? I give his biceps another glance. Patrick Swayze, he's definitely the Patrick Swayze Outsider. What was his name? Darryl!

"How long has your marriage been open?"

Thoughts of Swayze vanish from my mind as I blink at Alex, stunned. After spending hours together, this is the first time he's broached the subject. Why is he asking me this now? I hesitate, not sure I want to answer his question. But then I do. "Technically, six days."

"Not even a week?"

Alex laughs, and I'm mortified. I should have kept my mouth shut. Unmasked, he sees the real me. Now he knows I'm just a stupid little girl playing dress up. Deflated, I turn away, watching for a bus to come and take me home.

"Hey," Alex lays his hand on my shoulder, and his voice is soft when he says, "I'm sorry. I shouldn't have laughed. It's just that...I guess I thought...actually, it doesn't matter what I thought. I'm sorry."

His contrition sounds real. I glance at him over my shoulder and chuckle at the sight of his pitifully cute expression, Patrick Swayze with puppy dog eyes. All traces of my humiliation are gone in an instant, like magic. He's a magic man.

"So, tell me, in your six days of open marriage, have you acted on it?"

I'm acting on it now, aren't I? Clearly not in his estimation. I hesitate to be honest again, but eventually admit. "No, not yet."

"Interesting. A babe in the woods." He waggles his brow. Was that flirting? That seemed like flirting.

"I like your scar. May I touch it?" I flirt too.

His gaze changes from puppy to wolf, and he nods.

I rest my palm against his cheek and caress my thumb over the jagged scar that cuts through his left brow. Alex closes his eyes at the sensation of my touch, and the intimacy of that action excites me, inspires me.

It's time for me to act too. No more lists. No more waiting. I lean forward and press my lips to his. They're just as soft as I'd imagined, and he tastes like whiskey and mint toothpaste.

Kiss a stranger: check.

Alex pushes away from me, severing our connection. His eyes spring open, and he stares at me with a pained expression, as if my kiss has injured him.

Oh. God. Have I completely misread this situation? Quickly, I backpedal, "I'm so sorry. I can't believe I just did that. I shouldn't have—"

This time, Alex kisses me, and I mean he *really* kisses me. His soft lips smash against mine, and his callused fingers clasp my neck to pull me closer. My head spins at the sensations of new lips, new flavors, new motions. Even the way Alex's stubbled chin rubs against my cheek feels different, special.

My God, this kiss is everything: hard and soft, needy and generous, desperate and demanding. My kiss had been just a peck, a toe in the water. But Alex's kiss is a deep dive that takes me under.

Kiss a stranger: CHECK!

After a moment, we come apart and hover close, catching our breath. I shiver. I'm buzzing. I feel that kiss everywhere. I press my hands between my legs. "Felt that in my thighs."

Alex gives me a wide smile as he rubs the pad of his thumb across my lips. "Your bus is here."

I glance behind me, and sure enough, the number five is heading our way. Stupid bus.

Alex stands as it comes to a stop, and loads his bike onto the front rack. Then he joins me on the bus steps, and pays for both of our tickets.

"What are you doing?"

Alex nods toward a man sitting near the front of the bus. He's leaning against the window, seeming passed out. "Just going to make sure you get home safely."

We go to the bench in the back, me by the window, and Alex with his arm draped over my chair. The bus rumbles and whines as it moves north, and I think I might vomit. I feel every bump and bounce deep in my stomach. All the beer and liquor I've consumed sloshes from side to side. Groaning, I brace my hands on solid surfaces, one palm flat against the back of the seat in front of us, the other clutching Alex's thigh. Good lord, it's like he's made out of bricks.

At the sensation of my touch, Alex groans. I glance up, expecting to see those hungry wolf eyes again, but he looks injured, like I'm hurting him. With an apology, I release my hold on his leg and rub my palm against my own thigh, the sensation of touching him lingering long after I've let go.

The bus hits a pothole, and my head and shoulder knock against Alex's chest. I grapple for purchase, my hand once again landing square on his rock hard thigh.

"Sorry," I say, and pull my hand away again.

He seems amused, but by what? My awkwardness? My constant apologizing? The fact that every time I touch him, I squeeze? I find him increasingly confusing.

He ducks his head, like he's trying to hide his smile. The harsh overhead lights of the bus shine in his hair, and I am transfixed. I've never seen hair so beautiful. It's a riot of reds, as if each individual strand is a different shade, with some bits that sparkle like gems: rubies, garnets, topazes; and other strands that shine like polished woods: cherry, walnut, mahogany; adorned with metallics of bronze and copper. The length is not much longer than the stubble on his jaw, and I wonder if it would be soft or if it would prick in the same way his coarse beard scratched my cheeks. I want to touch it. I quell the urge, but just barely, having to sit on my hands to force them to behave.

Alex chuckles. "What are you staring at?"

Caught, I might as well admit it. "Your hair. You have amazing hair."

"Oh?"

"It's like fire. When it catches the light, it flickers like flames, and it's always changing."

"Like fire, eh?" Alex leans a little closer when he asks, "Are you saying you think I'm hot?"

If words had a texture, a flavor, that question would drip like honey and taste like sugar. I nod absently, staring at his mouth, wanting him to say more of his sexy, sugar words.

He laughs at me again. I shake my head to clear my drunken haze and snap to attention, suddenly defensive. "No."

"No, you don't think I'm hot?"

"No. I mean, yes. No. Shit." My head is a mess. The alcohol is obstructing my ability to communicate clearly, and it's amplifying my social awkwardness to eleven. "I'm going to stop talking now. Okay?"

"Okay." He chuckles again.

He keeps laughing at me, and I don't know why. I'm embarrassed, and I don't know why. As the silence stretches between us, my treacherous mind attacks, and my embarrassment morphs and grows into a full on shame-spiral.

What sort of alcohol-infused madness is this? We'd been having such a lovely time, and then there was that incredible kiss, and now I've ruined it all by jabbering nonsense about his fiery hair. Calling him 'hot' without meaning to, only to then call him 'not hot' without meaning that either.

I frown at where my thoughts are leading. I recognize this terrain. This is my quicksand. This is how nearly all of my social encounters end. I get social. I get chatty and put my foot in my mouth. Then I spend the next week in a quagmire of self-doubt, recollecting all the stupid things I'd said or done. With the weight of tonight's awkward encounters, my neurosis will be gorging for months.

"Are you alright?" Ever the knight in shining armor, Alex's voice punches a hole through the wall of my anxiety oubliette.

"What?"

"Are you alright?" he repeats, his eyes narrowed with concern.

I nod a little too vehemently, and the sudden movement sets my back teeth on edge as my vision wobbles, weaves, and doubles. Heh. Being drunk feels really weird.

"Are you going to be sick?"

His tone is so warm, it makes me want to curl up in his lap and purr like a kitten. Instead, I shake my head, much more slowly this time. "No, I'm just...tired."

"Well, let's get you home safe and sound before you fall asleep. Which is your stop?"

Oh right, I should be watching for— "Oh shit, this is it."

I yank the cord and the bus driver hits the brakes. We lurch forward, my face destined for a smash hit against the seat back in front of me. But with a quick swing of his bicep across my chest, Alex pulls a mom-seatbelt routine. I find my forward momentum stopped not by cold metal and molded plastic, but by warm skin and sensuous muscle.

I try not to hold onto him for too long as I clamber to my feet. Alex makes room for me to pass him in the aisle, then follows behind me, exiting when I do.

"What are you doing?"

"Walking you to your door."

"Why?"

Alex hesitates, then levels with me. "You're very drunk, and from what you tell me, you're new to drinking. I just want to see that you're safe."

"Oh," is all I can think to say.

Alex retrieves his bike before waving an all clear to the driver. In a flash, the bus is gone and we're alone on my dark street. I notice that Alex situates the bike between us as we walk. It's as if he's increasing the distance between us the closer we get to my house. Is this in some sort of deference to my husband? Perhaps it's some obscure proximity rule written into the Guy Code. Alex strikes me as the kind of guy who would adhere to the Guy Code. Or is it because I'm drunk? Alex also strikes me as the kind of guy who wouldn't take advantage of a drunk girl.

I glance at my house as we near it, the lawn well-trimmed, small path lights dotting the crushed granite walkway from the curb to the wide front porch. At the side of the house, the driveway sits empty. Greg isn't home, but of course he won't be home until last call, or later, depending on how his night goes.

I stop walking when I reach my mailbox, and gesture behind me at the modest bungalow. "This is me."

Alex glances over my shoulder to take in the sight of the house. A heavy silence sinks between us like a fog, neither of us seeming to know what to say next.

"So I—"

"Well—"

We both speak at once and stop at once. Alex raises his brow and dips his chin, urging me to continue.

"I just wanted to thank you, Alex. I had a wonderful night," I consider singling out his kiss as being particularly pleasant, but thanking a guy for a kiss is probably a bit weird. "I don't know what other plans you had for the evening, but I'm glad you, you know, changed them."

"Ariana—"

I sputter and cough at the sound of my full name on his tongue, and try to cover the noise with a demure giggle, but it comes out sounding more like a turkey gobble.

Alex smiles at me, the amber street lights twinkling in his eyes, and tries again, "Ariana, tonight has truly been a pleasure. I'm very glad to have met you." He swings a leg over the seat of his bike, preparing to leave. With a subtle bow of his head he adds, "Until we meet again."

"Is it likely? That we'll meet again?"

"For a big city, Austin is a pretty small town. I'm certain we will."

And that's it. He leaves, pedaling away without a backward glance. I watch him all the way to the end of the street, where he's just a speck of a white t-shirt lit by the moon. At the stop sign, he goes south and vanishes entirely. I stand there for a full minute longer, a big dumb grin on my face.

Smile more: check.

•   •   •

"There she is."

I wake to the sound of Jake's excited voice and blink my eyes open. I'm in the living room, passed out on the couch, a bit of drool under my cheek. When I sit up, my head rings like a bell, the walls of the room spinning like a ride at the county fair. I cover my face with my palms to try to make the spinning stop. "Whoa."

"Oh shit." Jake howls, too loud. "Hell has frozen over. Little Miss Goody Two Shoes is *drunk*. Fuck, where's my camera?"

"Did you have fun?" Greg asks.

"Yes. But also, whiskey really hurts." I collapse back onto the couch. They laugh at me as Greg shifts me upright to sit between them, looping an arm around my shoulders to help me balance.

"Well, you're not finished yet." Jake holds up a bottle of Jack Daniels with a pink bow stuck to the side in a half-assed attempt at gift wrapping. "We got you a debutante gift."

I put on a thick Southern accent. "For me? Why you shouldn't have."

"No way in hell you're getting through this night without drinking at least one shot with me, Two Shoes."

I can't think of a good argument, so I take the bottle of Jack from Jake. With a sigh of exasperation, I crack it open and swallow a big swig. It tastes different from the Bushmills, but hurts just the same. I gasp out a puff of hot air like a fire-breathing dragon. Greg and Jake both howl with laughter. Jake takes a swig from the bottle, then Greg, and we settle into the couch, continuing to pass the drink between us.

They ask me about my night, and I tell them, though I keep it vague. I make no mention of Alex or his kiss. As Greg listens, he rubs the pad of his thumb across the beard-burned spot that Alex's stubble left on my cheek. It feels strange to hold onto that secret. It's the first secret I've had in years. I thought I would feel guilty, but I don't. And that realization alone is more liberating than I could have imagined. With another swig from the bottle, I laugh. It feels good. I feel good. Tomorrow I will probably regret some or all of tonight, but right now, I regret nothing.

5—Christmas Eve,
Friday December 24, 2004

Greg is at the window, Jake on the aisle, and me in the middle. The flight is non-stop, thankfully, but bumpy. I'm a nervous flier, nursing my intense dislike for the loss of control with an airplane cocktail. The drink was Jake's idea, and it was a good one.

We hit a pocket of rough air and the plane shudders like it's nervous too. We make a jerky drop toward the earth and my stomach somersaults. I clutch the whiskey and Coke tighter in one fist, white-knuckling an arm rest with the other.

Greg coaxes me to release my death grip on the chair, lacing his fingers with mine, then proceeds to distract me by patiently explaining the science of flight. As he does, Jake pantomimes the concepts of propulsion and lift, and all of his gestures are x-rated. At one point, with his fist formed into "The Shocker," he pumps his hips up as far as his safety belt will allow in order to demonstrate 'thrust'. I giggle. Success. They've managed to distract me long enough for the whiskey to warm its way through my veins, and fog the fear out of my head.

On the ground, my legs are unreliable, stiff from holding such a rigid posture for the duration of the flight. Greg takes my hand and Jake takes my bag, and they patiently maintain the pace I set as we leave the terminal in search of my dad. He's in the no parking zone, waving frantically to get our attention as a traffic cop approaches. We hurry our hugs, handshakes, and hellos, then clamor inside the warm interior of the old SUV.

The drive isn't long from the airport to the house; still, Greg and Jake manage to pass out asleep in the backseat. On the radio, Hank Williams Jr is singing about family tradition. I turn up the volume and stare out the window. I recognize every inch of this road, every gravel driveway, every tree, bush and bramble. With the exception of a new gas station here or there, it's as if nothing has changed in the seven years since I moved from Knoxville to Austin.

Dad takes a left off the two-lane, and starts the trek up our mountain. It's actually more of a foothill than a mountain, and it's not really *ours*, but I still claim it. As a child, this was my domain, my kingdom of hills and dales. I didn't have a pack of siblings or nearby friends, but with my dog at my side, I explored every inch of this area, hollered from every peak.

I grin out the windshield as we approach the house. It's a modest ranch with a welcoming porch. Warm light emanates from each window, forming bright orange slashes against the glooming dusk.

Out of the car, I'm greeted by the soft whisper of wind through the boughs of the trees, and the jangle of Banjo the Beagle's collar as he tears around the corner of the house, his tail wagging excitedly. I hardly have time for a friendly bay of greeting from him before the front door swings open. Mom steps out onto the covered porch, wiping her hands on a kitchen towel.

"There's my girl," she says in her distinct East Tennessee twang, then gives a nod to Jake and Greg, "Boys."

"Ma'am," they respond in unison. They've had years of practice minding their manners around Mrs. Goody.

Mom clutches me close to her chest and says all sorts of sweet things as she hugs tight. She hugs Greg and Jake, too, then ushers us all into the house with a commanding, "Well, go on now, get in the house before you let all the warm air out."

"It's good to have you home, pumpkin," Dad says as he rests his arm over my shoulders and we walk up onto the porch together.

The house smells like cornbread and roasted meat. It's a familiar scent, like so many Christmases before. But, it doesn't feel as comforting as I recall. The potpourri of memory-infused sights, sounds, and smells weighs heavy in the air, cloying, and all I can seem to focus on is how out of place I feel here, and how foreign the word *home* sounds when Dad says it.

When was the last time I thought of their house as my home? I can't remember. Too many years and miles separate me from here. This house always stood as a landmark to help me find my place, should I get lost. But this isn't my place anymore. There's a treadmill in the corner of my old bedroom with more claim to the space than I have. It's been seven years since I settled in Austin, and in that time my definition of home hasn't changed, but my home has.

I do miss this place, though. I miss my family, and I miss the mountains. I miss the way I could see hundreds of trees and thousands of stars from my bedroom window at night. I miss the smell of winter, the changing leaves in the fall, the lush green of summer, and the tumultuous storms of spring. Hell, I even miss the Kudzu. But that's not homesickness, it's nostalgia; I don't miss my old Tennessee home, I miss my memories of it.

At dinner, Jake talks about his band's latest tour; Greg answers my dad's questions about Singapore; Dad details his upcoming hunting trip with my uncles; and Mom discusses what they're reading in her new book club. I pretend to listen as I sit and play with my food, but I can't seem to hear anything over the sound of my racing heart as I silently suffocate. It's impossible to breathe under the crushing weight of my deception. Because that's what my silence is, a deception.

I'm keeping a secret from my parents, and a secret is a lie of omission. That doesn't sit well with me. I've never hidden anything from them. It's part of why I was always such a Goody Two Shoes; I never wanted to keep the truth from them, so I kept the truth parent-friendly.

But now, my truth is changing, and how much of this new reality can I share with them? All of it? Any of it? Deep in my heart, I want to tell them everything. I want to grab onto the edge of the table, rocket to my feet and boldly announce: *Mom, Dad; I kissed a boy who's not Greg and*

I liked it and I want to do it again and that's okay and you should support me.

While the subjects of open marriage and the taste of another man's mouth hardly seem like healthy holiday conversation, my silence isn't fair to them. I'm behaving badly, withdrawn and harassed, but not because of any actual censure on their part. I've done it to myself, passed judgment on myself and then imagined that the gavel is in their hands.

I need to get out of the house, even if just for a moment. I need air. So when Greg and Jake indicate they're going out for a couple of drinks, I announce that I'll join them.

All eyes land on me. Mom and Dad look confused, unaware that their little girl has started drinking. Greg and Jake seem perturbed, like I've just climbed into their 'boy's only' tree house. But as the color drains from Greg's face I wonder if it's more than that. Was 'a couple of drinks' a cover story? For what? Does Greg have an actual date with someone? On Christmas Eve?

I consider my options for backpedaling, but before I can say anything Mom laughs delightfully—we have the same laugh, but I like it better on her. "Great! It will give your dad and me time to wrap your presents."

And so we go, walking out to the SUV single file, like mutinous pirates walking the plank. Once inside, Jake behind the wheel and me up front, I turn to Greg in the backseat and find him frantically texting. Who is he texting? I cringe at the thought.

"So, listen, Greg, I'll just hang out here, I don't want to…"

Greg glances up from his phone, his face a ghostly shade of green from the glow of the screen. "You don't want to…what?"

Cramp your style, I think, but don't say. "I'm just going to stay here, okay? Have a good night."

I hurry out of the car and look up at the house, I don't want to go back inside. I don't want to explain to my parents why I'm not out with the boys.

Instead, I walk toward the expanse of woods behind the house. I keep to the tree line at the edge of the property, so I don't alert Banjo to my presence in his yard.

A few hundred feet into the woods, I stop at an overlook. Already, I feel better. The crisp air is invigorating, even as it burns my nose. Overhead, the trees whisper their secrets to the wind. And off in the distance, I can see Knoxville. The city lights sparkle like citrines nestled in rich velvety darkness.

"Pretty, ain't it?"

I yelp and turn to find Jake approaching me from the woods. My heart racing, I breathlessly admonish him, "You shouldn't sneak up on people like that."

"Can't help it. I'm an Indian, we're physically incapable of walking loudly in the woods."

I smirk, but giggle. "Shut up."

"You just told me to make noise. Jesus, woman, make up your mind."

I laugh again. "What are you doing here?"

"This is where I want to be."

I stare at him, trying to read something in his expression, but he's blank, so I finally just ask, "Greg has a date tonight, doesn't he?"

After a long moment, he nods.

It stings. I'm not sure exactly why. Am I hurt because my husband planned a date at all, or because he planned a date on Christmas Eve...in our hometown...while we're staying at my parents?

While I was drawing a boundary between my life here and my life in Austin, clearly Greg was not. This is where those rules, which I never bothered to establish, would come in handy. If I'd made a rule, like: *Don't sneak out of my parent's house to fuck other women*, then none of this would have happened. But I didn't establish that rule. Technically, I have no cause to be angry. Yet still, I'm angry.

"She was his girlfriend in college, before he met you. Recently divorced and found him online, so..." Jake shrugs and kicks at a rock.

As I process the information, I pace. But the clearing isn't very large, and I'm just walking in small circles. I find a boulder beside a spiny hemlock, and sit. The stone is bitterly cold, the chill seeping through my jeans to nip at my legs. A biting breeze rustles through the trees, and sends a shiver through me.

Jake steps to the edge of the overlook and crouches down to pick up a rock. Analyzing it in the moonlight, he rubs at the rough edges, as if his touch can smooth them out. "For the record, I tried to talk him out of it. Then again, I've tried to talk you both out of this whole stupid thing without any luck."

I don't like the chiding tone in his voice, but I have no defense. Right now, it does seem pretty stupid.

"Why are you doing this to yourself? Isn't it tearing you up inside knowing he's out there with someone else? Why not just get a divorce? If you two are splitting up, why put yourself through this?"

"Who said anything about divorce? We're not getting a divorce, we're just giving each other—"

"Space?" Jake stands and hurls that rock he'd been holding into the blackness at the edge of the cliff. It plummets to the valley floor below us, but I don't hear the impact. "How's your *space* treating you now, Ari?"

Defensive, my words come out sharp as knives. "Fuck you, Jake! Why do you have such a problem with this? This has *nothing* to do with you. This is between Greg and me—"

"Nothing to do with me?" Jake paces in front of me, occasionally sneering and jabbing his finger in the air to make a point. "You guys are my best friends. You're the only family I have left. And one of you is off fucking his bitch ex-girlfriend, while the other sulks on the top of a mountain like some emo Von Trapp, and I'm supposed to, what, choose a side? Fuck you, Ari, I'm part of this too. Don't act like I'm not."

I want to argue with him, but, damn it, he's right. For as long as I've known him, Jake has been there for me; bolstering me when I needed support, challenging me when I needed inspiration, and helping me when I needed a boost. And, even before me, Greg and Jake have been inseparable since they were kids. Orphaned at fourteen, Greg's family practically adopted Jake. Greg is, for all intents and purposes, his brother, and I am his little sis. For him to watch this strange separation between us must be fraught with uncertainty, not knowing how he might be expected to split his allegiances should the worst happen.

"Jake." I rest my hand on his arm and coax him to sit on the rock beside me. "I'm sorry. I'm being a self-absorbed ass. You're right. This absolutely affects you."

Jake grins a little. "I don't need you to be sorry. I just need you to be careful. I can't bear the thought of you getting hurt, either of you."

The forlorn expression in his eyes makes me want to cry. It reminds me of the look my dad gave me the summer I graduated high school, and then again four years later when I graduated college and announced I was moving to Texas.

"I will. I promise." I squeeze his hand, then try to lighten the mood. "But if either of us here is an emo Von Trapp, it's you. The hills are alive with the sound of Jake whining."

Jake gives me his dazzling thousand-watt smile, the one that most people never get to see. "I love you, Ari."

I lean my head on his shoulder and stare out at the view. "I love you, too, Jake."

We both hear the sound of a branch snap, and Jake jerks into full alert, moving to block my body with his, ever the protector. I peek around his broad shoulders, shifting higher up on the boulder to see who's there.

A familiar figure steps out from beneath the darkness of the canopy of trees. The waxing moon kisses the highlights of his honey hair, and glints off the glass bottles he clutches in his hands.

"Change of plans," Greg answers before we can ask what he's doing here. "I went down to the county line, got us some refreshments. Figured we could hang out like old times."

I laugh. I'm not sure why. It just seems so absurd. Jake reaches for one of the bottles, reading the label. "Boone's Farm? You've got to be kidding me. Oh, Jesus Christ, it's Strawberry Hill. Dude."

"I got a bottle of Jack too. Figured we'd celebrate the holiday by getting drunk together like it's the first time." To Jake, "Strawberry Hill for you and me," then to me, "and Jack Daniel's for Little Miss Goody Two Shoes."

"Why did you"—I hesitate to ask, but I have to know—"change your plans?"

Greg blinks a couple of times, then cracks open the bottle of Jack and takes a drink. Finally, he answers, "Because it's Christmas, and I can't think of anyone I'd rather spend it with than the two of you."

Jake nods, a silent acceptance of Greg's peace offering. Slowly, I smile and nod as well. Jake passes me the bottle of apple wine already open, and I take a sip. I make a satisfied sound at the taste. Greg and Jake both let out a devilish cackle.

Greg settles beside me on the boulder, and together we drink and reminisce, our laughter echoing through the mountains. For a little while we forget that there is a tomorrow, and a flight home, back to the open marriage and a world outside of this moment right here on this mountain.

The New Year

6—Monday January 10, 2005

"Ari, you're going, even if I have to club you over the head and drag you there like a caveman." Sheryl's hands are on her hips, her bottom lip puffed out. She's serious.

"Fine," I pout back. "But I'm not singing."

"Ha!" She waves me away with a flourish of her wrist, her bangle bracelets clank along for the ride. "We'll see about that."

I have a new friend. Her name is Sheryl. I've known Sheryl for all of one week. We're complete opposites. She's the Rayanne Graff to my Angela Chase, and it works. It's weird, actually, how well it works. I always thought female friendships would take more time to cultivate, like a garden. And here I was with a brown thumb. But with Sheryl, it all comes so easy.

Take the way we met. It was during 'Free Week'—the week after New Year's when all the music venues in town host local bands and none of them charge a cover fee—at a metal show. I'd been in line behind Sheryl, waiting for the toilet. I liked her shoes, a pair of purple patent-leather platform combat boots, and told her so. She liked my shirt, Mastodon, and told me so. After peeing, we did shots, and voila, best friends forever.

"I'm not singing!" *Seriously, I'm not singing.*

Despite my protests, I'm eternally grateful to Sheryl for getting me out of the house tonight—the night of Greg's big date. After the Knoxville debacle, he'd wanted to make it clear that he was indeed going out. I appreciated the warning and candor, but I hate the images running through my head like one of those gory 'Death on the Highway' Driver's Ed videos: body parts everywhere.

It's nice, not being stuck at home alone. But still, I'm absolutely not going to sing. I don't do karaoke. In the great peep show of life, I'm a voyeur, not an exhibitionist.

Sheryl turns to Manic. "Barkeep, some liquid courage for my friend, please?"

Manic pours us two shots, then leans back and crosses his arms to watch us, seemingly half-amused and half-aroused by our mock cat fight. Clearly, he has a crush on Sheryl. But who doesn't, really? She's a tiny little dynamo of energy, a rock-hard, kick-ass roller girl with killer wit and the heart of a lion. This week, her hair is pink, the same shade as the bubble gum she spits out in order to take our shots.

Sheryl smiles at me, then shouts, "One, two, three—go!"

We toss the shots back and squeal as they burn. Sheryl hops off her seat—in her platform combat boots, she's still only about 5'4"—and gestures to her back as she crouches in front of me. "Your chariot awaits."

She wants me to piggyback? Shit, I've probably got twenty pounds on her. I scowl. This is a terrible idea.

She puts her hands on her hips again. "Any freakin' day now, Mrs. Hendricks."

I look to Manic, whose curiosity is piqued. With a shrug, I slide off my chair and wrap my arms around her neck. I hop up onto her back, and she hooks my legs through her elbows.

"Are you ready, Mrs. Hendricks?" she hollers over her shoulder.

"Wait." I move my hands so that each fist cups one of her breasts, and squeeze. *Okay, maybe I'm a tiny bit of an exhibitionist.* "Ready."

"Hell, yeah," Sheryl whinnies and bucks like a bronco.

Manic lifts an eyebrow. "What I wouldn't give for an hour alone with the two of you."

"Sorry, babe, it's girl's night out. No boys allowed." Sheryl rears back and gallops forward. I squeeze her boobs just to hold on.

Howling with laughter, we clamber out of the bar and nearly tumble to the pavement. A pack of frat boys walks past us, camera phones at the ready. *Annnnd done.* I slide off of Sheryl's back and grab her hand. We dart forward, running at full throttle up the block, until we've reached our destination. The door guy waves us inside, and there we find a lanky man with a mohawk, wearing a bright red skin-tight unitard, and singing Queen like he's channeling Freddy Mercury himself.

"See?" She moves her arm through the air in a grand sweep. "I told you it would be awesome."

"I'm going to need more alcohol."

It is pretty awesome, actually; not how I'd pictured karaoke at all. The crowd looks evenly split between Def Leopard and Abba fans, and everyone is standing at the foot of the stage, singing along.

"What do you want to drink?"

"Beer me."

I head for the bar. The bartender is cute, and he surprises me with a wink when I tip him. My hands full, I awkwardly blink in reply, then take the drinks to find Sheryl. She's secured us seats at a table, but it's already occupied by a guy.

As if reading my mind, Sheryl immediately defends her actions. "I know this is girl's night, but Stephen doesn't count."

"I think she just insulted you." I smile at Stephen as I slide into a seat across from him.

"Some things never change." Stephen gives me a huge grin. "You must be Ari. Sherrie has been raving about you for days."

"Sherrie?"

"God damnit, Stephen." Sheryl pouts at him.

He winks at me as if I'm in on some private joke. Just then, the Queen singer finishes up, and the DJ announces, "Ladies and gentleman, give it up for the one, the only, Mr. Stephen Lowe!"

The crowd goes wild.

"Ladies, if you'll excuse me." Stephen strides to the stage, confidently grabs a mic from its holster, and wraps the cord around his hand a couple of times. The opening strains of "Lust for Life" start up, and Stephen's body instantly changes. As if he's in a trance, he starts to twist and jump and shimmy and shake, laying everything out there as he rips through the song. And what an appropriate song for him—long haired and attractive, but with craggy irregularity, he looks every bit like a thirty-year-old Iggy Pop.

"Do you see why I'm in love with him?" Sheryl asks.

I nod.

"Sadly, he's gone monk."

"Gone monk?" I love Sheryl's use of language.

"He had some problems with drugs and drink and women a while back, so he's sworn it all off. He says he wants to put all of his energy into being a better person and creating art."

That's deep. I like it. When Stephen finishes, he returns to our table. I grin at Sheryl's wide-eyed smitten-kitten expression. She's got it bad.

Next up is the bartender. Interesting. Stephen high-fives him as he passes our table, and it's the first time I've really gotten a good look. He's more than cute; he's sexy—mid-height, with a strong build, and dirty blonde hair that he's constantly pushing out of his eyes. And oh, those eyes! When he takes the stage, looking out at the crowd, the lights catch his irises and they glimmer like emeralds.

As the song starts, I'm instantly charmed. He's chosen one of my favorites, The Animals' "House of the Rising Sun", and he sings it like a pro.

"Who's that?" Sheryl asks Stephen. "I haven't seen him before."

"That's my brother from another mother, Tom. He's a native, just moved back from L.A."

I listen to Stephen, but I don't take my eyes off of Tom. His throat muscles strain when he sings, and his hands clutch the microphone like it's a lifeline. He's intense. I like it.

"So, what song are you going to sing, Ari?" Sheryl's question catches my attention like a record scratch.

I frown at her. "None, *Sherrie*."

"God damnit, Stephen, now you've got her saying it." Sheryl pouts playfully at Stephen.

After a few more performances—none as notable as Stephen or Tom's—it's Sheryl's turn. She hops up, and never stops hopping as she sings "Cherry Bomb."

Stephen watches her with wonderment in his eyes and a slight grin on his lips each time she karate-chops the air and sings the chorus at the top of her lungs. Despite Sheryl's assertion that he's "gone monk," it's pretty clear that he likes her, which makes me adore him.

Sheryl is one of those women who intimidates the hell out of most men. The way she tells it, she's perpetually single. I'm convinced that's not a condition caused by lack of interest, but rather for lack of quality men with the guts to make a move. This guy, however, appears to be pretty evenly matched with her. I'd still put my money on Sheryl, but at least it'd be a fair fight.

"Your turn, Ari," Sheryl shouts when she bounces back to our table.

The DJ's voice crackles through the speakers. "Next, we have a newbie. Give it up for Ari. Come on up here and pick a song, sweetheart."

I will kill you, Sheryl. Kill. Murder. I will strangle your scrawny little neck until you are dead.

"You'll thank me later." She shoos me toward the stage.

"Don't count on it." I make my way to the DJ booth, select a song, and hesitantly climb the steps up onto the squatty stage.

This was never on my myriad 'To Do' lists. I have never sung in public before, nor have I felt the desire to do so. I'm not a performer; I'm a writer. The stage is not where I belong, it's not where I want to be.

My heart races, and my throat runs dry. How am I supposed to sing with no saliva? Oh God, what if my vocal cords seize up like unoiled pistons and I can't breathe, but no one knows because no one would expect a person to suffocate while singing on stage, so I collapse and die while the crowd watches, and some even clap, thinking it's part of the show? Will Sheryl notice? Will she even care that she's killed me with karaoke?

Just as I'm about to go into full panic mode, the familiar tune starts up. I watch the song recognition on Sheryl and Stephen's faces. He whacks her arm and gives me a huge smile. Sheryl looks a little irritated, but she smiles too when I launch into Steve Perry's "Oh Sherrie."

Surprisingly, my voice doesn't crack or shake. I manage to stay on key and alive, for at least the first verse. Slowly, my nervousness subsides, and by the time I reach the chorus, I'm actually enjoying myself.

The crowd loves my song choice, and most of them sing along. When I finish, the room fills with applause, and I hustle off the stage, buzzing with adrenaline and relief.

"Whoa, new girl's got some chops," the DJ announces as I return to the table.

Sheryl is on her feet, hugging me in her trademark chokehold of affection. "You were great. Oh my God, I thought you'd bomb, but you totally didn't!"

"I need a drink." I pull away from Sher and make a dash to the bar.

"You were really good up there." Tom says as he pours me a whiskey sour. "Something tells me that wasn't your first time singing."

"I sing all the time, but normally it's when no one is listening."

Tom smiles as he pushes my drink at me. "I'm Tom."

"Ari."

"Well, Ari, this one is on the house." He gestures to the drink. "The new girl special."

"Thank you, Tom." I awkwardly nod, stuff a few bucks in the tip jar, and turn back to the table.

Sheryl and Stephen are planning some sort of John Cusack-themed flash mob. It involves pub-crawling in trench coats while holding boomboxes that play "In Your Eyes" over and over. They're trying to figure out how to sync all of the boomboxes so that it's not, as Sheryl puts it, "a cacophonous clusterfuck." I only half listen, taking in the scene. The crowd is quirky and talented. And I just sang in front of them. I just sang *in public* and was applauded, and I didn't suffocate and I didn't suck.

After a moment, I realize Sheryl is staring at me, and when she catches my eye, she mouths, *You're welcome.*

Thank you, I mouth back with a wink.

7–Sunday January 16, 2005

"Ari!" Stephen waves at me the moment I step into the bar. Over by the pool tables, he's draped across one end of a couch, his arms stretched across the back and his legs spread wide like he owns the thing. Tom sits beside him, looking much more compact, scrunched against the arm on the far end.

I feel a frisson of excitement shiver through me when Tom looks up and slowly smiles. It's been almost a week since karaoke night, since meeting Tom, and something about the man's simmering intensity and those gem-green eyes has captured my curiosity. I run my fingers through my hair as if checking that it's still there. Yep, still there.

Stephen gestures emphatically at me, beckoning me to join them. I cross the room and crouch down to sit on the edge of a coffee table, facing them.

"Tom and I are having an argument about relationships. We need your opinion."

Well, color me curious.

"You see," Stephen starts. "I have this theory that relationships should not last more than three weeks. When you start dating, you should just be up front with the person and say, 'Let's only date for three weeks'. Then, at the end of that time, you both move on and remain friends. No need for horrible break-ups; just agree up front that the relationship will be short term, and enjoy yourself without the pressure of love and happily-ever-after and all that shit."

Isn't this interesting. I wonder what Sheryl has told him about me.

"Tom thinks that women would never go for that. So we need a woman's opinion."

"Well," I don't even know where to begin. "I'm probably not the best woman to ask."

"Why?" Stephen asks.

Clearly Sheryl has not mentioned my situation to him, probably because my *situation* is hardly worth mentioning. I've been decidedly chaste for a woman in an open marriage. It's been five weeks since Greg and I opened things up, and I've had exactly one kiss. Granted, it was an amazing kiss, a kiss I can *still* feel in my thighs, but one kiss does not an open marriage make.

I've turned down a few offers to shed my next first, all with the hope of seeing Alex again. But after a month with no sign of him, I'm starting to think he never really existed. Maybe my knight in shining armor was some sort of mythical fairy-God-kisser, sent to usher me through my first night out.

Regardless, I'm starting to get antsy. Greg is going out several nights a week, while I stubbornly hold onto the last breath of a first kiss. Perhaps the time is right to take that next leap.

"Well," I take a deep breath and dive in, "for starters, I'm married. But, it's an open marriage, so I'm probably a lot more open-minded about the no-strings stuff, or the low-strings stuff as the case may be, than the average single woman."

Stephen and Tom glance at each other, then back at me, seeming stunned.

"Well, Ari," Stephen points to Tom. "Have you met Tom?"

"I have had the pleasure, yes."

Stephen continues, "He's recently divorced and looking for some no-strings-attached fun."

I laugh, turning to Tom. "Does he always give you this sort of introduction, or am I special?"

Tom grins. "You're definitely special."

Stephen jumps up, announcing, "I need some water. Anyone want anything from the bar?"

When we both shake our heads, Stephen leaves me alone with Tom. We sit in awkward silence for a moment before Tom snaps to attention. "Shit. Where are my manners?" He straightens and pats the couch cushions. "Please have a seat, a proper seat."

I shift from the table to the sofa, leaving a respectable gap between us. We sit in uncomfortable silence. I need something to do with my hands. I inspect my fingernails.

Tom finally cuts through the awkwardness. "Open marriage, huh?"

"Yep."

"So you have sex with other men, and your husband doesn't mind?"

"In theory."

"In theory?"

"Well, we've agreed to the concept, but I haven't actually...you know."

"Ah," Tom nods slowly. "Whose idea was it, the open thing—yours, or your husband's?"

"Mine."

"Your husband must be a pretty chill guy. If my ex-wife had come to me with that idea, I'd have lost my shit."

"Sorry about the divorce."

He turns away from me, staring at the floor. "Yeah, it's been pretty rough."

We fall victim to another awkward pause. Tom seems to be losing himself in his thoughts.

Like a magician, Stephen reappears out of thin air, and plops down on the couch, sandwiching me between them. He drapes his arm across my shoulders, then looks past me to Tom. "So, Tom, have you and Ari established enough rapport to invite her to join us at 80s night?"

"Pretty sure you just did that, Stephen." Tom feigns embarrassment, but it's obvious the two have operated with this shtick before. It's endearing.

"Whadda ya say?" Stephen turns to me.

I shrug. "Sure."

With that, Stephen is on his feet again. "Let's go."

I take Stephen's extended hand and when he pulls me up, I let him drape his arm over my shoulders. He leads me out of the bar, up the block and around the corner, Tom following close behind.

At the club entrance, an enormous door guy lumbers off of his stool to fold Stephen and me into a suffocating hug. After releasing us, he shakes Tom's hand, then waves us all inside.

As we weave through the entrance, the first unmistakable notes of Modern English's "I Melt with You" grow louder. They weren't kidding about 80s night. We head toward the bright haze at the end of the hall and finally spill out into the shifting, multicolored light streams which gyrate to the beat. Before us is an expanse of wooden dance floor littered with swaying shadows.

I hadn't anticipated that we'd be dancing, I'm not a very good dancer. But that doesn't seem to matter as Stephen heads straight for the center, and once there, he takes my hand and spins me, then begins to dance me in circles. His every gesture is exaggerated and cartoon-like. It's fun and ridiculous and at some point, I stop caring that my movements are awkward and my feet tangled. I just dance, and I love it. I smile from ear to ear as I'm twisted and twirled around the floor. Then, with one mighty spin, I'm deposited directly into Tom's waiting arms. Tom doesn't miss a beat as he leads me backward, swaying us nimbly through the other dancers. He sings along with the song and twirls me once more before "I Melt with You" fades out and Spandau Ballet's "True" fades in.

We shift from fast dances, to slow ones; whatever the music calls for, never stopping, never leaving the floor. I'm in heaven. It's cathartic, a release of all my inhibitions and all my troubles.

Dance more: check.

Tom seems just as relaxed. Here on the dancefloor he's not a heartbroken divorcee, he's just a guy with a big smile and some killer moves. After my initial dance with Stephen, he's vanished. I suspect that, having set his friend up with an opportunity to get laid, he's left us to our own devices. And it's mission accomplished for Wingman Stephen. As we dance, laugh, and talk the night away, I find Tom's quiet charm and the way he moves his body increasingly irresistible. I'm pretty sure I'm going to sleep with him.

When I hear the familiar guitar riff and that laugh which starts Duran Duran's "Hungry Like the Wolf" the deal is sealed. I'm definitely going to sleep with Tom. It's time to let him know. I step away from him, still holding his gaze, then bite my bottom lip as I start to sway my hips to the steady rhythm.

With each beat, each shimmy, I come closer to Tom until I'm against him, shifting my hips across his front. His gaze turns hungry and his lips slide into a wicked grin. He traces his fingers down my neck as he leans close and whispers, "I want you."

I nod.

. . .

Tom pulls his truck into the gravel drive of a large house by the side of the highway. He shuts off the engine, but neither of us are quick to move, staring out of the windshield at the expanse of unmown grass that curves down toward the interstate as an eighteen-wheeler speeds by.

Finally, Tom shifts in his seat, kicking his door open to jump out. I take a deep breath, then follow where he leads. When he opens the front door to the house, it creaks. He turns to me, holding his finger to his lips, and whispers, "Four roommates."

We walk on our toes, silently weaving through hallways, across a mostly-clean kitchen and into a bedroom in the back. Seeing his bed— the knotted up sheets at the foot, a pillow folded in half against the headboard—makes it real. This is actually going to happen.

As if sensing my nervousness, he asks, "You sure you're up for this?"

I think about it for a moment, still staring at his bed. It's a lot to process. I've only ever had sex with one man, my husband, and that's about to change. But that's not the part of this which makes me nervous. The idea of sleeping with another man excites me. It's the nudity that makes me anxious. It's like stage fright, but worse: naked stage fright.

I haven't been naked in front of anyone new since I was eighteen. A lot has changed since I was eighteen. Standing here, staring at Tom's wrinkled sheets, I feel my age. I feel older than my age. I feel the force of gravity pressing down on the perky parts of my body.

In all the years I've been naked with Greg, I've never felt self-conscious. Greg has always enjoyed my body in an uncomplicated, wholly-accepting way. He likes to rest his head on the softness of my belly, and when he's in the area, he always kisses the dimple on my left ass cheek.

Will Tom appreciate the maturity of my curves in the same way, or is he expecting to unearth some svelte supermodel under these clothes? Do I care? A little, yes, but not enough to change my mind. I take a deep breath to center myself, then nod. Yes, I'm up for this.

I look over at Tom. He's trying to appear calm, but his eyes give him away. "I am. Are you?"

He considers—perhaps mulling all those same thoughts which just went through my mind—and nods. He steps away from the wall where he's been leaning and I do the same. We meet in the middle, and our lips touch for the first time. It starts softly, hesitant, like we're learning each other, but we shift closer as the kiss grows harder, more insistent.

My nervousness ferments into raw energy which wells up and begs for release. Naked stage fright forgotten, I move my hands to his body, working at the bottom of his shirt and unbuckling his pants. Tom fumbles with the zipper on my skirt. Once we've managed to strip in an awkward frenzy, he presses against me, stepping forward and moving me backward until I hit the bed and fall across the rumpled sheets.

Tom lands on top, and kisses me as his hands explore. He traces his fingers down my abdomen to between my thighs, then follows that same path with his mouth. God, it feels good. I gasp and moan and dig my nails into his back, not wanting him to stop. But he does, climbing back over me with a crooked grin as he reaches to the drawer of his side table for a condom. When it's on, he returns his attention to me, bluntly pressing his way inside.

I stare up at him, watching his face change with each stroke. I can't take my eyes off of him. This man, this near stranger, is the only man to be inside me other than my husband. It feels odd, so different. His rhythm, his scent, the sounds he makes, his eyes which go even greener with his growing excitement; it's all new and noteworthy. I want to remember everything. I try to commit as much to memory as will fit in my sex-addled brain.

Tom moves slow and then faster, finally balancing on his knuckles as he pounds hard into me. God, yes, I like the way Tom fucks. Building toward release, my moans grow louder. Tom falls heavy onto me, and covers my mouth with his hand; self-conscious of his roommates, I suppose. Regardless of the reason, it turns me on even more. I wrap my legs around his waist and drive my hips up to meet his.

I come with a scream, my voice muffled by Tom's fingers. His eyes grow large and oh so green, excited as he watches me. When I quiet, he moves his hand off my face, and gently kisses my lips. "I'm sorry about that. It's just...you're very vocal, which I like, but—"

"Don't apologize." I'm breathless, my voice just a whisper. "I liked it, the hand; it was hot."

His eyes flare and he suddenly pulls out, then turns me over and yanks my hips up to meet him, pressing back inside, taking me from behind. Oh, God, yes. Tom is a good fucker.

I brace myself against the headboard as I feel myself building again. From my thighs, it radiates through every muscle in my body. Everything clenches and I erupt. This time I bury my face in his pillow to muffle my sounds. It smells like him. Tom clasps my hips, and presses hard into me for a few more strokes before he groans when he comes. Then, spent, he collapses beside me.

Well, that was...awesome. I feel amazing. I feel free. I feel sexy. I feel everything. I'd feared that I would be overcome with guilt or regret, but there is none of that—only elation; awesome, awesome elation.

Have a one-night stand: check.

We both flop over onto our backs. Tom smiles and gently kisses me again. He props up on an elbow, and stares down at me, brushing errant strands of hair out of my face.

"Are you okay?" He's so sweet, treating me like a deflowered virgin.

"Are you kidding me?" I grin and brush his bangs out of his eyes. "I'm fucking fantastic."

He laughs, then curls against my side, laying his head on the softness of my belly—I can't believe I'd been worried about that. I run my fingers through his hair, enjoying this moment of intimacy, after all that relatively-anonymous sex.

Tom lifts his head and smiles at me. "Hey Ari, want to be my three-week-girlfriend?"

Have a one-night stand: check.

8—Friday January 21, 2005

"Jesus Christ, stop talking. You fucked the guy; I get it. I don't need a diagram," Jake says with a frown.

I suck down the last of my gin and tonic. I hate gin. Lesson learned. I order a vodka tonic this time. New drink in hand, I turn back around and join Jake in leaning against the bar, waiting for the band to start.

"So, aside from fucking every douchebag you meet, what have you been up to?"

"Stop exaggerating. There's been one guy, and he's not a douchebag. Actually, I think you'd like him."

Jake grimaces.

Okay, change of subject. "I tried pot."

He laughs. "And?"

"Meh. It made me giggle and cough. Nothing new."

Jake shakes his head. "I can't believe how much you've changed in just a couple of months."

"I'm still me."

"You're out fucking random dudes, and getting high. What's next, snorting coke, shooting up heroin?"

I frown.

"I remember when you used to spend your Friday nights writing. Are you still working on the book?"

I take a sip of my drink and look down, kicking at the corner of one of the floor's mismatched vinyl squares. The guitar player starts his sound check and the room echoes with a handful of chugging chords. I have to talk loudly to be heard. "I'm taking a break. Anyway, what good is a writer with nothing interesting to write about?"

"Why do you say that? Your mind is full of interesting shit. You know it's not about how many guys you fuck, right? Being easy doesn't make you more interesting."

"Is that what you think I'm doing? I'm not doing this to seem more interesting. I'm doing this because it interests me."

Jake looks like he has more to say, but the band picks that moment to start, drowning the room in a deafening roar of guitar and screaming vocals. I try to get into the music, bobbing my head to the beat, but I can sense Jake beside me, tense and tied in knots.

I glance over to see if he's still frowning at me, but he's looking past me now, his face twisted into a vacant frown. He inclines his chin, imploring me to turn and look at what's got his attention.

Greg.

He's just walked into the venue, standing at the top of the ramp which leads down into the crowd. And there beside him is a beautiful blonde, holding his hand. He leans close and says something to make her laugh. She has pouty Brigitte Bardot lips, and she wears her five-alarm fire-engine red dress like the actress too. Jesus, she's gorgeous, and so young.

The blood drains from my head, leaving me cold. But that only lasts for an instant before a rush of heat flushes my cheeks. I feel unsteady, like I might pass out. The music sounds discordant and too loud. It pierces my ears and rattles through my head. I need to get out of here, but Greg and his French girl are between me and the door.

"I need to pee." I don't wait for Jake to respond before I bolt for the bathroom. Inside, the music is mercifully muted, and I'm miraculously alone. I dive into the last stall to sit while I catch my breath, collect my thoughts.

My God, I'm so naïve. In all my philosophical musings about giving my husband space and freedom, I never anticipated that I'd be staring at his *freedom* as she looked so smoking hot in her fire-engine red dress.

But, this is good, right? I needed this dose of reality. This thing that Greg and I agreed to in the abstract, it's really happening. Can't pretend it's not. And it is a good thing. It's all above board. It's kosher. It's copacetic. So why do I feel like a piece of gum stuck to the bottom of a shoe?

I look around at the graffiti on the walls; anything to distract me. Written in giant letters on every surface of the stall—the walls, the door, the toilet paper dispenser, even the little tampon trashcan—are the words, "I Love Chris Nix," scrawled over and over again in large shaky letters. In between the myriad Chris Nix worship, other little thoughts pop up; pornographic drawings, hearts and initials, and right in the center of the door, in purple glitter block letters:

"Life shrinks or expands according to one's courage."
~ Anais Nin

I rub my fingers over the ink to see if it smudges, as if the words were written just for me, mere seconds before I sought solace here. The ink does not budge. The words echo in my head, then spill out of my mouth on the wave of a heavy sigh.

Courage. I wish I could say I had the courage to be honest with myself about how I feel right now. Am I hurt, or am I only reacting with hurt, because I think that's what I should feel? Yes. Maybe. No. A little? Ugh!

Someone enters the bathroom, and then another; a line is forming. I stand and flush the toilet, even though I didn't use it. At the mirror, I wash my hands and pretend to check my hair.

Now what? Should I talk to Greg or avoid him? Introduce myself and be the "cool" wife who doesn't mind that he'll probably be balls deep inside her before the night is over? Or do I leave without a word?

A line is forming for the sink now. I turn away from the mirror just as Greg's date steps into the bathroom, joining the line of ladies in waiting.

Really, Universe? My courage pops and hisses around the room like a deflating balloon.

I make my way toward the exit, having to repeatedly excuse myself as people slide out of my way in the cramped quarters. At the door, Greg's date gives me a guileless grin. There is a complete lack of recognition in her eyes. She has no idea who I am, and I'm not sure if that makes me feel better or worse about this awkward encounter.

Whatever. I can't breathe in here. I need out. It takes all the energy I have to return her smile as I fumble with the door handle and push out of the room. Out in the shadows of the hallway, I suck in a gulp of air and march toward the bright lights, thunderous noise, and suffocating crowd.

I aim toward the spot where I left Jake, and see Greg there, the two trying to talk despite the band. Greg spots me, too, and weaves through the thick crowd to come to me.

"Ari, I'm sorry."

Why is he apologizing? He's done nothing wrong.

"I didn't know you'd be here. I didn't plan this—"

I want him to stop explaining, so I interrupt, "For a big city, Austin is a pretty small town. This was bound to happen sooner or later."

My discomfort lightens briefly, when I remember the person who'd first said those words to me, Alex. God, if only my imaginary knight in shining armor would appear right now and save me from this awkward encounter. But, no, this is the real world, and in the real world you don't get the pleasure of a repeat visit from your fairy-God-kisser. No, in the real world, you run into your husband and his date.

Greg agrees with a nod, but his eyes keep glancing over my shoulder toward the bathroom door. Of course, he's watching for her. He's worried about having to introduce his date to his wife. Yep, this is definitely what it feels like to be a piece of gum stuck to the bottom of a shoe.

The walls start to close in, and the crowd seems to grow in height and frenzy. I gasp for breath, but the air in here is heavy and damp, and there's not enough of it. I need out of this conversation, out of this bar, out of this entire situation.

"Greg, I think the music is giving me a headache. Can you tell Jake I decided to leave?"

"Ari—" Greg furrows his brow with concern, but I cut him off before he spits out another apology or says whatever it is he thinks will improve this situation. It won't. The only cure for what ails me right now is distance.

"Greg, it's okay, really; it's just a little weird. I need to get some air, okay, some space." Funny, isn't *space* what this whole open-marriage thing was supposed to be about? Yet I've never felt so claustrophobic.

Greg doesn't respond, and I don't wait for him to. I turn and wave at Jake, whose face falls when he realizes my intention to leave without him. Before he can gesture to me, or protest in some other way, I head for the door and scurry outside. I feel like crying, but I don't. I won't. Surely I can muster enough courage not to cry.

I need a drink, some liquid courage to fortify my wavering spirit. I turn the corner and walk into one of my favorite bars. To my great relief, I spot a familiar face.

Tom.

"Boy am I glad to see you," I admit as I saddle up onto the stool beside him.

"Ari!" Tom's eyes grow huge, and he starts glancing around the room. "You can't be here."

"I can't?"

"I... I'm with someone."

"Not even a week and you're already cheating on your three-week-girlfriend? I see how you are."

It was meant as a joke, but Tom furrows his brow like he has no idea what I'm talking about. "Ari, please. She's in the bathroom. If she comes out and sees me talking to you she'll...I mean...she's not like you, she's—"

Do I look like I've been slapped across the face? Because I feel like I've been slapped across the face. "She's not like me? What does that mean?"

"I don't know...nothing. I'm sorry, Ari, but...*please*. I really like her. Please don't screw this up for me."

Gum on the bottom of a motherfucking shoe.

I nod and silently slide off of the stool to leave. I could stay, it's a free country, and men and women can sit side-by-side at a bar without it being an infidelity, but the air is starting to thin in here too.

Outside, I try, again, not to cry. God, what an idiot I've been. All I'd wanted from Tom was a one-night stand, and I'd gotten it. But, oh no, then I had to go falling for the sweet talk. I'd actually believed Tom when he'd asked me to be his three-week-girlfriend. I'd thought it could be fun. I look down at my hands, white-knuckled in tight fists, pressed against the rough bricks. *This is not fun. Lesson learned.*

My phone chimes, announcing a text from Jake: **Where'd you go?**

I'm just around the corner from where I left him, not sure if I want to reply. Do I really want him to see me like this? He already thinks this whole thing is a bad idea. If he were to see me right now, he'd be absolutely certain the idea is terrible. I don't reply, but it doesn't matter. He's looking for me, and he finds me.

Jake approaches with his head cocked to the side, a look of pity in his eyes, but he kindly doesn't say anything, just leans against the wall beside me. His presence is a comfort, desperately needed. And, despite all the awful emotions I've felt tonight, the one which surfaces now is pure love for Jake and his unwavering friendship. I turn and wrap my arms around him. The gesture catches him by surprise, but quickly he returns my hug.

"I told him about the show, but I didn't think he'd bring Kate." Jake sets his chin on the top of my head. "He told me she hates metal."

"Kate?"

Jake pulls back, just enough to frown at me. "The chick with Greg."

"Oh." I'd almost forgotten about her. Shit. What am I upset about here? Greg or Tom?

As if on cue, the door beside us opens and Tom steps out with a blonde trailing behind him. Tom's eyes meet mine, then flash to Jake, who still has his arms wrapped around me. Tom drapes an arm around his date as he silently walks away. My eyes follow them, and Jake watches with me.

"What was that about?" he asks once they've turned the corner.

"He's the guy."

"Tom is the guy you fucked?"

Jake knows Tom? Jesus, this city is small.

Jake grabs my arm and drags me in the direction of his truck. "Let's go get some pancakes."

• • •

This is our ritual. When his last band broke up, we ate pancakes. When my cat died, we ate pancakes. One plate. Two forks. Short stack. Blueberries, butter, and loads of syrup.

"About Tom," Jake says. "Why him?"

Shit. I was hoping he'd let this sleeping dog lie. I'd rather talk about the weather or sports or global thermal nuclear war: *anything* else.

"Why *not* him?" I twirl a forkful of pancake in the pool of syrup and take a soggy bite. Talking with my mouth full, I ask, "Do you really want a list of reasons?"

"No. I really don't." Jake plays with his food, but he's not eating.

I drop my fork on the plate and slouch in my seat. "Okay. Fine. What's got your panties in a bunch?"

Jake smirks. "My panties are in a bunch because I can't figure out why you're doing this. It's dumb. You're being really fucking dumb right now, which, for someone as wicked smart as you, is mildly alarming."

"Thanks...I think?" I'll go ahead and find the compliment buried in that backhand.

"The only thing I can figure is that Greg fucked up royally. Like maybe you're punishing him for cheating on you or—"

"No. God, no. It's nothing like that. Greg has done nothing wrong."

"Then why? And if you start waxing philosophical about *space* again, I swear to Christ, Ari, I'll vomit all over your pretty dress."

"We've already talked about this, like, a million times. Why do you keep wanting to rehash it?"

Jake just stares at me, waiting.

I stare back, like it's a contest. Eventually, I lose. "I stopped smiling. I stopped laughing. I stopped feeling happy or fulfilled, and I don't know why. It wasn't because I was sad or angry or...anything. I was just...numb. I asked Greg if we could open our marriage not because there is anything wrong with him, but because something is wrong with me. I don't want to be numb anymore."

"So it is punishment, but it's you you're punishing."

"It's not *fucking* punishment." I have to work to keep from shouting, there are other diners here. "I'm not punishing anyone, I'm...seeking."

"Seeking? And what has your little find and seek mission revealed, other than that men enjoy an easy lay?"

I frown.

"Because you definitely don't look happy now. And you didn't look *fulfilled* earlier when you were running away from your husband and his fresh squeeze."

I open my mouth to argue, but Jake talks right over me.

"And, hell, I get that you were feeling unhappy, or unfulfilled, or un-fucking-whatever, but couldn't you find a less self-destructive solution to your problem?"

"It's not—"

"Why not volunteer at a soup kitchen or join a goddamn bookclub? Most people, when they're feeling down, they get a new hobby, not a fucking STD—"

"Okay, that's enough. I'm done listening to this shit." I rocket to my feet and stomp toward the door. Jake curses in my wake, but I don't look back. I push through the exit, already scrolling through my contacts as I pace and shiver in the January chill.

Behind me, the diner door clangs open, and Jake hollers, "Where the fuck are you going?"

"Home," I answer as I select Yellow Cab and listen to the ring tone.

Jake jogs to catch up with me at the far end of the parking lot. He grabs my phone and snaps it shut. "What the fuck, Two Shoes? We were in the middle of a conversation back there."

I don't bother to control my volume out here. "That wasn't a fucking conversation, that was me sitting there listening to you hurl abuses."

"I wasn't—"

It's my turn to talk over him. "Let me be clear, Jake, because this is important. I've made a decision that I feel is right for me. *The end.* I don't have to justify it to you. And you don't have to like it, but if you want to remain my friend, then you damn well have to accept it. Now, give me my fucking phone back."

He huffs and his nostrils flair like an angry bull, but he gently sets my phone back in my hand.

"Thank you." I resume calling a cab.

"Ari, stop, please. I'm sorry, okay? I'm sorry." He huffs. "Jesus, hang up the damn phone. I'll drive you home, alright?"

I stare at him for a moment, then close my phone and slip it into my purse.

Jake isn't quite ready to leave though. He toes a loose chunk of asphalt with his boot, then kicks it clear across the lot where it crumbles on impact with the curb.

Finally, he speaks. "Look, Ari, you're the only living woman I love. When you hurt, I hurt. And tonight fucking hurt. I understand where you're coming from, I do; I miss your smile too. But...Jesus..."

Christ, he's going to make me cry. I hug him, squeezing his big shoulders as tight as I can. He stiffens, not expecting affection so soon after my anger, but quickly wraps me in his warm arms and lets out a shaky breath.

"Oh Jake, you big softy."

"Fuck off."

I chuckle and squeeze him tighter before letting him go. "You know, I'm not as breakable as you think, right?"

Jake plucks a strand of hair out of my eyelashes and pushes it behind my ears. "Yeah. Sometimes I forget that I'm the breakable one." He loops an arm around my shoulders and steers me toward his truck. "It's been a long night. Let's get you home."

9—Saturday February 12, 2005

The bar is on fire, or at least it feels that way. They must have the heat turned on, but it's not necessary. The wall-to-wall humanity acts as a furnace and charges the air with a sultry blend of pheromones.

This is nothing new for a Nebulous show. I attribute the sexual energy to Jake's lyrics. He writes like he lives; debauched and libidinous, yet moody and oblique. On the surface his songs are about pain and torment, but every syllable teases at something more erotic. It comes off as S&M, which I've never thought was Jake's style, but the dark double-entendres work for the crowd. Nebulous' fans tend to be a little kinky.

Around me, an assortment of latex and leather-bound bodies writhe and quiver despite the sweltering heat. This is nothing new either; it's the regular uniform of their crowd. What is new is that I'm dressing the part too.

Ditching my usual ensemble of denim mini, cotton tee, and oxford Chuck Taylors, I've stepped into a new role for the night. Squeezed into the black leather miniskirt and corset I borrowed from Sheryl. The shoes are hers, too, thigh-high patent leather stiletto boots that pinch my toes, but give me a few inches of height, as well as a boost to my confidence. I've pulled my hair back into a severe bun at the nape of my neck and kohled my eyes to complete the look, which lands me somewhere between hardcore dominatrix and those chicks in the Robert Palmer videos. I've left sweet, unassuming Ari at home. For tonight, I'll be playing the role of badass bitch. It's like Halloween, but on Valentine's Day weekend—Valloween.

I straighten my shoulders, steel my spine, lift my chin, and strut, which is the only way to walk when you're strapped into stilettos and leather. But, not accustomed to walking in heels, I start to wobble and stumble before I've even made it ten feet. A wave of panic rushes through me, and I look down at the beer-slicked concrete floor, wondering how much it will hurt when I ultimately go sprawling into a graceless face plant at the foot of the stage.

I reach out to the wall for support, but Sheryl swoops in to save me. She links her elbow with mine, gracefully guiding me toward the stage. I give her a mile-wide grin, seriously jeopardizing my status of badass bitch, but I don't care.

With a wink, she moves us forward into the morass. We are quite the pair tonight, perfect polarity. In compliment and contrast to my dark ensemble, Sheryl practically glows in her brilliant white latex dress and platinum blonde hair. She is the yin to my yang, the good to my evil, the naughty angel to my divine devil.

As we walk, Sheryl's attention is drawn to the stage, her gaze fixed on Jake. He looks like a warrior up there. He's plaited his hair into two neat braids that lay against his bare chest. Shirtless as usual, he's wearing only a pair of black leather pants. Even his feet are naked.

"Oh girl, I do *declare*, that man is *fine*." Sheryl drawls out her words like a southern belle. "You gonna hit that?"

"Are you talking about Jake, the singer?"

She nods and waggles her brow.

"Oh God no, that'd be like incest or something."

"Wait... He's your brother?"

"Not technically, no, but close enough. He's all yours, babe, and you're totally his type this week."

"Oh yeah, what's his type?"

"Blonde, boobs, and breathing," I say with a wink.

As if he can sense us talking about him, Jake's seeking eyes find us in the crowd, and his pensive expression turns to some combination of amused and awestruck. With a broad grin, he elbows Greg in the ribs.

And Greg, who'd been helping Jake lug his massive amplifier onto the stage, looks around. The moment he spots us his mouth falls open.

I guess that means Greg likes my Valloween costume. Good. I wore it just for him. After our awkward run in at the last show we'd both attended, Greg had made it a point to ask me out on a date to tonight's show.

Sheryl chuckles. "So that's the hubby, eh? He's pretty hot too."

Yeah, he is. Unlike me and my costume, Greg's gone with his usual simple style. But he still looks gorgeous in his basic black t-shirt and jeans. He jumps down from the edge of the stage, landing solidly on the soles of his heavy boots, and blazes a path through the crowd toward me. I practically purr as I watch his approach.

Sheryl makes a *meow* sound and winks at me. "Girl, I don't know what you're thinking leaving *that* unattended. If it were me, I'd be staking my claim so hard I'd be pissing on all the bitches sniffing around him."

I chuckle at the imagery, but ignore the comment.

When Greg reaches us, he scans me from head to toe, and back up again, then slowly licks his lips. I shiver all over and squeeze Sheryl's elbow a little tighter.

"Greg, this is Sheryl," I introduce them.

Greg is quick to shake her hand. "I've heard a lot about you. Ari said you're a roller girl. What position do you skate?"

"Jammer. I skate as Sher Nobyl. Ever seen a bout?"

"Flat or banked track?" Greg asks.

"Flat."

Greg nods. "Once, last season. Jake's band played the half time show, so I came out. Pretty cool shit."

"Fuckin' sweet! I'm trying to convince your wife to try out."

I guffaw. "After seeing me in heels, you can't seriously think I'd be anything other than a disaster on skates."

Sheryl doesn't say anything, just gives me that look that tells me she has big plans. That's my cue to leave. I get drink orders from them, and they return to their roller derby discussion while I head to the bar to place our orders.

Heel. Toe. Heel. Toe. Heel. Toe. I have to remind myself not to say the words out loud, or silently mouth them as I practice my sexy strut toward the bar. When I've finally got the hang of it, I look up at my destination and come to a full stop. I nearly twist an ankle and tumble onto my ass when I see who's bartending tonight.

Tom. Really, Universe?

When he spots me, he does a double take at the sight of my leather getup and gives me a crooked grin. He gestures me over to the opening beside the bar, so I meet him there. Not expecting much, I'm surprised when he hugs me. And I'm surprised again when he holds me a few moments longer than what's considered polite among former fuckbuddies. When we finally pull apart, his eyes go straight to my boobs, pushed up into the stratosphere by the corset. He subconsciously licks his lips, then clears his throat and finally looks up. "Hey, gorgeous, what can I do you for?"

My mind goes blank, and it takes me a moment to remember. "A Screwdriver, please, and two Lone Stars."

He holds my gaze for a moment longer before making me a top-shelf Screwdriver and popping the tabs on two Lone Star tallboys. When finished, he slides them to me and refuses my money.

"It's on me, but listen," Tom moves closer. I step back, but there's no room to maneuver in the crowd. "I want to apologize for—"

"Tom, it's really not necessary. You don't need to—" I nearly yelp when he places his hand on my forearm, his fingers tracing soft circles on my skin. The touch sends a shiver through me and I lose my train of thought.

"Ari." Tom leans in close so he can be heard over Jake's sound check. "About that night, when I saw you, I was an ass and I'm sorry. The rest of that night was miserable. Jennifer turned out to be..." He pauses, shakes his head then smiles at me. "Anyway, I regret that I didn't just hang out with you that night."

I don't actually want to hear any of this. I'd written Tom off weeks ago. I'd moved on. I figured I'd bump into him again eventually, but I wasn't expecting an apology, and it makes me uncomfortable that he's giving me one. This was all just supposed to be a mindless good time, a free-for-all fuck with no apologies and no regrets. I grimace. "Tom, I—"

"Shit," Tom interrupts with a gentle hand on my elbow. "Hang on just a sec, doll. Duty calls."

Doll? I frown. He squeezes my forearm and gives me a wink, then returns to the bar. I watch him, wondering why I'm still standing here. I should just walk away, go back to my date with...

Greg.

He's there. Standing at the bar just a few feet away from me. He's been waiting for the bartender to take his order. And while waiting, he's had to watch said bartender touch my arm and whisper in my ear in that way that only a lover would.

No, no, no, no, no, no! This is so wrong. This is supposed to be *our* night, *our* date. And here I am, talking to another man, letting another man lay his hands on me, flirt with me. My blood runs cold. I'm flooded with guilt. And fuck this city with its small-town complex. This place is like a goddamn Habitrail, the two of us a couple of hamsters constantly bumping into each other everywhere we turn.

Greg glances at Tom and orders a round of shots. As Tom pours, Greg watches him with a cold, assessing stare before his gaze returns to me.

I have no idea how to behave in this situation. I force a tight grin, and Greg does the same. When Tom finishes the drinks, Greg pays and pushes back into the crowd.

Tom returns to me, completely oblivious, and picks up where he left off, moving in too close for comfort again. "So, what are you doing after the show?"

"Tom—"

"Cuz, I'd love to get you back to my place—"

"Tom—"

"—bend you over—"

"Tom, listen—"

"—you can keep those shoes on while I—"

"Jesus, Tom, shut up!" *Badass bitch talking here!* Tom pauses and frowns at me, but finally he's listening. "I'm here with my husband tonight. That man you just served is my husband. So—"

"Your husband?" Tom shouts so loudly that several people turn to stare at us. Tom's eyes dart around the room in a near panic, and his skin goes ashen, like he might be sick. He takes a big step back, his face twisting into an awful scowl.

"I'm sorry." Why am I apologizing? Habit, I guess.

Tom stares at me, and I watch his eyes turn cold, the spark of whatever it was he felt for me extinguished as if smothered with a wet blanket. His expression turns rigid, and he shakes his head as he turns and walks away.

I take a deep breath, grab my drinks, and wobble my way back over to Sheryl and Greg, the stiletto strut not coming as easily this time.

Sheryl has watched the whole exchange, and gives me a supportive shoulder nudge when I hand her a beer. Greg, on the other hand, is studiously staring at the stage as if there is nothing else to see, still clutching the three shots he's bought.

"Wanna swap?" I ask, then want to kick myself. Oh, for want of better phrasing.

Greg frowns, and I hold his beer up, gesturing at the shots in his hands. He quickly understands and we exchange shots and drinks until all three of us are set with one of each.

"Well, cheers," I say.

We all drink our tequila, then wince at the burn. Sheryl collects our glasses and leaves to give Greg and me a moment alone. We stare at one another, Greg's expressionless mask firmly in place.

I step close to him, press against him, and move my mouth to his ear to say, "I'm sorry. That was not what it looked like, but I'm still sorry."

Greg pulls away just enough so he can look me in the eyes, then his gaze darts toward the man behind the bar. "Would you prefer to leave with him tonight?"

I laugh. Greg thinks I would abandon our date for Tom? "God no. Not even a little bit. I came with you, babe, I'm leaving with you."

Greg's eyes flash with heat as he leans in close and whispers, "You haven't *come* with me yet, sweet thing, but you will." Then he surprises me with a kiss. His lips are hard, demanding. It's a branding kiss. Let no man or woman here be confused: tonight, I'm his. I like it, his claim on me, and claim him back.

On stage, Jake's drummer Dillon starts in with a steady beat on his cymbals and tom. Soon he's joined by Ryan on bass, whose throbbing rhythm vibrates through the whole room. When Jake's guitar kicks in a chugging chord, Greg spins me around and pulls me into his arms, hugging me tight against him as we sway to the building beat.

Jake belts out the first line of the song. His provocative vocals ratcheting up the sexual tension, heating the room a few more degrees as everyone around us begins to writhe and twist, a maelstrom in the sea of humanity. Greg and I move as one, him holding me close and guiding my hips with his. I let him have his way with me, relishing the feel of his warmth at my back, his hands on my front and his mouth on my neck stealing little kisses and tastes.

Nebulous's set is longer than I remember. At the end of each song, I hope for Jake's customary goodbye to indicate that the show is over. But it's just song after sex-saturated song, building the tension up to thigh-clenching, member-throbbing, now-I'm-just-getting-sore levels. At my back, I can tell Greg is in the same state. I can feel his rock-solid erection pressing hard against my ass. His lips touch my ear and he whispers, "If I don't take you home real soon, I'll be taking you in the men's room."

I shiver at the thought, then practically cheer when Jake leans into the microphone and announces this will be their last song of the night. Greg squeezes me tighter to him, his dick goosing me in the ass. I yelp. Sheryl winks, seeming fully aware of the pants party happening at my rear, then goes back to dancing.

She's been dancing this whole time, flitting in and out of our radius like a firefly, buzzing with energy and light. I watch her, captivated by the sensual way she curves and twists, the way she closes her eyes and just feels the music move through her. It's gorgeous. I grin at my beautiful friend, and watch the faces of the wanton men and women who stare at her like she's a mirage in the desert, everything they want, but always just out of reach.

I'm reluctant to leave her alone. Greg grumbles about my concern. When the band finishes their set, Jake immediately comes down from the stage and Greg whispers something in his ear.

Jake smiles wide. "Hey Sheryl, I'm Jake. Greg asked me to make sure you get home safely so he can go home and bone his wife. Cool?"

I nearly choke on my tongue. Greg frowns at Jake. Jake smirks at Greg. Sheryl gives a big nod to all of us and says, "Cool."

Greg and I are a bit taken aback, but Sheryl shoos us away. "Well, go on, get!"

"Uh. Okay. Well, call me tomorrow, let's do lunch—" I yelp that last part when Greg grabs my hand and tugs me out of the building.

We're silent during the cab ride home. Greg has me tucked close to him, my head resting on his shoulder, my legs draped across his lap. He stares out the front window as his fingers gently stroke up and down my inner thigh, each lap inching further up my leg. I respond by spreading my thighs wider apart. He kisses my temple and whispers, "Naughty girl."

Once home, Greg kicks the front door shut, and with two long strides, he closes the distance between us. He covers my mouth with his, and practically devours me with a heavy, hard kiss. Still advancing, he pushes me backward until my back hits the wall. The air rushes out of me on a gasp and a moan.

Good lord, tonight I hardly recognize the man I married. This man before me, kissing and nipping at me, is an animal; feral, powerful, aggressive. I love it. I revel in it.

With me cornered against the wall, at his mercy and his pleasure, Greg attacks, his movements urgent, his breath ragged. He shoves one hand down the top of my corset while he cups my ass with the other. He bites at my lips, my jaw, my neck. I bite him back, anywhere I can reach. When I get a good nip at his ear, he hisses and pulls away from me. Grabbing hold of my hips, he spins me around and shoves me face-forward against the wall. The impact jostles a framed photo of us in our wedding whites and guileless grins, sending it rattling and lopsided, dangling askew from its nail.

Greg pushes the hem of my skirt up, and when he finds I'm not wearing any underwear, he growls in my ear. His cock, still in his jeans, jerks excitedly as he presses hard against my bare ass. I practically purr, rubbing against him as he works himself out of his pants and shoves hard and deep inside me.

The sex is sloppy, rough, and perfect. He fucks me hard and fast. He fucks me with his face pressed between my shoulder blades, exhaling humid, hot breaths down my spine. He fucks me like a stranger, not like my husband. Nothing about the man grunting behind me, gripping my breasts as he nails me against the wall reminds me of my husband. Tonight feels like a one-night stand, a single night of fire and desire, ephemeral and exhilarating, unsustainable, but a hell of a lot of fun.

I come screaming. Behind me, Greg slows his pace until he stops, still filling me, still breathing hard in my ear. He speaks, and it takes me a few seconds to recognize his words.

"You want to *what*?"

Greg moves inside me, a single maddeningly-slow stroke that takes him almost all the way out and back in again. I gasp and shiver at the sensation. Greg runs his tongue up the side of my throat. He nibbles at my ear as he admits, "A while back, I found a list you'd made. I shouldn't have read it, but I did." Another long slow stroke out and back in. "I know you want to try it. Please..." He moves inside me again. Slow, ever so fucking slow. "Please, let me fuck your sweet little ass."

I blink, stunned.

"I'll make it good for you, I promise."

I gasp when he moves inside me again. His deliberately slow pace is a literal cock tease, and extremely effective at keeping me amped up and horny and more amenable to letting him boldly go where no man has gone before. I bite my lip, nervous, but nod.

Greg kisses me hard, then drops to his knees behind me. I watch over my shoulder as he explores me with his mouth and fingers. He takes his time, working me until I'm not only ready, but desperate for him. He rises back up to his full height behind me, and I shiver and stiffen with nervous energy. Greg whispers in my ear, "Relax. You can trust me."

I do relax, because I do trust him, and that's when he takes me. The sensation is strange at first, something somewhere between intense pleasure and burning hot pain. Greg hisses in my ear, like it hurts him too. Then, slowly he starts to move inside. And—

I come...hard...really, really hard. I open my eyes and see stars. Every part of me shakes and shivers, like I'm having a seizure. It's total sensory overload. It feels like Greg is fucking every nerve in my body, and all the synapses in my brain fire in one ecstatic explosion. I scream in ecstasy, until my voice goes hoarse and silent. Greg comes, too, shouting, "Oh fuck," over and over again until his voice softens to a whisper, still repeating that same refrain.

Try anal: wow!

I might *try* that one again.

Slowly, we come apart and catch our breath. I start to laugh, a combination of nervous energy and an odd bit of embarrassment, like we've been caught doing something we shouldn't.

Greg grins wide, and it's beautiful. "Did you like it?"

I laugh. "What, are you deaf?"

He laughs, too, and takes my hand in his, leading me to the bathroom and helping me into the shower. We clean up together, then linger under the hot water: hugging, caressing, kissing. Here in this space—flush with our afterglow, the Valloween makeup washed down the drain, the flirty bartender long forgotten, inaugural butt stuff behind us—we relax together. For the first time tonight, Greg isn't my one-night stand, he's my husband again.

10—Friday March 18, 2005

"You weren't kidding; they *totally* sound like sex!" Sheryl shouts to be heard over the music. "They look like sex, too. *Meow*."

She's not wrong. I look up at the stage and sigh at the sight. The members of Mammoth each look different: some with beards, some without; some have long hair, others short; some are small, and some are tall; but all are hot...and Irish. Bonus points.

Sheryl and I are at the very front of the crowd, having used our innate charms to wiggle our way to the stage. Our arms draped over the audio monitors, we brace ourselves against the melee behind us.

After a particularly long growl by the singer/guitarist, their driving beat climaxes into a louder, faster frenzy, a stampede of sound. The crowd goes absolutely nuts, pulsing with energy and aggression, ebbing and flowing and swirling to the beat as the mosh pit punches and kicks at our backs.

Oddly enough, I love every minute of it. Somewhere deep inside me lies a gluttonous need for brutal contact. There is nothing quite like a metal show to make me feel completely alive, if a bit bruised the next morning—kind of like good sex. Jesus, am I in heat or something?

What is it about South by Southwest that has this entire city so hot and bothered? Austin is generally always sexually charged, but this festival is overflowing with sweaty bodies and horny hookups.

Cool down, Ari. I take a sip of my drink just as I'm body slammed from behind by someone in the pit. A splash of my cocktail sloshes into my face, and I laugh, wiping it away. All's fair in love and metal. When I hug myself tighter to the lead singer/guitar player's monitor, I see him glance down at me as he growls the lyric, "strong heart."

I hold onto his speaker for the entirety of the show, completely immersed in the experience, banging my head in perfect sync with each grueling beat. When the band finishes I feel equal parts spent and renewed; like I just cried and orgasmed all at once.

"Let's go meet them," Sheryl squeals and I furrow my brow. As if it's that easy. As if we can just walk right back stage and meet the band.

Apparently, when you're two cute girls in miniskirts, it is that easy. We head upstream through the tide of people drifting toward the exits, and make a turn at stage left to find the backstage door guarded by an honest-to-God mammoth of a man. My eyes go wide with panic at the thought of being sent packing by this guy. But when he spots Sheryl and me, he grins from ear to ear, gives us a nod and waves us through the door.

Backstage, the guarded inner sanctum, is really just a gravel-paved courtyard with a single wooden picnic table near the center. That's where we find the band. Two of the guys smoke cigarettes while the lead singer/guitar player and drummer talk about mistakes in the set.

Sheryl interrupts their conversation. "Hey. I'm not going to tell you guys how awesome you are. I'm sure you hear that all the time. I'm just going to invite you to an after party at my house."

They look bemused. "After party?"

The lead singer/guitar player seems to be watching me. I quickly glance away, but inside, I'm squealing: *Oh my God, Aidan Connor is looking at me!*

Sheryl actually does squeal, excited when they agree to come. I assume this means it will be a party of six—the four band members and the two of us. But when we arrive at Sheryl's house, there are cars lining both sides of the street, and the house is packed with people. Leave it to Sheryl to throw a party in her absence.

Incredibly, this is the first time I've been to Sheryl's house, and the place is exactly what I'd expect: an explosion of color and chaos. She has random mannequin limbs, painted in glittery jewel tones, attached to the walls and ceilings. The furniture is all mismatched and covered in brilliant swatches of fabric. Overhead, she's glued broken bits of mirror to the popcorn ceiling. The band is as amused as I am, turning in circles to try to take it all in.

"Feckin' mental," The drummer mumbles as he scrutinizes a lime green mannequin head with a orange wig and a pirate patch.

There are at least half a dozen dogs mingling with the party goers. I step over a sleeping pitbull as I find my way to the kitchen, looking for something to eat. All that remains is a browning bowl of half-gone guacamole and a bag of chip crumbs.

"Looks *manky*." Irish accent; oh lord, could it be? I look up to find that Aidan Connor has followed me to the grub.

Oh my God. Oh my God. Act natural. I blink at him, then awkwardly turn away and forage through Sheryl's fridge. There I find another bowl of guacamole wrapped in cellophane, still mostly green.

"Care to share?" *Oh my God.* Aidan Connor is staring into the fridge with me. What do I say? My brain struggles to process his words. Is he speaking English or Irish? He doesn't wait for my answer. Grabbing the bowl from the fridge and a bag of chips from the counter, he aims for the back door. "Come with me if you want to eat."

I follow.

The back yard is enormous and surprisingly empty—most people haven't made their way past the living room, where Sheryl has set the keg. It's just us and a few smokers hovering like moths near the porch light.

We wander to where the moon guides us, a large trampoline in the back corner. He pushes himself up onto the bouncy surface, impressively managing not to crush the chips in his maneuvers.

I follow his lead, awkwardly scrambling onto the trampoline, then roll onto my back so I can sit up. We both sink toward the middle, and there he opens up the food and takes a heaping mouthful of chip and dip.

"So, can you not speak?" He points to his throat, a sweet concern in his eyes.

Oh God, Aidan Connor thinks I'm mute. I nearly choke on a chip, then clear my throat and explain, "No. I mean yes. No. Sorry. I just get quiet when I'm nervous."

"Why are you nervous?"

Is he joking? Does he not know who he is? I mean, Jesus, he's the lead singer and lead guitarist of *the* hottest up-and-coming heavy metal band in the world. Chainsaw Magazine recently anointed him the Master of Doom Metal. His latest album is charting and there's talk of a Grammy nomination. Also, he's really good looking.

He's got jade green eyes, and fair skin that glows milky white in the moonlight. His hair and beard look midnight black in the dark. To be honest, I've never particularly liked beards, but on him, I do. And there in the void of his pitch black beard is his mouth, it's amazing. His lips are ridiculously huge, almost too big for his face, and perfect, so lush and kissable—

"Well, anyway, I'm Aidan."

"I know." *Shit.* I quickly correct, "I mean, I'm Ari."

Grinning, Aidan jabs his hand out for me to shake. His palms are soft, but his fingers are callused like Jake's, guitar-player hands.

An awkward silence falls between us, punctuated only by the sound of crunching chips. Within just a few minutes, we finish the entire bowl of guacamole. Aidan slides it all off to the ground, then stretches out on his back. I follow his lead, lying down to look up at the stars.

In spite of the fact that I'm at a raging party and hanging out alone with Aidan *fucking* Connor, I feel so relaxed I could drift off to sleep. Lulled by the gentle undulations of the trampoline beneath us.

Except that Aidan is moving too much. He slides his legs around in restless swipes and lets out a heavy sigh before he snaps upright, like a giddy schoolboy. "Let's jump."

"Oh God, I might vomit."

"Do you think guacamole looks the same coming back up as it does going down?"

I crinkle my nose and cover my mouth. "Now I'm definitely going to vomit."

"Well if vomiting is a certainty, then I'm definitely going to jump." He climbs to his feet unsteadily, and starts to hop. For an up-and-coming rock god, he's kind of goofy.

With each jump, I'm tossed into the air, arms and legs flying, like a cat trying to right itself. Finally, incredibly, I make it to my feet and start to jump with him. He reaches out and takes my hands, and we sync up.

I laugh as we get higher with each leap, but soon notice a heavy feeling in the pit of my stomach, then in my throat, then—oh shit, I'm going to puke. I yank my hands free from Aidan's grip and spin around. Falling to my knees, I vomit over the side of the trampoline.

"Feckin' hell, Ari. I'm such an eejit." Aidan dives to his knees at my side, and holds my hair as I retch up everything I've just eaten. "I'm sorry. I thought you were just letting on."

I finally stop puking. My eyes, nose, and throat burn as I wipe my mouth and try to catch my breath. "I thought I was too."

"Well, at least now we know the answer. Guacamole does look the same coming back up."

Despite myself, I giggle.

"I should tell ya, I thought I might kiss you tonight, but not now that you've made a right hames of things."

Now I full-on laugh. Aidan moves and the undulations send another wave of motion sickness through me. I cover my mouth, about to retch again.

"Let's get you on solid ground." He helps me off the trampoline and leads me to a set of concrete steps by the garage.

When I'm feeling better, I admit, "This is so embarrassing. I'm usually much better with first impressions."

"Aw luv, this wasn't your first impression. This was your fourth or fifth at least. You made a good first impression at the show. I looked down to find you cuddled up with me floor monitor, standing solid against the pit. Quite impressive. What's a little vomit after that?"

"There you are!" We both look up to see Sheryl stomping across the yard toward us. "I was starting to worry."

Sheryl pulls me up. I'm unsteady on my feet. Aidan notices and jumps up to wrap an arm around my waist and help me to stand.

"Sheryl, can I lay down in your bed?" I ask.

"No way! You two are not fucking in my bed."

Aidan laughs.

I explain, "No, not for sex. I just need to lie down."

Aidan helps, "She's unwell. She vomited."

Sheryl pouts. "Oh no, what's wrong, honey?"

Aidan pipes in again, "Entirely my fault. International trampoline incident. I was acting the maggot, as usual."

Acting the maggot? Sheryl mouths at me with a bemused smirk, then loops one of my arms over her neck. "Of course you can lie down. I have an extra toothbrush you can use too."

Aidan follows us inside. The rest of his band is playing beer pong with Sheryl's ex-boyfriend, but Aidan passes them, helping her get me to the privacy of the bathroom where I lean over the sink, splashing water on my face, and brush my teeth with her ex-boyfriend's toothbrush.

"Aidan, darlin, you need to give my girl some privacy." Sheryl shooes him toward the door.

"Oh. Okay. Sorry. I hope you feel better." He bows and closes the door behind him.

Sheryl holds my stare for a beat before we both crack up laughing. "Oh my God, you puked on Aidan Connor—"

"Not *on* him."

"In front of him, whatever, and yet he's drooling all over your shoes like a love sick puppy. That's pretty much *the best* SXSW story ever, and girl, I've heard some doozies."

"Guess I can check 'make a fool of myself' off my To Do List."

"Wait. You actually have a list?"

I nod and blush with embarrassment.

"And 'make a fool of yourself' is on it? Oh my God, I love you so hard right now, you big dork!" Sheryl wraps her arms around me and squeezes so tight she could break bones, then starts hopping up and down as she squeals.

"I love you too, Sher Bear, but if you don't stop jostling me I'm gonna barf in your hair."

With that she springs away from me and holds up her hands in surrender. "Okay, honey bun, take a shower and get some sleep. I'll sleep in the spare room, if I sleep at all. I'm working on Glenn, the drummer." Waggling her brow, she adds, "Maybe I should puke on him."

I smirk, but giggle.

Sheryl goes to leave, hollering over her shoulder, "Lock the door behind me. I don't want anyone sneaking in here and having their way with you." Once I've turned the latch, she yells through the wood, "Good night, lover."

· · ·

I wake to the scent of bacon. Out in the living room, there are a handful of half-naked bodies tangled together on the couches and the floor, and every surface that isn't covered with mannequin parts is littered with discarded cups and other party detritus.

I find my hostess in the kitchen, surrounded by drooling dogs; she's frying eggs in one skillet and bacon in another. Like the people passed out in the living room, Sheryl is barely dressed, wearing nothing but a pentagram-patterned apron, knee socks covered in skulls and a pair of red ruffle undies.

When she spots me, she taunts, "You have a *date* tonight."

Huh?

Behind me, a groggy male voice mutters, "Bacon."

Huh?

Sheryl scowls over my shoulder. "Hey, no shirt cocking in the kitchen."

Shirt cocking? Bacon? Date? What language is this?

I turn in my chair to find a tall, scrawny man leaning against the doorway. He's wearing an old Ministry t-shirt and absolutely nothing else. Whoa. I blink at his pale, hairy thighs and the dick dangling between them. Okay, well, that explains "shirt cocking."

Sheryl fearmongers, "What if one of these hungry dogs were to think that wiggly wiener is a squeaky toy and latch on?"

Shirt Cocker's eyes go wide as he watches the lazy, lolling-tongued dogs like they're a pack of vicious predators, and wisely clasps his hands over himself.

Sheryl shooes him away. "Go find yourself some pants, and then you can have bacon."

"Who's that?" I ask when he's gone back into the living area.

Sheryl shrugs, "No clue. Friend of a friend, I guess. He and about six others were too drunk to drive home last night, so I stole their keys."

"Did you steal their pants, too?"

Sheryl doesn't bother to answer as she dishes the food onto a pair of plates. The dogs whine and beg. "Anyway, you have a date with Aidan tonight."

"I do?"

"He insists he owes you dinner. You're meeting him at that Mexican joint at Twelfth and Red River at eight."

"Mexican food. Was that his idea or yours?"

"Mine." She shrugs. "He's a tourist; what'd you expect?"

"Was the date his idea or yours?"

"All his. He couldn't stop talking about you. He's cute when he's smitten."

I blush and change the subject. "Speaking of cute, how'd it go with the drummer?"

"Well," Sheryl brings the plates over to join me at the table. "After you help me kick all these people out and clean up the place, I have a date too."

"Oh? And where are you meeting?"

She grins. "His hotel room."

"Ho."

"Puke pickup artists who live in glass houses, uh, something about throwing rocks."

Shirt Cocker, wearing pants now, comes back into the kitchen. He's like one of Sheryl's drooling dogs, begging at the stove for her to drop him a bite, but the skillets are empty now.

"Oh, sorry, sugar." Sheryl's tone is so saccharine it hurts my teeth. "I didn't mean you could have *my* bacon. But, hey, now that your pants are on, it's time for you to go. Your keys are in a pile by the door."

• • •

"Pretty bold," I challenge him as I approach the table. "Asking me out on a date while I was unconscious. Didn't exactly give me the option of saying no, now, did you?"

"I think the word you're searching for is *brilliant*." Aidan stands and assists me with my chair. "And you could have easily said no."

"How would I have contacted you?"

"Not showing up would have been a pretty clear *no*."

"What kind of person would I be if I left you stranded and alone at a Mexican cantina in a foreign country?"

"A terrible person, indeed," Aidan laughs.

We give our orders to a beautiful brunette who can't take her eyes off of the metal god in our midst, clearly a fan. He hardly spares her a glance, studiously focused on his menu. But, once she leaves, he leans a little closer.

"I'm glad you came. And, might I add, it's nice to hear you say so many words, full sentences and everything. Do I no longer make you nervous?"

I heat with embarrassment at the reminder of my awkwardness last night, it was a new low, even for me. But, yeah, it does seem that I'm a bit more at ease here with Aidan today than I was yesterday. "Once a guy has held my hair back while I puke, what's left to be nervous about?"

Aidan chuckles and I like the way his large lips stretch into a smile.

Speaking of words, there are a few that I should go ahead and get out of the way tonight. "Aidan, before this goes any further, I need to tell you something about myself."

"Sounds mysterious. Crack on."

God, I'm starting to hate this part. "I'm married."

"Feckin' hell!" Aidan coughs down a sip of water. "That's no' what I was expecting."

"There's more."

"More? Jaysus."

"It's an open relationship, so I can, you know, be with other people." I stare at the basket of chips and ramakin of salsa set at the center of our table, then look back up at Aidan. "So, anyway, I don't know if you have anything in mind for tonight, but I wanted to get that out there up front."

Shit. Did I just suggest that we'd be having sex tonight?

"A *husband*, " he says the word like it doesn't fit in his mouth. "And your *husband* doesn't kill these other men?"

"He's too busy sleeping with other women."

Aidan's eyes go wide with surprise. "So it goes both ways then?"

"Of course it does."

He takes a moment to process what I've said, then gives me a salacious smile. "Fair play to ya. I'm gobsmacked."

Mercifully, our food arrives and provides a great distraction from the layers of personal information I've just shared with him. Oddly, I don't feel the usual anxiety that follows my big marital reveal. I'd been joking, before, about the vomit being an icebreaker, but maybe there's something to that. We've hardly spoken to one another, and yet I feel remarkably relaxed with Aidan. And, as I watch the way he chews and swallows his food with that glorious mouth, I become increasingly curious about him too.

"So," I hesitate, but only for a moment. "There is something I've been wanting to tell you. I'm curious about your opinion."

Aidan finishes the last of his meal, takes a long pull from his margarita, and waits for me to go on. When I don't, he dips his head so his eyes meet mine. "Yes?"

I take a deep breath and let it out. " I love your music. Love it."

"Thanks." He frowns. He clearly doesn't enjoy compliments.

Quickly, I continue, "I think it sounds like sex."

Aidan looks a bit stunned, like I've slapped him across the face. Then he laughs. "How does it sound like sex?"

He wants me to explain? He doesn't already know? How could he not know? He wrote the damn songs.

I take a long pull from my margarita and slide forward in my chair so I can speak in a hushed tone. Aidan stacks our plates at the far side of the table so he can lean a bit closer too.

Okay, here goes.

"Take the song 'Inside', for example; it opens with a guitar part that churns in this slow rhythmic build." As I describe it, I start to move my hips to the rhythm, like the song is playing in my head. Aidan notices, his eyes travelling down my body, his hands clinching into fists on the table.

"And then about six minutes in, the song hits a climax and churns louder, and everything gets bigger, harder, faster. The sound just keeps building and building until it ends with this explosion of notes. And you're growling your lyrics while Ian is screaming his. And...it sounds like really good sex...to me...so...uh...yeah..."

I finish that last part in a whisper, completely embarrassed that I've just pornographically dissected the man's song—a song which is actually about the evil of humanity—and described the whole thing like some horny teenager reading her fanfic masturbation material aloud.

Aidan blinks and swallows hard. When he finally speaks, his voice comes as a soft growl. "That's got to be the sexiest thing I've ever heard."

I let out a slow breath.

Aidan's eyes go feral and his gaze falls to my lips. "Let's get out of here."

· · ·

It's a short distance to Aidan's hotel. His room is dark, but the curtains hang open, providing a beautiful view of the twinkling lights below. I stand in front of the floor to ceiling windows, staring down at my pretty city, and half expect Aidan to approach from behind, wrap his arms around me and share the view. He doesn't.

I turn to find him watching me from the spot where he stands at the end of the bed. His jade eyes shine with a predatory intensity. His posture is predacious too, like a cat ready to pounce. But he doesn't. He doesn't move a muscle, just stares at me.

What is he waiting for? Me to lead? I hesitate, but just for a moment, before I cross the distance between us and come to stand before him.

Aidan is as still as a statue, marble in the moonlight, so I balance on my toes to reach his chiseled lips. I kiss him, and that's when he moves, a sculpture come to life. He lets out one of those noises he makes on the album, a deep metal growl, and wraps his arms around me, kissing me back.

Clearly, he'd been waiting for me to make the first move, and that revelation is oddly exciting. I'm in charge here. The sensation is new and neat. I've never had a boy to play with before; this could be fun.

To start, I push him. Aidan isn't expecting it and stumbles backward onto the bed. I almost apologize, but he looks amused so I stay silent. He props himself up on his elbows to watch me, like I'm about to put on a show for him. I guess I could.

It's another first for me, performing, sexually. Energy buzzes through my nerves, a strange mix of anxiety and empowerment. I take a deep breath to quell the anxiety, and exhale it in a slow blow to bolster the empowerment. Then I start to move.

The music is only in my head, but that's enough. I sway to it, moving mostly my hips, then letting the movement overtake me. I turn away from him, returning to stand in the window.

The view from up here is mesmerizing, all those thousands of lights winking and flirting with me from every corner of the city, like an adoring crowd. And so I perform, slowly unzipping my dress and letting it pool on the floor around my feet. Then I take off the rest of it too. Behind me, I hear that deep metal growl again—the perfect response—and it buoys my confidence. I turn to my private audience of one, letting him look his fill at my shadow, haloed with the aura of the city lights.

"Take off your shirt," I direct.

Half his mouth quirks in a cocky grin, but Aidan does as he's told, tugging it one-handed over his head to reveal pale smooth skin, sinewy tight muscles. With each step I take closer to him, his breathing accelerates, and those muscles rise and fall with anticipation. I settle onto his lap, my legs straddling his thighs, and feel his anticipation there, too.

When I kiss him, he tries to take control, cinching his arms around my waist, but I push him away again, landing him flat on his back on the mattress. I brush my hands over his chest, enjoying the feel as his muscles quiver and spasm in response to my touch.

Once I've teased him long enough, I reach for his hands and guide them to my breasts, letting him touch me now. He adores them, squeezing and kneading and hungrily taking them into his mouth. I wrap my fingers around the back of his head to bring him closer, to hold him there. He groans. He's clearly loving this, and, God, so am I.

I leave him and his chin follows me, silently begging for more, but he does not complain when I slide down onto my knees on the floor in front of him. He watches me tug off his boots and socks, and then I pull at the button fly of his jeans until it pop, pop, pops open. I find him uncircumcised (my first), ready, and waiting for me.

Aidan hisses like my touch burns, and sucks in a sharp breath when I open my mouth and swallow him deep. He tries to take control again, his hands clumsily grasping at my shoulders, my neck, the back of my head.

No. There'll be none of that. I peel his fingers away then move to my feet, crossing the room to the credenza by the window.

He starts to apologize, like what he's done has sent me away. But I soon return, having pulled a condom and my iPod out of my bag.

Tossing him the condom to take care of, I hold up the music player, "I want to prove my theory. Let's fuck to your music."

His brow furrows as he works the rubber, he lets out a nervous laugh. "Kinky."

"Too weird?" I come to stand between his legs at the edge of the bed, and watch his eyes trace over me.

He takes a moment to consider, then silently shakes his head.

I straddle his lap once again, this time allowing his hands to wander as he touches me everywhere. His callused guitar-player fingers feel exquisitely rough on my sensitive skin, a stark contrast to his soft lips, which trail wet kisses across my breasts.

While he's busy with that, I work the music player, pressing one earbud into my own ear and the other into his. I hit 'play' and wait for the first note of the song to—

There it is: that opening chord. I impale myself on Aidan's length and we both groan. He's large, and it hurts at first, but I start to move through the pain, riding him in sync with the slow, sludgy rhythm.

Soon the pain is gone, and all I feel—perfectly, intensely—is Aidan. He grabs my hips and moves me like I'm his instrument. After all, he knows better than anyone the tempo of this tune. He watches my face and grins at my gasps when he presses extra deep on every fourth stroke.

When the beat picks up, he moves faster, harder, and deeper. He flips me over onto my back, driving down into me with the growing ferocity of the music. Incredibly, the earbuds stay in place, but we hardly need to hear the song, the rhythm is rote.

I drive my hips up to meet his, increasing the pace and friction between us. We both pant and gasp and at one point, he growls just as he does in the song.

I can hardly stand it; I'm fixin' to pop and there are still two minutes left in the song. Aidan bites his lip, almost there as well, but we hold out, resolved to follow the rhythm until we get our release with the climax of the music.

Finally, just as the song is wrapping up, there is an explosion of sound, and we both let loose with the ecstatic build and release of the rhythm. He loses all sense of tempo as he pounds into me, growling when he comes. I dig my nails into his back and arch up as I scream out.

"Sweet Jaysus." He flops onto his back with a heavy sigh, then laughs up at the ceiling. "Did we prove your theory?"

I sound like the Kool-Aid Man when I answer, "Oh yeah."

When he's caught his breath, he quietly asks, "Does it make me an egotistical arse that I just fucked to my own music?"

"No." I stretch like a cat. "It makes you a songwriting genius."

He laughs with a low rumble that shakes the bed. I grin over at him, and find him smiling at me. "How many condoms do you have in your bag there, lass?" He slides up on his elbow and traces little patterns over my abdomen with the rough tip of his finger. "I have the entire Zeppelin IV album on my laptop."

"My, my, aren't we ambitious?"

He nods and circles his finger around my navel before sliding his hand lower.

We're going to need more condoms.

11—Thursday April 14, 2005

"Isn't it beautiful?" I ask as we settle onto Sam & Bea's park bench.

"Beautiful," Greg agrees as he kisses my temple and drapes his arm over my shoulders.

This is nice, just the two of us, together again. It's been so long since I've spent quality time with my husband. Shortly after Valentine's Day, he was called to Dallas for work, and he's been bouncing back and forth ever since. Between his constant travel and our rather busy social calendars, I've hardly seen him.

I sigh and nestle into his embrace as we take in the view of the tall trees, the babbling brook, and the lush green meadow thick with the bloom of spring. I'm content to sit here for the sunset, but Greg's knee is already bobbing.

"Bored?" I ask.

"Just hungry."

"Okay. We can go to dinner."

Greg squeezes me in a little hug then springs to his feet, pulling me up too, talking the whole time, "How about steak? I've been craving a good t-bone."

"You've been in a swanky Dallas hotel for weeks. How have you been deprived of the opportunity for a steak?"

"It was all about *sushi this* and *sushi that*." When he says 'sushi' he puts on an exaggerated voice, as if he's imitating someone, a woman. "Tonight, I just want a big juicy steak, and my wife. In that order."

I chuckle, "Well, let's see what we can do about that."

He leads me to his car at the edge of the park. His luggage is still in the backseat, and the center console is littered with half-drunk cups of coffee, one sporting a lipstick stain on the rim.

As we drive, I ask Greg about his work in Dallas, but his answers lack detail, so I stop asking and stare out the window, feeling oddly out of place at his side. It's a relief when I see our destination ahead. That relief is brief.

The moment we walk through the door of the steakhouse, I sense that something is terribly wrong. Warning bells ring shrill in my head as I watch Greg's posture stiffen, his forward movement stopping midstride.

I open my mouth to ask if he's okay, but I know he's not. He's gone ghost, the color drained from his face. Why? What has him so upset?

"Greg?" I hear my husband's name called out with bubbly excitement, but I'm too focused on his Casper-complexion to really notice. Then that same voice, now meek like the squeak of a mouse, sighs with disappointment, "Oh."

There is so much heartache in that one little syllable. For a split second, I stupidly wonder why. Following Greg's gaze, I turn my head, and it all becomes abundantly clear.

Kate.

I can hardly believe my eyes. Greg's gorgeous date from all those months ago is standing right in front of me looking shattered. Beside her, a handsome Latino man in a dapper suit stares at me with his mouth hanging open.

None of us move. We don't speak. It's as if time stands still, and we're frozen in place—a herd of mammoths mired in the tar pits, slowly dying.

Finally, it's Kate's companion who speaks. First to Greg, "Hello, I'm Antonio. I've heard a lot about you." Then he turns to me. "And you must be his *wife*."

The word 'wife' cracks like a whip. There's disdain implied in his tone, censure for a crime I'm not aware I've committed.

"Ari," I offer, and shake his hand.

"Charmed."

The restaurant door swings open and a party of women walk inside, all chatter and chirp, boxing us into the narrow lobby. The piercing sound makes me flinch, and seems to snap Greg out of his fugue state.

"I'm sorry," he says, but he doesn't direct his words to anyone in particular. Who is he apologizing to? What is he apologizing for?

The restaurant hostess returns to her stand and retrieves a handful of menus as she looks at Kate, Antonio, Greg and me, and cheerily asks, "Table for four?"

It's Greg who answers, "Uh, no, we're not together."

If it's possible, Kate's expression drops from crestfallen to a deeper place of hurt. She looks utterly heartbroken and I can't figure out why. I don't understand why all of this is so awkward. They went out, sure, but that was months ago.

It's then I notice that Kate's mauve lipstick matches the marks on the coffee cup in Greg's car. Did he take Kate to Dallas with him? I stare at her, scrutinizing, trying to piece together the jigsaw clues, and I don't like the picture that's emerging.

With the hostess staring at us impatiently, wondering what configuration to seat us so she can get us out of her lobby, and the women pressing in from behind, I start to panic. I can't breathe. I need out. Some sort of fight or flight response triggers within me, and my body makes the decision to flee before my brain can catch up. I turn and maneuver my way through the clutch of chirpy women, feeling everyone's eyes on me. Those five paces to the door are a humiliation.

Outside, I walk around the corner and lean against the limestone block wall to take deep, steadying breaths as I try to regain my composure. *Why am I so upset?* The rational part of my brain tries to answer that question, to make some sense of all this. But I'm deaf to logic, and I'm really fucking upset.

Greg appears around the corner and stops in front of me. He's got his hands shoved deep into his pockets, and his chin tucked tight to his neck like a lost little boy.

"I'm sorry," he says again, and I still don't know why.

I open my mouth, not quite sure what I'm going to say, but the words fire out like hot lead, "What just happened?"

Greg glances up, a shot of whiskey, then quickly focuses his gaze back on the span of pavement between our feet. He looks wrung out; racked with guilt, lashed with pain. *Why?*

I fume. "Why are you acting so strange?"

He seems to want to answer me, but can only manage to stammer and struggle for words.

"Is it Kate?" All I can think about now is her sad pout, matching the lipstick color on that coffee cup in his car. "Was she with you in Dallas?"

Greg jerks his head up and frowns at me, then he lets out a weird sort of laugh. It fills me with seething rage. I'm overwhelmed with the urge to hit him, to beat my fists against his chest, to scream as I kick and punch him.

"Yes," He finally speaks. "She's my assistant. She travels with me."

I blink, stunned, then I'm the one who laughs. The sound is hollow, brittle. "You're fucking your assistant? Could you be more *cliché*?"

The questions are rhetorical; still, I give him the opportunity to answer. He just nods. Not much better than a shrug, a nod is a lazy form of communication, too lazy for this conversation. It pisses me off. I could handle all of this so much better if Greg would just talk to me like a goddamn adult instead of acting like a sullen emo teen.

Rationally, my mind tries to piece the bits of information into a reasonable story. But I can't hear anything rational over the sound of my pounding heart, and the little voice in my head asking all the worst questions: *how long has this been going on with her? What does she mean to him? Is this just a long-term dalliance or something more? Is she in his heart? Am I still in his heart?*

It's that last question that hits the hardest. This was only ever supposed to be a physical exploration, sexual, not emotional. But Greg's odd behavior suggests this is much more than some no-strings fling. It feels like an emotional infidelity.

Infidelity? I squint my eyes shut and shake my head, trying to dislodge the thoughts snaking through my brain, pumping me full of venom. But it's no use. Now I'm an emo teen, too, a girl ready to rage at the boy standing before her.

But I don't. I keep my mouth shut. Some sliver of sanity stops me from saying things I'll surely regret. Instead, I put my foot down, literally, stomping my shoe onto the pavement where Greg has fixed his gaze. He glances up at me, and this time, he doesn't look away. He looks pitiful, wretched.

I can't bear the sight of him right now, so I look past him, over his shoulder to the city beyond. It is a forbidding tableau, built from rigid steel, heavy stone, and cold, sharp glass. The tops of the buildings cut a jagged line across the sky; teeth ready to bite. Yet when I focus on the ambient glow that turns the city sky a warm shade of amber, I see my solace there.

With a decisive nod, I take a deep breath, straighten my spine, clear my throat and announce, "I need some air. I'm going to take a walk."

Greg looks like he's about to speak, perhaps to stop me. His mouth opens and closes a few times, like a fish out of water, but he says nothing.

I frown at him and move away from the wall, away from him, taking two decisive steps toward the corner.

"Ari, wait." Greg closes the gap between us, and wraps his arms around me, crushing me against his chest. The air rushes out of my lungs as his arms cinch tight.

I want to squirm and struggle, to kick and claw my way out of his stifling embrace, but I don't. I push heavy breaths in and out of my lungs and steady my nerves, waiting patiently for him to let me go.

When he finally does, I don't move. I wait for him to speak, naively hoping he can somehow fix this, and magically lift the weight bearing down on my chest. But his only action is to caress my face. His fingers are rough, and I imagine his touch leaves marks, like streaks of Indian war paint across my cheeks.

Finally, I can't stand to be there any longer. I step away from him again, force a grin, and leave.

• • •

"Ari, how many boyfriends you got now?" Maggie asks.

The casual joke lands with a thud. I hide my wince as I slide up onto a bar stool. My walk here has been brief, as I made a beeline for the closest friendly face: Maggie—a cute little tattooed and pierced pixie chick, who's dubbed her style "granny core" due to her passion for baking and knitting. I adore her, and she adores my madcap stories of vice and debauchery, though never in great detail; more like weird little ice-breakers. She waits for one now, watching me with a wonky grin as she bites on the silver hoop in her bottom lip.

Not wanting to disappoint, I force a smile, waggle my brow and pronounce, "Aside from the husband, none. Why do you think I'm here tonight?"

There's a little more bite to my words than I'd been aiming for, but Maggie doesn't seem to notice. "Rawr, girl," she meows at me.

The bar is mostly empty, so we chat as she cuts fruit, me half-watching the movie that plays on the TV over her head. The mindless chatter and tequila shots are exactly what I need, and I already feel myself starting to unwind when I hear the door open and close. Maggie and I both turn to welcome the new patrons, and when I see who's come in, I smile.

Kelly O'Brien is one of the biggest flirts in Austin. I've come to know Kelly well. We chat whenever we land in the same bar at the same time, and it's always a pleasure talking to him, but nothing has ever come of it. Despite his many sweet smiles, smooth compliments, subtle touches, and occasional winks, he seems uninterested in making that one last move—the all-important line ("so, let's get away from all this noise," or "want to see my vinyl collection," or "let's go to my place and fuck like bunnies") which will take us to the next level.

Maybe tonight will be different.

As Kelly steps through the door, I notice another man enter behind him. Stuffing his ID back into his wallet, and his wallet back into his jeans, this newcomer follows Kelly toward the bar. The pair of them couldn't be more different from one another. Kelly is exceedingly tall and thin, almost gangly, though somehow he doesn't come off as awkward. He's light, with fair skin that nearly glows under the warm amber lights of the bar, wide blue eyes and a mop of pale blonde hair. The other man is average in height, but short compared to Kelly, and compact, his musculature tight and sinewy. He's darker than Kelly, too, with rich brown skin, jet black hair cut high and tight, and dark topaz eyes. Despite their disparate appearances, there is no question that the two men are together. They walk with a rhythm that comes from years of striding side-by-side; these two go way back.

The new guy subtly scans the room before his dark gaze settles on me. When he notices that I'm staring back, he gives me a devilish grin that promises nothing but trouble. Caught staring, I blush and glance away, back at Kelly and his lazy smile.

"Greetings, O'Brien," Maggie bellows. "And who have you brought us?"

Kelly's smile goes wide and he loops an arm over his friend's shoulders. With a nod to Maggie and me, Kelly announces, "Ladies, allow me to introduce Gabriel Martinez, my oldest and dearest friend." Then, in a stage whisper to his friend, "Gabe, whatever you do, do not piss off these women. Mags there can kick your ass with one arm tied behind her back, and Ari over here isn't nearly as cute when she's angry."

My jaw drops, and I can't help but laugh at the odd introduction. Then, feigning irritation, "Fuck off, you."

Kelly laughs, "Yeah, I'm a liar, Ari's always cute."

"I'll say." Gabe grins and takes the bar stool beside me. Without missing a beat, Kelly folds himself onto the stool at my other side, the two flanking me.

Once Maggie's taken their orders, Kelly leans over and rests his head against mine, an odd little show of affection unique to Kelly, and cats. "Hey there, sexy lady."

"Hey back."

"How's shit?"

"Shit's good." I grin. "How's shit with you?"

"Can't complain when you're around." Kelly beams a big smile. "Also, got my boy here in ATX for the next few days."

I turn to Gabe, who's curiously watching the interaction between Kelly and me. "Where are you visiting from?"

"Currently, I'm stationed at Fort Benning."

"Next month, Kandahar," Kelly adds with a frown.

Afghanistan. Oh shit.

"You're being deployed?" Maggie inquires.

"Yes, ma'am."

I don't know what to say that doesn't sound trite or patronizing—*sorry, be careful, thank you for your service, watch your ass over there and come back in one piece*—so I say nothing and give Gabe a somber nod. Gabe nods back, and I can tell he appreciates the lack of empty sentiment. That's not what he's come to Austin for. Note to self: for tonight there is no war, only love.

"Well, Gabe, it is a pleasure to meet you." I smile. "May I buy you gentlemen some shots?"

Behind me, Kelly laughs and insists, "Let's absolutely do shots, but I'm buying."

Maggie pours the drinks and lines them up. Gabe toasts, "To old friends"—a wink at me—"and new."

Speaking of old friends, I want to know how these two met, but before I can ask, Kelly shifts the conversation in a different direction. "So, Gabe, Ari here is married."

Gabe's eyes go wide. I nod, weary, steeling myself for a repeat of the same conversation I've had dozens of times. I explain my situation, and it's clear that Gabe's curiosity is piqued, but when given the chance to ask follow-up questions, the only thing he wants to know is, "Why?"

I take a good long minute to answer, thinking it through. "For most of my life, I lived like I was waiting for something to happen, for someone or something to come along and move me. Then one day I realized that there is only one person who can truly move me, and that's me. It's up to me to open myself to new ideas, experiences, and people. So I did...I do."

Gabe looks stunned. I glance from him to Maggie to Kelly and see the same look on all of them.

"I love my husband." I quickly point out, "But I need to love myself too, and for a long time, I forgot that part."

Silence. They are too quiet, and it makes me nervous. I don't like the scrutiny, so I look around the bar for an exit strategy. I find it there in the corner, wide and green and bathed in the light of a Tiffany billiard lamp. "And now, I'm moving myself to play some pool. Want to join me?"

Gabe nods eagerly. Kelly concurs. We play pool. It quickly becomes apparent that I've never really played before and don't have a natural talent for it. I miss all of my shots, and at one point manage to hit the cue ball off the table, sending it rolling across the concrete floor with Kelly chasing behind. I giggle, embarrassed. "Well, that happened."

Gabe laughs at me. Normally, I'd be self-conscious of someone laughing at me, but not the way Gabe does it. He has a great laugh, a throw-back-your-head-and-clear-your-throat-of-all-your-troubles sort of laugh.

Gabe comes around the table toward me, holding his arms out in a peace offering, "Let me show you something."

I shrug and he moves until he's standing behind me, then he bends me forward at the waist so I'm leaning across the table. The commanding move sends a warm rush of heat from my thighs to every part of me. Flushed with embarrassment and excitement, I glance up to find Kelly watching with a wicked grin, and Maggie, at her perch behind the bar, looks like her eyes might pop out of her head and roll across the floor like my wayward cue ball.

Gabe stretches his body over my back and covers my hands and the cue stick with his palms. His hands are warm and rough, hard-working hands. I imagine what those hands would feel like on other parts of my skin and nearly choke on the thought. Gabe moves the cue stick through our combined grip in a gentle, steady rhythm, and at my ear, he whispers, "It's all in how you hold the stick."

Kelly helpfully places the cue ball back on the pool table. Gabe adjusts our position a bit, grinding his hips against mine in the process.

"Slow and smooth." Gabe's words practically melt when they reach my ear. "Don't rush things. Just relax and focus on what you're aiming for, then hit it."

I nod, almost hypnotized by the soothing sound of his voice and the sensation of the smooth wood of the cue stick sliding through my fingers.

"Three ball, center pocket," Gabe whispers into my ear.

Suddenly, his arm jerks forward and the stick shoots through my palm, hitting the cue ball with a crack. The white ball ricochets off the green felt wall, hits the red ball and sends it into the middle pocket at my left.

"Fuck yeah!" I holler and jump up and down, throwing Gabe off my back so I can do a stupid little celebration dance. Gabe and Kelly watch me with delight, each giving me a high-five when I wiggle and shimmy past them on my victory lap.

Once settled, I try another shot and miss it, but I'm still grinning and so are they. We play hit or miss through one more round of pool before Kelly quietly suggests we go somewhere else. Gabe concurs.

I recognize this for what it is. All evening these two have been working me, lavishing me with smiles and winks, attention and compliments, coy glances and touches full of libidinous promise.

Individually, they've got game. Together they are unstoppable, and their dynamic duo act is working. When they suggest leaving, I don't hesitate. It never even occurs to me to say no. I want to join them, partly because I want to see where this night will take us, but mostly because hanging out with them feels easy, fun.

As we leave, Maggie catcalls and whistles at us. My cheeks flame with embarrassment. For some reason, her reaction makes this real. I am indeed leaving this bar to go home with two men who seem intent on sharing me. I'd put "threesome" on most of my myriad To-Do lists, but for some reason I'd always assumed my *ménage à trois* would come in the form of a girl-girl-boy tryst, not boy-boy-girl. But now, as I walk headlong into more than I've bargained for, I'm giddy with excitement. I flip Maggie the bird and she waggles her brow. I'll be interrogated about this later.

Kelly lives close, a short walk under the freeway to the east side and up the hill to a historic neighborhood near the state cemetery. He's in the bottom floor of an old Victorian-era house that's been sub-divided into apartments. The place is clean and airy, with twelve-foot-high ceilings and longleaf pine floors. It's clear that Gabe has been sleeping on the couch, but he makes fast work of moving his belongings off to a corner and straightening the cushions. Kelly walks over to a turntable and a milk crate full of vinyl, and puts on an old Fugazi album.

Then...

We all just stand there. It's awkward, each of us staring off in different directions, avoiding any accidental eye contact. I imagine that this is the point where most threesomes fail. I wonder if the same thoughts flooding my mind also inundate theirs: *who starts this? What do we do? What do we say? What if one of us needs to pee?*

Come to think of it, "Can I, uh, where's your restroom?"

Kelly and Gabe both look up at the sound of my voice, seemingly startled to find me still standing there, and point toward a doorway. I do my business then return to the living room where I find the guys in the same spots, unmoved, posed at awkward angles and staring into space.

Perhaps, as the 'F' in this MMF-scenario, it's my job to get things rolling. It would certainly assuage any concerns regarding consent if I were to grab the bulls by the proverbial horns. *Deep breath in annnnnnnnnnd out.*

Kelly is closer. I walk to him and he glances up, watching me advance. I'm used to sitting beside him, and when seated we're close to the same level. Standing up, he's a good foot taller than I am. I crane my neck up to look him in the eyes. It's worth the effort. His baby blues sparkle with excitement, and his Adam's apple bobs up and down on a big nervous swallow.

"Hi," I say as I smile up at him. I touch his arm, and slowly slide my hand down until our palms connect and we lace our fingers.

"Hi." He smiles too, and some of the tension drains from his shoulders.

I turn and walk toward Gabe, bringing Kelly with me. Gabe watches our approach with bated breath.

"Hi," I say to Gabe when I'm standing before him. He's only slightly taller than me, his lips within reach, and I want to kiss him. I've wanted to kiss him all night. I wait.

"Hi," he answers with a sweet grin, then looks over my shoulder to Kelly.

The two of them exchange a look, an understanding, something that only they share. I don't intrude. I understand that tonight is more about them then it is about me. After tonight, my place within their lives will be cemented, sure, but tertiary. I will forever be the woman they shared before Gabe went off to war. But for them, tonight means something completely different. With their long history, this could be an ultimate declaration of the bond of their friendship, or it could spell the end—all depending on how they react to one another naked. Finally, they share a silent nod, and that relaxes the remaining tension and uncertainty between us.

It's Gabe who makes the first move. With one elegant sweep of his hand, he touches my cheek and pulls me in for a kiss. His lips are soft and warm, and I moan at the sensation of him coaxing my mouth open, making room for his tongue to explore.

I bring my hand and Kelly's, still linked, and rest it on my breast. Kelly needs no further direction. With both hands on me now, he sifts through the fabric of my top in order to caress my skin as he licks and kisses my neck.

Someone, maybe Gabe, slides his hand down my belly to cup my sex in his palm. I gasp and let my head fall back, reveling in the ecstasy of overstimulation.

Kelly twists my head around to kiss him, and the sensation is so different from kissing Gabe that I luxuriate in the disparity. I switch between the two, enjoying the contrasting flavors of their toothpaste and liquor, the different textures of their lips, their varied styles and techniques; until it all weaves together in an erotic tapestry.

Someone, probably Kelly, starts us moving toward the bedroom. It takes a while, lots of stopping and starting, touching and tasting as we make our way down the narrow hallway to finally spill into the room and fall onto the bed.

Here, they strip me of my clothes. I seem to always be kissing someone, which helps as a glorious distraction from the cold, bracing vulnerability of nudity. I have Kelly at my mouth, when Gabe finds his way between my legs and coaxes me to sit on his face.

He works me with his tongue and fingers, and I come, quick and hard, nearly doubling over. Kelly is there to catch me and hold me up, pulling away from my mouth so he can watch me come. I gasp and hold onto his shoulders as I look down and find Gabe wide-eyed between my thighs, watching me as he continues to tease, milking those last gasps of pleasure from me.

It's then that I realize they're both still fully dressed. I shift away from them, and order, "Strip. Both of you. I can't be the only one naked here."

Well-mannered Texas boys that they are, they nervously oblige. Gabe licks his lips as he moves to sit up, then stands at the end of the bed beside Kelly. Off go their shirts, but that's the easy part. They hesitate to remove their pants, so I help.

I grab Gabe by the chain of his dog tags and pull him in for a kiss, tasting myself on his tongue, then use my hands to work at his belt. When his pants fall, he kicks off his shoes and socks and jeans as I move my fingers beneath the waistband of his boxer briefs. My hand finds him, hot and hard, and he hisses through his teeth at the sensation of my touch.

I shift mouths, still stroking Gabe, and with my free hand, I work Kelly's buckle and zipper until I have them each in a palm. I can tell that Kelly is the shier of the two, slower to touch and be touched, so I take him into my mouth first. His body quakes with the sensation and for a moment I think he might tumble over. But he manages to steady himself, placing his hands on my shoulders for support.

I continue to jerk Gabe, who seems perfectly content to explore my body with his touch as I suck his best friend. His fingers smooth down my back and over my ass and I vaguely hear him say, "Kelly. Condoms?"

There's a quick shift of movement. Gabe is gone, so I put both of my hands on Kelly's waist while I suck him deep and feel the bed indent behind me. Gabe clasps his fingers around my hips as he slowly enters me. I gasp, pulling away from Kelly to catch my breath as my body adjusts.

Behind me, Gabe moves in slow, steady strokes. I glance over my shoulder to see that he's got his eyes closed and his head turned up to the ceiling, working with touch as his only sensation. I turn and glance up at Kelly and the vision is completely different. Kelly's eyes are open, and focused on Gabe.

Gabe's pace quickens and I shift as if to take Kelly in my mouth again, but he stops me. He pulls my shoulders up until I'm balanced only on my knees, my arms hugged around Kelly's neck. Gabe doesn't miss a beat, clasping his palms over my breasts as he fucks me even harder from behind.

I am on the verge of coming again and dive forward to take Kelly's lips, kissing him hard as my breath comes more ragged and hot. He kisses me back, but something has changed. I open my eyes and see that Kelly is again looking past me, his eyes hooded, watching Gabe. Oh...

Kelly wants Gabe.

I look over my shoulder. Gabe's face is pointed down now, his vision fixed on the point where his dick plunges in and out of me. His callused fingers caress and tease as he works to coax another orgasm out of me. All of his focus and energy is directed at me, as if he's forgotten, or wants to forget, that there's another dick in the room.

Kelly wants Gabe. Gabe wants pussy.

The reality hits like a blinding light, so clear to me now I can't believe I didn't see it before. For Kelly, I'm a surrogate. Using me is the only way that Kelly can love his friend in the way he truly wants to, without losing him. I find the idea intensely romantic and endearing. I want to help. I want to share Gabe with Kelly. Hugging my arms tighter around Kelly's neck, I whisper in his ear, "Fuck my mouth. Pretend it's him."

Kelly jerks away from me, looking appalled and offended. When he catches the understanding expression on my face, though, he softens. Seeming stunned, he moves closer and nods slowly. I grin and kiss him, then work my way down, licking and nibbling as I go. When I take him in my mouth again, I suck hard and deep. Kelly spasms at the sensation and flexes his thighs to stand rigid.

Gabe pounds into me, his dog tags clattering against his chest in a syncopated rhythm. It doesn't take long before I come again. It's a good orgasm, and it has to be—this one's for me *and* Kelly. I scream and claw my fingernails into Kelly's ass and suck him deep into my mouth, even as I'm still quivering and shaking from the aftershocks.

Gabe continues to fuck me, chasing his own climax. I find Kelly's hands, braced on his own waist like he can't find anything better to do with them, and I move them to the back of my head. Kelly's fingers tense, but he doesn't hesitate. He fucks my mouth, matching Gabe's rhythm perfectly. I let him do what he wants, focusing my energy on breathing through my nose and trying not to gag when he hits deep.

Gabe starts to groan and grunt. His fists clutch tightly at my hips as he drives deep inside me and comes with a spasm. Instantly, Kelly comes in my mouth, shaking and shivering while I suck him dry.

We're all speechless and spent as we collapse on the bed in a tangle of arms and legs. Kelly has his arm stretched under my head, and Gabe is half draped across my stomach as we all lay there, catching our breath.

Gently, Kelly rolls his head to the side and kisses my temple, then whispers, "Thank you."

I smile and sigh, getting more pleasure from those words than from all of the evening's orgasms combined.

I stay the night. I tell myself that I'm doing this for Kelly and Gabe. That, without me here, the dynamic would shift, Gabe would return to his pallet on the couch, and this special night would be over for them. But when I send Greg a, "don't wait up," text and turn my phone off, I know my motives are not entirely noble.

12—Friday May 13, 2005

"You're friends with Jake Sixkiller, right?"

I frown and glance over at the unfamiliar man who clearly recognizes me. "Have we met?"

"Couple of times."

Shit. I have absolutely no recollection of this guy. "I'm sorry. I'm really bad with names and faces."

With a shrug, he introduces himself, and I nearly spit a mouthful of drink all over his t-shirt. "Really? *You're* Chris Nix? Oh my God, I thought you were a myth. Did you know that 'I love Chris Nix' is written in every ladies' room stall on Red River Street?"

Chris nods and seems slightly amused, but mostly, he's staring at my boobs. I'm wearing the black cotton top with the little cloverleaf eyelets, and if you look closely you can make out the color of my bra—blue. He's looking closely.

Chris Nix is not attractive. His mouth is too large and his eyes are too small. His long nose is bent at an unnatural angle, once broken and never set properly. His dark hair is shaggy, and his five o'clock shadow is inching toward half past eight. Yet despite all that, the devious glint in his eyes is weirdly appealing.

Clearly, this guy is a bad boy. Not one of those *good* bad boys, like Jake, on the surface a moody and aloof player, but with a heart of gold hidden underneath. No, Chris is a real, honest-to-God *bad* bad boy, the kind who leaves a trail of mugshots and broken hearts in his wake.

He's got a nasty cut on his chin, suggesting that he's recently been in a fight. That thing is going to leave a scar. Lord knows I do love a good scar. My mind flashes to Alex and his lightning bolt brow. I grin to myself.

Chris reads my smile wrong, taking it as an invitation. He touches my elbow to lead me through the throng of people to the large horseshoe bar. I consider saying no. I consider walking out the door and never looking back. I've known this guy for about half a second, and he's already got my creep radar in the red zone. But it's Friday the Thirteenth, and I'm in the mood for a little freaky Friday action. Besides, Greg's out on a date…with Kate, Jake's in Houston playing a show, and Sheryl's detoxing for her derby bout this Sunday, so what else is there for me to do?

Read a book! Try to write! Talk to any other guy here! Literally, any other guy would be a better bet than this creeper! Despite my better judgment, I follow him, curious to see where he leads.

There are people stacked three deep waiting to be served, but Chris finds a small gap behind the beer taps with one stool available. He pulls the stool out and wedges me in front of him. Then he sits and moves his stool forward until I'm pinned against the bar, his thighs spread out on either side of me. What the fuck? I glance behind me, turning as much as I can in the tight space between his legs, and see him grinning…at my ass.

I look back to the bartenders and feel Chris's breath on my ear as he instructs me, "Order a Lone Star, a shot of Jameson, and whatever you're having. Put it on my tab."

I turn to nod at him and find his lips too close to mine. But he doesn't try anything, just grins at me with that huge mouth, like the Cheshire Cat. I turn away, blowing out the breath I'd been holding, and give my full attention to the bartenders, trying to catch someone's eye.

His hands are on me. At first, I hardly notice. His entire body is practically cocooning me, and that has my head overloaded, flustered, so I'm a little confused by the addition of a new sensation. But there it is, his palms pressed against my waist and moving down. His fingers are long and warm as they trace over my thighs, stopping at the hem of my skirt. I freeze, not sure what he's doing and not sure how I feel about whatever it is he's doing. Slowly he starts to pull up the front of my skirt. I gasp and look back at him, but he just gives another damned wink.

For whatever reason, curiosity maybe, I don't tell him to stop. I don't say a thing. I turn back around, feeling renewed vigor to catch the eye of a bartender. Finally, someone walks over to take my order. As I open my mouth to speak, Chris moves his hand up to my underwear, and then beneath.

"Two Lone Stars and two Jameson shots," I cough out, my eyes wide. The bartender seems amused by my flustered demeanor. Oh God, does she know what he's doing to me? What if Chris is known for finger-banging his conquests in public places? Maybe that's how he earned so much bathroom wall space. Jesus, I'm in way over my head with this guy.

"Put those on my tab," Chris calmly adds.

Two by two our drinks are set before us. Chris doesn't skip a beat, grabbing one of the two whiskey shots with his free hand, he clinks his glass to mine and downs his drink. I watch him multitask, stunned and maybe a little impressed. I down my shot. The fire burns my throat and helps me to keep my face from giving away what's happening down under. Goddamn, am I going to come right here in the bar? Before I can, Chris pulls his hand away and pushes my skirt back down my legs.

"Gotta leave you wanting more," he says as he not-so-subtly licks his fingers.

He doesn't ask me to leave with him, but when he clasps his hand over mine and heads for the door, I don't protest. The walk to Chris's car takes ages, as he seems incapable of walking a block without yanking me into an alley, pressing me against a wall, and kissing me. His mouth is so massive he practically swallows me whole, and he's so much taller than me that he has to alternate between picking me up off my feet to reach his lips, or splaying his legs out to the side, bringing himself down to my level for these intensely tactile make out sessions.

I'm not used to public displays of affection, and certainly nothing on this level. Chris Nix is a powder keg ready to explode, and he doesn't seem to care where he is when that explosion comes. More than once I hear, "Get a room," lobbed at us from passing cars.

At his house, he practically pushes me into a bedroom and kicks the door shut, then strips me like a NASCAR pit crew, operating as if every second counts. He hasn't even finished stripping his own clothes off before he's on his knees, his face buried between my thighs. I wobble and look down to find him furiously jerking himself off while he eats me out. This guy is unreal.

Just then, his bedroom door flies open. A large woman with Einstein hair steps inside, and her face turns white as a ghost when her wide eyes survey the pornographic scene. In a panic, I jump backwards onto the bed, covering myself with my arms and crossing my legs. Who is this? His wife? It occurs to me that for the first time since I started this open-marriage thing, I didn't bother to tell Chris Nix my whole life story, nor did I ask for his. Oh God, what if—

"Don't you know how to knock?" Chris asks the woman in a nonchalant tone, his dick still in his hand.

"I," she stammers, "I thought you were alone."

"I'm not. What do you want?"

"Pot."

"Desk drawer." He points to the desk in the corner.

"I'll come back later." She glances at me, then retreats, closing the door behind her.

I'm stunned, frozen to the spot. Chris shakes his head, half-amused and half-annoyed, then gets on his knees and comes toward me.

"Who was that?"

"My mom."

He lives with his mom? What kind of *bad* bad boy lives with his mom?

He seems unmoved by her appearance, and with that same pit crew speed from before, he lifts me off the bed and brings me down to straddle him. I am only just able to get in my protest before he tries to shove inside me.

"Condom!"

"What?"

"Condom."

He pouts. "I fucking hate those things."

Yeah...and? I stare blankly at him, unmoved by his whining. He scowls and dumps me onto his bed as he stands, kicking off his sneakers and the tangle of jeans wrapped around his ankles as he grumbles and digs a condom out of a drawer.

It's green. His dick looks like a cucumber. I almost laugh, but he's already pissed that I'm making him wear it. Probably shouldn't laugh at how it looks on him.

Stifle laughter: check.

Back at the side of the bed, he grabs my ankles and yanks me toward him, then spins me so carelessly that my head nearly hits the headboard. I press my hands against the wood veneer to brace myself as he bores into me.

He fucks me at a furious pace, my ankles at his ears, but he's not making a sound. On the other hand, I can't seem to hush. I grab his pillow and hold it over my mouth.

His mom is on the other side of that door, Ari.

His mom can hear every sound you make, Ari.

His mom can hear the vigorous squeaks of the bed springs, Ari.

His mom can hear the headboard banging against the wall, Ari.

Shut the fuck up, brain.

I can't come. I can't stop imagining his mom standing in the doorway, Chris with his cucumber dick in his hand. Also, he's fucking me with such relentless vigor that I've dried out from the friction. It's starting to chafe.

I stare up at him. He's not even looking at me, staring at the wall over my head with a distant, bored expression. Who is this guy? He was so passionate before; now he's like some emotionless fuckbot. Jesus, at this rate, we could go on for hours. I'll be raw and bloody before he finally comes. I reach up and scratch my fingernails on his chest. He looks down, watching my hands. I pinch his nipples, and he moans.

Ah. Okay. He just needs a little extra stimulation. I slide up on my elbows, and he leans back to sit on his heels, pulling me up to straddle him. I take the opportunity to grab two fistfuls of his hair, tugging hard. He moves his head back and groans, fucking me even faster now. *Wow, so before, that was the slow speed?*

"Please," he begs.

"Please what?" I grin as I imagine what kind of kinky requests he might have.

"Let me take the condom off."

"What?"

"I can't feel anything."

"No." I frown. He can*not* be serious. "No condom means no sex."

He suddenly pushes me off of him, flips me over and spins me around, nearly hitting my head on the wall this time. He presses into me to continue fucking me furiously, but now in a new position. "If you're worried about pregnancy, I can pull out."

There is nothing less attractive than a man trying to negotiate his way out of a condom. I pull away, and his dick falls out of me with an unceremonious slap on his thigh. He's barely even hard anymore. His cucumber looks more like a pickle now.

"It's about a lot more than just pregnancy." I point at his pickle dick. "I don't know where that thing has been."

He scowls like a stubborn child. Is this what bad boys are like? Whiny little crybabies? I'm sorely disappointed.

"Look, I'm sorry, but I insist on it with everyone." Why am I apologizing to this man-child?

He shakes his head and pulls the rubber off. It slingshots from his hand and hits the wall right next to me with a juicy splat. Okay, that does it.

"I'm out of here." I climb up from the bed and hurriedly dress.

Chris scowls as he silently watches me. When I loop my purse over my shoulder and head for the door, he stands and stalks toward me, planting himself directly in my path. I try to sidestep him, but he clasps a fist around my bicep and pulls me toward him. "Where do you think you're going? I haven't finished."

"No. We're done." I try to wrench my arm from his iron grip, but his fingers only tighten more, squeezing so hard I wince. "Let go of me."

"Least you can do is suck me off."

I try twisting my arm in his bruising grip again, but he won't let go. I demand again, "Get your hands off me right now, Chris, or I'll—"

"Or you'll what?" He juts out his jaw, looking obstinate and amused as he mocks my struggle to get free.

I expect panic to wash over me at any moment as I stand here facing off against a groping douchebag man-child who is at least a half a foot taller and fifty pounds heavier than me, but I remain relatively calm and collected. I've been practicing for this. Ironically, it's Jake, Chris's supposed friend, who's been training me.

"Hit me, baby, one more time." Jake would sing, channeling Britney Spears, then bounce around on the balls of his feet while pushing and whacking and generally harassing me until I would hit him. Then the critique would begin. "Not bad, but keep your thumb outside your fingers, tight, but outside. If you hit hard with your thumb on the inside, you'll break it. Also, don't lead with your knuckles. You want to hit with the flat part of your fist; the added surface area means a better impact. Remember, too, to keep your wrist straight. You want a straight line from your fist to your elbow, then throw the punch from your shoulder. The power should start in your shoulder move through your arm and slam straight into your opponent. You have a lot more power in your arm than you do in that tiny little fist, Two Shoes, so use it."

Here and now, faced with a *bad* bad boy clutching my arm in his punishing grip, I hear Jake's lessons repeat through my head as I curl the fingers of my free hand into a fist, thumb on the outside, and straighten my wrist. Chris doesn't even notice, too focused on my face, watching me with a cruel grin as if he's waiting for me to start crying.

I take a deep breath like I'm about to yell at him, and Chris smirks, ready to mock anything I have to say. I blink. He laughs. I pull my arm back. He frowns. From the shoulder, I power a punch straight at the scabbed injury on his stupid fucking chin.

Thwack.

The satisfying sound bounces against the walls, echoing through the room as everything seems to slow way, way down. I watch that scab on his chin spring a leak and gush blood down his neck. Chris's stupid face changes with each stage of his reaction. His shock wears off, and anger sets in as he realizes he's just been sucker-punched by a woman and is now bleeding all over the place.

"You hit me, you *bitch*!"

I don't wait around to hear him rant and rail at me. The moment his grip loosens, I wrench my arm away and run past him to the door. I feel awash with relief to be out of there and admittedly a little self-satisfied to be leaving Chris stunned, naked, bleeding, and alone.

In a hurry, I sprint through the living room, silently passing between Chris's mother and some reality show on the television, then jog out the door and up the street, wheezing and sucking in huge lungfuls of air as I make my great escape.

I sprint for ten blocks before I realize no one is chasing me. I double over, my chest blazing with fire as I try to catch my breath and calm my pulse. When my heart and lungs settle, I pull out my phone and scroll through my contacts. I hover over Greg's number, but I don't want to call him. I don't want to have to tell him *why* I'm calling him. I'm already awash with shame for ignoring my better judgement and getting into this situation; I don't want Greg or Jake to know about it. I move down my contacts to Yellow Cab's number and hover, then close my phone and slip it back into my purse. There is nowhere I want to be right now, so I might as well just walk.

Overhead, the sky hangs low. I breathe deeply and the air fills my lungs with a warm, wet, earthy scent that promises rain. The downpour starts gently, a cleansing shower to wash away the memories of Chris's massive mouth, grabby hands, and pickled dick. I turn my head up and open my mouth, washing away the taste of him.

Soon, though, the rain comes harder, its thick drops pelting me and soaking through my clothes. I flinch and lower my face, trying to ignore the torturous assault as I walk to the interstate and the diner at the corner.

The door triggers a chime to announce my entrance, and the waitress by the cash register smirks as she takes in the sight of me—my dripping tangle of hair, black lines of mascara marking my cheeks, damp mini skirt and shirt plastered to my skin. Shit, I must look like a half-drowned whore. Certainly I'm not the strangest sight this waitress has seen in here, but I'm probably the strangest sight she's seen tonight.

I do as the sign instructs and seat myself, taking a booth in the far corner by the expanse of plate glass windows. Outside, an eighteen-wheeler sprays the median with a tidal wave of rainwater as it rushes past.

"What can I getcha?" The waitress hovers, drumming a pencil on her order pad.

"Blueberry pancakes, please."

She nods and returns with a carafe, pouring me a cup of coffee that I don't want.

"And a glass of water. Please," I call after her as she heads toward the kitchen.

I glance around at the dated décor and notice that the only other customer, a scruffy old man with a stained overcoat, is watching me from the row of stools at the counter.

"Wet one out there," the man hollers hoarsely across the gulf of plaid berber carpet between us.

I nod and look down at my table. The waitress returns with a water, and my plate of pancakes. I dive in, slathering the short stack in butter and drenching it in syrup. I eat almost half of the plate before the scruffy man slides into my booth.

I don't look up, don't engage. I mumble down at my plate between bites, "Please leave me alone."

"Rough night?" He smells awful, and his breath reeks of whiskey.

"Leave me alone." My words louder this time, gruff but shaky. I'm closer to tears than I'd like to admit.

"No need to be a bitch. Just tryin' to be friendly, one down-and-out to another." It doesn't escape my attention that this is the second person tonight to call me a bitch.

I frown at the man and see that he's sneering at me, his eyes on my boobs. My stomach turns. My appetite gone, I look down at the mangled pancakes and drop my knife and fork into the pool of syrup. I shove the plate at him and leave him there, moving to the counter to pay my bill. Dialing Greg's number, I look back at the smelly man devouring what's left of my food and press call.

"Ari?" He answers on the second ring.

"Are you busy?" my voice wavers.

"What's wrong?"

"Can you come get me?"

There is a pause, and I consider backing out of the request. I could just hang up and call a cab. But before I can say anything, Greg asks, "Where are you?"

I give him directions to the diner and feel a warm wave of relief when I hear his keys jangling over the static of the stormy reception.

We hang up, and I melt into my seat, finally finding some relief from this terrible night. That relief is short-lived. Having finished my meal, the smelly man returns to the counter, sliding up onto the stool beside me. The sensation is eerily familiar to my usual Friday night routine, though this freaky Friday-the-Thirteenth version is like the funhouse mirror reflection of my life, deformed and twisted, but still a reflection. My stomach does a somersault. Is this my future; the drenched slut picked up by the smelly drunk at an interstate diner? I jump up and head into the bathroom, practically running.

Standing at the mirror, I stare at the person reflected back at me. I watch her eyes blink, her throat tighten when she swallows, her chest move when she breathes. But I don't recognize myself in her.

Tears prick the backs of my eyes, but I refuse to cry. I busy myself instead, rinsing my face, detangling my hair, and straightening my clothes—as if alterations to the surface will fix what I'm feeling underneath.

My phone buzzes. It's Greg. I answer and his voice booms over the roar of the rain hitting the roof of his car, "I'm out front."

"I'll be right there." I hang up and take one last look at the stranger in the mirror before I trudge outside. I make a mad dash to the car, my arm a sorry excuse for cover from the torrential rain coming down in sheets outside.

The car is warm and smells like Greg. I close my eyes as I breathe in the comforting, familiar scent.

"Are you okay?" Greg coaxes, resting his palm on my damp thigh.

I exhale a long, sharp breath. "Yeah."

"Did someone hurt you?" His voice sounds rough. I turn to see the rigid lines of his jaw and anxious look in his eyes. Shit. He thinks...

"No. It's not what you think." I bite my lip. "I'm sorry. I didn't mean to alarm you. It was just...a bad night."

Greg scrutinizes my profile while I stare straight ahead at the wipers moving across the windshield. With a soft exhale, he turns his attention forward and drives home.

Once at the house, however, his focus is back on me. He helps me out of my cold clothes and into a hot shower, noting my swollen knuckles, as well as the bruise on my arm and another on my hip.

I don't give him an explanation for the marks on my skin or for my panicked phone call. At this point, I'm starting to forget why it is that I called him. It's not like I couldn't have called a cab just as easily. Why did I turn to Greg tonight?

Since the "incident" with Kate last month, Greg and I have barely spoken, at least not about important things. We've kept our conversations light. When he hasn't been traveling or spending the night elsewhere, we've coexisted more as roommates than spouses or lovers, orbiting in each other's periphery, rarely making actual contact.

So why had my first instinct been to call Greg? On the drive home, I hadn't been able to piece it together. But now, standing naked in the bathroom, watching Greg strip off his own clothes to join me in the shower, it's as clear as day.

I'd called Greg because he's my goddamn *husband*. Greg is the man who's been by my side for twelve years. He's the man who's seen me through every crisis, every meltdown, every bad night of my adult life. He's the man I *should* call when I need someone. Somehow, in all the madness of the last six months, I've forgotten that, I've forgotten him.

But right here, right now, with Greg's hands delicately working a thick lather of shampoo into my hair, I remember. I remember us. I close my eyes and hug my arms around his waist, finally letting myself cry. When I can catch my breath again, I whisper to him, "I've missed you, Greg."

13—Friday May 20, 2005

"So, what's new?" Sheryl asks.

I don't want to talk about that awful night last week—at least not until I've had more to drink—so I reach a bit further back, offering with a smile, "Well, I fucked a vampire."

"You fucked a vampire?"

"I fucked a vampire."

"And where, pray tell, did you meet a vampire?"

"Really, that's your first question?"

Sheryl shrugs.

"I met him online. Online dating is weird?"

"Wait. What? Why are you dating online?"

"I'm not anymore. This was, like, two weeks ago."

"So?" Sheryl raises a brow, "How was your foray into online dating?"

I consider the question, then launch into a rant, "You know, back in my day, no one had cellphones, cameras used film, and the last thing you'd want to do was hand over a film canister full of nudies to the guy manning the photolab drive-thru window."

"Got a bunch of dick pics, huh?" Sheryl says with a pitying pout.

"Got a bunch of dick pics," I admit with a smirk. "Seriously, what's that about?"

"Welcome to dating in the 21st century, Grandma Hendricks."

I groan.

"Circling back to the vampire fuckage and suckage," she waggles her brow, "leave nothing out."

I giggle, then launch into the story. "I should have known from his username..."

Sheryl cants her head in curiosity.

"Dracula69."

Sheryl howls with laughter and the sound echoes off the tin ceiling of this weird little hole-in-the-wall shot bar, turning a few heads.

"Surprisingly, for a vampire, he was really boring. He kept talking about his modeling career. He was really good looking, by the way."

"Oh?"

"Yeah, but, like, too good looking, you know?"

She nods. "I hate that."

I nod too.

"So, get to the good part where Vlad impales you on his big hard stake."

Now I'm the one laughing. "Yeah, that part was less boring. Let's just say, vampire boys have quite the oral fixation."

"Meow!"

I open my mouth to tell her more, but lose my train of thought as a gaggle of girls come rollicking through the door wearing matching wedding veils, chanting, "shots, shots, shots."

I forget all about my Lost Boys story, my attention riveted to the bachelorette party, watching them like an anthropologist observing some newly-discovered tribe. Sheryl starts to giggle and dance along with their bizarre little "shots, shots, shots" dance.

I'm instantly and completely obsessed with these ladies, their bald enthusiasm a narcotic I want to overdose on tonight. I nudge Sheryl as if to ask, "you game?" To which she winks and excitedly nods, silently agreeing, "let's do this."

We watch them as they flutter about the bar, squealing and dancing and checking items off a scavenger hunt list. They appear to all be in their early twenties, all blonde except for one brunette, all super skinny except for one big girl, and all wearing matching pink dresses except for the pending-bride, who's in white. One of them—not the bride, brunette, or big girl—takes charge. She orders in a booming voice that stops all other conversations in the bar. Clearly she was a cheerleader at some point in her life. *Ready! Okay!* "Five Flaming Dr. Peppers!"

The party of five squeals and giggles and woots and jumps up and down, hugging one another like they've just won Wheel of Fortune.

Sheryl grins and I shout, "Seven Flaming Dr. Peppers! And the drinks are on us!"

Party of Five gasps, then glances at us and squeals even louder. They come at us with their giggles and their wooting and their jumping up and down, hugging us now too. In an instant, they've adopted us as part of their crew. They seem to love my shoes, a pair of Chuck Taylors covered in silver glitter, and they rave about Sheryl's bright pink hair, which matches their dresses.

I'm a bit stunned by their easy affection and inclusiveness, and even more surprised by my own spontaneity. Why the hell am I buying flaming shots for a bunch of complete strangers? Why do I want to join their party?

Behind the bar, the tender gets busy lining up pint glasses half full of beer, then pours the shots of amaretto with the 151 rum floaters. While we wait, our new friends introduce themselves—all Candies and Mandies and Sandies and Brandies. I immediately forget the details, but the details are hardly important.

They could be any bevy of bachelorettes and I would feel the same way about them. I like them. I want to be near them. Their optimism is refreshing. I smile when they go all dreamy-eyed talking about the future, and wax poetic about true love. They all speak glowingly about James, the groom-to-be, as if they are all in love with him, or at least the idea of him. He is the archetype of their fantasy future husbands. It's all so simple and sweet. It's the saccharine sort of thing that might normally make my eyes roll and my teeth ache, but tonight it's a salve that soothes me—mind, body, and soul. Sheryl seems to sense this, and makes a concerted effort not to roll her eyes when the women get particularly chirpy and excitable.

The bartender gestures for us all to move aside from the line of fire, so we do, watching her ready the butane lighter in one hand, and dip two fingers from her other hand into a shot glass full of 151. I hold my breath, waiting with anticipation, equal parts nervous and excited about what's about to happen.

In one smooth movement, choreographed like a circus act, the bartender sucks in a big breath, lifts her wetted fingers in a narrow vee to her mouth, and flicks the lighter on. She blows through the spread of her flammable fingers and over the top of the lighter...*ignition.*

Suddenly, there's fire, a big stream of flames shooting out of the bartender's mouth. The ball of fire hits the seven shot glasses stacked carefully in a squatty pyramid, igniting the 151 that floats on their surface. We all stare at the blue flames dancing in the drinks, mesmerized. I'm so excited by the display that I squeal with delight, as do Sheryl and the rest of our girlfriends, who are howling and doing herkies all around us.

The bartender blows out the flames on the shots and sets them all carefully in front of the half pints of beers to indicate they're ready for our consumption. We drop the shots into the half-pints and toast to love and marriage. I pound my shot, finishing second behind Sheryl, of course. It really does taste like Dr. Pepper.

The ladies titter like little birds circling around us as Sheryl and I close our shared tab, tipping the bartender a well-earned one-hundred-percent. Then we join the gaggle and head for the next bar.

· · · ·

"To punching the dick right in the pickle!" Candie, the bride, shouts as she toasts us all. Apparently, my storytelling hour at the last bar was a success. I frown and Sheryl smirks, then we drink the shots. I burp and vow not to drink anything else tonight that's pink and tastes like watermelon Jolly Ranchers. Strictly tequila shots from here on out.

As we sit at the bar, our new friends fan out to finish their scavenger hunt. We've added a few new items to their list, so now they're looking for a man named James who will give them each a lap dance. Also, they have to kiss someone's tattoo; any tattoo will do. We can hear Brandie, the former Dallas Cowboys cheerleader, hollering half way across the bar, "Anyone here named James?"

"You two are on thin ice." Manic frowns at Sheryl and me. "And I'm not giving any of them a fucking lapdance."

"Wait." I gasp, "Is your name James?"

Manic scowls and walks away.

Before we can inform our friends that Mr. Personality is in fact named James, someone hollers, "I'll be your James for the night, babe. Name's Bond, James Bond. Want to see my gun?"

Sheryl and I collapse into a laughing fit, only settling down when Manic slams a couple of beers on the bar in front of us. I wrinkle my nose at the thought of drinking beer, then drink it anyway. After a few gulps, I turn to Sheryl and wave her on. "Anyway, you were saying?"

"Oh, right." She nods and slaps her hand on the bar top then clutches her beer in her fist and gestures with it as she speaks, "I read about it once. It's called the paradox of hedonism."

I raise an eyebrow, giving her side eye over the rim of my glass, defensively asking, "Are you calling me a hedonist?"

"Yes. But also not necessarily, you could also call it the paradox of pleasure or the paradox of happiness." Sheryl flaps her hands when she gets excited, she's doing that now. "Basically, it's this theory that if you spend all your time seeking pleasure, you'll have no time to actually enjoy it."

"I'd say I'm enjoying my pleasure quite well."

It's Sheryl's turn to raise her eyebrow now. "Debatable."

I scoff, but after last week's Friday-the-Thirteenth Horrorfest, she sort of has a point.

She continues, "Think of it like this. You know those fat cats on Wall Street? They're working themselves to an early grave for more money, more money, more money. But why? What good is money if you don't spend it on the things that make you happy, right? But these guys are so focused on the process of accumulating wealth, they've lost sight of the actual value of wealth."

"So, what are you saying, for me?"

Sheryl frowns, pity in her eyes like I'm an idiot. "I'm saying, you gotta slow down, girl. Take some time to smell the roses. Stop trying to force yourself to be happy all the time, because only misery lies that way."

I frown.

"You're actually extremely good at being happy, did you know that? It's your natural state of being. Laughter practically bubbles out of you like crude oil." Sheryl softens her tone when she adds, "But earlier, when I asked if you were happy, you said 'yes...but' and then you followed it with a list of things that make you unhappy. You say that you're exhausted. You're having some communication issues with Greg and Jake. You can't talk to your family about what's going on in your life. That's a lot of really heavy shit you're juggling, and all in the name of happiness. Seems kind of backwards, if you ask me."

I blink and sniff. *Allergies.*

"One day, you know what I want?"

"What?" I manage to ask, despite the lump in my throat.

"One day, in the not-too-distant future, I want to ask you 'Ari, are you happy?' and I want you to say, 'yes.' Not, 'yes...but,' just plain old 'yes.'"

I sniff and wipe at my eyes. *Definitely allergies.* Despite the quick tears, I smile and laugh awkwardly. "Sheryl, how did I get so lucky to meet you?"

"Oh shut up." She shoves at my shoulder playfully. "I'm the lucky one."

"No, I am." I shove her back.

"Nuh uh, me." She shoves me again, and...ouch, that actually hurt.

"Okay, okay," I hold my hands up in surrender. "We're both ridiculously lucky. Truce?"

"Truce." Sheryl nods and drains the rest of her drink.

"We have a James! Ladies, ladies, we have a James and he's giving lap dances upstairs by the pool tables," One of the Candie/Brandie/Mandie/Sandies shouts from the back of the bar.

"Oh thank Christ," Manic mutters.

Sheryl and I both howl with laughter.

"Speaking of hedonistic scavenger hunts, how is your mid-life crisis bucket list coming along?" Sheryl asks with an exaggerated wink.

I hesitate, but finally admit, "Just one item left."

"Let me guess..." Sheryl holds her finger to her chin, considering, then shouts loud enough for all the bar to hear. "Anal!"

I bowl over with laughter again when Manic nearly swallows his tongue, stops what he's doing, and leans in to hear more of our conversation.

"Actually," I pause for dramatic effect, then declare, "that cherry's been popped."

Manic sways and pales, looking like he might pass out.

"Wait. What? With who?" Sheryl's eyes grow as big as saucers.

I bite my lip, faking coy as I try not to laugh.

"Okay, we'll put a pin in that topic for later." She claps her hands together, back on point. "So, if it's not buggery, then what is the last item on the list?"

I giggle nervously. "Well…" I blink. Shit. This could get weird. "It's to, uh, kiss a girl."

Sheryl slowly grins. "Really?"

I nod.

"Any particular girl in mind?"

Truth be told, I've sort of wanted to kiss Sheryl since the moment I met her. I wonder if she would kiss like she hugs, brutal embraces that leave bruises, or if she'd have gentle lips. I hadn't put a ton of thought into it, but the idea had most certainly crossed my mind a couple of times.

I nod again, slowly.

I think I hear Manic praying, but I don't want to look away from Sheryl to find out.

She holds my gaze too, as she considers, then asks, "Wanna make out?"

I nod and gasp when Sheryl hops off her bar stool, moves to stand between my legs, clasps her palms against my cheeks, and presses her lips to mine. It starts as just a peck, nothing overtly sexual. Just a little kiss amongst friends. But when Sheryl melts against me, her hands clutching a little tighter at my face, I kiss her back…and I mean, I *really* kiss her back.

To answer my own question, Sheryl's kiss is nothing like her hugs. Instead of the intense, violent affection I brace for, I'm greeted with only tenderness. Her lips are soft as pillows. Her tongue tickles like a feather. And she tastes sweet, like watermelon Jolly Ranchers. When she tilts her head to deepen the connection, I let out a moan and lose all of my senses to the kiss—consumed by it, addicted to it, loving every moment of it.

Eventually, we come apart and I blink my eyes open. Sheryl grins widely, her lips a little kiss-bruised, and hoots, "Whoo wee! Girl, that was some kiss." Yeah. Ditto on that sentiment.

Kiss a girl: sigh.

Hovering behind the bar, wringing the neck of a Bushmills bottle with his tight fist, Manic groans and wipes a palm down his face, shaking his head as he mumbles, "Swear to Christ, you two will be the death of me."

I glance around to see that our pink ladies have flanked us in a semi-circle, eyes wide and mouths agape, looking shocked and more than a little intrigued by what they've just witnessed.

"Was that on our scavenger hunt list? I don't remember seeing that on my list," Sandie, or maybe Mandie, quietly asks her cohorts.

Sheryl and I both giggle like schoolgirls, then turn to Manic and demand a pair of tequila shots. As he pours our drinks and pushes them across the bar to us, Sandie/Mandie takes notice. To Manic, she says, "I like your TARDIS tattoo; can I kiss it?"

I laugh so hard my face hurts and I descend into a coughing fit. Sheryl too is howling beside me.

Manic hesitates for a moment, scowling as he considers the request, then shrugs and holds his forearms out in front of him across the bar. Our girls seize upon him like the Brides of Dracula, each kissing either his TARDIS tattoo on the left forearm, or his USS Enterprise tattoo on the right.

I watch with a big dumb grin, a little bit astounded by the direction the night has gone. With a wink, Sheryl clinks her glass against mine, then toasts, "To the paradox of hedonism."

The Summer of Love

14—Friday June 10, 2005

Not even halfway through the door, I hear a deafening squeal, and Rebecca, Jake's ex, pounces on me.

"Oh shit. Hi." I try to talk, but my words come out mumbled and indecipherable when she smothers me in an all-consuming hug.

"Oh my God, you *have* to let me buy you a drink." Rebecca says as she adjusts her massive boobs and fluffs her blonde hair.

"Uh." I flinch. I barely know Rebecca. Sure, Jake brought her to his shows, but I'd never particularly liked her, and usually avoided her, something I'd very much like to do again now. After all, the only reason I've come out tonight is to hang out with Jake. Despite my icy body language, Rebecca laces her arm through mine and drags me toward the bar.

I try to be subtle as I pull out my phone and text Jake a quick warning message: **Danger, Will Robinson! Rebecca's here and she's buying me a drink.**

Jake's reply is instant: **Fuuuuuuuuuuck. Text me when you can shake her. I'll meet you elsewhere.**

I frown at Jake's message, then paste on a smile for Rebecca when she hands me something with vodka in it and introduces me to her friends.

I've somehow managed to step right into the middle of a man-hating pity party, a reality that becomes apparent as I meet each member of the menagerie of misery. In addition to Rebecca, there is Allison (who found her boyfriend cheating on her last month), Stacy (who slept with a guy last Saturday and he hasn't returned any of her phone calls), and Tara (who's getting wasted because she was dumped earlier today via text message).

I will kill Jake for convincing me to come out tonight.

Considering I only know Rebecca because she dated Jake, it's incredibly awkward listening to her trash talk him in some misguided effort to win me to her side in the post-breakup custody battle.

"Does he ever talk about me?"

"Uh, he doesn't really talk to me about that kind of stuff," I lie.

She smirks. "Well, I know he was cheating on me."

"Oh, I don't think so. He's a lot of things, but a cheater is not one of them."

"Then why did I find the box of condoms on his bookshelf instead of on the nightstand where he always keeps them?"

She looks at me, expecting an answer. I suck down a gulp of my free drink. Free, my ass; this drink is costing me my sanity.

"Fucking Jake! You know what he said when he broke up with me?"

"I have absolutely no idea."

Rebecca launches into a diatribe which I mostly ignore. At my right, Tara, the really drunk little brunette, teeters against me and grins wide. "I got dumped today," she slurs as she reminds me of what she told me five minutes ago. This time, though, she adds an addendum, "But it's'okay. It's'okay because"—she points—"I'm totally gonna bag that guy over there."

I nod, struggling for an appropriate response, and glance over in the direction she's gestured—

Oh my God, it's Alex.

I blink my eyes, like I can't believe what I'm seeing. There he is. After all this time. He's real. I didn't imagine him. My fairy-God-kisser is real.

As if I've called out his name, Alex picks that moment to look my way. Our eyes meet for the first time since that night oh so many months ago.

I will kiss Jake for convincing me to come out tonight.

"He's hot, right?" Tara interrupts my reverie.

I mumble a reply, not really sure what to say other than, "Yeah. He sure is."

He sure is. With that fiery red hair, his perfect dusting of five o'clock shadow, those piercing blue eyes, his incredibly sexy scar, and those amazing lips, he's just as remarkable as I remember. I smile, and he smiles back and it hits me like a bolt of lightning straight to the spine. If there is one guy in all this time who I've most wanted to see again, it'd be—

"...Oh, and his obsession with big boobs. I wonder if his mom had big boobs, cuz you know she died when he was a teenager, and I was reading where boys who lose their moms tend to..." Rebecca's anti-Jake rant burps its noxious noise into my lusty fog. I frown and turn to scowl at her, silently pleading that she leave her theories about Jake's oedipal issues unexpressed for tonight. Fortunately, she moves onto some other topic, never even noticing my discomfort.

I glance back at Alex and find him walking my way. Beside me, Tara does a strange, drunken version of the happy dance.

Alex, ever the knight in shining armor, charges into the fray to rescue the damsel in distress from a fire-breathing dragon. Or rather, he gallantly steps forward and attempts to interrupt Rebecca. "I told you we'd meet again, sooner or—"

"Excuse me, I was talking!" Rebecca doesn't even spare Alex a sideways glance as she swats her hand up to halt him mid-sentence, coldly dismissing him.

My eyes go wide and my jaw drops. I look to Alex, who appears more bemused than pissed. He just winks at me, then shrugs as he returns to his original seat. Rebecca doesn't even skip a beat, diving right back into her rant.

At my side, Tara swoons and slurs, "I want to blow him."

Rebecca's monologue ends like a record scratch. "Who do you want to blow?"

"That guy you smacked."

"What guy? I didn't smack any guy. Girl, you are da-runk!"

"Rebecca!" I blurt out her name like my ass is on fire, then grimace when half the bar turns to stare at me. More quietly, I add, "I'm going to go get another drink."

Rebecca frowns, but nods and the other women fold together like origami, continuing their chatter. I shimmy and slide my way through the small gaps between them until I'm finally free.

Tempted to flip my arms up in a triumphant gymnast's dismount, I glance at Alex, who's watching me. He gives me a grin and a golf clap, clearly amused.

Taking his constant eye contact as an open invitation, I cross the room and slide up onto the stool beside him.

"Hey, Alex," I whisper, surprising myself by how shy I sound.

He waits a beat before he answers back, "Hey, Ariana."

That rabble of butterflies in my stomach—which I haven't felt in months—flutter at the sound of my full name on his tongue. No one calls me that now. Even Manic eventually got used to calling me Ari. Hearing it brings back memories of that first night. I remember the gurgle and slosh of too much drink, the minty taste of Alex's kiss, the raw burn of his stubble on my cheek, and the hope that I'd see him again.

And now, here he is.

For a brief moment, it's as if no time has passed. I feel like I did before—nervous and new, looking for adventure, and lucky to find a wonderful guide along the way. But...

Time *has* passed.

It's been six action-packed months, and here I am, looking much the same, yet hardly recognizable from the person he met back on that cold December night. No longer the girl he knew; what if he doesn't like the woman I've become?

I squeeze my hands between my thighs. His eyes follow the movement, then flash with warmth as he brings his gaze back up to meet mine. Oh good God, those eyes. They sparkle like the waves of the Caribbean sea, transfixing.

"I was beginning to think you'd make a liar out of me."

"Huh?" I blink to break the spell.

"The night we met, I said we'd surely meet again." He smirks. "But months passed and I didn't see you."

Was he looking for me? I've been easy to find. He knows where I live, for fuck's sake. But then, it's not like he could just knock on the door and ask, *Can your wife come out and play?*

"I thought maybe you'd given up on the open marriage thing."

"No. I'm still openly married."

He laughs, then looks a bit bashful when he says, "I asked Manic about you once. He went off about some wannabe vampire you were dating...though he didn't call it dating."

"Oh for Christ's sake. Fucking Manic." I nervously laugh and hide my blushing face behind my hands. But soon the humor's gone. I try to look him in the eyes when I admit, "I'm afraid I'm not the babe in the woods you met all those months ago."

"Shit. Ariana, I wasn't judging you. I'm sorry if it sounded like I was."

We share an awkward smile, like two nervous teenagers on a first date. And just like before, when I'm embarrassed, he seems to know just how to ease the tension. He winks at me and the butterflies in my belly go absolutely bonkers. I giggle and Alex's warm smile widens. *God, is it weird that I've missed him?*

Over his shoulder, I spot trouble. Tara watches us, staring daggers at me. Crap.

"Uh...hey, so I should introduce you to Tara."

"Who?"

"Tara." I gesture over his shoulder. "She likes you."

He shakes his head, and without even looking at her, states. "I'm not interested."

"But—"

"No buts and no introductions." Alex cocks an eyebrow as he leans closer to me. "I'm perfectly happy right here with you, Ariana."

Tara who? No. Wait. "But see, I shouldn't even be talking to you like this. I'm totally cock-blocking her right now...or cunt-blocking...or whatever the term is for chicks that poach dudes from other chicks."

Alex laughs. "Cock-blocking? Really?"

"Well yeah, I'm literally cock-blocking." I lean in close to whisper, "She told me she wants to blow you."

Alex coughs out another laugh. "Really? Well, shit, why didn't you say that before?"

He moves to stand, but I grab his arm to pull him back. He falls against me, still laughing, and his joy is contagious. I laugh too.

"Well don't you two look cozy?" Rebecca interrupts. She stands behind our barstools like a schoolmarm about to enforce the PDA rules of separation: *Make room for the Holy Spirit, kids.*

Alex and I glance over our shoulders, looking sheepish, like we've been caught misbehaving. Wearily, I turn in my seat to face her. Alex follows my lead, and when we settle into our new positions, he drapes his arm over the back of my chair, resting his palm on my shoulder.

"Uh. Hey. So. Rebecca and Tara, this is Alex."

"Hi," Tara says as she awkwardly wedges herself beside Alex. We both ignore her; it's Rebecca we're watching. She looks like the cat who ate the canary, unnervingly self-satisfied and ready to burp yellow feathers all over us.

"So it's true. You and Greg really are sleeping with other people?"

I feel Alex's arm tense around my shoulders.

Rebecca keeps talking, "Jake said something about it, and I just couldn't believe it. You and Greg always seemed so solid."

I swallow hard, as if to speak, but Rebecca's not finished.

"I mean, don't get me wrong, to each his own. I was just wondering if you and Jake...you know..."

"What?" I'm blindsided, completely confused.

She clarifies, "Well, he dumped me for you, so I just wondered if...you know..."

Again she drags out a vague, winking 'you know,' but I'm still stuck on the first part. *She thinks he dumped her for me?* "What are you talking about?"

"Oh come on Ari, no one buys the *just friends* act. I just wondered, I mean, now that you and Greg are screwing around, are you and Jake—"

"No! Jesus. No. What do you mean, no one buys the friend act? What act? Jake is like a brother to me. I love him like a brother."

"Well, that's not how he loves you."

"You don't know what you're talking about."

"Oh come on, a blind man could see it. He's in love with you. It's so obvious."

I'm dumbfounded, speechless. She keeps talking, but the grenade she's just thrown in my lap must have shredded my ear drums. I'm mostly deaf now, catching only bits and pieces, "...dumped me the day after Greg told him...can't be a coincidence...if you mean what you say about the brotherly love thing, you should...so he'll open his heart to someone else..."

No. I'm done listening to her bullshit. I rocket to my feet, unsteady. I see Alex jump to his feet too, and hear him call my name, but the sound is muffled, distant. The room seems to be getting smaller, darker; the air heavier. It's as if I'm sinking into a mire, my lungs filling with mud. I need air. Now.

I run away. But I don't get far, barely making it around the corner to the alley when I start to collapse. Dizzy. I need to lean against something, anything. Just need to catch my breath. I aim for a dingy wall covered in something green and slimy. But before my shoulder makes contact with the hard brick, I find myself engulfed in a warm, solid embrace.

"Whoa. You okay?" Alex says as he pulls me against him, one hand clasped at my waist and the other gently stroking my hair. "Just breathe. That's it. Just breathe."

I do as instructed, and eventually, it works. My vision steadies, my heartrate calms. I frown up at Alex, confused. "What are you doing?"

A smile tugs at his lips. "I'm holding you."

"Why?"

The smile grows wider, and a laugh rumbles through his chest. "Because I want to. Do you want me to stop?"

No.

Alex brushes his thumb across my cheek like he's wiping away a tear. Oh shit, am I crying? I touch my cheeks and find them wet. I look down as I dry my eyes, embarrassed. I must look like a stark-raving lunatic to him right now. "Jesus, what must you think of me?"

Alex doesn't say anything; he just keeps touching me, and it feels so good. His hug is warm, and I burrow even deeper into his protective embrace. His fingers sooth, with gentle strokes up and down my back. I press my cheek against his chest, listening to his heart beat loudly, and I am transported out of this alley, out of this awkward moment, out of Rebecca's crosshairs to somewhere else, somewhere nice. Then Alex clears his throat and ruins it all when he asks, "Who's Jake?"

I can't have this conversation right now. Clearly, Jake and I need to have a talk, but I'm not ready to think about it. I frown up at him as I pull away. "Listen, Alex, I should go."

He frowns too. "Wait. What? Why?"

"Because," I huff, "look at me, I'm a mess."

"Nonsense. You're beautiful."

He's a terrible liar. "I'm all red and puffy and a basket case."

"Yeah, but you're a *beautiful* red, puffy basket case."

I can't help but laugh.

Alex closes the distance between us. "Ariana, please don't go. Stay with me tonight."

"Why?"

He shakes his head, like I've asked a dumb question. I blush and look down at where he's gently entwined our fingers, and notice that my purse is slung over his arm.

"Why do you have my purse?"

Alex glances at it as if he's forgotten it's there. "Oh. Yeah. You left it at the bar. I was bringing it to you."

I giggle awkwardly and take it from him. "You really are a knight in shining armor."

Alex's eyes light up at that. "Does that mean you'll stay?"

"Okay."

"Okay?"

"Yeah."

"Fuck yeah." He drapes his arm over my shoulders, and leads me out of the alley to a small hole-in-the-wall bar on Seventh Street.

"I don't know about you, but I could really use a shot." Alex grins as he holds out a seat for me at the bar then slides onto the stool beside me, his warm gaze never straying from mine. "Still shooting whiskey?"

"Oh God, no. Tequila. Herradura, please."

His smile grows wider and he nods at the bartender as he holds up two fingers. When the drinks are laid out, Alex toasts. "Here's to keeping a smile on that beautiful red, puffy face."

I burst into laughter and nearly choke on the shot.

Alex smiles wide, then turns to the bartender. "Dean, this is Ariana. Take good care of her. Whatever she wants, it's on me."

When he stands up, I frown.

He explains, "I left my credit card at the last place. I'll be five minutes, tops. Please don't leave. Okay?"

I nod and watch Alex jog out the door, and my gaze lingers even after he's disappeared.

Oh boy. I think I really like this guy. All this time, I'd attributed my warm feelings for him to the fact that he was my first kiss. I figured being first had its privileges. But what I'm feeling now has nothing to do with a kiss we shared months ago. This is all about him, now, and the way he smiles and laughs and hugs me while he's carrying my damn purse.

I sigh, all girly-like, and turn around to find Dean scrutinizing me.

"So you're *her*?"

Her? I'm not sure I've heard him correctly, but before I can ask for clarification the door swings open and Alex returns. Behind him I spot Rebecca, Tara, Allison, and the other one whose name I've forgotten. Their approach would be cinematic, were they not so drunk. They fan out around Alex like an estrogen and alcohol-infused version of the Reservoir Dogs, making their way in slow, stumbling motion toward the bar.

"I was followed." Alex frowns as he slides onto the stool beside me.

Rebecca somehow manages to spin my chair around and pins me against the bar. Before I can react, she squeezes me in another of her suffocating hugs. "Oh my God, Ari. I'm so sorry. I didn't mean to upset you."

Really, Rebecca, then what exactly was your goal? "It's fine. Let's just drop it, okay?"

Rebecca nods, "But I'm buying you a drink. I owe you that much."

Oh lord, not another *free* drink. "Give me a sec." I turn to Alex. "I need to go close my tab too. I'll be right back."

Alex's expression falls slightly, but when I mouth, *I promise*, he seems to relax.

I waste little time closing out my tab, and walk back up the hill to find Alex sitting exactly where I left him. Even with his back to the door, I can spot exasperation in the hunch of his shoulders. The chair I'd vacated is occupied by Tara, and I hear Alex speak to her, sounding apologetic when he says, "I'm sorry. It's not you, it's her. I'm crazy about her."

Her again? Who is this *her*? He couldn't possibly be talking about me, could he?

Realizing that I'm behind him, Alex jerks around. "Hey, all set?"

I nod.

Since Tara is camped out in my seat, Alex rises to his feet. He seems nervous—his hands shoved deep in his pockets, scuffing the toe of his boot across the concrete floor—and his uneasiness makes one thing abundantly clear: I'm *her*.

"So," he asks, "are we going to pretend you didn't hear that?"

"Yes," I answer with relief.

"Okay. We'll play it your way." He scowls then shakes his head. "No, fuck that. I hate playing games. Let's talk."

Alex clasps my hand, lacing our fingers, and leads me into the next room. The old bar is made up of a series of adjoined cave-like spaces. Rough-hewn stone walls and dim lighting add to the subterranean ambiance. He leads me down a set of steps to a dark back corner, lit only by the glow of a dozen candles flickering inside the mouth of a craggy old fireplace.

He settles onto a low couch near the hearth and waits for me to join him. I sit a respectable distance away, my knees wedged between us, thighs firmly clinched, hands resting in my lap, every bit the demure lady.

Too nervous for eye contact, I stare into the hearth, watching the flames flicker hypnotically. Alex touches my cheek, his caress so soft it send shivers through me, and his fingers on my chin bring me to face him.

That's when he says, "Ariana, I'm crazy about you."

I stare at him, dumbfounded, expecting him to continue, but apparently it's my turn to talk. What am I supposed to say? I panic, and utter the only word that surfaces. "Why?"

He frowns and opens his mouth to answer, but I've thought of more to say.

"Alex, you don't even know me."

"I know enough."

"No, you don't."

"Ariana—"

"And even if you think you know me because we once got drunk together and shared a kiss, I've changed since then. I'm not the same person you met six months ago."

"Neither am I."

I frown.

"Ariana…" He takes a deep breath like he's about to dive underwater. "That night when I first met you, I had a girlfriend—"

"Oh God. I'm sorry. If I'd known, I wouldn't have—"

"Don't be sorry. Please don't apologize. Just hear me out."

Shell-shocked, I nod.

"I didn't tell you that to make you feel bad. If anything, I should be thanking you. Before that night, I wasn't happy. I wouldn't exactly say I was *unhappy*, but I know I wasn't happy. For two years, I stayed in a mediocre relationship because staying was easier than leaving." He lifts his hand to brush a few strands of hair behind my ear. "Then I met you, a brave, beautiful breath of fresh air." Alex's fingers linger as a gentle caress down my neck, sending more shivers through me. "You inspired me, challenged me. You made me want to at least *try* to be happy." He narrows his eyes when he says gently, "I ended things with Nicole the next day."

I sit in stunned silence, trying to process what he's just said. When I'd suggested to Greg that we open our marriage, I'd never thought of the action as brave. In fact, I'd generally thought that my actions all along were ruled by fear, not courage. Yet Alex has found inspiration in me. He thinks I'm brave. He's going to be so disappointed when he gets to know the real me.

"Alex, I'm not brave. When you first met me, I was a naïve little girl talking big and pretending to be bold, but it was an act. I didn't have a clue what I was doing. And now…"

And now…what? When I think back to the blind optimism and naivety of that night with Alex, it feels like a lifetime ago. That was the night before it all began. The night before I was buried beneath a mountain of unsolicited dick pics, and smothered by an avalanche of smarmy pickup lines. It was the night before I started my adventure quest through the bars and bedrooms of Austin, seeking self-actualization and instead finding, well, I'm not exactly sure what I've found.

And isn't it interesting that I put Alex *before* that line of demarcation. All the other men who came after, they didn't just follow after Greg, they came after Greg *and* Alex.

"And now?" Alex patiently coaxes me to continue.

"And now," I huff, "that little girl is gone."

Alex grimaces. "Ariana, you were never a naïve little girl. You were bold and brave back then, and you are still. Maybe you don't see it in yourself, but I see it as clear as day."

"I'm not brave." I frown at him. "And I can't believe you're telling me that you dumped your girlfriend of two years for me...a married woman."

"Jeez, when you put it like that—"

"Alex—"

"Ariana, let me be clear, I didn't dump Nicole... Can we not say 'dumped' it sounds awful? I didn't end my relationship with Nicole for you, I did it for me. You were the catalyst, yes, but not the reason. You were my inspiration. Your decision to shed comfort and complacency for this big unknown thing called *happiness*; that was incredibly brave. And it inspired me."

"God will you stop saying that? I'm not brave."

"Yes, you are."

"No, I'm not."

"Yes, you are."

"No, I'm not."

"Yes, you are, and you're as stubborn as a mule."

"No, I'm not."

Alex lets out a slow rumbly laugh. "My God, I'm absolutely crazy about you."

"First you say you didn't break up with Nicole for me." I lift my chin at a stubborn angle, challenging him. "And now you say you're crazy about me?"

"That night, remember when I asked you how long you'd had an open marriage? You answered, *six days*, and I laughed."

"I remember," I grumble.

"You thought I was laughing at you, but I was laughing at myself. By that point, I'd already made the decision to end things with Nicole, so learning that you were brand new to polyamory was a little surprising. In that moment, on the bus bench, I started to second guess my decision." He grins. "And then you kissed me."

Alex leans toward me, and for a moment I think he might kiss me, but he doesn't. I watch the candle light dance over his lips and reflect in his fiery gaze. He's so close that I can feel the tickle of his breath when he whispers, "Your kiss changed me."

Oh. My jaw drops and I let out a shaky breath.

Alex's gaze falls to my mouth. "I've given it a lot of thought. I've thought of little else these past months. All I can figure is either your mouth is a drug and I'm addicted, or..."

Or? I don't dare ask, struggling to swallow the lump in my throat.

"Or there's something more between us."

I gasp when Alex clasps his palms on my thighs, his thumbs tracing delicate little infinity shapes over my skirt.

"That night, you felt it too. Didn't you? Felt it in your thighs, as I recall."

I shiver, practically panting now.

"I still feel it, Ariana. Just being near you is electrifying." His eyes meet mine. "You still feel it, too, don't you?"

Oh God, I really do.

"Ariana." His voice is so quiet that I almost need to lean forward to hear him. But if I were to lean any closer, we'd be— "Kiss me."

I do. No hesitation, no second thoughts; I press my lips to his. His hands come off my legs to cup my cheeks, holding me closer, angling my mouth so he can kiss me harder, deeper. My head spins with sensation— the touch, the smell, the taste of him—leaving me dizzy, drunk on him, drowning in him.

That first night, I'd thought the kiss between us had been amazing, but I hardly had anything to compare it with. All I knew was that it felt different from kissing Greg. But, good lord, kissing Alex is different from kissing *everyone*. There is something more between us; he's right about that.

As fast as the euphoria hits, so too does reality come rocketing back. I'm struck by a barrage of emotions: guilt, as if this kiss is a betrayal of Greg; anger, because why do I feel guilty about this; and shame, for feeling anything other than pure bliss at the sensation of Alex's kiss. It's all too much, overwhelming.

I pull away and feel the loss acutely. Alex drops his head to my shoulder, his breath fanning out in warm gusts across my skin.

"Alex," I sigh, weary. "I'm married."

"I know."

"How am I supposed to do this?"

He lifts his head to look me in the eyes. "Do what?"

"This," I gesture between us. "I don't do *this*."

"We'll figure it out." He tries to kiss me again, but I hold him off.

"Alex, my life is already so complicated and now you're wanting me to…to…what…what do you want from me anyway? Because if you want me to leave—"

"Ariana, stop, *please*." He brushes his palm across my cheek. "You're making this much more complicated than it needs to be."

"But—"

"No buts. Just answer me this—do you like me?"

"Yes, but—"

"You like me." He leans in and places a delicate kiss on my jaw. "And I like you." Another mind-numbingly soft kiss, this one at the corner of my mouth. "This is all very simple."

When he kisses me this time, I don't protest. I kiss him back, taking his mouth as he takes mine. The last gasp of hesitation drains from me, though one nagging thought remains: this thing between us, whatever it is, is definitely *not* simple.

15—Saturday June 11, 2005 2:18 AM

Alex disappears through a darkened doorway, and I take the opportunity to look around his space. His house is old, but spacious and clean, and very obviously in the midst of a massive remodel.

In the front living room area, the carpet has been pulled up to reveal the original hardwoods. They're scraped and discolored, needing a good sand and polish. There's no trim around the brand new front door—the gap overflowing with spray foam insulation to keep the insects and weather outside. The wall around a large hearth has been gutted, leaving gaping holes in the drywall, but he's already started framing to install a pair of windows, which will add a ton of natural light to the space. I nod with approval at his craftsmanship. The daughter of a home builder and the wife of a structural engineer, I notice these things.

Across the room is a large fish tank. It's almost as tall as me, and about five feet wide. Inside, there's mostly just a lot of rock and bits of colorful coral, but not much else. Perhaps it, like the rest of the house, is a work in progress.

"You don't have very many fish." I holler.

Alex reappears with two glasses of water from what I presume to be his kitchen. "I'm not really into fish."

"Then why do you have a *fish* tank?"

"That, my dear, is a saltwater aquarium, and there's a lot more to the ocean, and a good aquarium, than just fish."

I give him a quizzical look and he grins.

"Check it out." He sets our waters down and joins me, bending slightly to look into the tank. He starts pointing, as he lists off the names of coral, fish, and crab. I try to follow along as my attention is riveted to his profile and the way his mouth moves when he says the word *Goby*.

He's in the middle of pointing out a little spiny shrimp when I reach over and brush my hand through his hair. It's longer now than it was six months ago, and there's a slight wave to the texture, hinting at curls.

Fish forgotten, Alex gives me a wolfish grin, then comes at me, kissing me hard and hungry. He walks me backward until I hit the wall with a gasp. Pinned, he lifts me off my feet, and I wrap myself around him as he carries me to a chair and lowers me into the seat.

Alex falls to his knees on the scuffed hardwoods in front of me, and before I can wonder about his intentions, he's on me again. He takes my mouth with another deep kiss, then leaves me gasping and breathless as he licks his way down my neck. Slowing way down, his movements turn tender as he unbuttons my shirt, revealing my bra beneath. His teeth are a surprise, teasing as he licks and nibbles at me through the red lacy fabric. And when I moan at the sensation, he bites just a little bit harder.

Distracted by his mouth, I hardly notice when his hands venture down my body and under my skirt. He moves me, pulling me to the edge of the chair, and strips me of the little scrap of red lace which separates us there. Then he pulls away, sliding back onto his heels to stare at me.

Panting and breathless, teetering at the edge of my seat, I shiver with nervous energy, and look down at myself too. He's pushed my clothes aside and left my legs spread wide, completely exposed. I feel the heat of embarrassment and move to close my legs, but he clasps his hands around my ankles, holding me open. Then, sensing my insecurity, Alex kindly covers my nakedness with his mouth.

He's a master with his tongue, wordlessly assuaging my embarrassment. I go boneless, a blissful slouch. He slides my legs onto his shoulders, and loops his arms over my thighs to keep me where he wants me. And good lord does it feel like he wants me, consuming me with ravenous intensity.

But he teases me too. Each time I'm about to come, Alex stops and watches me with a grin, licking his lips. He can read my body well, seeming to know the precise moment to cut me off, delighting in my desperate anticipation.

Finally, I beg, "Please."

Like he's been waiting for that word all along, he gives me a waggle of his lightning-bolt brow and dives back down, eager to oblige. I come almost immediately, arching my back and screaming as every muscle tenses and releases. When I settle down, I find Alex smiling at me as he catches his breath. I give him a coy grin and say, "Felt that in my thighs."

His laugh rumbles deep and draws me to him. *It's your turn now, you beautiful man.*

I slide off the chair to straddle him on the floor, ready to explore him like he explored me. I tug at his shirt, and he lets me pull it over his head. And—

My jaw drops as I stare at the most magnificent tattoo I've ever seen. There's no color, it's in grayscale, and what's perfectly depicted in all that lightness and shadow is a giant squid. The big beast's body stretches across Alex's well-defined pecs. It's tentacles curling up toward his neck, down his abdomen, and around his side. And there, encircling his left nipple, is its mouth, a ring of razor sharp teeth.

I want to touch it, so I do. I trace a finger over the lines of the beast's tentacles. And when I reach the mouth of the creature, I twirl my finger around the ring of teeth and finish with a flick of my nail across his nipple. He hisses sharply, and I watch as his tight chest fills with air, breathing life into the monster.

"Like the tattoo?" Alex asks, his voice thick.

I nod and lick my lips, then bend forward and trace one of the monster's tentacles with my tongue, moaning as I answer, "Uh huh."

Alex's breath goes ragged and he clenches his fingers on my hips so tightly they'll leave bruises. God, I love the way he responds to every little thing I do. Like a tuning fork, one flick of my finger, or tongue, and he's humming.

When I reach the ring of the squid's deadly mouth this time, I tease his nipple with my teeth, then bite down, and gently tug like he'd done to me before.

Alex bellows, "Oh. Fuck. Yes!" Then with a frustrated groan, he pushes my shoulders back, severing my tooth-hold.

That monster on his chest moves with each excited breath he takes. His nipple is hard as stone and still glistening from my wet kiss. I crane my neck, wanting to have my mouth on him again, but he holds me at bay.

"Please," he begs, pausing to catch his breath, "you have to stop."

I surface from my pheromone-induced stupor to frown at him. Why is he telling me to stop just when things are getting so good? Clearly, he likes this; every part of his body is hard for me, his hot touch is practically electric on my shoulders. I lean forward again and he lets me. I go to his other nipple now. I get in one lick, then two and delight as Alex's fingers squeeze me tighter and his head falls back on his shoulders. I nibble, then bite—

"Ah fuck!" Alex groans as he holds me at arm's length again, breathlessly mumbling. "It's too much. Any more of that and I'll forget my manners and fuck the ever loving shit out of you."

Wait...what? Record scratch. "Isn't fucking the ever loving shit out of me kind of the point?"

Alex steadies his breath and gently brushes a hand over my hair, as if trying to focus his attention on my non-erogenous parts. "I didn't bring you here for sex, Ariana."

A strange silence settles between us like a fog, blotting my thoughts. I don't understand. How can he say that when he's just made a meal of me? We stay like this, frozen in the awkward moment like insects trapped in amber, each watching the other as if waiting for something to happen. When one of us finally moves, it's Alex, grimacing as he gently slides me off his lap, then climbs to his feet.

Completely dumbfounded, I frown up at him as he offers a hand to help me stand. "Wait. I'm not following."

"Are you hungry?"

Subject change not accepted. "What do you mean, you didn't bring me here for sex? Then why did you bring me home with you?"

"Jesus," He runs a hand over his face, looking weary and frustrated. "Listen to what you're saying."

I flinch and look away, shamed by the censure in his tone. Ignoring the hand he holds out toward me, I climb to my feet on my own. We stand like this for a moment, hovering just out of reach.

"Ariana," Alex's voice is gentle again. He steps closer to me. I stare down at his boots, a well-worn pair of steel-toes. "Will you please allow me the honor of cooking you a meal? I'm fairly good at making macaroni and cheese from a box."

I glance up to find him grinning nervously, his puppy dog eyes sexy as hell. Jesus, it's impossible to stay irritated with this man. And now that I think about it, I am kind of hungry. In all the hubbub with Rebecca and my reunion with Alex, I'd forgotten dinner. After an extended think on the matter, I shrug, then nod.

"Great." Alex's posture relaxes, and he gives me a wide, boyish grin as he leans down to the floor, picks up my underwear, and hands them to me. "I'm going to start the water. Make yourself at home."

I glance down at the red lacy drawers in my hand, and nearly laugh at the absurdity. Turning my attention to Alex, I watch him cheerily unlace and kick off his boots then whistle as he walks into the kitchen. I'm overwhelmed with an urge to laugh...or possibly cry. This night has been so topsy-turvy that either would come naturally at this point. But something about his boyish charm and the way he looks as he heads to the kitchen, shirtless and barefoot and whistling the chorus to Kenny Roger's *The Gambler*, lightens my mood.

Laugh. I choose to laugh. So I giggle as I shimmy back into my underwear and kick off my shoes.

"Hey," I holler, "do you have a pair of socks I can borrow?"

Alex peeks around the corner from the kitchen, one eyebrow raised. "Socks?"

"If I'm going to make myself at home, then I need socks. I'm a sock person."

A wide smile slides across his lips, and he stares at me for a few seconds before he jogs down the hallway, emerging moments later with a pair of bright red socks. "To match your bra and undies." Then he jogs backwards to the kitchen, still whistling.

I slide the socks on, button my shirt back up, then go to find Alex. I can hear him moving around in the other half of the house and follow the sound.

Unlike the living room, which is clearly still a work in progress, the kitchen is finished and it's amazing. The large space is simple in its design, yet spectacular. On either side of the room are long, matte black soapstone counters, topped and bottomed by simple Shaker-style white cabinets. The appliances are all restaurant-grade and stainless steel. Along the back wall, a giant set of glass doors open to a deck illuminated by a spray of twinkly Christmas lights entwined in the arbor overhead.

I sigh and mumble something like, "Ohmygodyourhouseisamazing!"

Alex grins as he turns away from the sink, a pot full of water in his hand, and walks it over to the stove. "You like?"

"I love."

Alex stops in his tracks and smiles at me, then takes a look around the room as if seeing it anew. After a thoughtful moment, he resumes his path to the stove. With the water heating, he crosses to one of the cabinets by the fridge.

"Guess what I have," he teases as he retrieves a bottle of Herradura and two shot glasses.

"Whoa. Tequila shots?"

"Yes, for our drinking game."

"We're playing a drinking game?"

He sets the tequila and glasses on the counter and turns to me, wrapping his arms around me as he gives me a spirited kiss. "You bet your ass we're playing a drinking game."

I giggle. When did he become so playful? It's as if I'm only now getting a glimpse of the real Alex. And Real Alex is completely adorable. Feeling increasingly relaxed with him, I hike myself up onto the counter, swinging my red-socked feet in front of me.

Alex gives me a sidelong glance as he pours the shots. "You look incredibly cute in my socks, you know that?"

"Well, duh."

He chuckles and sets the shots between us. "Okay, so you say I don't know you. Let's fix that. Here's how this game works. You ask me a question, anything you want, and I either answer or I take a shot. Then I get to ask you any question I want, and you answer or take a shot."

I shrug. "Okay. Game on."

"Ladies first."

"Hmm." I scrunch my face, pretending to be considering my query, even though the question I want to ask is on the tip of my tongue. "Why don't you want to have sex with me?"

He smirks and slowly shakes his head, "Vicious! Not even a warm-up question, you go straight for the jugular." He pauses, then grabs a shot and drinks it.

I'm surprised, not expecting that to be an off-limits question. "Whoa. What are you hiding?"

"I'm not hiding anything. Just not ready to answer that yet. Ask me again later." He slaps the counter. "My turn." He goes straight for the jugular. "Are you happy to be married?"

I scowl at him as I consider how to answer. Am I happy? Right this minute, yes, I'm happy. Am I happy being married? Where do I even begin to answer that question? Things are complicated in my life and in my marriage, and those complications are not all good, they don't always make me happy. However, given that I'm married to a man who grants me the freedom to find my happiness, wherever it may be, I'd say yes; I'm happy in this marriage. But that's not really what Alex is asking. *Do you wish you weren't married?* That's the real question he's dangling between us. I stare into his waiting eyes.

He scrutinizes me, but he doesn't grow impatient. He waits with a Zen-like calm, and it urges me on to answer him the best I know how to. "It's complicated. And yes, the fact that I constantly have to deal with *complicated* when what I really want is *simple* can get frustrating. It's not easy. Being married is not easy, and being in an open marriage is doubly difficult. But, yes, right here, right now I am happy, and I don't regret any part of the journey which has brought me here."

Alex raises an eyebrow at me. "Heh. That doesn't really answer my question, but the judges like your answer, so they're going to let it stand."

I let out the breath I didn't know I was holding. "Okay, my turn." I grin wide. "Why don't you want to have sex with me?"

"Nuh uh. No repeats."

"You told me to ask you again later. It's later."

"Smart ass. You're just trying to get me drunk and take advantage of me." Alex raises an eyebrow as he downs the second shot. He pours out two more drinks. "Why did you open your marriage?"

I've told this story a hundred times, at least, and I have about a dozen versions: the curt and *cliché* version, the long and rambling version, the funny version, the heartfelt version, even the 'shut up and fuck me' version. But I don't want to give Alex a *version* of the story. I only want to tell him the truth.

"I was suffocating. I needed air."

Alex nods, his expression turned sad, as if he knows that exact feeling. "Are you getting the air you need?"

"Oh no you don't; it's my turn." I give him an evil grin. "Three guesses what my question is."

"Oh for fuck's sake, you're like a broken record." He fights a smile. "Fine. I don't want to have sex with you *yet*, emphasis on 'yet', because I want more than just sex. It's not enough for me...not with you. If all I wanted was a lay, I could get that with any woman and you could get that with any guy." He shakes his head. "I don't want to be just any guy to you."

Once again, he renders me speechless, and he uses the opportunity to get in his next question, quickly changing the subject back to me. "Are you getting the air you need?"

I shrug. "Sometimes."

"That's not a satisfactory answer. Elaborate or drink."

I think for a moment and realize I have no real answer for him. Sometimes, in the midst of all this madness, I feel free, I can breathe easy, take a step back and enjoy the view. But other times, it's like I'm drowning. And, if I'm really honest with myself, it's not the sex that sets my spirit free, it's exploring my boundaries in so many other ways. It's the first time I sang karaoke; meeting new people and visiting new places; it's my friendship with Sheryl and all the new relationships I've built. Sure, sometimes the sex is great, but that's not what helps me breathe. When I open my mouth to explain all of this, the words stall in my throat, so my answer remains: *sometimes*.

I look at Alex, grab one of the shot glasses, and drink. *Ouch.*

A sympathetic smile crosses his lips, but he says nothing. It's my turn again.

"If it's not about the sex, then why did you go down on me?"

He laughs. "I went down on you because I wanted to go down on you."

I throw his words back at him, "That's not a satisfactory answer. Elaborate or drink."

Alex thinks for a moment, his fingers slowly turning the last tequila shot like he might drink it. So when he speaks, his words surprise me. "You can learn a lot about a person by the way they come." His eyes narrow. "And I've wanted to make you come since the first night I met you."

Whoa. I shiver but quickly recover. "What did you learn about me?"

"No, it's my turn."

"No more games." I shake my head, grab the last shot from his grasp, and down it. Gasping for air, I gesture for him to keep talking.

Alex smirks and licks his lips, as if he can still taste me there. He steps in front of me and presses my knees apart, making room for his hips between my thighs. He rests his forehead against mine and speaks softly, just above a whisper. "You scream when you come. It's incredible to hear—primal and base and damn sexy. You open yourself up completely, and that's especially exciting considering how closed off you are the rest of the time. It's like you're constantly bubbling under the surface, and just waiting to boil over. Which reminds me..."

Alex holds up a finger as if to press pause and pulls away from me. He turns to the stove and dumps the pasta into the simmering water, stirs for a moment, sets the timer, then nestles his way back between my legs.

He brushes a few strands of hair behind my ear and continues, "Then, after your incredibly sexy primal scream, you let out this sad little whimper. Like you wish you hadn't come, because once you have, then the moment is over and you're back to where you started. You close yourself back up until you're suffocating again."

I'm stunned. Not sure if I'm excited by his reading of my body, or upset by how accurate his assessment is.

"Ariana, I don't want to have sex with you tonight because I don't want that moment to be over either." He takes my face between his palms. "While I'm absolutely certain that sex with you will be fucking incredible, I want more."

I swallow hard and blink, trying to process his words.

"When the time is right, I will have you, but today is not that day." He quirks half a smile at my grimace. "But I'm a patient man, and I think you're worth the wait."

I'm stunned silent, dumbfounded. How do I respond to that? How do I feel about that? What does that even mean? He talks like we have all the time in the world, like we have...a future.

Alex watches me as the thoughts play through my mind. He's not expecting a response, which is good because I don't have one. He kisses me, and this time it's not starved or sex-laden, but achingly tender, a demonstration of his determination and patience.

The timer buzzes and we come apart with a jolt. Alex takes a moment to catch his breath before he pushes away from the counter and tends to the pasta. I watch his every move. The way he slants his head as he shakes the strainer over the sink. How he uses his teeth to rip into the packet of cheese. The way his muscles flex as he mixes it all up.

I smile when he serves our meal in the saucepan with two forks. He finds his way back between my legs, holding the pot between us as we each scoop up forkfuls of the delicious food. It is by far the most scrumptious macaroni and cheese from a box served in a saucepan I've ever had, though that might have something to do with the cook.

16—Saturday June 11, 2005 8:43 AM

"Fuck!" Alex hisses.

I wake with a jolt, trying to get my bearings in the unfamiliar room. Alex is in a rush, hurriedly detangling his arms and legs from me as he climbs out of bed. He's wearing nothing but boxer briefs, and I can't help but ogle as he scrambles to slide on the jeans he discarded last night.

"What's going on?" I rub my eyes and stretch.

The doorbell rings, followed by a loud knock. It's an intimidating sound, full of force and authority, the sort of knock you'd hear just before the police kick the door in and wrestle you to the floor. My heart skips a beat. But Alex doesn't look concerned. Why isn't he concerned?

"Relax." He grins. "It's just Pete."

"Who's Pete?"

Alex doesn't explain. He just winks as he leaves the bedroom, closing the door behind him.

I listen to the bell ring again, and hear the knocking continue until Alex opens the front door. It's another male, I can just make out the sound of their voices, though none of the specifics of what they say. Then, the voice of the other man comes near and I hear him distinctly.

"You got someone in there?" he asks.

"You've got shit timing, Pete," Alex replies.

The man speaks louder, practically yelling when he says, "Come on out, sweetheart, I won't bite."

Panicking now, I scan the room, finding my blouse and skirt rumpled on the floor. Do I really want to wear my walk-of-shame clothes from last night to meet this mysterious Pete? But what are my other options? One of Alex's t-shirts? His robe? Does Alex even have a robe? And who is Pete?

The bedroom door opens. I quickly lift the sheet to cover myself as Alex steps in and closes the door behind him.

"What's going on?" I ask in a whisper.

"My friend Pete's here. He does this sometimes."

"Does what?"

"Shows up out of the blue." Alex tries to act annoyed, but it's obvious he's not. Clearly, Pete is important to him. My panic only increases with that revelation.

Alex seems to sense my fear. He sits beside me on the bed, running his fingers up and down my arm. "Don't worry. He already likes you."

"You've told him about me?"

"Uh. A bit."

"When?"

"Come on, get dressed. I want to introduce you two."

"What am I going to wear?"

"Your clothes." He laughs.

"But—"

"No buts. Trust me. He's gonna love you. You have nothing to fear. Now come on." His expression is gentle and sweet, and it soothes my jangled nerves. I oblige, climbing out of bed and letting Alex help me back into my clothes.

When I'm dressed, he runs his fingers through my hair, taming the bedhead, and kisses me sweetly on the forehead. Then he clasps my palm in his and leads me out to the living room.

"Ariana, this is Pete, my oldest and closest friend."

I see Pete before he sees me, and I'm immediately impressed. He stands at the aquarium, looking in at Alex's strange pets. With his back to me, I can only assess that he's tall, statuesque in build, and black. At our approach, Pete turns and I get to see his face—his features handsome, his eyes keen, a hint of a grin on his lips. For a moment, he just stares, his curious eyes looking me over, assessing. I hold my breath, not sure what to say or do. Finally, Pete smiles widely.

"So you're her, then."

Her?

As he crosses the room, I offer my hand, but instead of a handshake, he gives me a bear hug and lifts me off my feet. *What the hell?*

"I like her, man. She's cute," Pete addresses Alex over my shoulder as I'm crushed against him, my feet dangling at least a foot above the floor.

"Dude," Alex laughs. "Put her down."

Pete does, and when I'm safely grounded, he crooks his neck down and grimaces at me. "What's the matter, sweetheart, cat got your tongue?"

Shit. I haven't spoken yet. "Sorry, I'm still a bit sleepy."

"Sorry about that. As I was explaining to Alex, it's tomorrow in Japan, so my internal clock is a bit off. Didn't mean to wake you love birds."

"Japan?" I ask blankly.

Pete nods as he moves into the kitchen, and soon returns with a glass of water. "Place is looking real good, my man. Coming right along." He takes a long sip, then keeps talking. "Yeah, so, my relief was thirteen days late. I was afraid I'd miss the big day. But Finn showed up just in time, so here I am."

To me, it sounds like Pete has strung a bunch of nonsense words together, but Alex seems to follow. "Finn's still second? Thought he'd be first by now."

Huh?

"He is first. So am I. Dude, didn't I tell you? This last time I sailed as first engineer."

Enough. "What language are you two speaking?"

Alex and Pete both look at me, and Pete's hearty laugh fills the house. "Sorry, sweetheart, mariner speak."

Still completely confused.

Alex tries to help, "Pete's a merchant marine. I was for a few years too."

"You were a marine?"

"No. A merchant marine, a mariner," Alex explains, but it's all Greek to me.

"Oh." I give up trying to understand.

"So?" Pete looks between us. "What are your plans for the big day?"

"Big day?" I stupidly inquire.

Pete looks at me like I've sprouted a second head. Then to Alex, "You're shitting me. You haven't told her?"

"Told me what?"

Pete gestures to Alex with his half-drunk glass of water. "Our boy Balfour here turns the big three-oh today."

My eyes go big, and I turn to see Alex looking embarrassed and shaking his head. "It's your birthday? Why didn't you say something?"

Alex shrugs.

Taking pity on the new girl, Pete offers, "If you two don't already have plans, and if I may presume to invite myself along for the day, I suggest we partake in pool, more pool and booze."

I turn to Alex and see that he's already looking at me. "Will you join us?" he asks quietly.

Pete has the good grace to pretend he's focusing on the fish tank again. I smile at Alex. "How could I deny the birthday boy? But I need to change clothes and brush my teeth."

"No, sweetheart," Pete chimes in. "What you need is a bikini."

"A bikini?" I ask.

"Well yeah," Pete shrugs, nonchalant. "Unless you want to swim buck-ass naked. Which, I'm completely fine with. In fact, I love the idea, but it means we'll need to head out to Hippie Hollow rather than Barton Springs."

Alex gives Pete the stink eye as he speaks to me. "We'll stop somewhere on the way and get you a swimsuit."

But I have a swimsuit...at home. I recognize what this is, Alex clearly doesn't want to take me home. He'd prefer to avoid running into my husband. And who can blame him? However, the solution the guys have worked out doesn't solve my two key problems—namely my hellacious mac-and-cheese morning breath, and my rumpled walk-of-shame ensemble.

I consider protesting, but one glimpse at Alex has me ready to agree to just about anything. It's his thirtieth birthday, and he so easily could have gotten laid before the sun even rose on his new decade, but he'd abstained. He'd given me a screaming orgasm, then whispered "today is not that day" when it came to his turn. For this strange and noble man, I will gladly suffer the indignity of halitosis and the social stigma of a bedraggled fashion victim.

"Okay." I grin.

I'm rewarded with a warm hug from the birthday boy. He and Pete quickly change into swim trunks and t-shirts before ushering me out the door. In short order, we hit a mercado where I pick up a swimsuit, as well as a flirty little sundress, a toothbrush and paste, and a bag of *polvoróns* from the bakery.

"It's like a normal swimming pool, except it's huge and the bottom is covered with algae and there's salamanders and crawdads and shit. Basically, it's a spring-fed creek inside a pool." Pete chomps on another cookie and wipes powdered sugar off his lips before adding, "Oh, and the water's cold."

I frown.

Alex catches my look and adds, "It's not *that* cold." He opens his mouth and I stuff another *polvorón* in.

Barton Springs, like Sixth Street, is a place I've heard plenty about, but have never been. No matter how much the guys have tried to prepare me, the reality far exceeds my expectations. Pete wasn't exaggerating. It looks like it could fit five or six Olympic pools inside it. Its rich green water, sparkling in the morning sunlight, stretches as far as the eye can see.

The pool looks like a natural creek in places, but on the east end there are long swaths of concrete which straddle both sides, a pool deck dotted every few feet by lifeguard stations. A creek within a pool, just as Pete had said.

I stop short when I get through the gate, and try not to trip and fall down the stairs as I take in the view of the enticing water, as well as the lush green landscape. Immediately digging for my new camera—my new hobby—I start shooting photos. The pool is in a small valley, with grassy berms on either side dotted by massive oak, pecan, and cottonwood trees that provide welcome respite from the blazing Texas sun. It's a wonderland, an urban oasis.

Ahead of me, Pete and Alex charge down the steep steps, toss their towels under one of the giant oak trees, and strip out of their shirts and shoes like someone has issued the challenge, "last one in is a rotten egg." And in they go.

I try to shoot action shots as Pete performs a graceless back flop, and Alex pulls off a powerful cannonball, both sinking deep as they splash high. They reemerge howling and whooping, their glee filling the valley with the echoes of their shouts.

I take my time to reach the water's edge, tug my sundress over my head, then settle onto the grass, enjoying the feel of the sun on my skin as I people-watch.

Across the pool, there is a man playing a banjo. His back wedged against the base of one of those mighty oak trees, he strums his instrument and fills the valley basin with a lilting tune, just barely audible above the morning song of the birds up in the trees. At the far end of the pool, awash in the low slung rays of the morning sun, another man is twisted into an impressive yoga pose. In the water, a handful of fit and fast lap swimmers forward crawl past a clutch of old ladies in floral swim bonnets, paddling and chattering over their kickboards.

The boys have made their way to the diving board on the opposite deck. I watch with a grin as they take turns impersonating Greg Louganis with increasingly outlandish and daring jumps. Pete's good, a strong swimmer, and absolutely gorgeous in his skivvies, sporting a sexy pair of piercings in his nipples that glisten in the sun and shine against his dark muscled chest; yet my attention is absorbed by Alex. An Adonis and a damn merman, never still, always diving, swimming, or somersaulting in the water. And his tattoo? Even sexier when it's wet.

At one particularly good backward flip dive, I judge it as a perfect ten and hold all my fingers high. He chuckles and winks, "What are you doing out there? Come in, the water's great."

I smirk, but stow my camera in my bag and make my way down to the water's edge. I hesitate for one moment, then jump in—

Holy Mary Mother of— "Jesus Christ!" I sputter, squealing like a banshee when I surface. The water is cold, really cold, glacially cold.

Alex and Pete judge my jump a perfect ten, but I ignore them. My teeth chattering, my hair plastered to my face, I whine, "For the love of God, you said it was cold, but you didn't say it was *coooooold*. I think I'm getting hypothermia."

Alex laughs. "It's seventy-degrees. You'll live."

"I can't feel my feet anymore."

"Aw, sweetheart, this is nothing. Try surfing in Alaska then talk to me about hypothermia," Pete adds helpfully.

Alex nods in agreement. *Wait, they've surfed in Alaska?* He turns to me, looking very authoritative as he insists, "Just be patient. Trust me. Your body will adjust and then it will feel amazing."

As if to punctuate his point, the cluster of little old ladies with their pastel swim caps come paddling past me, slowly moving between us like a flock of Easter-tinted ducks.

"It's nice to see you boys again. Alexander, how is your mother?" one of the old ladies asks cheerfully.

"She's good, Mrs. Mitchell." Alex nods politely.

"Peter, so nice to see you," she say to him.

"Pleasure's all mine, Gladys," Pete answers.

I try to suppress a laugh, but can't. "Alexander and Peter?"

Pete hoots. "That's right, sweetheart, you're in the company of 'The Greats.'"

I frown, confused again.

Alex explains, "Alexander the Great, Peter the Great..."

Pete adds, "When we were young, anytime there was a new kid in school, we'd hoped his name was Ivan so we could make him our friend and be 'The Great and Terribles.'"

I laugh and the sound echoes throughout the whole valley. The group of old ladies all smile at me, and I smile back.

"Still cold?" Alex asks.

That's when it hits me, I'm not. Actually, the water feels wonderful, perfect, even. I slowly grin.

"You see? You've just got to be patient." Alex winks, "Some things are worth the wait."

Are we still talking about swimming? Without clarifying, Alex gives me a gorgeous smile, then flops backwards into a somersault under the water. I drift, allowing myself to just relax. I float on my back and watch the leaves rustle in the trees, grinning when a flock of feral parakeets fly overhead, squawking and chirping. I swim a slow breaststroke and listen to the banjo music.

I don't know how long we stay at the pool, could be hours or days, but when we leave, I feel different. Like a baptism, all my troubles have been washed away by the cleansing waters. I've shed some of the weight I was carrying before, and now I'm just a simple girl in a simple dress with my hair drip drying down my back as we find a place to drink margaritas and play pool.

• • •

"UNREP," Pete slurs. "It means underway replenishment. It's where you've got two ships pulled up side-by-side and we pump fuel to them, and lift food and supplies to them."

"Oh." I nod loosely; those drinks have worked through me faster than I expected. "And what is your job?"

"First engineer." Pete nods too. We're all nodding. "My job is to make sure the lights are on and there's hot water in the showers."

"Oh."

"It's more involved than that," Alex elaborates. "He's got to keep everything running on the ship."

"Oh."

"Pick a different vowel, sweetheart, for the sake of variety." Pete presses his hands together, praying.

"Ah," I oblige, and they both laugh.

The more I get to know Pete, the more I like him. He's got 'tough guy' written all over him, but he's a big softy who clearly values his friendship with Alex. After hours of pool—where I lost every single game—then enchiladas and margaritas, I find an easy rhythm in our conversation. It makes me appreciate their friendship, and the way they're making room for me within it.

"I gotta take a piss," Alex exclaims, then climbs over the back of the horseshoe booth and vanishes down the stairs, presumably to find the restroom.

This is the first time Pete and I are alone together. Turns out, Alex is the glue that binds us. Without him, our easy rhythm suffers.

"What are your intentions with my boy?" Pete asks as soon as Alex is out of earshot, sounding significantly more sober than he did a moment ago.

"I honestly have no idea." I'm more sober too. "My situation is...complicated."

"He told me you're married."

"Did he tell you it's an open marriage?"

Pete nods.

"In my head, this has all been so simple. I had my husband over here, and my, uh—"

"Side dudes," Pete interjects. Surprisingly, his tone is judgment-free.

"Uh, yeah, husband over here and side dudes over there. But with Alex, I don't know, it's jumbled up."

"Why?"

"He's...different."

Pete tries to suppress a smile. "Not just a side dude?"

I let out a heavy sigh, exhausted by the mere thought of trying to put my feelings about Alex into words. Do I even know what my feelings are? Finally, I just say, "Things with Alex are...confusing, and very new. So I don't have a good answer for you."

Pete nods. "I respect that. I just don't want to see him get hurt."

"I appreciate how protective you are. It speaks highly of him that he has such a good friend."

Pete shakes his head like I have no idea what I'm talking about. "I owe my life to Alex, literally. Protective doesn't even begin to describe how I feel about him. I'd do anything for the guy."

"You owe him your life? Care to share the story?"

"No ma'am," He chugs his beer, then wipes his mouth on his arm before adding. "That story makes me look like an idiot, and it makes Alex look fucking golden, so I rarely elaborate."

"I'll tell you what happened," Alex interjects. I turn to see him, three shots of tequila in hand, slide into the booth and distribute the liquor. "Pete was mouthing off about Crocodile Dundee at a bar in Sydney, and some guy swiped at him with a broken bottle. Would have sliced him in the neck, but I tackled Pete out of the way. Nearly lost an eye." He points to his brow, to the bolt of flesh that cuts through it. Oh holy hell, that's how he got his scar?

"Sydney, Australia?" I ask.

They both nod.

He got his scar from a bar fight in *Australia*? My jaw hits the floor, and Pete shakes his head, as if he still feels guilty. I give him a sympathetic grin and say, "Well, Pete, if it makes you feel any better, that scar led to our first kiss."

"Really? It was my scar? Not my charm or devastating good looks? You were into me for my fucking scar?" Alex huffs.

I shrug. "I wanted to touch it."

"That's right." Alex laughs and waggles his scarred brow. "She started stroking it, and then boom, she kissed me. Kind of blew my mind."

"Well in that case, you're welcome." Pete grins wide and lifts his shot of tequila. "To war wounds and battle scars and a life well-lived."

We drink and then pause as the tequila percolates at the backs of our throats. I watch Alex as he stares back at me. Without permission this time, I slide my hand to his cheek and run the pad of my thumb over the flesh of his scar. Just like that first night, Alex closes his eyes and I steal a kiss. Only this time, Alex doesn't flinch. He kisses me back.

"Jeez, get a room, you two," Pete grumbles.

We laugh, but we don't stop kissing.

• • •

We say our farewell to Pete at the bar, he'll be spending the night at his mom's house. Like our hello, he sweeps me off my feet with his hug. This time, I giggle. He chuckles, then speaks to me, his voice too quiet for Alex to hear.

"I'm glad to finally meet you. You're a sweetheart, and cute as hell, and you make him happier than I've ever seen him." His words stun me, but I don't have time to reply before he sets me on my feet and turns to hug Alex.

I don't object when Alex takes me back to his place. I'd more or less assumed I'd be spending another night with him.

At his house, I make my way to Alex's bedroom where I snoop. Taking a look at the photos on his wall and dresser top, I learn that he gets his hair color from his dad and he has his mom's eyes, that he and Pete have got a hell of a lot of funny stories left to tell me, and that he's a dog person. I grin and move to his bookshelf, scanning the titles—an assortment of maritime history, some science and math texts, and a handful of fantasy and sci-fi novels to round it out. Behind me I hear Alex approach. I grin to myself as he laces his arms around my waist and hugs me tight, planting a soft kiss on my temple.

"Sleepy?"

It's early still, but I yawn and nod.

Alex leads me to the bed and helps me out of my clothes, leaving me in just my undies and a fresh pair of his socks. Then he strips down to his boxer briefs and invites me to crawl into bed with him. We tangle together, arms and legs entwined. It's a nice feeling, being wrapped in Alex's sleepy embrace.

Once settled, we kiss, slow and deliberate. The kiss itself is a form of conversation, wordlessly speaking volumes. When it ends, Alex pulls away just far enough to stare at me, his thumb rubbing my cheek in gentle circles, tracing infinite loops over my skin. He plants a kiss on my forehead before he reaches back and turns off the side lamp. In the darkness, we curl together again, and he takes a long, deep breath as he settles in to sleep.

"Alex..." I exhale his name on a long sigh.

"Mmm-hmm."

"Happy birthday."

Alex squeezes me tighter and kisses me again, then settles against me with a contented sigh.

"I like Pete," I whisper.

"Yeah. He's good people."

"How long have you known him?"

"Since I was twelve, when I moved here."

"Where did you move from?"

"Aren't you tired?"

"Not anymore." I stroke my fingers over his chest, and he shivers in response before he takes my hand and kisses my palm.

"I lived in San Diego. My dad was in the Navy. But he died. So we moved to Austin to live with my mom's sister. Pete lived in the house next door. We got into a fist fight the first week I moved in, but after that, we were inseparable. It's pretty much been Pete and me versus the world ever since."

"Alexander and Peter, The Greats." I grin as I say it.

Alex chuckles, "The way we do things, it was always a bit of the Great and Terribles."

I giggle and Alex squeezes me a little tighter against him. Slowly his breathing starts to even out. He's falling asleep.

"Alex," I whisper.

"Yeah?" he whispers back.

"I'm sorry about your dad."

He hugs me tighter, "When I was a kid, he used to take me surfing off of Coronado Beach." With a chuckle, "You don't know cold water until you've been in the Pacific in January."

I smile at the airiness in his voice. "Alex."

"Yeah?"

"I really like you."

Alex's breath catches in his lungs and his arms tighten around me. He kisses me again, another of his long, deep, conversational kisses. When he pulls away from me, he whispers. "I really like you too."

17—Sunday June 12, 2005 10:52AM

I open my eyes, and have to shield my face from the mid-morning sun pushing through the blinds. It takes a moment to recognize my surroundings.

"Hey, Sleeping Beauty." Alex is stretched across the bed beside me, propped up on an elbow, fully dress.

I blink at him. "Have you been watching me sleep?"

"Only for a few hours. That's not creepy, is it?"

I frown. *Uh, yeah, it's kind of creepy.* He winks and chuckles. *Oh, good, a joke, and so early in the morning.*

"What time is it?" I grumble and rub my eyes.

"Eleven. Clearly you are not a morning person."

"Clearly you are."

He chuckles. "Eleven ain't morning. Get your ass up. We're burning daylight."

I flop onto my back with a groan, and smile when Alex's eyes flair wide at the sight of my bare breasts. He reaches for me, thoughtfully tracing the edges of the nearest nipple. "So, you got any plans for today?"

I try to remember what day it is. I haven't been home since Friday. I *should* go back, check in with Greg, do the laundry, balance the checkbook... I shake my head. "Nope." With one caveat. "I do need to go home tonight, though."

Alex nods.

"Oh," I bolt upright, "I have an idea. There's somewhere I want to take you."

"Well, take me. I'm all yours."

I crawl out of the bed and quickly dress, wearing the same clothes as yesterday. Next time, I should pack an overnight bag.

Next time? I'm making plans. I'm thinking about our future, together. It's a seductive thought, future nights sleeping with him, and mornings waking at his side. I shake my head to chase away the schoolgirl fantasy, and spot Alex waiting for me by the door. He watches me with knowing eyes, like he can read my mind. He smiles and my breath catches in my lungs.

Yep, definitely need to pack a bag for next time.

• • •

"Have you been here before?" I ask as we stare up the one hundred and six steps that lead to the top of Mount Bonnell.

The name "Mount" is being kind. Mount Bonnell is not an actual mountain, more a foothill. Compared to the mountains back home, it's a molehill. But you work with what you have, and in Austin, I have Mount Bonnell. The summit is exactly one hundred and six steps up from the road—actual rock stairs, not a natural trail. Still, it's a lovely local spot with a great view.

"I have, but it's been years. And besides," he winks at me, "I like exploring with you, even if it's ground I've already covered. You have this uncanny ability to make old experiences new again."

My cheeks warm and I giggle bashfully, then catch myself. Jesus, I'm like a lovesick teenager. I set aside my timid nervousness and excitedly rub my hands together. "Ready?"

"Ready for what?"

I crouch down and plant my feet, a runner at the starting blocks, turn to Alex, and issue the challenge. "Last one to the top is a rotten egg."

Alex laughs at me and shakes his head, but he doesn't move. Me, on the other hand, I practically fly up those stairs, the first twenty anyway. Scaling the second set of twenty is a bit rougher. By the sixtieth step, I'm huffing and puffing and dragging my feet. That's when I see Alex again, beside me, not winded at all, still laughing at me. "I remember when I was a kid, my mom would read me the story of the tortoise and the hare. Guess which one you are."

I laugh and nearly miss a step. Alex grabs my arm to steady me. Feeling my second wind kick in, I taunt, "Whatever, Tortoise, eat my dust."

I make the next twenty steps my bitch, but have to struggle to get up the remaining stairs. Alex catches up with me again, helpfully offering, "I can carry you the rest of the way if you can't make it, Little Hare."

One-hundred and four, one-hundred and five, one-hundred and six—I reach the summit, breathless and wheezing. Alex, ever the gentleman, waits to reach the last step with me, allowing us to tie. Then while I'm doubled over to catch my breath, he picks me up and carries me to a spot of shade under the arbor.

I squeal as he settles onto a wide rock bench with me on his lap. I'm not accustomed to this level of affection. I can't seem to stop giggling or squirming. Alex cinches me against him, his arms a strong band around my waist, and holds on until I finally relax.

It's a bright June day, and everything glitters with heat, like a mirage in the desert. From our spot at the top of the mount, we have a breathtaking view of the city skyline to the east, the sparkling lake waters to the south, and the backyards of multimillion dollar mansions directly below us.

The voyeur in me likes to stare down at the rich folks in their pools and on their chaise lounges; the writer and budding photographer in me finds inspiration in the panoramic vista. It looks hot down there, but up here in our shady spot, there's a constant breeze which keeps us cool and whips my hair like a flag around our faces.

After a few moments, Alex quietly asks, "Tell me, Little Hare, why'd you bring me to this of all places?"

I lean back against his chest, getting more comfortable in his arms. "Last night when you were talking about surfing with your dad, I realized how alike we are in that way."

Alex raises a brow, interested.

"You clearly love the ocean. You miss it, don't you?"

Alex shrugs.

"Whatever. You're wicked obvious with that tattoo and the fish tank—"

"It's an *aquarium*."

I giggle. "Anyway, I figure we're the same in that way. Only for me, it's the mountains. Where you have Barton Springs and the lake for your local water, I have this place for my local mountain."

I turn to catch a glimpse of Alex's face. He's frowning.

I frown too, and, suddenly embarrassed, try to backpedal, "It's dumb, I know. I just—"

"No, it's not dumb at all. It's..." He clears his throat. "You brought me to your mountain." His expression softens and he squeezes me even tighter against him. "Thank you."

"Well, actually, there's a mountain in Tennessee that is *my* mountain, but this is as close as I can get in Austin."

Alex's whole expression seems to light up. "Tennessee, huh?"

"Born and raised."

"That explains the accent."

"I *do not* have an accent." I whine and pout defensively. Very mature.

He laughs. "You hide it pretty well when you're sober, but it comes out when you drink. The other night, when you asked me why I went down on you, you stretched 'down' into about three syllables." He impersonates awkwardly, "Duh-ow-n."

I scoff.

"Ah. I mean no offense, Little Hare. It's adorable."

I don't know what to say, so I just grin.

"What brought you to Texas?"

"Greg got a great job offer and Jake wanted to move here for music, so here we came."

"Greg..."

"My husband."

He nods. "And Jake..."

"My best friend."

He nods again. "So they brought you here, but you didn't want to come?"

"I love it here."

"That's not what I asked."

"I didn't hate the idea, but it was a big change." I haven't thought about those days in a long time. "It was hard to leave my family behind."

"So you'd come here to your new mountain when you were feeling homesick?"

"No. I only started coming here a few months ago. This oasis is new to me," I add. "Back when I first moved to town, I would write or go for walks, but never walked this far. It takes me two bus rides and a mile and a half walk to get here from my house, so it's really more of a special-occasion oasis."

Alex frowns, confused. "Why don't you drive?"

"No car." I backpedal, "Well, I mean...we have a car. Greg has a car. It's just...me...I don't drive anymore."

"Why not?"

I shrug. "I don't know. Just got out of the habit, I guess. When we moved here, I was working from home, I still do, and it's not like I went out to socialize a lot. There wasn't anywhere I wanted to be that Greg or Jake couldn't take me. And car insurance is expensive. So, I don't know, I just stopped driving."

"You haven't driven yourself anywhere in seven years?"

I shake my head, then do the math. "Almost eight years."

Alex raises his chin and his eyes narrow in a pitying look as he tries to tame bits of my wild hair, recapturing the tangled locks from the wind to tuck behind my ear. When he speaks, it's not much more than a whisper, but I hear it loud and clear. "No wonder you feel suffocated."

I frown at Alex's revelation and my cheeks turn red with embarrassment. I feel too exposed, too vulnerable; I've revealed too much of myself.

Alex sees the change in my demeanor and works to ease my discomfort. Like tit for tat, he gives me a piece of himself in exchange for what I've just given him. "When my dad died, I started fighting. I was angry all the time, so I'd pick a fight with anyone over anything. I feel like a total shit when I think about it now; Mom having to deal with her delinquent son, so soon after losing my dad.

"We moved here because my Aunt Jackie was a therapist. Mom thought she could knock some sense into me. She was right. Aunt Jackie's therapy for me was Barton Springs Pool. Every morning, weather-permitting, she'd take me to the pool at the crack of dawn and make me swim laps until I didn't have the energy left to fight. Between that and Pete keeping me out of trouble, I straightened up pretty quick."

Again, I'm speechless; constantly surprised by his openness, with how much of himself he's willing to give to me. I turn to look at him, and see he's staring out at the view, wearing a distant expression, lost in his thoughts. I want to thank him, so I kiss him. Just like our first kiss, it takes him by surprise. He startles, then just like our second kiss, he kisses me back and it takes my breath away.

When we come apart, I turn back around to look at the view and Alex rests his chin on my shoulder. Together, we stare out at our city, the city we each landed in by happenstance but love all the same.

The companionable silence we share is nice, comforting. I lose track of time, hardly taking notice as the sun treks through the sky. We sit there through lunch and most of the afternoon, barely speaking, hardly moving. Only when my stomach starts to rumble do we make our way back down the hill.

Alex offers to take me to dinner. I consider it. I want to join him for one more meal, one more shared moment before our little bubble bursts. But...

"I can't."

Alex nods. "I need to go see my mom anyway."

"Bet she can't wait to wish you a happy birthday."

Alex raises his sexy brow. "What she can't wait to do is talk about you."

"Me?"

"Oh yeah, you can be sure that Pete has made you the talk of the *cul-de-sac* by now."

"Oh no."

Alex chuckles.

"What will you tell her about me?"

"The truth."

"What's the truth?"

Alex grins. "You can't handle the truth."

I laugh at his poor impersonation of Jack Nicholson, knowing full well that it's a distraction technique. And he's likely right, I *can't* handle the truth right now, so I let it go.

"You're still licensed to drive, right?"

The question takes me by surprise. I nod hesitantly.

"Great, then you can drive." Alex tosses me his truck keys.

I don't catch them. I stand there, stunned, as the keys fly right past me and land in the gravel by the side of the road. "What?"

"I only vaguely remember where you live, so instead of navigating, why don't you just drive?"

I see what he's doing. He's trying to get me to crawl out of my hermit shell a little bit. It's annoying. I huff, but pick up the keys and open our way into the truck. My fingers tremble as I try to fit the key into the ignition. Alex clasps his steady hand over mine.

"Ariana, you don't have to do this. But I'd really like it if you'd try."

Try? What if I try and fail and wreck your pretty truck? I take a deep, calming breath and get the key in the hole. The truck roars to life beneath us, and the sensation of all that power at my fingertips, sends a frisson of excitement and panic through me. I blink a few times to clear my vision, then carefully back out of the spot and put it into drive.

"See? You've got this. Now, just drive like you're the tortoise, not the hare."

When I arrive on my street, I park a few houses away. My hands are shaking. I'm buzzing all over with energy. I'm like a livewire, sparking. But, my God, I just drove! It's such a simple thing for most people, but for me it's monumental, herculean. I'm embarrassed by what a big deal it is.

"Thank you," I say to the steering wheel, though the words are meant for Alex. I glance over and find him smiling at me, like he's proud. But he doesn't say anything, and I'm thankful for that too.

I slip out of my seatbelt and shift across the front seat to kiss him, and kiss him again, and just keep kissing him. I don't want to say goodbye. I'm not ready for this to be over.

When I pull away, my breath ragged and my cheeks beard-burned, Alex presses his forehead to mine and whispers, "Can I see you tomorrow night?"

I don't hesitate to answer. "Yes."

Alex kisses me again, then says "Eight o'clock, meet me where it all began."

Where it all began, such beautiful words. It's the sort of thing you say about the start of an epic adventure or a fairytale romance. A story which ends in *happily ever after*, should start with *where it all began*.

Tomorrow night, we will go back to where it all began.

18–Sunday June 12, 2005 6:38PM

Greg steps into the front hall from the kitchen, looking weary. "You're home."

I nod.

"My calls went to voicemail."

"Oh shit." I dig my phone out of my purse. "My battery died. I'm sorry. Is everything okay?"

"Yeah. I just... I was hoping we could talk." Greg's voice is uneven and hollow. Talk? About what? That awkward sentence jangles my nerves. Greg swallows hard, and the bob of his Adam's apple serves as a measure of his discomfort.

What the hell is going on here? Something is clearly not right, but I can't put my finger on what the problem is. I've stayed out multiple nights before, so that's not what has him rankled. I wonder if it's Alex, if he can tell that I'm planning to see him again. That's new. Since Tom and the three-week-girlfriend debacle, I've kept my forays to the one-night-stand or one-weekend-stand variety. With Alex, things are different, we've made plans. Can Greg tell? Like an alpha dog, can he smell his rival on me?

His rival? I frown at my own wayward thoughts. They are not rivals. This is not a competition, so why is my mind going to that place? Maybe it's the jagged edges of this transition from Alex to Greg, from a day of blissful, shared peace to this strange exchange.

Whatever it is, it's mucking with my head, so I do what's always come so naturally for me: I detach. I compartmentalize. I draw a line in my conscious mind and shove all thoughts of Alex to the other side of it. That part of this day is over. That part of my life is outside, on the other side of the door.

"I'm making spaghetti." Greg announces, bringing my focus back to him. "Are you hungry?"

My stomach growls in response, and I cross the room to hug my husband. It's awkward, our movements stilted and out of sync. We nearly tap foreheads when we both go left. I giggle. He smirks. Some of the pall between us is lifted.

In the kitchen, I sit in my usual spot at the table. Greg dishes the meal onto two plates and sets us up with wine and cutlery. When he sits down, he glances at me briefly, then starts to shovel forkfuls of pasta into his mouth like he's starved.

I become increasingly alarmed by the extended silence. Hadn't he wanted to talk? I could ask him what's the matter, but I don't. Perhaps I'm afraid I won't like the answer. There's a lot that's gone unsaid between us lately. Do I want to open this Pandora's Box? So I watch him, and try to eat, though I can't seem to swallow with the lump in my throat.

When Greg finishes his plate and still hasn't uttered a single word, I can't take the silence anymore. "Is everything okay?"

Greg's shoulders slump, silently answering with a resounding: *no, everything is not okay.* He won't look at me, keeping his gaze on his empty plate. His fists still clutch his knife and fork as if holding on to a lifeline. "There's something I need to tell you."

My throat goes dry, and I need to drink a sip of wine just to swallow my bite of food. I wait for him to speak, but he doesn't say anything. The silence between us grows heavy and suffocating. I can't bear it anymore.

"Yes?" My voice is meek, weighed heavy with worry.

His eyes glance up, then away again. "Ari, I think I might be falling in love with someone else...with Kate."

The air seeps out of my lungs. A cold chill moves through my body. From my fingers and toes, the ice hardens up my veins, heading straight to my heart.

Kate. Of course, it's Kate.

Since that date night gone afoul two months ago, we have not spoken much about Greg's girlfriend-slash-assistant. We've skillfully danced around the subject. But despite our careful minuet, the specter of her has lingered between us, like the Grim Reaper lurking in the corner, scythe in hand, saying, "Don't mind me, I can wait."

I sit frozen, waiting for him to say more. Finally, he does. "I don't know what to do." Greg brings his eyes up to meet mine, and I can see his sincerity as he pleads, "I love you, please know that. But I can't help these feelings I'm having. And I don't know what to do about it."

I consider what to say, but nothing comes to me, so I say nothing. The silence between us is suffocating. The air grows stale in my lungs. I can't sit here anymore. I'll die. I stand up, my chair screeching across the floor, and I leave.

I find myself in the bathroom, in the shower. As the warm water steams up the room and scorches my skin, my thoughts run wild. I go through every emotion at once. I wish we could rewind to the moment just before he said those words. I consider begging him to forget her. I imagine walking out of the bathroom, naked and dripping, informing him that the marriage is now closed, and fucking his brains out until I'm all he can remember. I consider the prospect of sharing him with her. I ponder escape. *How difficult would it be to sell the house and divide our assets?*

I cry, but it's an empty gesture. My tears mix with the scalding water, and my sobs are drowned out by the squealing pipes. Tears are pointless, so I stop.

In a bathrobe, my hair dripping over my shoulders, I stare into the foggy mirror, seeing only a pale, featureless blur where my face should be. My gaze bores holes through the strange reflection as I try to see inside, to extract my thoughts, but there is nothing there. I am blank.

I open the door and step out into the hall, leaving humid footprints as I tiptoe to the bedroom. Greg's already there, slumped on the end of the bed, his posture like a damp towel draped over a clothesline. I walk past him to the closet, digging out a change of clothes.

When I turn to leave, I find Greg there, held upright by the doorframe, blocking my exit. I stare at his feet, wordlessly urging him to move. He doesn't budge.

"Ari, please say something."

"I don't know what to say."

"Are you angry? Hurt? Glad?" *Glad?* "I can't read you. Please talk to me."

"Do you want to split up?" I look at him, but I can't bear the scrutiny, so I return my gaze to the floor.

"No." Greg lifts my chin. "Ari, no, that's not what I'm saying at all. I'm saying I screwed up. I let it get out of hand, and now I don't know how to fix it."

"Are you asking for my permission to love us both?"

"Ari, if you want me to stop seeing her, I will. You're my wife. I haven't forgotten that." He says *wife* as if it means something, as if those four letters grouped together carry some intrinsic, sacred value.

"And how would that make you feel about me, if I asked you to stop seeing her?"

He doesn't answer, and his response is in his silence. His brow is tight with anguish, his lips pointing down in a stiff frown. He watches me closely, as if trying to read some tell I don't know I have. Then he presses against me, kissing me hard. It catches me by surprise and I push him away.

We stand awkwardly for a moment before I suddenly pounce, my mouth on his. He stumbles backwards, but quickly recovers, lifting me off my feet to carry me to the bed.

It's heartbreakingly tender, the way he frames my face with his hands and whispers, "I love you. Please know that I love you."

I know he does. Or, at least, he thinks he does. He's not one to lie, and I've always loved that about him. But his words ring hollow in my ears.

Greg tugs my robe open and fumbles with his own pants, then presses deep inside me. I cry out at the invasion. It feels foreign. He feels unfamiliar. I stare at his face and barely recognize him. As he moves inside me, he repeats his affirmations of love, seemingly afraid that I'll stop believing he loves me the very instant he stops saying it.

I can't feel my body, not the way I normally do during sex. We move through the usual motions from rote, not passion, and my heart breaks at the thought that we've lost this connection between us. The sex had always been so good. *Fuck, don't fail me now.*

"...I love you. I love you, Ari—"

"Shut up!" I surprise us both with my outburst. But, *Christ*, I don't want to hear any more words right now.

Greg freezes inside me, his mouth hanging open in shock.

"Don't stop." I wiggle my hips, imploring him to continue. "Fuck me," I beg, but he doesn't comply.

His stilled weight crushes down on me, and when he inhales, my lungs collapse. Only one of us can breathe here. I panic and cry out, clawing at him to get off of me. He scrambles away, pulling his body to the far side of the bed, watching me with terror, like I'm a wild animal freed from my cage.

"I'm sorry, I just..." I don't know what to say. Words fail me again. I rub my palms over my face and move off the bed, to disappear into the closet again, dressing. When I return to the bedroom, Greg is sitting on the end of the bed, his pants zipped back up, his hands working through his hair as if he can wring a solution to this problem from the strands. I stare at him, observing his discomfort with a detached gaze. My voice is flat, my words emotionless and matter of fact. "I need some air. I'm going for a walk."

• • •

My phone is dead, so I left it at the house. Left my wallet, too. I walk alone through the empty streets with nothing on me but my keys. I drift east because the traffic lights keep turning green in that direction. I don't want to stop for red. Not paying attention to where I go, my feet seem to have a mind of their own, bringing me to Jake's apartment.

Relieved, I climb the stairs and use my key to let myself in. *I probably should have knocked first,* I realize when I hear Jake having sex in his bedroom. Or rather, I hear the sex sounds stop abruptly, followed by, "What the fuck? Stay here, uh, Stephanie."

"My name is Jennifer." *Stephanie* corrects him, and I smirk.

"Whatever. Just wait here. Someone's in the apartment."

"It's just me, Jake," I holler, as I cross to the couch, and sit.

I can hear the rustling of clothes and bare feet slapping the tile floor, then Jake appears at the mouth of the hallway with a Louisville Slugger in hand, ready to bunt his intruder.

"You have got to be kidding me," he grumbles, and combs a hand through the tangles of his long dark hair. His half-zipped jeans hang open, exposing a lot of skin, coated with a sheen of sex sweat.

I look away quickly. "I'm sorry. I didn't mean to interrupt anything."

"What the fuck, Ari? This is a flagrant violation of the friends-with-keys policy."

"I know. I'm really sorry. I just needed to talk."

"Sort of in the middle of something." Jake gestures with a thumb over his shoulder just as Jennifer emerges beside him, fully dressed except for the pair of heels she carries in her hand.

Jennifer glances between us. "I'm, uh, gonna go."

Jake just nods, and the two of us stare at each other until she leaves. With a curse, Jake dumps the bat at his feet and leans against the wall. I try not to stare at his bare chest and open fly, and finally huff with frustration. "Jake, please put on a shirt. I can't talk to you like that."

Jake looks down at himself, gives a curt nod, and disappears into the darkened hallway. He soon returns with his jeans fastened and wearing his Master of Puppets t-shirt, his hair combed and pulled back at his neck. He walks past me to the kitchen, hollering over his shoulder, "You want a beer?"

"Yes, please."

Jake returns with two long necks. He pops the caps off using the edge of the coffee table, and hands one to me. "I heard a rumor about you the other day."

I quirk an eyebrow.

"Chris Nix, the singer from Donkey Death Punch, was talking like he got in your pants."

Seriously? "I can't believe that asshole would brag about that."

"Wait." Jake frowns. "Jesus, it's true?"

"Barely. He was awful, I mean really, really awful, and his mom walked in on us. It was absurd. I left before either of us finished."

"Christ, Ari..." Jake looks like he's going to vomit.

"What?"

"What the fuck were you thinking? Chris *fucking* Nix? Really? He's trash, and you know, the fucker didn't even remember your name? He kept calling you Angie as he bragged that he'd boned you. I thought he was full of shit. I fucking defended you. Guess I gave you too much credit." Under his breath, he grumbles, "Fuck's sake, woman, have some dignity."

My heart sinks. My blood runs cold, and all I feel, from the top of my head to the tips of my toes is shame...and rage.

"Oh fuck you, you fucking hypocrite!" I spring to my feet and pace the room, stomping and scowling at him as I let loose. "Fucking Christ, Jake, not even ten minutes ago, you called Jennifer by the wrong name, and now you have the fucking gall to lecture me on *dignity*? Fuck's sake, *man*, how about *you* have some goddamn dignity. I mean, shit, Jake, you can call me a slut all you want, but look in the fucking mirror while you do it, because this double standard shit is total fucking crap. I'm a consenting adult who can and will fuck who I want to fuck when I want to fuck them, and that doesn't compromise my motherfucking, goddamn dignity. This is me, Jake—slutty, easy, shameless, fuck-happy me. Take it or fucking leave it, you fucking prick."

Wow. Where did that come from? Granted, I've got a lot pent up right now, but *damn*. Still, it feels cathartic to get it off my chest, like a pressure valve letting out steam. I fall onto the couch with a harrumph and cross my arms over my chest, waiting for Jake's inevitable argument. When it comes in the form of a laugh, I glance over to find him smiling at me.

"Damn, Two Shoes." Jake takes a slug of his beer. "Sweet rant."

"What? No rebuttal?"

"Nah. You're right. I was out of line and I'm sorry."

Jake doesn't do apologies. This is notable. I stare at him, stupefied, like he's speaking Greek.

"But for the record, I never called you a slut."

"You didn't have to—"

"I never said it because I never thought it." His expression is dead serious. "I don't think that about any woman."

I blink, a bit stunned.

"Look, I just worry about you." He huffs out a heavy sigh. "You tend to see the best in people, even when they don't deserve it." Jake slants me a side eye. "And for the record, Chris Nix doesn't deserve it. He's a piece of shit. The guy is criminally sexist, casually racist, and he drives drunk all the time."

"Ew, really?"

Jake nods. "You're so much better than him, Ari. I just want you to be careful who you trust."

I smirk, "Yeah, well, lesson learned." I give Jake a big grin, "And you'll be happy to know that I punched him in the face."

Jake nearly spits out his beer with a laugh. "Really?"

I nod.

"That's my girl," Jake smiles wide and reaches for me, looping his arm over my shoulder and hugging me against him. I freeze, Rebecca's words echoing through my head, *He's in love with you. It's so obvious.*

Well, while we're getting everything out on the table, might as well cover this ground, too. "Jake, are you in love with me?"

Jake nearly chokes on his beer again, coughing as he asks, "What?"

"On Friday, when I ran into Rebecca—"

He groans. "Oh Jesus."

"She said I'm the reason you broke up with her, because you're in love with me."

Jake rolls his eyes and huffs. "Such bullshit. Okay, first of all, I broke up with Rebecca because she made me miserable when she was sober, and she was always slapping me when she'd get drunk." With a squeeze of his arm around my shoulders, he adds, "And as for you and me, of course I love you, but not like she's talking about. You're my best friend, which makes you my number one girl, but I'm not *in* love with you."

I exhale with relief and snuggle a little closer to Jake.

He keeps talking, "I mean, sure, when we first met I had a thing for you, but that was years ago."

"You did?"

Jake laughs. "Why the hell do you think I invited you to all my shows, dumbass?"

My eyes go wide, remembering. I'd been working with Jake at the bookstore in the mall for three weeks when he first started inviting me to his shows. I'd just thought it was a bit of shameless self-promotion, nothing more. Then one day, I accepted the invitation. I liked the music, sure, but I felt completely out of place, wondering what I was doing there. It wasn't until I spotted the rhythm guitar player next to Jake—his warm whiskey eyes watching me—that I relaxed and really enjoyed the concert.

After the show, Jake introduced me to Greg, and I was instantly smitten. I almost laugh now when I think of Greg's words to me at the end of that night, *Are you interested in Jake?* I'd frowned, confused, and shook my head no, and that's when Greg kissed me for the first time.

My God, how could I have been so blind? "Jake, I had no idea."

"Stop it. Don't look at me like I'm some heartbroken hanger-on you friend-zoned. It was never like that. It was obvious from the beginning that there was something special between you and Greg, so I backed off. I found where I fit in this whole thing, and it works. You guys are my family. You're my best friends. I can't imagine my life without either of you." I grin at him, and he squeezes my shoulders, but then slants me a look when he says, "Though in a weird way, you are the reason I broke up with Rebecca."

Huh?

"When Greg told me about the decision you two made, it got me thinking about my own life. I didn't like what I saw, so I made some changes. Rebecca was one of those changes."

And that would be the second time this weekend I've been told I'd inspired a breakup. I'm a regular wrecking ball, wreaking havoc on the relationships of Austin...including, possibly, my own marriage.

The tears hit me like a tidal wave. One minute, nothing; the next minute, a flood. I let out a sob and Jake frowns, terror in his eyes. He presses his hands gently to my shoulders, like he's accidently broken an irreplaceable vase and he's trying to piece it back together. With horror in his voice, he asks, "Ari, why are you crying?"

"Greg's in love with Kate," I blurt out on a miserable sob. "He told me tonight. And I don't know what to do. I don't even know what to say to him. I came here to—"

"Wait." Jake stiffens and frowns at me. "You left Greg to come here?"

I sniff.

"Ari."

I sniff again and wipe the tears away.

"The whole time you've been here, Greg's been sitting at home alone, fretting?"

I slowly nod. Jake's frown sinks deeper.

"Ari, you need to go home, now. You need to talk to *him* about this, not *me*."

"But—"

"Now."

"But—"

"Look, I get it. I do. That's a hell of a pile of shit he laid on you. You freaked and you ran like you always do."

"I do not—"

Jake laughs a little. "Two Shoes, you avoid conflict like it's the fucking plague. But you can't run from this. This is between you and Greg and it's important and you need to go home and face the music."

I blink, a bit stunned and stung. *I run from conflict?*

Jake stands up from the couch and grabs his keys off the table. He disappears into the kitchen and returns with a paper towel that he hands to me to use as a tissue.

He's still frowning at me, disappointed. And he's right to be. Running away is exactly what I did. It's what I always do. When the going gets tough, I get going in the opposite direction. I'm a fleer, not a fighter, and as soon as things don't go my way, I'm out the door.

"Come on, Two Shoes, I'll drive you home."

• • •

Home.

The word doesn't sound right in my head, and the concept somehow feels off, like in a dream where you know you're in your house, but it doesn't look like your house at all. There is carpet where your wood floors should be, the stark gray walls are now adorned with paisley-patterned wallpaper, or suddenly, your bedroom is a submarine being crushed beneath the weight of the ocean. A Talking Heads' moment: *this is not my beautiful house.*

I hear the strum of a guitar in the bedroom and make my way down the hall, leaning against the doorjamb to watch him play. In just boxers, Greg leans against the headboard, his eyes closed as his fingers work the frets. When he hears me come in, he stops and looks up, relief washing over his expression.

"You came back."

Of course I came back. Did he think I wouldn't?

I nod then gesture at the guitar. "Working on something new?"

Greg looks down at his instrument and shakes his head. "Remembering something old, actually."

He starts to play a tune that I immediately recognize—the song he wrote for me. It was so many years ago, but that melody is forever etched in my memory.

I smile at the same time that tears well up, threatening to spill. I move to the bed and settle beside him, listening as he plays the whole song.

When he's finished, I ask, "What's going to happen to us?"

Greg thinks for a moment, but admits, "I don't know."

More silence, so awkward and stifling it makes my skin itch and my lungs burn. I want to stand up and move, pace, walk...out the door. But I stay. As if I'm tied to the bed, I stay. Jake was right, I can't run from this.

"I never thought this would happen. It was the last thing I would have expected." Greg sounds sheepish, apologetic.

My God, we'd been so naïve. Such arrogance and ignorance to think that we could rein in our experience. That we could sit down and have a logical conversation with our hearts, explaining that this little adventure of ours doesn't involve them.

"Do you regret it?" he asks. "Now that this has happened, do you wish we hadn't changed things?"

It's a strange question, and I give it a good amount of thought, and when I answer I can honestly say, "No. I don't regret it."

Greg just nods. I don't know what answer he was looking for, but that's the truth.

I think about my life before. I had been content and comfortable, but stifled. And looking back, it's clear to me now, it hadn't been Greg holding me back, it had been me. I'd been suffocating under the limitations I'd placed on myself. Then I stepped out of that comfort zone. No, more than stepped out, I *nuked* my comfort zone. And I'm glad I did, but is my marriage part of the fallout? Have I sacrificed Greg to save myself?

"Listen, Greg." I turn my body to face him, wanting to be sure he understands me. "I want you to know that it's okay."

He furrows his brow, confused.

"It's okay that you're with her. And it's okay that you love her. I am glad you told me. I know that was hard to do. And I'm sorry I didn't say any of this before. I guess I needed some time to think. But it is...okay. Okay?"

Greg sets aside his guitar and moves his body to face me too. He takes a deep breath and touches my face, brushing a strand of hair behind my ear. "I still love you, Ari. You know that, right?"

I nod, but I don't know that; not really, not anymore. This is all new. Our journey together has brought us to a strange land with unfamiliar terrain and a foreign language: polyamory. Okay, sure, we've been fucking other people all this time, and that's polyamory, too, but this is different.

Going from sex to love is a great emotional leap across a chasm of molten lava, and somehow, apparently, we've jumped it. But now we find ourselves dangling at the precipice, holding on by our fingertips.

I look at Greg for guidance, for instructions on what to do next. But he's as much a tourist here as I am. Still, I ask, "So, what now?"

Greg furrows his brow and shakes his head and says, "I don't know. I guess we'll figure it out."

We'll figure it out. Alex's exact words to me. For the first time since walking through the front door, I allow myself to think about him. I think about my complicated feelings for him, adding yet another layer to this mess. I turn to Greg and ask, "When did you realize that it was love with Kate, that it was more than just a fling? How did you know?"

I watch his expression change. He doesn't want to talk about her with me; it's written all over his face. I'm not sure if that's his hang-up or if he thinks it's mine. I consider rescinding my question, but I want to know the answer. He doesn't speak for a long time, and I start to suspect he never will.

Finally, he clears his throat and says, "I don't know how to put it into words." A cop out. I almost sigh, but he continues, "I remember when I knew with you, though. I watched you laugh at something Jake had said and it was so beautiful. It was this"—he runs his thumb up my throat in a touch so gentle it almost tickles—"the curve of your neck. You threw your head back and laughed up at the ceiling and I couldn't take my eyes off of your neck. I was in awe. That's when I knew."

I let out a shaky breath, stunned.

"After that, I was constantly trying to make you laugh, just so I could see it again. Jake called it my 'awkward phase.'"

I chuckle. "I remember. God...that awful joke...what was it?" I attempt to impersonate Greg's voice as I recite it, "The past, the present, and the future walk into a bar..."

In unison, we both say, "It was tense."

I laugh, not even realizing that I've thrown my head back. Greg's thumb strokes my throat again and when I look back at him, his eyes glisten with unshed tears. He leans in and kisses me softly. "I still love you, Ari Beth. That hasn't changed."

19—Monday June 13, 2005

"You alone?" Alex hugs my waist and kisses my neck as he repeats the first words he ever spoke to me.

"Oh holy hell, is this the big surprise?" Manic crosses his arms over his chest and slouches against the wall as if to demonstrate disappointment, but the smile on his face gives him away. "Well, this guy is definitely an improvement over that prick parade you were making time with." Manic pours three shots, then lifts one of the glasses to toast Alex. "Happy belated birthday, fuckwit."

"Best birthday I've had in a long time." Alex beams.

We all drink, and Manic moves on to other customers.

"Prick parade?" I grumble.

"His words, not mine." Alex laces our fingers and rests our linked hands on his knee. "So, how was your day?"

Complicated.

"How so?"

Did I say that out loud? "It's stuff you don't want to hear about."

"What makes you think that?"

I hedge. "It's...marriage stuff."

Alex settles into his seat, like a therapist preparing to listen, "So let's talk about it."

"Alex," I sigh. "When I'm with you, the last thing I want to do is talk about my marital problems." Oh shit, did I just admit to marital problems?

Alex's eyes go wide.

Yep, I did. I panic, and rush to fill the silence that falls between us. "Please, can we talk about anything else? My favorite flower is the Stargazer Lily. My favorite holiday is Halloween. I hate peas..."

"Ariana, part of being in an open relationship is being *open*. Keeping everyone in your life in separate silos isn't a healthy long-term approach, and it's a lot of stress for you to carry alone." Alex says this with a strange sense of authority. Authority that I immediately feel the need to challenge.

"You're an expert on the subject?"

"I'm not an expert, but I've been in an open relationship before."

"You have?"

He nods. "Plus, I've been reading up on it."

I blink at him. "Why?"

He rolls his eyes. "Because I care about the things that affect you."

"Why?"

"Really? You have to ask?" Alex chuckles, then clasps my cheeks between his palms. "Because I'm crazy about you. We've covered this."

"You hardly know me."

"We've covered that too." Alex groans, then he comes at me, pressing his forehead against mine, staring long and hard into my eyes. "I understand that you're scared. I get it. You want to tell yourself that I'm just a stranger because you don't want to admit that you feel *this*"—he presses our joined hands to my chest, right above the rapid beat of my heart—"just as much as I do."

My eyelids flutter like I'm some Victorian damsel on the verge of fainting. God, he's so intense. I gulp, and when I can breathe again, I exhale a soft moan.

That little sound is enough to set him off. He pulls me into a long, deep kiss. I forget for a moment that we're in a bar. His kiss transports me to somewhere else entirely; up in the stars, on a planet built for two, with an atmosphere that smells like mountain rain, where everything tastes like tequila and spearmint, and the celestial body is ringed by a gorgeous pair of biceps—

"Hot! Can I get in on that action?" Sheryl interrupts.

I break away from Alex to find her grinning at me, her hands on her hips. She has blue hair this week, which perfectly complements her royal blue corset and pencil skirt. Her boobs are like blown bubbles, fixing to pop out of the tiny top.

"Sheryl! You look like a piece of candy," I squeal as I hug her.

"And I taste like one too." Sheryl hops up and down with me wrapped in her tight embrace, only to stop abruptly as she glances over my shoulder. "Alex?"

Sheryl knows Alex? I turn to see that he's watching us, his eyes as wide as saucers.

"Hey Sher," he offers gingerly.

"Wait." Sheryl looks back at me. "Oh holy shit! *You're* his Ariana?"

What?

"I can't believe I didn't put it together. I mean, I know you as Ari, not Ariana. It didn't even occur to me. And anyways it's not like you guys have been dating each other this whole time, right? I mean, well, Ari you've been with—"

"The prick parade," Manic offers unhelpfully.

"Yeah. Exactly." Sheryl nods.

"Sheryl, what the fuck?" I frown.

"It's just...I'm just...dude."

"Start making sense right now," I demand.

"Ariana..." Alex's voice is calm, but he's squeezing my hand so hard I'm starting to lose sensation in my fingers. "Sher is friends with my ex-girlfriend."

"Friends is a stretch. We're teammates."

I blink at Sheryl and gape at Alex. "Your ex is a roller girl?"

"She skates as Arson Nic," Sheryl offers.

"Wow." Is all I can seem to muster.

Sheryl turns to Alex, "She told me you left her for someone named Ariana, but I didn't meet Ari until later and never put two and two together."

"Wow." I say again, my brain scratching like a broken record.

"Come here." Sheryl grabs my hand and tugs until I follow her into the cubicle-sized bathroom at the back of the bar. Once the door's shut, she squeezes me in one of her suffocating hugs, squealing, "This is so awesome."

"What?"

"Honey, Alex is tops."

"You're not upset?"

"Why would I be upset?"

"Because he dumped your friend or teammate or whatever."

"Oh honey, no. Nic is, well, she's a handful. She can be kind of a bitch, actually, and I say that with love, or something akin to love, a love-like substance... But I digress and that's not the point. The point is: Alex is perfect for you."

"What?"

"He's all thoughtful and sweet, just like you," She bats her eyelashes at me like she's flirting. Then her whole face changes, as she stage whispers, "Though I didn't think you would be so into the kinky stuff."

"*What?*" I squawk.

"Oh shit." Sheryl covers her mouth.

"What kinky stuff?"

"Listen, Alex is a total keeper. Don't let me get your head all screwed up."

"Sher, what are you talking about? What kinky stuff?"

"Have you two not..." My answer must be apparent from the expression on my face. "Oh wow."

"Talk. Now."

Sheryl crosses her arms over her chest, and I do the same. We both stare at each other, waiting for the other to crack first. I always win this game.

After a few moments, Sheryl sighs dramatically, then loses with grace when she finally says, "Okay, fine. I'll just say this: I've heard a few things, nothing specific, just that sex with Alex is really good, and, uh, not vanilla."

My eyes go wide. There are rumors? Alex's prowess in the bedroom is a topic of discussion? And exactly how kinky are we talking? I'd imagine that in order to be the subject of roller-girl rumors, he'd have to be either really, *really* great in bed, or really, *really* kinky...or both.

Sheryl eyes me like she's afraid she's turned me off of him.

Au contraire, ma Sherrie, my curiosity is piqued.

I exit the bathroom, Sheryl tight on my heels. Alex watches me like a deer in headlights. I flop into my chair with an exhausted sigh and crack a smile. "This town is too fucking small."

Alex grins, Sheryl exhales the breath she's been holding, and Manic pours a round of shots for four. We all down the drinks in silence, and the awkwardness lessens as the tequila soaks in.

"Sher, honey, why are you dressed like Willy Wonka's Wet Dream?" I ask.

"I'm meeting Stephen at karaoke." Sheryl's eyes light up. "Oh my God, you guys should totally join us!"

"Okay." Alex accepts the invitation and hops to his feet, ready to leave.

With a shrug, I agree. We say our farewells to Manic then head up the block. Sheryl skips ahead, while Alex and I couple hands and bring up the rear.

"What'd you guys talk about in the bathroom?" Alex aims for an air of nonchalance, misses.

"Wouldn't you like to know?"

As we approach the club, he pulls me against him. "Yeah, I would."

"Well, apparently, Sheryl thinks we're perfect for each other."

Alex lets loose a dazzling smile.

"Also, she mentioned something about you not liking the taste of vanilla."

Alex's mouth falls open, and his eyes go wide.

"Is that the real reason you won't have sex with me? Afraid you'll scare me off if you let your freak flag fly?" I don't wait for an answer. I just grin and turn away, following Sheryl inside. Alex stumbles after us, a bit dumbfounded.

The bar looks much the same as the last time I came to karaoke. The red-unitard wearing Queen singer is now wearing a leopard print unitard, and still singing Queen. A few other familiar faces stud the room too.

Sheryl bounds down the ramp toward Stephen, who's secured his usual table at the center of the room. Stephen hugs me and shakes Alex's hand, apparently they know each other. When Alex turns and nods at Tom behind the bar, I gawp.

"You know Tom?"

Alex nods. "Pete and I went to high school with him and Stephen."

This town is absurdly fucking small. How it took Alex and me six months to reunite boggles the mind.

Alex steals a quick kiss. "What are you going to sing?"

"The perfect song." I wink and pull him to the DJ booth. We thumb through the selection books, each finding a song, writing the details down, and handing them to the DJ.

We watch a few more singers; some great, some okay, one tone-deaf guy who nearly swallows the mic as he bellows out a Metallica tune. Tom sings a heartbreaking rendition of Chris Isaak's "Wicked Game." Up next, is Alex, and *that's* not a weird juxtaposition at all.

Alex calmly ascends the stage and stands in a cat-like crouch, ready to pounce, staring straight at me as he drums his heel on the floor to the opening beat. It's a song I immediately recognize as a favorite from my teens. When he belts out the first lines of The Cult's "Fire Woman," my insides ignite.

Good God, the man is hot, and I am in his thrall, if that's a thing. I hold my breath and cross my legs and watch his every move, every ripple of muscle, the way his eyes focus on me, the way his fingers caress up and down the microphone stand, touching it in all the ways I know he wants to touch me.

Yep. I am in his motherfucking thrall.

When he's finished, the room erupts, and I can hardly move. My thighs are jelly, and my jaw hangs slack. I glance at Sheryl, who watches me with a knowing grin plastered on her face.

After a few more numbers, Sher and Stephen are a hit with their duet of X's "Los Angeles," Sher is especially popular as she jumps up and down, defying the laws of physics when she miraculously manages to keep her boobs in that corset. Tough act to follow.

The DJ calls my name. Really?

I bite my lip as I nervously approach the stage. I gather the mic in my hand and wait for the song to start. When it does, I watch Alex's eyes grow large with surprise and his lips curl into a wicked grin. I guess my choice of Journey's "Any Way You Want It" was not as subtle as I'd intended it to be. But, hell, I picked this song to flirt, so by-gosh, that's what I'm going to do. I lock eyes with Alex and sing to him, letting the sex drip from every verse.

His gaze narrows on me, the eyes of a predator stalking his prey. I go breathless and nearly falter over the lyrics. I look away and lock eyes with Sheryl, who clearly also gets the inside joke. Her furtive glances between Alex and me almost crack me up.

It's a miracle that I finish the song without a mistake, and the crowd gives me a warm applause as I leave the stage. But it's Alex's reaction I'm most anxious to see. He pins me with his wolfish gaze and gives me a sexy smirk as I approach from the stage. Before I have time to sit, he's on his feet and whispering into my ear, "Let's get out of here."

I quickly nod and grab my purse. Sheryl grins and gives me a dainty wave goodbye as Alex pulls me toward the door.

Outside and around the corner, in the relative privacy of a dark side street, Alex pivots and presses his body against mine. With two strides he walks me backward until I hit the wall with a gasp.

"Yes," he breathes into my ear. "Part of my reluctance is a fear of letting you see that side of me."

He leans back to look in my eyes, and I can see the trepidation on his face. I want to ease his concerns. I lean up and balance on my toes to kiss him. The kiss is timid at first, but quickly grows in intensity, his desire overwhelming his fear at least for a moment.

When we pull away to catch our breath, I whisper, "Show me."

"Do you even know what we're talking about here? How specific was Sher? And for the record, I don't have a clue what she'd know about me. I've never so much as kissed her."

"She just said you were kinky."

"And what do you think that means?"

"I have no idea." I scowl. "I'm hoping you'll show me."

He exhales an exasperated breath, "What's the kinkiest thing you've ever done?"

I grumble, but it's clear that Alex has no intention of showing me anything until he knows what he's dealing with. "I don't know...anal? And I had a threesome with two guys at the same time..."

His eyes go wide as saucers. "Double penetration?"

"No. The anal was a different night. The threesome was just oral and, you know, vaginal."

He coughs out a laugh.

"What?" I frown. "What's so funny?"

He laughs again. "It's not funny. It's just...listening to you say 'vaginal' is incredibly hot and kind of cute at the same time."

"Well?" I raise an eyebrow at him. "Did I pass your little kink test?"

"With flying colors."

"Now will you show me?"

Alex shakes his head. "Not tonight, Little Hare."

"Why not?" I pout like a petulant child.

Alex grins and runs his finger across my bottom lip as he quietly answers. "Because we've both been drinking." He leans in close and presses his forehead to mine until all I can see are his translucent eyes. "When I have you, you'll be sober."

The word *sober* has never sounded so sexy. My toes curl in my boots.

Alex still has me pinned against the wall with his body, his chest moving against mine with each breath he takes. I watch him closely as he watches me, then finally he speaks. "Tomorrow night. But only on one condition..."

I nod anxiously. I'll agree to anything at this point.

"You can never again say we don't know each other."

20—Tuesday June 14, 2005

We stand in the hallway of Alex's house—me waiting, Alex stalling. His hand rests on the knob to a door I'd come to consider a closet, since it had always remained closed when I was here. Guess it is a closet of sorts—behind this door, Alex hides his secrets.

He eyes me nervously, making it clear why he always keeps this door shut. I shiver with anticipation, but tilt my head and give him my best coaxing grin. "Alex, please."

Hours, I've spent getting ready for this. After Alex and I made out like teenagers in his truck and he drove me home last night, I was too amped for sleep. I completed three freelance writing jobs and started on a fourth before passing out close to sun up. When I woke, I converted the bathroom into a spa—soaking, waxing, and plucking every part of me. Then there was that hour spent hovering in my closet, looking for the perfect thing to wear.

I haven't been this nervous since that first night out, the night when I met Alex, when my kiss changed Alex. Now, standing here, I wonder how I'll be changed by what lies on the other side of this door. Before I can work myself into a panic, Alex turns the knob and swings the door open.

Inside, the bedroom is large, and the style of the textured walls and popcorn ceiling suggest this is the last room to be remodeled as he works his way through the house. Overhead, the dome light looks older than me.

Okay, clearly I'm stalling. I'm cataloging all the wrong details of the room. I blink my eyes, take a deep breath, and focus on what matters: the furniture.

On the far wall is a mahogany chest of drawers, and beside it, a peg board littered with an assortment of paddles and whips. The adjoining wall sports a large wooden x-cross with a pair of leather cuffs mounted at the top. In the center of the room is a narrow table that appears to split open about halfway up the middle, with cuffs at the head and foot. Here by the door, is an innocuous-looking leather bench, and beside it is something that resembles a bright red pommel horse.

But it's what's at the far end of the room that really catches my eye. Dangling from the ceiling, like S&M stalactites, are a pair of heavy-duty chains attached to the joists with large lag bolts. And hanging from the ends of the chains, yet more restraints.

My jaw drops as I take in all the sights. Well, what do you know; my knight in shining armor has a dungeon.

"Who gets chained and whipped? You or me?" I ask.

He shakes his head. "You don't ever have to—"

"You or me?"

"You, but—"

"I want to try it."

Alex frowns.

"I like to try new things, and I want to try this."

He stares at me, scrutinizing, reading the sincerity in my eyes. Slowly, his rigid expression relaxes. "Okay." A predatory grin creeps onto his lips. "You want to play, we'll play."

Alex closes the door behind us and leads me to the center of the room. There, he kisses me, his lips gentle and soothing; it's oddly romantic, all things considered. Then he stops, and he's all business.

"We need to establish a safe word."

"Okay."

"It's important that you have one and you use it if you need to. If at any point this gets to be too much for you, you say that word and we will stop immediately."

"Oh," My eyes fall to the pegboard of pain behind him, and a strange little hiccup of fear bubbles up like a shiver.

"Ariana, if this isn't something you want to do—"

"No," I stop him. "I want to try it. I'm just a little nervous."

"Okay," He nods as he scrutinizes my face. "What would you like for your safe word to be?"

I have absolutely no idea. I try to be clever. "How about...Godot?"

"Godot?" He tries to stifle a laugh, but fails. "No, that's not a good safe word."

"Why not?"

"Because it sounds like *God* and *oh*. You don't want a safe word that sounds like a word you might shout out during sex. It could get confusing."

"Oh. Okay, how about...stegosaurus."

Alex laughs. "Now I'm imagining you shouting that out during sex."

I raise an eyebrow.

Alex quells his laughter. "Stegosaurus has a lot of syllables; usually people just go with 'red'. It's short and synonymous with stop."

I shrug.

"Okay, how about this? If at any time you want me to stop, you say either 'stegosaurus' or 'red', and I will stop immediately."

I nod.

"You can trust me, Ariana." He takes my chin in his fingers to force eye contact, "I need to know that I can trust you too. I need you to promise that you will stop me if it gets to be too much. The words 'stop' or 'no' won't work. I won't stop unless you use a safe word, so promise me you'll use one if you need to."

I nod again.

"Stop nodding, I need you to say the words."

"I promise."

He studies my face, reading the honesty in my expression. When he's satisfied, he takes a deep breath, straightens up and steps one pace backward away from me.

"Turn around," he commands.

I'm taken aback by the change in his tone. Gone is the sweet, gentle coaxing voice, replaced by an authoritarian tone that's both startling and sexy.

I do as I'm told and turn around.

He smooths his hands up my sides and his fingers clasp the zipper of my dress, tugging it down. The dress yawns open.

"Turn to face me," he commands again.

I do.

He stares, his eyes moving up and down my body. I fidget beneath his gaze. He seems to delight in my nervousness, waiting for what feels like whole minutes before speaking again.

"Take off your dress."

I do, letting it slide off my shoulders and pool on the floor around my feet. Underneath, I'm wearing a new lingerie set, black satin with red lace. A smile flashes across his lips, but he suppresses it.

"Turn around."

I quickly oblige and rest my fidgety fingers against my thighs, trying to calm my nerves with deep breaths. For a long time, there is only silence. I imagine him standing perfectly still behind me, staring at my ass in these lacey black and red hip huggers.

Finally, I hear movement and have to stay myself from turning to see what he's doing. Drawers slide open and shut, items are moved and removed. I hear his slow steps toward me. His fingers brush my neck, and I flinch at his soft touch as he moves my hair to my back.

A cool fabric slides across my shoulder and down my front. It is satin or silk and long. I can't help but glance down at the black strip of material as he tugs both ends and raises it to my eyes. Oh. Uh. Okay. He gently ties the blindfold behind my head, then turns me to face him and tugs at the fabric, making sure there are no gaps for peeking.

Alex's fingers trail down my cheeks to my neck, over my front, to finally come to rest on my breasts. He caresses and teases, hardening my nipples through the lacy fabric. I moan, and he's suddenly against me, his mouth at my ear. He breathes one word, a command, with a long slow hiss. "Hush."

My breath comes out in a shiver, but I hush. My God, this is fucking hot. Why would I ever want to stop this with my stegosaurus safe word?

Alex's fingers glide across my stomach and around my ticklish sides. I wiggle, and he presses himself against me again, this time commanding only, "Still."

I straighten, and he continues. Moving his fingers to my bra, he springs the clasp and pushes the straps off my shoulders to fall down my arms. Next, he hooks his thumbs into the waistband of my underwear and slides them off my hips until they, too, fall to the ground.

Nervous, naked, and blind, I try not to fidget but it's impossible. Alex glides his fingers back up my ticklish sides, and I can't help but shiver. When his palms cup the undersides of my breasts, I suck in a sharp breath and almost moan at the pleasure of his delicate touch. His fingers reach my nipples, rolling them gently before he pinches them hard.

"Ouch," I yelp. He doesn't stop. Flinching under the blindfold, I squeeze my eyes shut until he releases his grip. I breathe hard and feel the pain subside, replaced by a warm tingle that soothes and comforts me more than I expect it to. Alex's fingers tenderly massage my breasts until I relax my posture. That's when he grabs both nipples again, and pulls.

"Fuck!" I hiss and cock my head back. He tugs harder, and I move my hands to stop him.

Alex snaps his grip from me and grabs both of my wrists, shoving my arms behind my back and pressing me flat against his chest. It's bare. When did he take his shirt off? He whispers in my ear, "If you want to stop me, you know how. No hands."

I nod slowly.

He releases one of my wrists and turns, guiding me to a new spot in the room. He arranges my hips to stand in a precise place, then circles around me. I feel his bare chest against my back, his mouth at my ear, his breath warm across my cheek, as he commands, "Practice your safe words. Say them for me now."

I stammer, "Stegosaurus."

"And?"

"Red."

"Yell them. Make me hear them."

I feel silly, but comply, "STEGOSAURUS."

"And?"

"RED."

"Don't forget them." His words are so calming, even as he slowly lifts my left arm over my head. "Now, stand on your toes."

I raise my heels off the ground and balance on the balls of my feet. As I do, I feel a leather cuff clasp around my wrist and the tug of his fingers as he fastens the strap high above my head. *Okay. Wow.*

When he moves away, I remain there, dangling like a cockeyed Christmas ornament. My fingers explore the edges of the thick leather cuff and the heavy gauge chain that pulls taut above. Next, he takes my right wrist and cuffs it over my head too.

I am fully suspended, rendered helpless, completely at his mercy. And this is how I remain for a long time. I'm not sure how long it is—time moves differently when you're naked, blindfolded, and suspended from the ceiling. It could be minutes or it could be hours that I wait. It feels like it's been days that he's not touching me, not moving, not making a sound.

I can't help but fidget, feeling unnervingly vulnerable and exposed in my new captive state. But I resist the urge to shout a safe word. I don't want to stop, not before we've even started. I want to see this through. I want to know this side of him, and I want to know this side of me.

As if he can hear my thoughts, he touches me, and rewards me with a sweet, soft kiss. Was he expecting me to break? I can feel the relief and joy in his lips as he recognizes in me a willingness to play this game with him. And with that, I am centered, ready, even excited about what is to come.

•   •   •

Spanking.

I've never thought a spanking could hurt so good. With each whack of his palm, he expresses every ounce of desire he has for me. And between the slaps, he gently runs his fingers over the inflamed flesh. I'm sure there are brilliant red palm prints on each ass cheek, and I warm at the thought of his marks on me.

He develops a rhythm, and before each swipe, I wince with anticipation. Then, always one step ahead, he varies the pattern, and I don't know when to expect a hard pat or when to expect a gentle pet. My initial winces and yelps turn to moans and purrs as the skin warms, and the sharpness of the slaps is replaced by a tingling thud. Each of my moans is answered by a groan from him. This is the most intensely erotic and intimate act I've shared with anyone in—

Smack!

Moan.

Groan.

. . .

Tickling.

He has something in his hand. It's cold and metallic, and sounds like a spur ringing in its cradle. He presses it to the flesh of my arm and I flinch. It pricks. With gentle ease, he rolls the spur down my arm and along the sensitive skin of my side. I yelp and try to wiggle, but the restraints are taut and there is nowhere to go. I try to turn away from him, and he stays me with one hand on my neck, while he continues the prickly tickling torture. I gasp and yelp, and finally, I giggle. He presses the metal harder against my skin until it hurts and uses his free hand to smack my ass. My giggling ceases.

. . .

Teasing.

Between the tickling torture, the spanks and the occasional tug of a nipple, Alex moves his hand down my abdomen, sliding his fingers between my legs to tease me. He massages me in slow circles, always bringing me right to the brink of orgasm before he stops, usually with a hard slap of the ass. I shiver and wiggle and beg, but he won't let me come.

"Alex, please..."

Alex slips a finger inside me as he purrs in my ear, "Please, what?"

"Fuck me," I moan and whine and wiggle. "*Please.*"

"You want me to fuck you while you're chained to my ceiling?"

I nod slowly, my head lolling like I'm stoned, panting and begging shamelessly. I'm so close to coming, just a moment more—

Alex pulls his fingers away from me and I cry out with the loss. He moves against me, pressing hard into my back so I can feel his erection evident through his jeans, rigid as steel and thrust against my ass. "You want my cock inside you?"

"Yes."

"No."

"Alex, please," I cry. "Please. I want you—"

He spanks me again. Hard. I wince and stop begging.

• • •

For what seems an eternity, though it could be mere seconds, he leaves me. With the lingering sting of that last spank, he steps away from me. I can't feel him, can't hear him, I'm not even sure he's still in the room. I feel his absence acutely. I turn, as far as my arms will stretch, straining to listen for him. I hold my breath so I can hear his, but there's only silence. I start to panic. I shiver, suddenly feeling cold, exposed...I whimper, about to cry.

In an instant, Alex slides against me, soothing me with the comfort of his presence. He hugs me tight, one arm wrapped around my waist, one hand cradling my head, his fingers caressing my cheek. His bare chest, pressed up against me, is warm and slick with a sheen of sexy sweat. I sigh with relief.

"I'm here," he whispers into my ear, his words and the comfort of his nearness warming me all over. "You've been a very good girl. You've earned a reward." He slides his hand down my neck, my chest, my abdomen until his fingers are again between my legs. I groan.

Not again. I try to wiggle away, overstimulated and sexually frustrated, not wanting to be denied anymore. He hugs me tighter, holding me in place as his fingers move over me, then inside me.

I pant and groan and wiggle as I feel my orgasm building again. I expect him to stop once more, but this time he only increases his speed as my groans turn to moans.

Alex presses his lips to the shell of my ear. He gives me a soft kiss, then commands, "Come for me, Ariana. Now."

As if waiting for permission, my body erupts. The orgasm courses through me like hot lava, scorching everything in its path. I scream until my throat goes hoarse. I shake like I'm having a seizure. I see stars where before there was just the black cloth of the blindfold. And when it's burned through me, I crumble like ash.

Sated and spent, every muscle in my body quits at once. I sink against him, my weight hanging from the wrist cuffs, my hands numb within the restraints.

With one arm wrapped tight around my waist, Alex reaches up and fumbles with the cuff clasps until he releases first one arm, and then the other. He catches my weight as I drop.

I'm floating. No, wait, he's carrying me. I curl into him, breathing in his scent. I stick out my tongue and lick a bead of sweat off his chest. I moan at the salty, sweet taste of him.

He hisses a curse through his teeth, then asks. "Did you just lick me?"

"Mm hmm," I mumble.

Alex chuckles as he shifts me in his arms and lays me down on a surface, something soft...his bed. I whimper when I don't feel him against me anymore, but quickly the surface of the mattress indents near me, and I feel he lie down beside me.

I can see again when he gently tugs the blindfold off. I blink and squint from the light of his bed side lamp, and when I focus my vision I'm treated to a perfect view of Alex's beautiful, smiling face. His eyes are warm, full of light, affection, adoration.

"That was incredible." He kisses me, slow and sweet. I relish the contact, so sated I'm nearly unconscious, and yet still wanting more of him, anything I can get. He touches my cheek, running his thumb over my lips, lingering for a moment before speaking again, whispering, "The way you respond to me...it's fucking incredible."

Then Alex sits up and starts to rub the reddened skin of my right wrist. It feels amazing. He lifts my hand to his lips and showers gentle kisses over the skin where the cuff had shackled me. Working his firm fingers up my arm, he rubs the strained muscles all the way to my shoulders. *God, has anything ever felt this good?* When he's loosened up that side, he moves to the other and repeats his gentle affection.

I'm so overwhelmed with bliss from his touch, I hardly hear when he asks. "How was the experience for you?"

I have trouble forming words. Alex smiles, patiently watching me as I search my mind for what I want to say and the words to express it. It was incredible, to steal his word. I've never felt so stripped and vulnerable, yet cared for and safe in my life. I've never been more needing of a single person's touch and nearness, nor felt more brave and independent. In that time, I found myself and I found him. I want to be his, my own self—independent, strong, and brave—yet completely his. Finally, I speak, but all that comes out is, "It was awesome."

Alex chuckles and a wide smile spreads across his face. After a moment, he slides down the bed to rub my feet. Circling his thumb over my instep, he massages pressure points that affect me elsewhere. I wiggle and grin lazily at him. He does the same for the other foot, then cares for my calf muscles, rubbing them until they loosen. As he does the same to my thighs, he gently parts my legs and slides down to cover every inch of my pelvis with soft kisses. With a sighing moan, I completely surrender to him, letting him have his way with me, any way he wants me.

I feel his tongue teasing me as his fingers press inside, and it's like nothing I've ever felt before. Every cell in my body is primed and ready. As tired as I am, my body is fully awake, and I come quickly, bucking my hips, arching my back, twisting my legs around him. He continues, driving me to the brink of madness as orgasm after orgasm surge through me.

When I can't take any more, I moan his name, and Alex slides up to me, a wide grin on his face as he cradles me in his arms and pulls the covers up around us. I entwine my legs with his and lay my head on his chest, the sound of his heart beat soothing me to sleep.

My last thought before lights out is sobering and strange, but I don't have the energy or inclination to question it; not after the exhausting and enlightening bonding experience we've just shared. My last thought: *I could easily fall in love with this man.*

21 - Wednesday June 15, 2005

I wake very early to the sensation of Alex nuzzling against me, whispering my name as he gently runs his fingers over my back until I stir.

"Unless you want to spend the day at my house, which you're perfectly welcome to do, I need to drive you back to your place."

I rub my eyes and nod as I struggle to sit up. The sun isn't even up yet. "What time is it?"

"It's 6:00 AM. Morning comes early in construction."

"Construction?"

"Yeah. I'm an electrician." He laughs. "This would be the part where you tell me that we hardly know each other. Oh, but then you can't, now can you?" He winks.

How can he be so damn charming this early in the morning? I can't help but smile.

"Well, now you know one more thing about me. Have dinner with me tonight, and I'll tell you all sorts of other inconsequential details."

"I can't." I frown, and so does he. "I promised Jake we'd hang out tonight." Suddenly, I'm struck with a brilliant idea. "Oh! You should join us. I think you'd like each other." *Jake is going to kill me.*

Alex blinks, then he smiles, and finally, he nods. "Yeah, I'd like that."

I try to climb out of bed and stumble. My calf muscles, sore from balancing on my toes last night, are hardly working this morning. I amble toward the bathroom like a zombie who desperately needs to pee. Alex chuckles behind me, but I don't give him the satisfaction of blushing with embarrassment. I relish the ache and the memories it evokes. It hurts so good.

We drive to my house in companionable silence, and when we reach my street, I don't want to let him go. I steal kiss after kiss. We smile between each one like we're sharing a secret. Eventually, he cuts me off with something about not getting fired, and we part with plans for tonight.

Then I return to the other half of my life—the separate compartment. Only Greg isn't home, either already at work or still asleep somewhere with Kate. I'm a little surprised when the thought of the latter doesn't send my stomach into knots. And I'm even more surprised at the sense of relief I feel to find myself alone.

Once upon a time, the prospect of being alone depressed me. I hated the quiet. Now, I relish it. I don't turn on music. I don't set the television to a dull murmur for background noise. I let the quiet sink in and surround me as I walk through the house, stretching my sore arms and legs. I strip out of last night's clothing and stand in front of the mirror, twisting around to catch sight of the marks that still linger on my ass. I run my hand over the long purple lines left by Alex's fingers. They are still warm, still inflamed; a tender reminder of our incredible night together. My lover's signature, left here on my body, just for me to see.

It turns me on, almost as much as it did last night. With one hand still stroking his marks on me, I slide the other between my thighs and tease myself almost as nimbly as he did the night before. Within a matter of moments, I come, hard and loud. I wobble and nearly fall when my legs turn to jelly.

With what little strength I have left, I stumble into the bathroom and run a hot bath. The near scalding water stings those sexy welts and bruises, and it turns me on anew. I give myself another orgasm. Jesus, I'm like a cat in heat.

When I recover, a bit dazed from some combination of lack of sleep, piping hot water, and intense sexual satisfaction; I lean back, close my eyes, and let the warm water loosen my tight muscles. In the quiet, I remember last night. I remember our weekend. I remember the way

Alex winks at me when he's being cheeky and the sexy way he says *sober*. I remember the feel of his touch, cruel and kind and pure bliss. And my God, my ass hurts; it hurts so good.

• • •

"Don't hate me." I wince as I sit down next to Jake at the bar.

"I could never hate you, Two Shoes." Jake sips his beer.

"Well good, because I invited someone to hang out with us tonight. It's a guy."

Jake spits a mouthful of beer all over the bar. Manic raises an eyebrow and frowns as he pulls the towel out of his back pocket and wipes the mess clean.

"You what?" Jake squawks.

"I think you'll like him. His name is—"

"Are you fucking kidding me? I do not want to hang out with one of your boy toys. Period. End of story. Fuck you very much."

"Jake, please—"

"Greg is my best friend too, Ari. Why would you make me meet some dude you're fucking on the side when you step out on him?"

"Normally, I wouldn't, but Alex is...different."

"Oh my God, he's *different*? Really?" Jake laughs. "Jesus, you are such a girl." Jake impersonates my voice, but goes so high-pitched, he sounds more like Betty Boop, "Oh Jake, he's so dreamy."

"Fuck you. I didn't even say that."

"Might as well have. He's so *different*. Total fucking chick thing to say."

I'm a little annoyed. But Jake is smiling, really smiling, showing me the deep dimples that most people never get to see on him. So I smile too.

"Do your parents know about this open marriage shit?"

What a random question. I shake my head.

Jake chuckles. "That should make things interesting this weekend."

"Fuck!" I shout. "I completely forgot about our trip."

Jake laughs. "Really?"

"What am I going to do? They're going to know something is up. You know my mom; she's a freakin' bloodhound when it comes to secrets."

"Is it a secret?"

"Well…no. I mean, no, but can you imagine how my dad will take the news that I have a husband and a boyfriend?"

"Boyfriend?" Jake gawps.

Well, that just slipped right out there, didn't it? "Wait. Rewind."

Jake shakes his head. "Nice try, Two Shoes, but what has been heard cannot be unheard."

I huff, "Jerk."

With a grin, Jake asks, "Well, lay it on me, Two Shoes, what's so *different* about this *boyfriend* of yours?"

Before I can chide him for saying "boyfriend" again, the door opens, and it's Alex. I immediately recognize him. Even backlit by the bright glow of the afternoon sun, I notice his confident posture and the way he moves his hips when he walks. I damn near need to fan myself just taking in the sight of him.

"He's here. I'll be right back." I launch myself off the stool and hustle across the room to greet Alex.

When he sees me coming, he gives me a wide grin, and I smile right back. It's been too long since I saw him last. Whole entire hours have passed without the sound of his laugh, the glint of his eyes, or the smack of his hand on my ass. During those hours of separation, I've managed to laugh and sing and come, but I want to do it all again and again with him. I'm a glutton for him.

"Hi," my voice lilts, all girly-like—maybe Jake has a point. I dive into his arms to kiss him hello.

"Hey," Alex's voice practically purrs.

"I missed you."

"I missed you too. Twelve hours without you is too damn long."

"Twelve hours and twenty-two minutes."

The smile he gives me lights up the room. "How's your ass?"

"It's perfectly sore."

"Well, you've got the 'perfect' part right," he says with a wink.

Blushing, I angle toward the bar. "Come meet Jake."

Alex laces our fingers and follows. Jake's been watching us, and he sits up a little straighter as we approach.

"Jake, this is Alex." I slide into my seat and Alex sits on the stool beside me. "Alex, this is Jake, my best friend."

They shake hands, and Alex says, "I know you, right? You're in Nebulous."

Jake works his memory, then points at Alex with shared recognition. "Derby championship. I thought you looked familiar."

I glance between them, a little lost.

Alex helps. "My ex booked his band to play the halftime show at a derby bout last season."

Really? This fucking city is so damn small.

Of course, Jake doesn't help to ease the tension when he sputters and excitedly asks, "Arson Nic is your ex? Damn, dude." What the hell is that supposed to mean? Oh Lord, save me from this horrid conversation.

As if to answer my silent prayer, Manic breaks in with, "Bedding them in pairs now, Ari?"

"No," I scowl and I gesture to Jake. "This is Jake, my best friend, I just wanted him to meet my boyfr—" I cut myself off before I let the b-word slip out again. "I wanted him to meet Alex."

Despite my quick recovery, they all hear the word I didn't finish. I glance over at Alex to see a warm smile spread across his face. He clearly likes what he's almost heard. Manic winks at me as he fixes a round of drinks for us, and we all just sort of sit and watch him work, not sure what to say next.

"So," I break the silence, turning to Jake with an icebreaker. "You'll never believe this, but Rebecca sort of helped to bring Alex and me together. I mean, she didn't actually introduce us so much as she bonded us together with the power of her bitchiness."

Jake laughs. "Oh I believe it. You could light entire city blocks with the power of her bitchiness."

I then commence with telling the story of how I met Alex on my first night out, and Rebecca's role in how we met again only a few days ago. Wrapping up with, "So in the middle of her rant about you, Alex tried to talk to me and she swatted at him like this." I do my best impersonation. Alex nods, verifying my account of events. Jake snorts with laughter.

I stop there, at a loss for what to say next. We fall back into an uncomfortable silence, as if we're all holding our breaths and balancing on shaky legs in the middle of a minefield.

Enter Alex, ever the knight in shining armor. "How'd you two meet?"

Jake laughs and gestures for me to start, so I do. "This was back in Knoxville, Tennessee. I was seventeen; a senior in high school. My parents thought that I should have a job to teach me about responsibility, so I got a part time gig at the bookstore in the mall." I crook my thumb in Jake's direction. "And this jackass was the assistant manager."

Jake picks up the story from there, "Here was this cute little thing all decked out in goth gear, but she was boring as hell. She was so serious; it cracked me up. I figured there was probably a crazy wild child under all those layers of seriousness, but no, she really was *that* boring, and unbelievably stubborn about it too. She was so stubbornly boring that she became utterly fascinating to me. I made it my mission to try to get her to loosen up."

"It's true." I shrug. "Every time we would work a shift together he'd try to get me to smoke a bowl with him in the breakroom, and insist I come see his band play."

"Didn't think she'd actually come to a show."

"I didn't think I would either, but I did. That was how I met Greg. After that first night, the three of us have been practically inseparable ever since then."

Alex doesn't flinch at the mention of Greg, keeping his expression neutral, ever mindful of Jake's presence.

Jake nods. "When she graduated high school, she moved in with us, and I thought for sure she'd turn into some crazy party girl. College does that to people, you know? But no, instead she wrote a goddamn novel. It's a good book, don't get me wrong, but, Jesus, I couldn't even get her to drink a beer."

I lift my drink. "Cheers."

We all clink glasses, the mood between us remarkably relaxed.

"You wrote a novel?" Alex asks me.

I nod.

"Did you get it published?"

I nod again.

Alex's grin grows into a wide smile, and his eyes fill with adoration. "What's it about?"

I sigh and fidget. "It's about time travel and history and there's a love story. It's dumb."

"Don't listen to her. It's good. I'll lend you my copy next time I see you."

Wow. Jake likes Alex. I soak in the moment, and Alex squeezes my hand as he, too, recognizes that a connection has been made.

The happy moment is short-lived. In an instant, something changes in Jake. His posture stiffens, and he lets out a quiet "Uh oh" under his breath. At the same time, Manic slides near and knocks his knuckles on the bar. "Alex. Trouble. Six o'clock."

Alex turns toward the door, and though I can't see his face, I feel his body tense and his grip tighten. I immediately know why when I spot the woman standing a few feet behind him. She's tall and lean, with short dark hair, enormous green eyes, and a deep frown marking harsh lines across her face as she pins Alex with her icy stare.

This must be Nicole.

Well, she's pretty. There's no getting around that. Oh, who am I kidding? She's downright gorgeous, with sharp sexy features and those verdant doe eyes. She stands rigid, her stiff posture exuding confidence. By comparison, I feel hunched and boneless, like I could just melt off this stool into a puddle on the floor. I sit up a little straighter.

My mind races as I watch her watching Alex. What do I do? What's the protocol when your boyfriend's—there's that word again—ex-girlfriend shows up for the first time; especially when she's been described as "kind of a bitch"?

Nicole doesn't hesitate to approach. Moving with a cat-like grace, she stalks up to us and stands directly behind me. I turn in my seat to see her, and Alex and Jake both stand, flanking me like sentries.

"So you're Ariana." Her voice is sexy, though harsh and cold.

I nod. "And you're Nicole."

She looks me over, her expression twisted in judgment, her eyes narrowed with contempt.

"Okay, you've met her. Now what?" Alex asks.

Nicole flinches at the cold tone of his voice. She flicks her gaze to him, but he says nothing more, just sets his jaw in a hard line, grinding his teeth together. For a moment, as she stares at her ex-lover, I can see through a crack in the hard mask she's wearing. There is so much sadness in her big green eyes, such longing.

My heart breaks for her. To love and lose someone like Alex must be absolutely devastating. I can't bear the thought of being where she is, in love with this beautiful man, and not loved by him.

In that moment, I panic. I want to run for cover, protecting myself from ever feeling the sort of pain that Nicole is carrying. Yet, in that same instant, I want to stay; I want to entrust Alex with my heart. As terrifying as that leap of faith may be, something tells me I'm safe in his hands.

Nicole grimaces, and in an instant her defenses are back up. She smirks at Alex, scowls at me, gives Jake the once over, then turns and heads toward the patio out back.

When she's gone, I exhale the breath I've been holding, as does everyone else. Alex slowly sits back down, rubbing his palm over my thigh and giving me a concerned look. I lean into him for a slow, sweet kiss, and feel him relax against me.

On my other side, Jake is still wound tight. He doesn't sit, leaning against the bar and looking away from us as we kiss. Awkwardly, he interjects, "Well, listen, I'm going to bail, give you guys some space."

Alex apologizes, "I didn't mean to invade your time together."

"No sweat. We'll get plenty of time to hang when we're in Tennessee this weekend." Jake's tone is casual, as if he's accidentally slipped that mention of our trip in there, but the hint of a grin on his face tells me he's being his usual troublemaker self.

They politely shake hands and say their farewells, and Jake leaves me alone with a rather confused and cautiously irritable Alex to contend with. His body tenses, his hand tightening on my thigh. In a weary tone, he asks, "Tennessee?"

In a rush, I explain, "An old friend is getting married, so we're flying out there for a few days, and we're going to visit family while we're there."

"Why didn't you say something?"

"I completely forgot." I grin, trying to rouse a smile from him. "I've had *other things* on my mind lately."

Alex's knee bounces up and down. "How long will you be gone?"

"Saturday morning through Monday afternoon."

Alex groans. "This is going to kill me. I barely survived the twelve hours and twenty-two minutes without you today, and now you're leaving me for days."

I open my mouth to apologize, but yelp when a hand comes down on my shoulder. I look up to see who's tapped me and it's Kelly O'Brien. What is this, "Ghost of Christmas Past" night at the bar?

With a big grin, Kelly's voice booms when he says, "Hey there, sexy lady."

"Hey back." I repeat our usual introductions as I give Kelly a hug.

"How's shit?"

"Shit's good." I grin. "How's shit with you? How's Gabe? Is he in Afghanistan now?"

Kelly slowly nods, then smiles ear to ear. "I'm good. Gabe's good. He's stationed in Kandahar, and keeping his head down. So...all's well and good." Kelly's gaze falls to Alex, who hasn't moved from his chair, but watches us with cautious curiosity.

I glance between the two, then find my manners. "Kelly, I'd like to introduce you to Alex. He's, well, sort of my boyfriend now."

Kelly's face softens, and he raises his eyebrows in some combination of amusement and approval. He turns to Alex, who looks more surprised than anyone to hear about his new title.

"Sort of, eh?" Kelly says to Alex as they shake hands. "I'd say 'boyfriend of Ari' is a title worth acquiring."

Alex drapes an arm over my shoulders and hugs me to him as he says, "That's the plan."

"Well, glad to hear it. And I guess that's my cue to stop flirting with you, sexy lady." Kelly gives me an exaggerated wink and Alex a magnanimous grin, then walks away.

"Sort-of boyfriend," Alex hugs me, and his lips tickle the shell of my ear when he says, "I sort-of like the sound of that."

He tosses some cash on the bar and grabs my hand. "Come on. Let's get out of here."

"A quick errand," he calls it. But then he takes me to his house and won't let me come inside. I wait in his truck, the engine running, AC blasting. A few minutes pass before he returns with a blanket under one arm, and an insulated cooler under the other. Then he drives us back downtown.

"Where are you taking me?" I ask when he parks in a lot and ushers me toward the entrance of a mid-sized office building, the cooler and blanket under one arm; me under the other.

"You'll see," he answers when we've reached the portico. He lets go of me long enough to pull a set of keys from his pocket and unlock the door, locking it behind us when we're inside.

He guides me through the darkened lobby to an elevator at the back. Inside the small wood-paneled Otis box he presses the button for the top floor, and the elevator lumbers upwards, dinging at each level, until it shudders to a stop. The doors slide open to reveal a large empty space under construction. The floorplan is wide open, with metal studs that differentiate where one room will end and the next will begin. Strung from the ceiling are strands of electrical wire, dotted every few feet with dangling light bulbs in plastic shatterproof cages.

"Where are we?"

"My job site. I'm foreman for the electrical crew. We're wiring for some internet company's offices." He leads me around a corner to a darkened stairwell, illuminated only by the fire exit signs on each level. He points up, and I ascend the steps until they dead end at a heavy steel door. The hinges groan in protest when Alex pushes it open, and a warm breath of June air rushes inside.

It takes a moment for my vision to adjust to everything I'm seeing. He's brought me to the roof, a wide flat deck covered in waterproof membrane and bordered by a parapet wall. I step outside and gasp as I catch the view. The twelve-story building is ringed by giant towers on all sides—massive monoliths of glass and steel that hem in the open space with their glittering reflections and colorful accent lights.

Alex steps up behind me and wraps an arm around my waist. "It's not a mountain, but it's the best I could do on short notice."

"Oh my God." I shake with some strange combination of excitement and amazement. My eyes tear up and my breath hitches in my lungs: it's pure enchantment. I step out of his embrace and circle to take it all in, my mouth hanging open and my arms swinging at my sides like I'm Julie Andrews. "Alex...this is...unbelievable. It's so beautiful up here. It's so...God! How did you get it so exactly right?" I glance over at him, his smile beaming back at me. "You're imaginary, aren't you? You can't possibly be real. No one is this perfect."

"I'm far from perfect."

"Not from where I'm standing."

Alex chuckles and shakes his head as he walks to the center of the wide roof, spreading the blanket out and setting the cooler beside it. He turns to me and beckons me to join him. "I made some sandwiches. Thought we could eat while we watch what's left of the sunset, and then count the stars."

He made sandwiches? I go weak in the knees and stumble a bit as I approach, placing my hand in his and letting him pull me down to sit on the blanket beside him. Alex rummages through the cooler, pulling out two sandwiches carefully wrapped in little baggies. *He made sandwiches!*

"Alex, why are you so good to me?"

"Isn't it obvious?" He grins as he traces his thumb across my jaw, then promptly changes the subject. "Do you prefer strawberry or grape jelly on your PB&J?"

I stammer, still overwhelmed, but recover to answer, "Strawberry."

He hands me one of the two sandwiches, and we both quietly eat and watch as the sun closes in on the horizon. The sky is streaked with a smattering of clouds which transform before our eyes, from ordinary white squiggles into flamboyant, feathery sky boas of yellow, orange, pink, and finally blood red, before the color fades and the light dims.

When the sun has set and we've devoured our sandwiches, I curl forward onto my hands and knees and crawl to him, climbing into his lap and wrapping my arms around his shoulders. In my sexiest voice, I flirt, "So what's for dessert, big boy?"

He grins. "I brought cookies."

I laugh and the sound echoes between the surrounding buildings. Then I pinch him. Hard.

"Ouch. What did you do that for?"

"I'm pretty sure this is a dream. I'm pinching you to see if you're real."

"You're supposed to pinch yourself." He pinches my arm hard and I squeal. "See? You're not dreaming. I'm very real, and that's going to leave a very real bruise."

I stutter, "I just...I can't...I mean...you're too perfect. You've got to be a figment of my imagination."

"I'm not imaginary and I'm not perfect; I'm just falling in love with you."

I can't believe my ears. I shiver and gasp and close my eyes. Alex hugs his arms around me possessively, as if he's afraid I'll run away. But there's no way I could run. My legs are as useless as the rest of me; I'm completely stunned. I don't know what to do or say or feel. All I can muster is a weak, "Why?"

"That's a dumb question, Ariana." He inhales a deep breath and lets it out slowly as his thumb traces a line down my throat. "You know, after that first night, that first amazing kiss, I was pretty sure I was in love with you, but I wasn't certain. During those months without you, I second-guessed it a lot. I knew I liked you, but that was a confusing night, and with the turmoil of ending things with Nicole, I thought maybe it was all playing tricks with my head. It wasn't until the night we met again, when you called yourself a 'sock person.' That's when I knew I was completely head over heels in love with you."

I laugh.

"I'm serious." His thumb traces the line of my collarbone. "I pictured you at eighty, a pair of striped knee socks drooping on your wrinkly, spider-veined legs—"

I smirk and smack him in the chest, but he just smiles a wide, toothy grin and cinches his arm tighter around my waist.

"There you were in my head, all wrinkled and blotchy with liver spots, and I thought, holy shit, I want to be around to know the old-lady version of this woman."

"Jesus Christ, Alex." His words knock the breath right out of me, but still I can't help the smile and the laugh that erupt. "You're so...weird."

"Tell me something I *don't* know."

Alex's smile is sweet and genuine, and he's not waiting for me to say the words back to him. He seems happy just to have said them. And I have to admit, I adore that about him—his bald honesty, with no expectations attached.

"Hey." He glances up at the sky. "Let's count the stars."

I nod, and we shift down onto the blanket. The sun's rays are fully extinguished from the sky, but what's left is still lit—an orangey haze of urban darkness. At first, I can't spot any stars through the city's ambient glow, but the more I look, the more I see the ancient light of faraway suns prick the velvet sky and shine through.

I don't bother to actually count the stars. I don't do anything. And it feels good, just laying here, still and serene, as Alex squeezes my hand, and the warm breeze flirts with my hair. I'm not anxious or bored or looking for the next adventure. Right now, I'm exactly where I want to be. I take a deep breath like I'm smelling the roses, then let out an embarrassed giggle.

I turn my head to look at Alex and find he's already staring at me. And here we remain, transfixed with one another, occasionally raising our hands to touch and explore. I trail my fingers over his jaw line. He caresses the curve of my lips. I tenderly touch his scar, and he brushes stray bits of hair behind my ear.

"Alex, you scare me." It's three words, not the ones that matter, but it's all I can say at the moment and it's certainly honest.

He gives me a smile and a soft chuckle. "Ariana, you scare me too."

22 - Thursday June 16, 2005

"Spill it," Sheryl demands from her side of a graffiti-carved picnic table beneath the boughs of a littering cottonwood tree. She's wearing scrubs from her day job as a veterinarian at the animal shelter. They're blue, like her hair, and covered in cats.

"Spill what?" I know exactly what she means, but I'm going to make her work for it.

"Don't give me that crap. What happened after you two left on Monday night? You've gone radio silent, which can mean only one thing."

"And that is?"

"That you can't answer the phone because there's a huge cock in your mouth."

I laugh, but keep my mouth shut.

"You bitch. You're not going to kiss and tell, are you?"

"Not this time, nope."

"Why not? You tell me everything."

"I don't know, this time it's...different." And there I go again with the girly sigh that Jake was noting.

Sheryl's jaw drops. "Oh. My. God! You like him."

"Of course I like him. I wouldn't spend my time with him if I didn't."

"No, you *like him* like him. Oh my God, this is so awesome. He's so right for you. He's totally the one!"

"What?"

"Totally."

"Huh?"

"He's the yin to your yang, the zig to your zag, the Captain to your Tennille...baby girl, he is your *soooooooooulmate*." She performs that last word, going loud and long, and a few of the other food court patrons glance our way. Sheryl, oblivious, finishes her outburst with a doozy. "Face it, honey pie, Alex is your true love."

"Okay, first of all, you're insane," I huff. "And for the love of God, will everyone just shut up about love, already? I've been dating him for less than a week. It's too—"

"Whoa. Whoa. Whoa!" Sheryl interrupts. "Who is this 'everyone'? Who else has been talking about love?"

I press my lips together in a thin line. *Whoops.*

Sheryl is too smart to be fooled. She gasps dramatically, then squeals, "Oh! Fuck! Oh fuck! Ohfuckohfuckohfuckohfuck! It's Alex, isn't it? Did he say *the words*?"

My mind flashes back to last night, to his rooftop confession: *I'm not imaginary and I'm not perfect; I'm just falling in love with you.* I'd been awestruck and speechless and excited. But now, with a little distance and perspective, I feel the weight of it all.

"Sheryl, what am I going to do? He's getting so serious."

"So he did then, he said the words?"

The guy at the taco truck picks that moment to holler, "Sheryl, order up."

Sheryl retrieves our lunch, and I dive into my food, grateful for the distraction.

"So what'd you say back?" Sheryl asks, her mouth full of *carne asada*.

"Nothing."

"Nothing?"

I shrug. "I told him he was weird."

Sheryl laughs at me and shakes her head.

Suddenly feeling defensive and overwhelmed, I rant, "Sher, it's too much, too fast. I mean it's been just a few days and he's already talking about love."

"How long did it take you to know with Greg?"

Just a few days. But I was seventeen and single and things were simpler back then. This is different, isn't it?

I ignore her question. "And then, this morning, when he drove me home, we had our first fight. Well, it wasn't really a fight. I sort of snapped at him and then he kissed me. It was so weird."

Sheryl quirks an eyebrow, encouraging me to continue, so I do.

"He's mad because this weekend I'm going to Tennessee with Greg and Jake, so he expects me to cancel tonight's date night with Greg and spend the evening with him. When I explained to him that Thursday is always date night with Greg, he got quiet and things got weird and I got defensive and said, 'Stop trying to control every minute of my time. I have a whole life outside of you.'"

"Oh Ari, you didn't."

"I did. It was a shitty thing to say and I regretted it immediately, but he didn't even argue with me. He just touched my face"—I rest my palm where his had been—"and he leaned in and gave me this *amazing* kiss, and just as I was sliding closer to him to, you know, kiss him some more, he reached past me and pushed the passenger door open."

Sheryl looks half shocked and half amused.

"And he said, 'If you change your mind, you know where to find me.' He waited for me to get out, and then he just drove off, no goodbye or anything. It was so...*weird*."

Sheryl looks pleased. "Giving you a taste of what you'll be missing tonight."

"I just hate how we left things."

"Well, yeah, that's because he left you wanting more. Smart man."

I groan and dump my face into my hands. "What am I going to do?"

"Well, you could start by cancelling your date with Greg and spending tonight with Alex."

"But—"

"Ari, why can't you just admit that you're seriously into him? Why are you fighting it so hard?"

Irritated and weary I slump and frown at her, "So what if I am? So what if I'm falling for him? Then what? It's not as simple as fitting my foot into a glass slipper and riding off into the sunset. This whole thing is so much more complicated than that."

Sheryl takes another bite of her lunch, and it's hard to make out her words as she flashes a sympathetic frown and asks, "Complicated how?"

"Well, for starters, I'm married. Remember?"

Sheryl rolls her eyes. "Oh, Ari, give it a rest, will ya?"

"What?"

"Please! Who are you kidding with this open marriage nonsense? This is your way of having your cake and eating it too."

"Having my cake and eating it too? Really?" That hurts.

"Ari, I've got several friends who are polyamorous, and you, my dear, are not one of them." At my scowl, Sheryl sets her food down, and holds up her hands in defense. "Before you get mad, just hear me out."

I take a deep breath and listen.

"I've known you for, what, six months now? And in that time you've been, like, this terminal patient with an epic bucket list and a ticking clock. You've had this urgency about everything. It's like, deep down, even you know that this whole thing is temporary, and at any moment this life you're living could be taken away from you. But guess what, honey, the doctor called, turns out the tumor is benign. So now what?"

"Cancer? You're comparing my life to cancer?"

"I said it was benign."

"And what does any of that have to do with polyamory?"

"Babe, poly people are poly for life. It's not an adventure for them, it's just how their hearts are shaped."

I frown, completely confused now.

"Look, all I'm saying is you've clearly been searching for something, and honey pie, you've found it. So start being honest with yourself and stop making this whole thing more complicated than it needs to be."

"I'm not making it more complicated than it needs to be, you are trying to make it more simple than it is. I don't know what the hell you're talking about with all this cancer and heart-shaped shit, but Sher, the fact remains that I'm married! M-A-R-R-I-E-D! Married! And Greg's a good and decent man. Things with him are"—I'm really starting to hate this word—"complicated. I admit that. But I can't just up and not be married anymore, not on a whim, not for a crush. I like Alex a lot, sure, but I've been dating him for less than a week. I've got *twelve years* of history with Greg."

"The key word there is *history*. Girl, it's time for you to focus on your *future*."

I huff. I picture Greg, guitar in hand, playing the song he wrote for me all those years ago. I remember the words he whispered to me: *I still love you, Ari Beth.*

Still. That word hadn't bothered me at the time he'd said it, but it bothers me now.

Still: regardless, in spite of, nevertheless.

Still: stagnant, motionless, unchanged.

I don't want to be *still*, not in any sense of the word. For a moment, I consider that Sheryl might actually be right, that my future may no longer resemble my past. Then snap back to attention when I realize Sheryl's talking again.

"...in the two years they were together, Alex never told Nicole that he loved her."

"Why not?"

Sheryl gives me a pitying expression, like I'm a complete moron. "Because, honey, Alex doesn't say things he doesn't mean. If he says he's in love with you, then he's in love with you, and you need to take that seriously."

That's when it hits me like a tidal wave. This thing that I've been exploring with Alex is, yeah, *complicated*, but it's also *different*. It's something special, and it's something I need to tell Greg.

· · ·

The lasagna is in the oven, bubbling and browning. I've cleaned the house from top to bottom. I've showered and changed into my favorite dress. Everything is neat and tidy, in place. I'm ready.

I feel good, my mind clear and my heart lifted. The revelation of today still buzzes in my head. The reality of a future that is messy, sure, but so damned exciting has me practically giddy.

Tonight, over Date Night dinner, I will tell Greg about Alex. I am resolved. Greg had been brave and honest with me with regard to his feelings about Kate. I owe him the same courtesy with regard to Alex. And I owe Alex the courtesy of recognition.

I hate this wait. I pass the time in my study. I've opened *the book,* adding notes here and there, rereading and writing whole chapters anew. It's something I haven't done in over two years. It feels good, like sliding on a pair of shoes that fit just right—

I hear the front door close loudly, and jolt upright, book forgotten. No, wait... I hit the 'save' button. Now, book forgotten, I pause for a moment, staring at the open doorway to my office, expecting to hear Greg call out. When there is only silence, I go find him.

He's in the kitchen, at the counter, with the door to the liquor cabinet hanging wide open. His shoulders hunched, Greg pours himself a glass of whiskey. I wait for him to finish, to turn and see me. When he does finally turn, his eyes are closed. He slouches backwards against the counter and slugs his drink. He looks terrible, his posture stooped and heavy, his skin sallow and waxy, like he's sick.

"Are you okay?" I ask.

He opens his eyes slowly and stares at me. He looks lost, disoriented. He furrows his brow, turns, and pours himself another drink. When he swallows it all without answering my question, the answer is clear: *no, he is not okay.*

"What's wrong?"

He stares at me again, looking crushed by the weight of some unseen force. I flinch, expecting terrible news. Is everything okay with Grandma Millie? His parents? His brother? Jake? Finally, after a painfully long pause, Greg quietly admits. "It's Kate. We broke up."

Wait. What? "Why?"

He shrugs. God, his posture; he looks like he's been trampled. I wish I could help. I wish that I could fix this, but something tells me I don't possess the cure for what ails him.

"May I ask..." I pause, afraid to overstep my bounds, which is completely absurd considering I'm talking to my husband about his breakup with his girlfriend. "What happened?"

Greg's shoulders fall. He blows out a gusty groan and collapses into a chair at the table, his empty glass in one hand and the bottle of whiskey in the other. Quietly, he admits. "We had a fight. She asked me to choose."

He doesn't look at me when he says it, and that's probably for the best. I'm not capable of hiding my surprise. My jaw drops and my eyes go wide, absolutely stunned. *I'm the reason they split?*

I wait for Greg to say more, but that's all he offers, and I'm left to draw my own conclusions. Kate wants him to leave me. She doesn't want to be his other woman; she wants to be his only woman. I don't know why I'm surprised by this. There are some people who thrive in open relationships, but they seem to be a rare breed. For the rest of us, it's a stasis, not a status. It is the act of being "still"—still married, still attached to another. How long had we expected Kate to tolerate that limbo? And how odd is it that I find myself identifying more with the latter group, than with the former?

I shake that last thought from my head as I cross to the table and slide into the seat across from Greg. I tilt my head to catch his gaze as I rest my hand over his, clasping the bottle of booze. He frowns at me and I frown back, my heart twisting in my chest from the guilt. "Greg, I'm so sorry."

With a smirk, he glances away, down at the table as he quietly says, "You have nothing to apologize for."

But I do. I look across the table to Greg, slumped in his chair, drowning his pain in whiskey, and I feel awash with guilt. I owe him so much more than an apology. This is my fault. I'm the reason he's hurting. I led him into this emotional minefield and then I left him to navigate his own way out. Sure, Kate had been the one to hurt him, but I'd put the weapon in her hands.

When I'd suggested to Greg that we open our marriage, I could never have imagined that we'd end up here. But here we are. And had this been our eventual destination all along? Had either of us actually been interested in embracing the polyamorous lifestyle? Or were we just curious and bored?

Finally, I understand what Sheryl meant about having my cake and eating it too, and it leaves a bad taste in my mouth. I stare at my husband, the man I've loved for twelve years, and I see a stranger. I see another woman's man. He's not looking at me; his gaze is focused elsewhere. His thoughts, his heart, are elsewhere as well. Yet, when Kate had asked him to choose, he'd chosen me. *Why?*

"Greg, why did you choose me?"

Greg looks up, his eyes finally meeting mine. He purses his lips as he scowls. "Because you're my wife."

"But you love her."

"I love you too." He scrutinizes the expression on my face, as he runs his callused fingers over the bottle in his hand. "And you never asked me to choose."

I let out a shaky breath. There it is, the real reason. It wasn't for love, or even for loyalty, but stubbornness. Greg had chosen not to be hemmed in by an ultimatum.

Kate is in his heart, that much is evident, but Greg has never been ruled by emotion. He's not swayed by tearful demands or manipulations; issuing an ultimatum to a man like Greg is not going to produce the desired result. I nearly smile at my stubborn, predictable husband, but the flicker of amusement quickly fades as he downs another dram of whiskey straight from the bottle.

"Greg—"

"Ari, do you mind if we postpone our...night?" He mumbles, "I think...I just...I need..." His voice fades to nothing and he takes another drink.

"Um, yeah...I...I'll go." I watch him, worry filling me with each drink he takes. He doesn't want to talk to me right now, and that's fine, but I can't leave him alone. I pull my phone out of my pocket and text Jake a quick 911 from under the table: **Greg and Kate split. At house. Drinking with death wish.**

An instant later, my phone vibrates to announce his reply: **FUCK. OMW.**

I slip the phone back into my pocket and move to stand, mumbling nonsense to fill the silence. Stuff like, "If you get hungry, there's lasagna." Brokenhearted? Here's some pasta. I want to kick myself for how lame that sounds. But I have no idea what else to say, or how to behave. This is new terrain.

I shut my idiot mouth and cross to the stove, pulling out the pasta and turning off the heat. When I swing back around, I find Greg is standing now, moving toward the hallway on shaky legs. I don't let him pass me. When he's close enough to hug, I reach for him and loop my arms around his neck. He freezes, then slumps against me like the strength has melted out of him. After a moment's pause, he wraps his arms around my waist and squeezes me tight. We stand there, embraced in silence—me trying to lend him support, him trying not to need it.

"Greg, we'll figure this out, okay?" I whisper. "I'm so sorry you're hurting. I never wanted you to get hurt by any of this."

He pulls away from me, frowning, seeming confused by my words. But he says nothing, just lets out a tired breath and plants a soft kiss on my cheek before he walks away.

I let him go, though I want to follow. I want to talk this out. There is so much I should say to him right now. My initial plan for tonight had been to tell him about Alex, and now more than ever, he needs to know. If he'd known about Alex before, would he have responded to Kate differently? But it hardly seems appropriate to spring the old, *hey babe, sorry about your breakup. By the way, I think I'm falling in love with another man.*

I gasp at the revelation. There it is, that word that I've denied to everyone including myself. It's a bit of an epiphany, and the timing couldn't be worse. I watch Greg amble to the bathroom and shut the door, listening to the shower come on. I remain frozen in place, not sure what to feel or how to react to any of this. I stare at the clock until my eyes drift out of focus, the red numbers becoming a blur as they change from minute to minute.

At some point, Jake arrives. He lets himself inside and joins me in the kitchen. Standing over the stove, eating forkfuls of lasagna straight from the pan, he asks me for details I don't know.

My phone rings. The cab I don't remember requesting has arrived. I give Jake a kiss on the cheek in farewell. He frowns. I know what he's thinking: I should stay. I'm running again, he'd say, and he'd be right.

The going gets tough, and there goes Ari, right out the door. But what good would staying do? With all that booze, Greg is in no shape to talk. And despite being completely sober, neither am I.

•   •   •

"I thought you had a date tonight."

Alex's icy reception sends a shiver through me. He doesn't sound hurt or angry, but he isn't smiling like he usually does, and he hasn't moved to let me inside his house either. He just stands there, shirtless and barefoot, waiting for an explanation for why I've turned up on his front porch.

"Things changed," I say.

"What changed?"

"It's a really long story."

"I've got all night."

"I don't want to...can we not...talk tonight? I just want..." Why am I stuttering and babbling senselessly? Why am I so nervous? Why am I here? I take a step back, and consider turning around and running away. Again. But where would I go this time?

Sensing my skittishness, Alex steps out onto the porch. His sudden approach is startling and I take another step back. But he moves faster than me, cornering me, his body pressed hard against mine. With his mouth to my ear, his voice practically growls with predatory menace when he asks, "What is it you want, Ariana?"

The summer evening air flushes my skin, and everywhere that Alex's body touches mine is branded with his heat, burning the thoughts from my mind and the words from my mouth.

The lingering rays of the setting sun shine in his eyes, fire on a calm, clear lake. And I can see everything there, such honesty, every brutal truth laid bare. He's hidden nothing from me, while I've hidden everything from him, from everyone.

Why can't I be honest with him? Why do I stutter and stammer and close my mouth when I should be telling him what he needs to hear. Finally, I mean to do just that. I open my mouth and I answer his question. *What do I want?* "You."

Alex considers my answer. The prolonged silence makes me feel vulnerable, exposed. I open my mouth to fill the silence with something, anything that will relieve this tension between us. But Alex has his own ideas about how to relieve the tension. "Have you had anything to drink tonight?"

I shake my head no.

One corner of his mouth lifts in a devilish grin.

• • •

"Try to touch your elbows together?"

I try to do as he says, but Alex reads my pained expression and adjusts my arms until I feel relatively comfortable. But *relatively comfortable* is a strange concept when you're wearing nothing, and your arms are tied behind your back in a series of complex knots.

Alex continues to loop the rope around my arms and then around my chest, isolating each breast in a taut knot. Holding the remaining length of rope like a leash, he guides me to a bench in the middle of the room. I sit, and he positions my hips at the edge of the leather cushion, then pushes my legs apart in a wide spread-eagle. I tremble with nervous energy as he loops the rope over my thighs in ornate knots, like exaggerated fishnet, and ties each of my calves to the wide legs of the chair.

When he's finished, Alex settles on the ground in front of me, running his palms over the flesh and rope of my legs. Unable to move and splayed wide open, I feel too exposed. My breathing goes ragged as panic rises up within me. Alex watches this change and moves to calm my nerves. He kisses me and his fingers lightly graze my cheeks as he whispers, "Do you have any idea how beautiful you are?"

I swallow hard and shake my head. Alex stands and leaves the room without a word. My nervousness ratchets up, and I shift as much as I can to watch the doorway for his return. I don't have to wait long, relaxing slightly when he reenters the room. Then I see the large mirror in his grip. He sets it against the wall in front of me, angling it to reflect every inch of my body. At the first sight of myself, I avert my eyes.

"Don't look away," Alex commands.

I let out a frustrated breath but comply, raising my eyes to meet my own reflection. Seeing myself like this—bared naked and spread open—is overwhelming.

Alex walks to me, circling behind the chair he's bound me to. He lays his hands on my neck and bends down to speak in my ear. "With you like this—your soft skin bound by my coarse rope, your body open to me—I've never seen anything so beautiful."

I hold my breath as Alex sits behind me, his legs straddling mine. I can feel his jeans and the erection they contain with the tips of my fingers. He leans into me, his warm, bare chest pressing against my bound arms as he slides his hands down my front. His fingers trace the lines of the taut rope around my breasts and follow the crisscrosses that lace down my belly. I catch sight of his grin in the mirror as his fingers leave the rope at my thighs and slide between my legs. His words come as a whisper, when he tells me, "I'm going to make you come, and you're going to watch. I want you to see what I see."

His fingers circle, slow and gentle, and I moan. I can't seem to watch, though. I dip my head back, letting it fall against his shoulder as my eyes close.

Alex stops, "Open your eyes, and keep them open."

I open my eyes but turn my head to look at him.

He shakes his head, with his voice stern, he commands. "Watch."

I let out a meek whimper, but swivel my head back to the mirror, flinching at the shocking sight of myself.

Alex's fingers return, and I moan with pleasure, even as he warns, "I will only touch you if you watch. Close your eyes again and I'll stop and leave you here alone."

At that, my eyes go wide.

"That's a good girl," Alex purrs in my ear. His lips slide into an erotic grin. His hand moves again, those slow, deft circles. I watch. And after a moment, I really see. I see the way he touches me, the very tips of his fingers plucking me like an instrument, strumming until I hum. I see the way I respond, my breaths growing shorter, my skin flushing pink. As Alex's rotations increase in speed and pressure, my chest rises and falls with my ragged breath, and the undulations of my breasts pull the ropes tauter, pinching in places. The pain is an exquisite compliment to Alex's gentle touch, and only serves to excite me more. My eyelids flutter and droop, but I don't close my eyes.

Alex brings his other hand around, sliding one finger and then two inside me. I moan. Alex groans in my ear as his fingers work their magic.

In the mirror, I see my cheeks turn rosy and my pupils dilate. I'm going to come. I can see it written all over my face. Alex watches me through the mirror, too, reading me. His hands move faster and harder. I moan and groan and wiggle. My eyelids grow heavy, sinking, about to shut. I fight the urge, actually *wanting* to watch now as my orgasm builds.

"Come for me. Watch yourself come for me," Alex whispers. It's all I need to send me over the edge. I come, loud and urgent, and I watch the dawn rise over my face. My eyes go wide as if surprised, my lips curl back, and my throat strains as I cry out for God and Alex in the same breath.

He's right. It is beautiful. That moment of pure bliss is powerful to watch. I like watching Alex, too. His excitement is evident as well. It's like he's come along with me, not literally, but he's definitely enjoying my orgasm. I shudder all over, and the ropes pull in response. The sensation almost makes me come again.

Alex's hands continue to work me, wringing out every last drop of bliss. His lips find my ear, and he nibbles as his ragged voice whispers, "I can't wait to make you come with my cock buried inside you."

Feeling bold, and ready for anything he has to give me, I challenge him, "Why don't you?"

Alex abruptly pulls his hands away and stands. I nearly collapse backwards, having to splay my fingers out in order to prop up my sated and exhausted body. I watch Alex in the mirror as he crosses the room to the chest of drawers. He pulls out a blindfold, as well as a few colorful toys and what looks like a snakebite kit. Then he moves over to the pegboard of pain.

He takes a riding crop off its hook and examines it. Knowing full well that I'm watching his reflection, he swipes it through the air a couple of times and swats it on his own hand. The stinging sound of leather thwacking skin sends a shudder through me. He sets it aside with his collection of items, then runs his fingers through the long leather strands of some sort of whip, after a moment of consideration, he pulls this off its hook as well.

My pulse quickens as I look at the assortment of items he's collected. I guess we're not finished playing.

Alex turns and his eyes meet mine in the mirror, the blindfold dangling from his fingers as he walks toward me. His intense stare is so magnetic, I couldn't look away even if I wanted to. When he stops, he's standing right behind me, staring down at my reflection.

After the long silence, I don't expect a response to my question—damn near forgot I'd asked one—so when he answers, it's a surprise. "I've given you my heart, and you've given me your body."

My eyes widen at his naked words.

"But that's not enough for me. I want it all, Ariana. The day you decide I'm in your heart, that'll be the day you can get in my pants."

With that, Alex's grin grows mischievous, and he raises the blindfold in his hands. The last thing I see before he slides the fabric over my eyes is his brow waggling and a cocky grin. "Until then, I'm having a very good time playing with your body."

• • •

"How did you get into this lifestyle?" I ask when I can finally form coherent thoughts again.

"Do you really want to know? It involved another woman." Alex rubs my back. He's still wearing his jeans as he straddles my hips, massaging the tension from my newly-freed limbs. I can feel his erection pressed against my ass, but he refuses to let me touch him. And that seems kinkier than any of the naughty things he's done to me tonight.

"Yes," I moan as his fingers work out a particularly tight muscle in my shoulder.

He laughs, but keeps applying pressure with his thumbs as he starts his story. "About six years ago, I was living in Seattle and working as a mariner—we were rehabbing an old Navy ship at the dry dock—and I was seeing this woman, Danielle, who was a Dominatrix. It was her job. Guys would pay her to treat them like furniture."

"Furniture?" I giggle, and he tickles my side, making me giggle even more.

"Yeah. She'd sit on them like they were a bench, or put her feet on them like they were an ottoman."

"Strange."

"It's not my thing, but who am I to judge?"

"So you were never furniture?"

"No. I wasn't into being a sub. She could tell that right away, so she started training me to be a Dom. She wanted to employ me. She took me to S&M parties, introduced me to potential clients. But that wasn't my thing either." He pauses and moves his hands further down to work the muscles of my lower back. "I do this because I enjoy it. The idea of doing it for money left me cold. But it was all a moot point anyway, because my aunt got sick and then she died, so I quit my job and moved back to Austin."

"I'm sorry." I turn to look at him, and he shifts off of me, moving lower to massage my legs.

"It was rough on my mom. They were twins, and very close. It was hard on her when she lost my dad, but losing Jackie nearly broke her. So I moved back here to be closer to her."

"You're a good son."

"She's a good mom." He shrugs. "Anyway, Danielle told me about a group here in Austin who hosts S&M parties. I started going, playing around, and I guess it took."

"Was Nicole a sub?"

Alex hesitates, probably as surprised by my question as I am, but he answers, "Sometimes, but sometimes we'd switch it up."

"Switch it up?"

"Sometimes she'd top, I'd bottom. You know, switch roles for a night. Whatever she needed."

"What do you mean?" Well, look at me, being all open-minded and asking about the kinky-bondage sex he had with his ex-girlfriend.

"Nicole's had a rough life, and the Dom/sub thing can be a form of therapy, if you let it. I would try to give that to her." He finishes the massage and lies down beside me, running his fingers in soft circles over my back.

"What about you? Is it therapy for you?"

He chuckles. "No. For me, it's about having fun, exploring my limits and my partner's limits. I like the control, sure, but it's not because I have some deep-seated need to dominate women. I'm not working through childhood trauma or wrestling with my inner demons. I'm a simple guy with simple motivations, and I tend to get bored easily. The kinky shit challenges me."

His words hit home. I turn onto my side to face him. "I get that. I think that's part of why I wanted to open my marriage. I wanted to challenge myself. I think I wanted to know if I could step out of my comfort zone."

"It's what first attracted me to you." He grins, and his eyes light up with humor. "Well, I mean, aside from those big brown eyes and the sound of your laugh."

I laugh and bury my face in his side.

He tickles me to elicit another laugh when he says, "Besides your eyes and your giggle, your courage is pretty damn hot."

"Courage?" I raise a brow and frown.

"I know you don't believe it, but your decision to open your marriage was incredibly brave. From what I can gather, you had a comfortable married life which you stepped away from in order to explore the great unknown. That took guts. I'm more than a little bit in awe of you." He grins as he traces his thumb across my lips, but his expression sinks when he adds, "But it's that same part of you that scares the shit out of me."

"Why?"

"It's not often that I feel insecure, but with you I feel completely out of control. It's as if I can't get my hands on you. Even when you're right here with me, tied up in my fucking bed, part of you is still out of my reach."

I don't know what to say. I could admit to him that I feel more for him than I'm letting on, and I want to. I want to assuage his fears. I want to press my hands to his cheeks and insist: *You can trust me, Alex!* But can he? Can I promise I'll never hurt him, even as my husband is at home drinking himself into a stupor, nursing a broken heart? And were I to start making those promises, what next? How would I react were Alex to slap me with an ultimatum like Kate did to Greg? She'd asked Greg to choose, and he'd chosen me. If Alex were to ask me to choose, who would I pick?

Alex lets out an awkward laugh. "Maybe I do have some inner demons to wrestle with after all."

23 - Friday June 17, 2005

"Yeah, he's here. He's comatose on the couch." Jake's voice sounds like a shrug.

"Comatose?" I'm flooded with concern. "Is he okay? Have you checked on him lately?"

"I held a mirror under his nose a few hours ago. He was still breathing."

"What?" My concern ratchets up to full-blown panic. I search for a pair of shoes to slip on. "I'm coming over there."

Jake laughs, but it's without humor. "Cool your jets, Two Shoes. I've got this. Greg's fine. He's just sleeping it off."

I sink onto the couch, still tugging on my sneakers. "I'm just so worried about him."

"I get it, but you need to give him some space. I brought him over here last night to clear his head and figure some shit out. You can talk to him on the flight, or whatever, but for now—"

"But—"

"Ari, I'm serious. You're the one always talking a big game about needing space. Well, now it's time for you to give him some. You feel me?"

My shoulders slump and I want to protest. Greg and I hardly ever see each other anymore, how much more space could he possibly need?

But Jake is right, it was me who was always waxing poetic on the subject, so I can't rightly deny that to Greg.

I numbly listen as Jake rattles off a set of instructions for me to pack bags for Greg and myself, they will swing by to pick me up tomorrow morning at nine on the way to the airport. Just as I think we're about to hang up, Jake surprises me when he says, "Oh, and next time you want me to keep a secret for you, you need to fucking *tell* me it's a secret."

Stunned, I stutter, "What secret?"

His answer is just one word, but his tone is so sharp it slices right through me. "Alex."

My blood runs cold and drains from my head, leaving me dizzy.

"He was pretty surprised to find out that not only does his wife have a boyfriend, but that I've had a beer with the guy. How could you not tell him, Ari?"

"I was going to—" I stop when I realize I'm about to make an excuse. Excuses won't help. I should have told Greg. I didn't. I fucked up. Period. Tears fill my eyes as I imagine how my clumsy omission has hurt him, a kick in the gut when he was already down.

His voice thick with emotion, Jake continues, "You know what his first question was?"

I cringe.

"He asked me if you're happy."

The guilt overwhelms me. I let out a whimper as tears overtop my lashes and streak down my cheeks. I hug an arm across my chest, but all I really want to do is hug my husband and apologize to him.

"You tell me, Ari, are you happy?" He waits a beat, then hangs up.

That's when the dam bursts and the tears wash over me in suffocating waves. I curl up on the couch and bawl like a baby, gasping and wailing and moaning in all my ugly-cry glory. There's no fear I'll be heard.

In space, no one can hear you cry.

• • •

The phone rings and I startle, realizing that I've lost track of time, comatose on the couch, staring at the wall. I answer without checking the screen to see who's calling.

"I'm cutting out of work early." It's Alex. "Can I see you one more night before you leave tomorrow?"

I pull my eyes back into focus and realize I've been staring at the wedding photo hanging on the wall beside the television. It's a candid shot, taken without our knowledge as we'd danced during the reception. I still remember the moment. Greg had whispered in my ear about how quickly he planned to get me out of my dress. I'd smiled wide and thrown back my head as I'd laughed. Greg had smiled too, then kissed my throat. That's when the photographer had snapped the shot. It's always been my favorite photo of the two of us.

"Yes," I answer, "but I have an errand to run."

I briefly explain the details, and Alex sounds excited. "There is nothing I'd rather do than watch you take your clothes off. But I have one condition."

"What?"

"If I'm going to go dress shopping with you, then I get to pick the dress you're going to wear to the wedding."

I accept his terms, and then he hangs up and I'm alone again in the silence of this empty house. I shower quickly, washing away the tracks of my tears, slip on a sundress, and feel a little more at ease when I hear my phone chirp with a text.

Out front, it reads.

I practically run to his truck, which is parked in his usual spot, across the street and two houses away. Inside, Alex greets me with a tight hug and a sweet kiss. I melt into him and let his warmth soothe my jangled nerves.

"You alright?" He asks as he runs his thumb across my cheek. "You look like you've been crying."

"I'm fine."

Alex doesn't look like he believes me. He turns his gaze to the house, to Greg's car still in the driveway, as if he's still there. "Did he do something? Did he hurt you?"

"No," The word fires out of me, sounding too defensive, sounding like a lie. But it's the truth. I'm the guilty party. I've hurt everyone. "Can we just go?"

He frowns at me, watching me closely, but says nothing more as he shifts the truck into gear and takes us south.

At the shop, we walk single-file through the narrow aisles, hemmed in by tall racks that burst with colorful dresses. I can't seem to focus, my mind scattered between all the different compartments in my head. I drift aimlessly, touching fabrics and running my fingers along the tops of the hangers as I wander.

"What happened to make you cry?" Alex asks when there's no one else around us.

It's a long story, I almost answer, but I know that Alex will just want to hear it all. "There was a miscommunication with Greg...and Jake."

Alex nods. "But, you're all still going to Tennessee together?"

I frown at him over my shoulder. "Yeah."

"Hmm." I hope he'll drop the subject, but no. "How often do you go back there to see your family?"

"Usually just at Christmas. But, with Grandpa Chuck's funeral and Ben & Cassie's wedding, we're traveling home quite a bit."

"Do they know?"

"Know what?"

"About the open marriage."

"Oh." I frown over at him. "Uh. No. I've kept it under wraps with my parents."

"Are you going to tell them?"

I don't know, am I? When the open marriage was just a bit of fun, it wasn't something I'd ever wanted my family to know about, but now...things are different. How can I possibly hide all of this from them? And why would I want to hide any of it? What's happened to Greg and me in the last few months has been monumental, and what's happening with Alex is important to me. I need to tell them, but how on Earth do I explain everything?

"I don't know." I try to change the subject by modeling a blue dress against my chest. Alex shakes his head disapprovingly.

"What do you mean, *you don't know*?"

"If it comes up, I'm not going to lie, but if it doesn't..." I'm not sure how to finish that sentence, so instead, I yank a hideous pink gown from the rack and hold it up. Alex shakes his head and smirks.

"Ariana, what do you see for your future?"

Shit.

"Will you stay married? Get divorced? Close your marriage? Keep it open?"

Shit. Shit. Shit.

"Do you see me there?"

"Alex…"

"Do you see me there, Ariana? It's a simple question." Alex leans close. "Because when I look to my future, I can't see past you."

My breath hitches in my lungs. I slump and lean back against a stand full of satin party dresses in a rainbow array of colors. "Alex, it's so—"

"Complicated." He smirks. "You know, this 'complicated' shit would be a lot easier to stomach if you gave me some indication of where I stand with you."

Is this the ultimatum? I turn away, heading up the aisle to a different rack of dresses, but Alex quickly catches up with me, moving to block my escape.

"Christ, stop running away from me." Alex's words whistle through clenched teeth as he tries to keep his voice low, avoiding attention from the other shoppers. He moves me until my back is against the wall, and we're partially concealed by racks overflowing with sequins and silk. I try to look at my feet, but his hand catches my chin and pulls my gaze back to his. He closes his eyes and presses his forehead against mine.

"Ariana, I'm not trying to make your situation more difficult than it already is. I know your life is complicated. I get it. But goddamn it, I'm having a really hard time with this. The thought of letting you go, even for just a few days, is killing me. And I'm not a possessive man, so this is really fucking with my head."

"I'm sorry."

"Don't be sorry. I don't want you to be sorry. I just want you to be honest with me. I want to know where I stand with you. Are you going to tell your family about me, or am I your dirty little secret? The kinky bastard you keep hidden in your closet?"

"You're not a secret." Jake had called him that this morning. A twinge of guilt shivers through me. I squeeze Alex's hand in mine as I reiterate. "You're not a secret. I want to tell them about you. You make me happy, and I want them to know that. I just have to find the right time. I mean they don't even know about the open marriage yet. It's—"

"Complicated." Alex lets out a flat, hollow laugh. He seems to think for a moment, before his eyes fix on mine and a small grin creeps across his lips. "I make you happy?"

"Yeah, I thought that was obvious." I quickly change the subject, aiming for humor to lighten the mood. "You are a kinky bastard, though. You got that part right."

That gets a laugh out of him, a good one. Alex lets out a heavy breath and places a chaste kiss on my forehead before he turns to take in the assortment of dresses around us. I watch him thoughtfully flick through hangers until he comes to a full stop. He glances at me and nods as he pulls a gown off the rack.

"This one." He holds up a shimmering taffeta dress. The fabric seems to change colors in the light, from copper to topaz to deep chocolate and rosy garnet. It's a color I never would have considered wearing. However, when Alex holds it up, the array of colors match his hair. I smile wide, instantly charmed. I find my size and head to the dressing room; Alex on my heels.

"You're not supposed to come back here with me," I whisper.

"Says who?" Alex nods at the fitting-room monitor stand, which is unmanned at the moment. "We're all alone here. I could shove you into any one of these little changing rooms and fuck the ever-loving shit out of you, and they'd be none the wiser."

"With the amount of noise I make, they'd be the wiser."

Alex chuckles, "Good point. I'll have to gag you."

I giggle, thinking it's a joke, but he surprises me when he pushes me into the last cubicle, latches the door shut behind him, and pins me to the wall for a breathtaking kiss.

When he pulls away, he instructs, "Turn around."

Practically panting with anticipation, I do as I'm told. His fingers slide up my back to the zipper of my sundress and bring it down. He nudges the straps off my shoulders until it falls around my feet. Then he pushes the copper dress at me. "Let's see what it looks like on you."

Wait. What? I frown and turn to find him grinning at me with a cocky smirk. Pouting, I mutter, "Tease."

"Don't make me spank you."

"Promises, promises."

He tries not to smile, fails, and swats my ass, "Try on the damn dress."

I give him a dramatic sigh, but I do as I'm told, stepping into the dress and holding my hair aside so he can zip up the back. Then, stunned, we both admire my reflection. Wow. I look really hot.

"You look amazing," Alex says in a whisper.

He brushes a few strands of hair off my shoulder and kisses my neck, his eyes meeting mine through the mirror. But then his expression changes, his smile sinks into a frown and he balls his fingers into fists. With a sharp inhale, he steps away from me.

"What was I thinking? I should have found you an ugly dress. If your husband sees you in this, he's going to come to his senses. Take it off."

He acts like the dress is radioactive, rushing me out of it. Before I can get back into my own clothes, he's got the dress in his fist and he's out the door. I stand there, half-naked and stunned silent, then slowly put my own dress back on. Just as I've zipped it up, I hear a soft knock.

"I've found the perfect one for you."

I slide the lock open, and Alex steps in, carrying a hideous floral-patterned dress.

"Strip," he orders as he pulls the thing off the hanger.

I oblige, and he gets it on me. It's awful, really awful. Black with giant blue and yellow flowers, it's boxy and baggy and better suited to a schoolmarm twice my age.

"Ah." Alex gives me a cockeyed grin in the mirror. "That's more like it."

"You want me to wear this to the wedding?"

"Yep."

"It's hideous."

"Yep."

"But—"

"No buts. We had a deal. I get to pick the dress, and this is the dress I pick." He crosses his arms over his chest and nods with self-satisfaction.

"Oh for fuck's sake." I shake my head and roll my eyes at him. "You act like you've just won something. This isn't a competition."

He scoffs. "Isn't it?"

I frown at him in the mirror. There goes our good mood, again.

"Tell me something." Alex works the zipper down my back. "Have you told Greg about me?"

I can't hold his intense gaze through the mirror, so I glance down at the floor. He reads me like a book.

"Do you ever plan to tell him about me?"

Greg already knows about you, it just wasn't me who told him. I cringe at the reminder and the sting of guilt, and start to babble, grasping desperately for some sort of defense for my inaction. "That was the miscommunication. I was going to tell him about you last night, but then his girlfriend broke up with him. I couldn't dump all of this on him when he'd just had his heart broken. And then Jake accidentally told him, so he—"

"Wait." Alex's head snaps up and he scowls at me. "He has a *girlfriend*?"

"What's the big deal? I have a *boyfriend*, remember?" I gesture at Alex's chest as if to remind him of his status.

"No," Alex corrects me, "I'm your *sort-of* boyfriend."

I frown.

"She broke his heart," he mumbles, like he's thinking out loud. Then, looking almost sick, asks me, "Is he in love with her?"

I nod before I think better of it. *Dumb.*

Alex stands rigid as he stares at me, too still, the calm before the storm. And then the storm breaks.

"You have got to be *fucking* kidding me." Alex groans loudly and rubs his face with his palms, then he skewers me with a cold stare. "Ariana, I've tried to be patient. I've tried to keep my mouth shut, but this is bullshit. Your husband is a *fucking* idiot, and he doesn't deserve you."

I'm stunned and feeling defensive, but when I open my mouth to argue, my voice comes out meek and pathetic, "Please don't talk about him like that. You don't know him. You don't know the situation—"

"The situation?" He seethes, "He's in *love* with another woman, and you're protecting him. You're defending him from me while you keep *me* at arm's length."

His icy tone has me close to tears again. All I want is to get out of this dress, out of this store, and out of this conversation. But Alex stands between me and the door; he has me trapped.

"Why are you yelling at me?" I'm exaggerating, he's not actually yelling.

"Because I'm angry." Okay, now he's yelling. "Because I want you and he has you, and he doesn't *fucking* deserve you. Because I *love* you, and you love *him*."

I can't contain myself anymore. I collapse backwards onto the little triangle chair in the corner and jab the heels of my palms into my eyes as the tears start to roll down my cheeks.

"What do you want from me?" I sob.

"I want *you*."

"You have me," I insist.

Alex lets out a sardonic laugh as he paces in the tiny space. A step forward and then back is about all he can manage as he fists his hands in his hair.

"You do have me, Alex. As much as I can give you right now, you have it, but I understand if it's not enough for you. I know you're tired of hearing me say that things are complicated, but they are. If that bothers you so much, maybe this isn't going to work."

Alex's shoulders slump and his face falls. "Ariana...fuck."

I straighten my spine and try to wipe my face dry, but I'm too far gone. I need out of this place right now. "I want to leave."

"Wait. I'm sorry. Shit."

"Now," I bite out between a sucking breath and a sniff.

Alex blinks.

"I want to leave right now!"

"Okay." Alex tries to touch my shoulder.

I shrug him away. I don't want him to touch me. I don't want him to be sweet. I just want to be angry with him. It's easier to just be angry with him.

"Let's get you out of this dress." Alex's voice is gentle and he tries to touch my arm again, but I push his hand away.

"Please, just give me some space. I'll be out in a minute."

Alex exhales a shaky breath, but he leaves the dressing stall, leaning against the wall outside to wait for me. I yank the dress off and toss it over the door at him.

"Ariana."

"What."

"Here are my keys. When you're ready, head on out to the truck and wait for me there. I'll be out in a minute. Okay?" He gently lays his keys on the floor just inside the stall.

When I have my sundress back on, I look at the mirror and wipe the tears from my cheeks. I look like a goddamn raccoon. I resent those women who can cry pretty. I cry like I come—loud, wet, and messy. It's not pretty. And that's fine when I'm home alone, but not here at a shop surrounded by people. I take a few deep breaths and fan at my face, but it's no use.

Resigned, I retrieve Alex's keys from the floor and start toward the exit. I keep my head low, avoiding eye contact as I rush toward the door and through the parking lot. Once inside Alex's truck, I can't help when the sobs come again. *What is wrong with me?* I moan in desperation, wishing for once to not be a simpering sop.

I see Alex leave the store and walk toward the truck with a garment bag slung over his shoulder. Seriously? He actually bought that hideous dress?

Shaking my head at him, I sort of laugh, which somehow ends the tears. Sliding across the seat, I unlock his door. He hangs the dress from a hook in the back, then settles into the driver's seat. He sits very still for a long moment. Even with the AC blasting, the heat of the summer night suffocates. I break into a sweat and the sensation ratchets up my anxiety. I feel gutted, exhausted, and now I'm damp too.

"Ariana." Alex's voice registers just above a whisper. "I'm sorry."

"I know."

"This is really hard for me."

"I know."

"I know it's hard for you too." His breath comes out heavy. "I shouldn't have said those things. And, Ariana, I can handle *complicated*. Okay?"

I don't know what to say, so I say nothing. He glances at me, and I give him a firm nod. He stares for a moment longer before he shifts the truck into gear and heads north. We travel in absolute silence, so consumed with our thoughts that neither of us thinks to even turn on the radio.

When we reach my street, Alex parks the truck in his usual spot, and shuts off the lights. He unstraps his belt and slides close to me, but stops when I shrink away.

"Ariana, talk to me, please."

"I don't know what to say." I can't hold his eye contact. I look at my hands. "I just need to get away for a few days and clear my head."

"Shit. Please tell me I didn't just fuck this up. Please tell me this isn't the end for us." He moves closer to me and captures my hands in his. "Ariana, I'm in love with you, and I know you feel the same way. I know it's a messy situation, I get that. I'm sorry I snapped. Just...please come back to me. Go clear your head, if that's what you need to do, but please come back to me."

I glance up and immediately regret it. The pained look in his eyes pulls at something deep inside me. I've hurt him. I've hurt everyone.

My tears come again, and my voice falters with a sob as I say, "I have to go."

Alex's jaw tenses, but he doesn't argue. With a curt nod, he releases my hands and scoots away. He reaches over his shoulder to pull the garment bag across the seat, and silently hands it to me.

I stare at it for a moment before lamely offering, "Thanks."

With that, I climb from the truck and walk slowly toward the house. It's empty, dark and quiet, too quiet. I can't bear the silence so I turn on the television just for the noise, a distraction from all the empty *space* around me.

In the bedroom, I carefully pack a bag for Greg. Then I pack one for myself, mindlessly dumping clothes into the luggage. When it's nearly full, just enough room to roll up the dress and shove it on top of the rest, I rip the plastic garment bag open and gasp. Inside, instead of the hideous floral thing, I find the beautiful copper dress.

Oh. God. My knees give out, and I fall onto the bed. I curl up into a ball beside the dress and the tears come again, in long, heavy sobs that shake the mattress. I weep and shudder, and want to cry myself to sleep, but sleep won't come.

I urge my mind to blank, to empty; but it's no use. I'm full of words now. They swirl around me like a maelstrom, sucking me down into an abyss. I'm drowning in all the words I should have said...to Greg...to Alex. All the words I should have said, but didn't.

24—Saturday June 18, 2005

Any hint of emotion is gone now, wiped clean from Greg's face like yesterday's makeup. He wears his mask of impassivity like he wears his sunglasses—protection, a shield. But this mask is the face I know. This stoic, aloof man is the one I've woken up beside for over a decade. And looking at him now, it's almost impossible to recognize the man I'd watched drown his troubles in whiskey just two nights ago.

He's clearly still hungover, though, the evidence of his prior meltdown apparent in the purple circles under his eyes, which peek out beneath the dark lenses of his sunglasses. His clothes are rumpled as if he's slept in them for two days, which, of course, he has. And his hair is a spiky mess.

Jake, too, is not looking his best. His eyes are heavy-lidded; his skin sallow; and his hair is plaited into hastily woven, sloppy braids.

Not that I have room to judge. I look like warmed-over road kill. I had considered makeup this morning—staring into the mirror, frowning at my tear-streaked cherry red cheeks and puffy, bloodshot eyes—but it had seemed like too much trouble.

The drive to the airport is silent. Greg grunts a vague hello and helps me heft the luggage into the truck bed, then waits for me to take a seat and strap in before handing me a breakfast taco. Jake just nods.

At the airport, we amble through check in and security to find our gate. The effort drains what little energy we have, and, exhausted, we collapse into the plastic seats set in front of a giant window at our gate. Jake stretches his long legs out in front of him, and leans his head against the rigid chair to nap. Greg scrunches forward, his elbows on his knees, his nose buried in a book. I stare out the window, my unfocused eyes gazing blankly at the distant horizon, squinting in the harsh light of day.

On the plane, I take the seat by the window. This is new. Before, I would always sandwich myself between my boys, avoiding the view outside. But today, I want to look. I want to see the world with eyes wide open.

Greg frowns at my seat selection, but doesn't say anything. He sits beside me and reopens his book—Kerouac. On his other side, Jake folds himself into the aisle seat, smirking irritably as he tries to stretch out and get more sleep. I turn away, focusing outside. I watch the ground crew perform the essential minutia of air travel, then we back out of the terminal, and slowly slalom toward the runway.

As we take off, I watch, wide-eyed and a little giddy. The ground falls away and my city, my home, shrinks to nothing and disappears behind us.

Gliding ever higher, my bird's eye view becomes a God's eye view. The topography becomes an abstraction, an indecipherable mass of greens and browns and grays, just shapes and textures, until that too is blotted out by the blinding white glare of powder puff clouds.

From up here in the heavens, everything seems so simple. All those little dramas, and the big dramas too, are a million miles away, or at least thirty-thousand feet below. Soaring above it all, I am removed, exempt. With silent lucidity, I am given perspective, a wider view. Yet, all I can see is the look on Alex's face when I'd told him goodbye last night.

I close my eyes, hoping to wipe the image away, but it's branded on the backs of my eyelids. His face tight with strain, his blue eyes sad. His lips twisted and pinched, holding in all those words left unsaid. With a heavy sigh, I rest my cheek against the window.

It seems only an instant later that I wake with a jolt. Swallowing a loud yelp, I scramble to sit up and blink my bleary eyes to see. Out the window, a glittery river zig-zags across the land. Is it the Mississippi? How long have I been asleep?

I turn to find Greg watching me, his hand gently caressing mine. When our eyes meet, he lifts a corner of his lips in a sheepish grin.

"Sorry. I didn't mean to startle you."

I rub the sleep from my eyes.

"You're not afraid anymore," Greg says in a hushed voice. When I frown in confusion, he clarifies. "Afraid of flying."

"Oh," I glance out the window and grin. "I guess not."

Greg's lips tease at a smile, but it doesn't happen. His expression stays in neutral when he says, "I feel like such a shithead, because I sort of miss it."

"You miss my fear of flying? Why?"

Greg links our fingers and brings my hand to his lips for a soft kiss. Then in a whisper I almost don't hear, he admits, "It made me feel needed."

Not sure what to say, my mouth flounders open and closed. Finally, I whisper, "Greg—"

The speakers crackle overhead and a member of the air crew begins issuing instructions for landing. Jake wakes with a snort and straightens his seat. Greg returns his tray table to its locked position, his mask of impassivity firmly back in place. I reach for his hand, lifting it to my lips, returning his gentle kiss. He gives me a forced, toothless smile.

· · ·

I, Ariana Elizabeth Goody, take you Gregory Christopher Hendricks, to be my husband

    To have and to hold from this day forward

    For better or for worse

    For richer, for poorer

    In sickness and in health

    To love, honor and cherish, until death do us part

    I want to cry.

Why does the memory hurt? Why does remembering that beautiful day bring sadness? I shake my head, trying to dislodge the thoughts, but they keep coming—a barrage of smiles in silk, laughter in lace. I remember every moment in excruciating detail. There's Greg's sweet smile as he watches Dad guide me down the aisle to be by his side. I can still feel the sensation of Greg's shaking hands as he slides the ring on my finger. I can taste his kiss, our first as husband and wife. I feel the gentle sway of our first dance, and hear The Cure's "Just Like Heaven" playing in the background as Greg holds me tight and we circle across the dance floor.

As if he can read my thoughts, Greg presses his hand over mine and laces our fingers together. I glance at him, expecting to see his usual placid expression, unruffled and unmoved. But his mask is off. The muscles of his face are tight, pinched, and his eyes are sad, the brilliant amber irises dulled.

My heart twists and squeezes in my chest, the guilt almost overwhelming. I furrow my brow, confused, and he gives me an empty smile, a poor attempt that doesn't reach the corners of his mournful eyes. He looks back toward the front of the room to where Ben and Cassie are saying "I do." I stare at Greg's profile for a moment before I, too, look away.

I want to cry.

· · ·

"I knew her first, brother, I introduced you," Jake shouts into the microphone. It whines with feedback and he backs off a bit before continuing. He's wearing a sleek black suit, and his jet black hair is plaited in twin, tight braids, the bottoms wrapped in leather. He looks drunk and deliriously happy, a goofy, wide grin spread across his face. "I said that to Greg a lot when these two first met. It was the best blackmail I had and I used it all the time." To random chuckles and guffaws, he elaborates. "For example, if Greg were going into the kitchen, I'd shout, 'Make me a sandwich.' Well, I think you all can imagine the colorful responses he gave me." The crowd snickers. Greg shakes his head and rolls his eyes, but he's smiling. "So I'd say, 'You only know her cuz of me, brother, you owe me.' And apparently Greg

couldn't argue with that, because he made me a lot of sandwiches that fall—

The crowd laughs at something Jake has said in his toast to Ben and Cassie, and the ruckus shakes me out of my reverie. I blink back the flood of memories and push a faux smile out as I scan the room.

Why does every detail of this wedding resonate—each special moment ringing my head like a bell? Nothing about this event is similar to my wedding to Greg. The colors are all different. The time of year is off by a few months. There's a roof over our heads, whereas Greg and I married under the stars. And yet, I'm repeatedly battered by a torrent of vignettes from my past. Up front, Jake has the microphone, the cord wrapped around his fist as if he's about to start singing, and my mind takes me back yet again.

"To this day, the song Greg wrote for Ari is my favorite song to sing, so that's what I'm going to do." Jake turns to us and winks, then takes a deep breath and launches into an a cappella version of the song Greg wrote for me, serenading us.

The tears come, too many to stop. I use the handkerchief Dad gave me to mop up the mess before it mucks up my makeup, but I don't really care. I sway, and lean against Greg. He hugs an arm around me and we stand together, listening to our best friend sing the song my husband wrote for me. It's one of the most beautiful moments of my life. Greg feels it too, squeezing me tight and beaming that thousand-watt smile. When Jake finishes, we all raise our glasses and toast. I take a sip of champagne and kiss my new husband.

$$\cdot \quad \cdot \quad \cdot$$

It starts with a poppy beat from the drummer, then the guitarist joins, and with a flourish of showmanship, the synth player of Ben and Cassie's wedding band hits those iconic first few notes of The Cure's "Just Like Heaven." It's our song. I freeze, then nearly jump when I feel Greg's hand on mine.

He leans in close and asks, "May I have this dance?"

When I nod, Greg guides me to the parquet dancefloor at the front of the ballroom, and there we dance to the first song we ever danced to as a married couple. It feels nice, to relax in his arms, to lean against him, to feel his heartbeat against mine. But it's different now, less intimate somehow; we're disconnected even as we're tangled together. The lyrics of our song seem different now, too, so much more sad than I remember. Yet, still, we sway together, dancing in the deepest ocean, lost and lonely in a sea of memories.

. . .

"Damn, Ari." Mason, the groom's little brother, folds me into a stifling hug. "You look amazing as ever. Nice dress."

I look down at the copper dress and nearly laugh. *Fuck yeah, it's a nice dress.*

I'd had second thoughts about wearing it tonight. It felt strange to wear the dress my lover bought me to attend a wedding with my husband, like the act of wearing the dress was a betrayal of Greg and our marriage. But wouldn't *not* wearing the dress have been a betrayal of Alex?

Alex. I sigh, dreamy-like, then shake my head and frown as I try to remember what Mason had said to me. Oh right, the dress. *Fuck yeah, it's a nice dress.*

"Wow. You've grown up, Mason. You're a man now." I press one hand to his stubbly cheek, the coarse hairs remind me of Alex. With the other hand, I tilt my champagne flute up and down the rest of my drink. Okay, so it's possible I'm drunk.

Greg and I both seem to be searching for answers at the bottom of a bottle tonight. We've been drinking almost non-stop since the ceremony ended. And then, at some point, we separated. I don't recall the exact moment when Greg's hand was no longer holding mine, his presence no longer a constant at my side. I just remember spotting him up near the front of the room by the bandstand, while I leaned against the bar in the back.

At this very moment, Greg and Ben, the groom, slur their way through an Irish drinking song up near the stage, the wedding singer having to smack Ben's hand every time he tries to steal the microphone. Meanwhile, I sway with Ben's little—though not so little anymore—

brother Mason, who is getting a bit too friendly with his hands. But who can blame the kid for his roaming touch? In this dress, I'm completely irresistible. He's drawn to me like metal to a magnet, like a leech to engorged flesh, like a white cat to black pants—

"Whoa there, watch the hands, you little fucker. You might be as tall as me now, but I can still kick your ass." Jake's voice shines through the champagne fog.

I turn to give him a wide grin and sing his name. "Jaaaaaaake."

"May I have this dance, Ms. Drunky Pants?"

"That rhymed," I giggle absently.

Through Jake's laughter and Mason's whining protests, I feel hands replace hands in a changing of the guard and collapse against Jake as we sort of shuffle to a Whitney Houston song.

"What the hell is wrong with you?" Jake asks as he holds my limp form upright.

"Such a good question." I sigh. "Hey Jake?"

"Yeah?"

"How do you know when you're in love?"

"Oh Jesus Christ."

"I mean, is it like, 'Freeze Frame: I'm totally in love' or is it like a rash that just spreads and spreads and itches and shit."

Jake howls with laughter. "Okay, Two Shoes, I think it's time for you to pass out for the night. Let's go."

With that, I'm on the move, up and in Jake's arms.

"Put me down."

"No."

"Please?"

"No."

"Hey Jake?"

"Yeah?"

"Why am I such an asshole?"

"You're not an asshole, Two Shoes. You're just drunk."

"No. I don't mean right now. I mean...always."

"Honey, you're not an asshole."

"Hey Jake?"

"Yeah?"

"I love you."

"Oh for fuck's sake."

"Not like I love him, but I do love you."

"Him?"

"Him." I sigh the word.

25–Sunday June 19, 2005

I wake with a jolt, and the sudden movement assaults my head like a hammer. Squinting, I look around the room to find Greg splayed out beside me, on top of the sheets, still fully dressed, shoes and all.

My amazing dress is across the room, draped over the chair in the corner, and I glance under the covers to find I'm wearing only my bra and undies. What the hell?

I vaguely remember the end of the night, nothing solid beyond Jake chasing Mason off and us dancing to Whitney Houston's "Greatest Love of All." Shit. I hope I didn't say or do anything stupid or embarrassing.

I climb out of the bed and hobble to the bathroom for a shower. When I'm clean, I slip on a robe and go out to the balcony to sit in one of the lounge chairs.

Our room has a spectacular view of the Cascades Lobby of the Opryland hotel. I stare down at the indoor waterfall, and rotating bar now serving Bloody Marys and Mimosas for brunch cocktail hour. I take in the sounds of the space—the roar of water and the rumble of tourists—which volley off the sun-soaked glass ceiling that spans the chasm between buildings. The whole scene hurts my head, but I don't retreat to the darkness and quiet of our hotel room. I sit and take it.

"Ouch." Greg's voice greets me before I see him. I look up to find him frowning at the bright light of day. He looks like a member of the brat pack, his tux wrinkled, his bow tie draped open around his unbuttoned collar, and his hair spiked every which way. He plops down into the chair beside me and squints in my direction. "Damn, I don't think I've had that much to drink since...well, Thursday."

I laugh at the awkward joke, finding relief in the levity.

Greg squints and grimaces. "It's way too bright and noisy; what are you doing out here?"

I shrug and look down at the scene below. There's a bright orange carp circling in the shallow pond at the base of the waterfall.

"I'm watching Giuseppe," I answer.

"Who?"

"That carp." I point and Greg strains to see. "He's the orange one with a fleck of red on his top."

"I see him."

"Giuseppe."

"Giuseppe the carp?" Greg grins.

"He's new to the pool. The other fish don't know what to make of him. They're jealous of his fleck of red."

"Well he's clearly prettier than the rest. Are they bullying him?" He sounds concerned.

"No. The fish of Nashville are as friendly as the people—they don't bully, but they are a little suspicious of the new fish in their midst. They're watching him from afar to see if he's cool or not."

"Sounds lonely."

"You have no idea." I'm on a roll. "There was a girl fish at his last pond, Lucy, but he had to leave her behind when he moved here."

Greg glances over, pinning me with those doleful eyes. "That's sad. Will he ever see her again?"

I realize this story has gone off the rails, but I can't seem to stop my mouth. "Probably not, but there are plenty of other fish in the pond."

Greg grimaces. "You know, coming from a romance writer, that ending is kind of depressing."

"Might be why I haven't written a new book in eight years," I joke. But the humor drains out of me when I add, "You don't think the ending could be happy?"

Greg frowns at Giuseppe, but says nothing.

"I think it could be happy; it could be anything. It's full of possibilities."

Silence falls between us, getting heavier by the minute, a pall thick with words left unsaid. Finally, when I can take it no more, I speak up. My voice cracking when I ask, "The thing with Kate, is it irreversible?"

Greg watches me carefully, then says just, "I don't know."

"You should talk to her."

Silence.

"If you love her—"

"The thing is," Greg pauses and looks down at his lap where his fingers play with the cuffs of his sleeves, like a little boy forced to wear stuffy, grownup clothes, "I don't think it's mutual."

I frown, but listen, waiting for him to continue. When he remains silent, I speak up. "But... I mean, her ultimatum... She wants to be with you. She wants you all for herself."

He shakes his head, still not looking at me, and quietly counters. "That's not love. That's control."

"But..." I search for my words, not sure what to say next. I bend my head, trying to catch his eye. He glances up at me, waiting, anxious to hear my thoughts. How surreal is this? "I think... I mean... Our circumstances aren't exactly normal. Not everyone is cut out for the poly thing."

Greg lets out a brittle laugh. "Very true. I'm pretty sure *I'm* not cut out for it." His laughter subsides and his wistful smile slips a bit when he asks, "What about your guy, how is he handling it?"

My guy. I'm surprised by the subject change, and Greg's casual mention of Alex. He's keeping his expression flat, his emotions carefully tucked behind that familiar mask, but I know he's hurting. Guilt cracks my chest open. "Greg, I'm sorry. I should have told you about Alex sooner. You should have heard it from me, not Jake. I meant to tell you, but—"

"I know." Greg gives me an appeasing nod. "You were going to tell me Thursday night, weren't you?"

I nod. I watch him for a moment before adding, "And to answer your question, he's struggling with our situation too."

Greg grimaces at my use of the word "our" and I nearly laugh at the absurdity of it. Who exactly does "our" encompass—me and Greg, me and Alex, or me and Alex and Greg and Kate? After all, we're all four of us in this, *our situation*. As if Greg has just gone through the same thought process, his eyes soften with empathy.

"Struggling? How so?"

"We had a big fight about it on Friday night. I don't even know if..." I can't finish. I don't want to say the words.

Greg nods absently as his gaze drifts back down to Giuseppe. Our carp has joined his pond-mates as they school in a mad feeding frenzy at the edge of the water, where a small boy is throwing pellets of food at them. Quietly, Greg speaks again, "If I asked you to leave him and close our marriage, would you?"

I look at Greg, but he won't meet my gaze. My eyes bore holes in his profile as I try to determine if this is his ultimatum to me. And if it is, shouldn't he look me in the eyes when he issues it? Finally, my throat parched, I ask, "Are you asking?"

Greg finally looks at me. "No. But would you?"

Wedding vows cover all the extremes: rich and poor, sick and well, life and death. But no one ever tells you where most marriages really live: the in-between. Most marriages are boring. My marriage had been boring, until I'd strapped us into this roller coaster ride, the thing jerking us through a series of peaks and valleys, making us want to puke one moment and howl the next. Staring at my husband, who waits patiently for my answer, my stomach bottoms out as I'm once again turned upside down on this screaming ride.

"I was suffocating. I needed air." That's what I'd told Alex when he asked why I'd opened the marriage. And I had been, suffocating, that is. Naïvely, I'd thought all I needed was to come up for air, like Guiseppe in his pond, puckering and gasping at the surface of the water. I thought I'd catch my breath, have a look around, then tuck back into the murky depths of my marriage.

On that day in December, naked on the couch, bare and vulnerable, I'd been bubbling with nervous energy when Greg and I agreed to open the marriage, hardly noticing that we'd also agreed to close our marriage were anything to cause problems between us.

"You and me, Ari, that's what's important here." That's what he'd said, and that's what I'd believed at the time. But things have changed since then, we've changed since then. I stare at Greg, and hardly recognize him anymore. And when he stares at me, who does he see—the girl he says he still loves, or the woman I've become?

When I'd started this journey, I hadn't realized I was lost, so I hadn't planned to find myself. But find myself I had, and in so doing, somewhere along the way, I think I lost Greg.

I blink back tears. I know he's waiting for an answer to his question, but I think we both already know what that answer is. Still, I say it, "No."

There is no visible reaction on Greg's face. He doesn't seem surprised. He just nods as his gaze drifts back down to Giuseppe. Eventually, it's Greg who says the words. "It's over between us, isn't it?"

I turn to look at him and find he's staring at me, a blend of sadness and exhaustion in his topaz gaze. He's beautiful when he says goodbye.

My eyes sting with tears. "Yes. I think it is."

"This has been coming for a while."

"I think it has."

"It wasn't just the open relationship."

"I don't think so." I fist the sleeves of the robe I'm wearing in my palms and squeeze, needing to hold onto something. "I think that just delayed the inevitable."

Greg nods, we both do. "I can't remember a time when I didn't love you, Ari. I think a part of me always will."

The tears push forward. It's not my usual loud, ugly cry. These tears are silent, rolling down my cheeks to dampen the collar of my robe. I find myself on my feet, wrapped in Greg's arms. I melt against him with a sob. "I still love you, too, Greg. A part of me always will."

He holds me tight, rubbing his hands down my back in gentle strokes. It soothes me, even as the tenderness breaks my heart. I try not to think that this will likely be the last time he holds me like this. I try not to think about how disturbingly easy it has been to end our twelve-year-long relationship.

Just a few words. After years together and months of all this complicated bullshit, for the end to be so simple seems like the punchline to a lame joke. How can it be so easy? And how can something so easy hurt so much? Does it hurt *because* it's so easy? We're not even fighting. Twelve years together, and neither of us sees fit to fight.

. . .

"But what does this mean?" My mom asks, her face a study in motherly concern.

I'm not sure how else to explain it. I look to Dad for support, but he's giving me his worried-dad look too.

With a sigh, I slump deeper in my chair. "There's not much more to say. Greg and I have decided to separate."

"You say that like you've just added an item to a grocery list. This is a big deal, Ari Beth. Aren't you upset?"

"Of course I'm upset, Mom, but I've cried enough for one day."

We sit in a stretch of silence that feels a mile long before Mom talks again, crossing her arms over her chest, eying me suspiciously. "You know, I thought something was wrong. It's been impossible to get you on the phone lately, and when we did get to talk to you, you seemed so distant and distracted. But you kept saying everything was fine."

"I'm sorry, Mom. It's been a crazy time, and I just needed to figure it all out."

"Where are you going to live?"

"I don't know. I suppose we'll share the house for now. We haven't gotten that far. We just agreed to a separation this morning."

"You know, I never liked that house."

I laugh, relieved by the subtle shift in subject. "What's wrong with my house?"

"I don't like how the kitchen is separated from the living room. It's too chopped up. I always thought you should have knocked out that middle wall."

Dad nods in agreement, and I roll my eyes. "Well, I'll keep that in mind on future house hunts."

"Honey," Mom's tone softens and almost turns to begging, "why don't you move back home?"

Oh my God, what?

"We still have your old room. It's just like you left it. Well, we can move the treadmill."

"Dad, please tell Mom that it's considered a step in the wrong direction to move back in with your parents when you're 30."

"You're 29 for a few more months, dear." Mom's on a roll. "You could write your books here. You know, you might have more success here anyway. Maybe this is where your mojo is."

"My mojo?" I can't help but laugh. Then, serious again, argue, "Mom, I'm not moving back here. I have a life in Austin. I have stuff to go back to."

"Stuff? What *stuff*?"

"Kathryn, leave the poor girl alone." Dad tries to help.

The front door bangs open and closed, and we all turn to see Jake come into the dining room with a big grin and a wide glance at the food on the table. "Mr. and Mrs. Goody, hope you don't mind if I crash dinner."

"Didn't Greg's mom feed you?" I ask.

"Well, yeah, but I always have room for Kathryn Goody's fried chicken."

"Jake, sit down, fill a plate." Mom grins, and Dad shakes Jake's hand as he slides into the chair across from me.

Mom gives Jake a sly grin. "Maybe you can help me talk some sense into Ari. Don't you think she'd be better off if she moved back home?"

"Mom," I huff, "for crying out loud."

"Sweet. I'm just in time for the Goody Family Circus." Jake settles into his chair, dropping a dollop of mashed potatoes on his plate as he winks at me.

"Maybe you'll tell me," Mom turns to Jake. "What's this *stuff* Ari Beth has to go back to in Austin?"

Jake's eyebrows shoot up and he glances at me, not sure what he's supposed to say. So I relieve him of the torment and answer for him.

"There's a guy. Okay?"

"What?" Mom's voice hits an octave I've never heard before; a shriek so loud it startles Banjo the Beagle awake with a frightened yelp. "A guy? But you and Greg just separated this morning."

"It's really complicated."

"But—"

"Mom," I plead. God, I do not want to have this conversation right now. Given that the fight with Alex is still hanging over my head, and the breakup with Greg is so fresh, this seems like the absolute worst time to be talking about this.

"Honey," Mom's tone completely changes, sounding sweet and motherly as she reaches over and touches my arm. "You know you can tell us anything, even the complicated stuff. We love you, and we just want you to be happy."

I'm brought nearly to tears and whimper, "Ah, Mom."

"So, what's his name?" she demands.

I laugh a little at her Jekyll and Hyde routine. "His name is Alex."

Mom grins, seeming oddly excited by that detail. "How'd you meet? I mean, you're married, how'd that happen."

I consider hedging, finding yet another reason to avoid discussing the matter at hand, but I don't. I owe it to Alex and I owe it to myself to finally be honest.

"I met him in a bar," I start, and then I just keep going. I tell them everything, including the complicated parts. Well, not *everything*. I gloss over a lot of the story, leaving out the prick parade to focus on Greg and Alex. And even when it comes to Alex, I parent-proof the story. They don't need to know about my knight's dungeon of love. When I'm finally done, and they're mostly up-to-date, I feel a lightness in my chest, a heavy weight off my shoulders, to have it all said.

"Okay. Well...wow." Mom stumbles over her words before venturing to ask a question, "So, this is pretty serious then, you and Alex?"

I think back to that awful fight, to the look on Alex's face when I last told him goodbye. "I don't know."

They all stare at me, but it's Jake who speaks up, "What do you mean you don't know?"

I groan. "I think he thinks we broke up."

"Why would he think that?"

"Well," I flinch. "We sort of had a huge argument about Greg, and I told him I need time to think and then I left town."

Jake laughs. "Ari, get your head out of your ass." To my mom, he adds, "Pardon my French."

My mom just laughs too. I pout. "You're not helping."

"Seriously? You need help with this problem?" Jake shakes his head. "Jesus, Ari, how do you manage to make everything so complicated? It's simple—he's in love with you, you're in love with him—just fly back home and tell him."

"Who said anything about love?"

"You did, last night when you were drunk."

I frown.

"Do you deny it?"

I frown deeper, and then, weirdly, I feel the urge to cry. My vision blurs, and it's only when I shake my head and a few of the tears spill over that I can see clearly. No, I don't deny it. I'm falling in love with Alex. I smile, even as I wipe my tears away. Glancing around the table, I see they're all smiling too.

For the first time in a while, Dad speaks, "It's good to see you happy, Ari Beth."

"I'm crying, Dad."

"That you are, pumpkin, that you are."

26—Monday June 20, 2005

God, it's hot out here, and too sunny, and this dress doesn't breathe very well. The tangled limbs of live oaks aren't long enough to reach over the road, leaving the asphalt blacktop to bake for hours in the summer heat.

The rush-hour of neighborhood joggers and dog walkers all stare at me as they pass. I'm hard to miss, shining like a new penny in the hot Austin sun. I'd captured the fascination of most of the passengers on the bus too. Should have taken a cab, but I wasn't thinking when I left, or rather, I was thinking too much.

I see my destination up ahead, but it shimmers in the heat like a mirage in the desert, and so I quicken my pace, anxious to arrive, practically running when I reach Alex's front door. I knock like Pete, urgent and loud, demanding and desperate.

There is something truly magical about the way a man looks at the woman he loves. In that first instant of recognition, Alex's expression softens and his eyes fill with warmth, a light that glows brighter than the sun. "You came back."

I nod.

Alex doesn't move, like he's frozen to the spot, stunned and just staring at me with a smile stuck on his face.

"Alex, can I come in? I'm melting like a wicked witch out here."

Alex smiles wider and quickly steps aside. "Yeah. Of course. Sorry."

The air conditioning is a gift from God, a snow-capped breeze that blows down from the ceiling. I close my eyes and take a moment to feel it.

I hear Alex moving around me, and then he pushes a glass into my hands. It's water, and I drink it all in a few sloppy gulps.

"Did you walk here?"

I nod as I wipe my lips with the back of my hand. "And took the bus."

"Why didn't you call? I just got off work, I would have come to get you."

Because some things should be said in person, not over the phone while arranging a ride. I open my mouth to launch into my memorized monologue, but my thoughts derail as I stare at the kitchen. The wall which used to stand in the way is gone, demolished into dusty piles of rubble on the floor. "Holy shit, Alex, what happened?"

Alex chuckles, "Since I had a whole weekend to myself and some, uh, issues to work out, I thought I'd go ahead and take the wall down." He gestures at the space. "I've been meaning to open this up for a couple of years. Never liked how the kitchen was cut off from the living room."

"Oh man, my parents are going to love you."

"Your parents?"

I blink, and my mind comes back online. "Alex, we need to talk."

Alex holds up a hand to stop me and his mouth flounders open for a moment before he says, "Before you say anything, I just need to tell you that I'm so sorry about the things I said to you. I've been playing that night over and over again in my head, and I'm...so...sorry. I promise you, I won't put you in the middle like that ever again. I know this isn't a competition and I know the situation is complicated, and I don't care. All I care about is you, and—"

"I love you."

He blinks. "What?"

"I love you, Alex."

Alex's entire body stiffens. His breath sucks in, and his eyes go wide, as if I've surprised him, as if he really hadn't expected those words. It takes a moment for them to sink in, and I watch as the dawning comes over his expression. His slight grin slides into a smile, and the smile widens until lines fan out around his brilliant blue eyes.

"Ariana, my God."

A nervous breath saws out of my lungs as I realize, *my God, indeed*, I've said it. I've made it real. And the look in his eyes is powerful, it's overwhelming. It makes me nervous, the butterflies in my belly all aflutter. Suddenly, I feel the need to explain everything, every word I need to say ready to come out of me all at once. The hours I'd spent planning and practicing my memorized monologue are wasted when he unravels me so thoroughly with that awed expression on his face. And so I stand there in the midst of the rubble on his floor, and ramble breathlessly.

"I'm sorry I didn't tell you before. I felt it, I did, but... I've only ever said those words to Greg and Jake and my parents. And it mattered to me to be sure, even though I *was* sure, I still, I don't know, I waited. And maybe I waited too long, but it's out now. I've told everyone about you. You're not a secret, you were never a secret. You were a surprise, though. I never expected... What we share is so different, and it's all happening so fast. And it's not at all what I thought would happen. I mean, when I started all of this, I never thought... It's important that you understand that I never meant to leave my husband. That was never my intention. And I did love him very much, and a part of me always will—"

"Wait," Alex holds up a hand again to stop my babbling. "Leave your husband?"

I stutter before I answer plainly. "Greg and I have decided to separate."

"Ariana, my God," he repeats. He takes a few steps closer to me. "Are you okay?"

If there is a more perfect question Alex could have asked in this moment, I don't know what it is. The sweetness in his expression and the concern in his eyes absolutely confirm every emotion I feel toward him. He is a good man, and I love him dearly for that.

"Yeah. I'm okay."

Alex stands in the middle of his living room staring at me with his jaw hanging open, looking absolutely stunned. But it's only for a moment, before he crosses the room in three long strides and kisses me senseless. *God, yes!* The power of his mouth is exquisite, gentle and demanding, and it feels like heaven. His taste and scent, wintergreen, is like heaven too.

He pulls away too soon, grinning like a fool, and begs, "Say it again."

I grin like a fool, too, and say it again. "I love you, Alex."

Alex closes his eyes and takes a deep breath, like my words give him life. And when he opens his eyes again, he's a new man.

There's a wolfish grin on his face and a wicked twinkle in his eyes when he grabs me and slings me over his shoulder, a caveman carrying me back to his den. I yelp and squeal as he makes his way down the hall to his bedroom.

"What are you doing?" I ask with a giggle, when he smacks to my coppery-taffeta ass and sets me back on my feet.

"Are you ready to get into my pants?" Alex asks casually as he strips his shirt off and starts to untie his boots. "Because I'm absolutely desperate to fuck you right now."

I nod like a bobble-head doll and smile so wide I must look completely mental. Alex reaches around me to get at the zipper of my dress, yanking it down, and in no time at all I'm stripped bare before him. I hardly notice, all of my attention focused on the button and fly of his jeans.

Hands twitching to touch him, I yank at the waistband until the button pops open, then fumble with the zipper. My wide-eyed gaze follows the trail of auburn hair down, down, down, and my anticipation ratchets up, up, up with each notch of the zipper teeth unfastened, each inch of his flesh revealed. Never in my life have I wanted to set eyes on a man's dick more than I want to set eyes on this man's dick right now. Finally, his jeans are open and I reach in, ready to make—

Contact. I gasp and Alex groans. I wrap my fingers around his thick, warm length and slide my hand from base to... Oh wow. Oh my God, he's pierced.

With my free hand, I push his clothes down so I can get a good look, and find a magnificently beautiful dick with a thick gage barbell pierced through the tip: a Prince Albert.

"It's lovely," I mumble as I touch it, running my fingers over the cool metal and down his warm shaft. Alex tilts his head back with a groan.

"Why did you pierce it?" *What on Earth would drive a man to let someone stick a needle into his urethra?* I turn the piercing, tickling at the holes where the metal penetrates his flesh.

He groans low, and his fists clutch at my hips, but still, he manages to answer my question, "It increases sexual stimulation."

I squeeze my hand over his shaft and execute a long, slow stroke as I use my thumb to play with the ring. "It increases stimulation for you or your partner?"

"Both," he hisses through clenched teeth.

Both. Wow. I'm overwhelmed with the urge to take him into my mouth. I want to taste him—all of him, metal and man. Not even fully conscious of what I'm saying, I start to move down to my knees as I mumble, "Good things come to those who wait."

"The wait's not over yet, Little Hare." Alex says as he pulls me back up. He kicks his jeans the rest of the way off, then carries me to his shower. Inside, he turns me around so I'm forced to keep my eyes and hands to myself as he washes my hair and gives my body a full scrub. Then he cleans himself behind me, while I wait. It's torture, the waiting—masterful, glorious, exquisite, perfect torture.

•   •   •

"What would you have me do to you?" Alex whispers in my ear as he carries me, dripping wet, out to his bed. "Tell me."

I purr and stretch like a cat when he lays me down. Then he lays on top of me, covering me with his weight, patiently grinning as he expects an answer. "I would have you pierce me with your mighty sword, good knight."

Alex chuckles and rolls us until he's on his back and I'm on top. He stares up at me like he's saving the image to his memory forever. Then, with a quirk of a grin, he reaches for the drawer of the bedside table and pulls out a whole lot of condoms. Ripping one off he tosses it to me, waggling his brow suggestively. The instant I've maneuver the thing out of its wrapper and onto Alex's length, he laces his fingers around the nape of my neck, and pulls me down to deliver a scorching kiss. And while he's working me into a frenzy with his mouth, he bends his knees, presses his feet into the mattress for leverage and proceeds to pierce me with his fucking sword.

Oh. My. God! Ooooh, holy shiiiiiiit! I can feel the piercing. I sever the kiss with a gasp, seeing stars as I try to catch my breath and adjust to the exquisite sensation of Alex inside me, filling me, that erotic barbell rubbing me in all the right places as he pushes deep.

Alex, too, seems overwhelmed with sensation. His eyes roll back as he curses and squeezes his hands on my hips, holding me still against him. After that lingering first connection, he doesn't move for a long moment. We stay just like that, perfectly connected, and it feels like completeness, like finally fitting that last piece of the puzzle in place. And then he stirs inside me.

"Oooooh my God, what did you just do?" I gasp and press my hands to his chest to steady myself, a little lightheaded and seeing stars.

Alex grins. "What this?"

He makes a quick flick of his hips beneath me, and I nearly come right then and there. I yelp and gasp and Alex chuckles at my reaction. He does it again, a minimal movement that touches me *just* right. It's the piercing, it hits me in exactly the right place to send me over the edge. "Oh my God, you're hitting the spot."

"Which spot?" He plays dumb, "This spot?"

"Fuck!" I squeal and start to tremble when he hits *the* goddamn spot again.

"If you like that, you're gonna love this." Alex stirs his hips in a circle beneath me.

"Oh! Fuck!" I scream as I collapse onto his chest, on the verge of orgasm.

Alex rolls us over again and laces our fingers together, pulling my arms up over my head until I'm stretched out beneath him. He moves within me, and it's unreal. I revel in every sensation: the perfect rhythm of his steady pace, the way that metal stud rubs against me as he pulls out and presses back in, his fingers clutching mine, his weight balanced on our linked hands, his jagged inhalations breathing life into the monster on his chest.

It's a matter of just moments when I come the first time. I arch up and scream out in ecstasy. When I come down and open my eyes, I see him staring at me in awe, enraptured.

"The way you react to me..." Alex grins as he slows his pace and gathers me in his arms, hugging me tight as he rolls onto his back, continuing to fuck me from below. I come again, clinging tight to his neck as I scream and pant. When he slows his pace this time, he sits up, me in his lap, watching me with worried eyes. "Are you okay?"

I blink, confused.

"Hey." He pushes strands of hair out of my face. "You're hyperventilating."

I am? I try to catch my breath, but they come in shallow, nervous bursts.

"Breathe with me, okay? Deep breaths. In and out. In...and out. That's it. Just breathe with me."

I do as I'm told, and watch his face as the look of concern slowly starts to ebb. He stares at me with such tender eyes, such affection; it's overwhelming. With his hands caressing my face, his body still inside me, wrapped all around me, and now breathing with me, I've never felt so connected to another person in my life. I've never felt so...much.

"I feel it," I whisper with awe, like it's a revelation.

"You feel what?"

"Everything." At that, I cry. Not a lot, just a few big fat tears that streak down my cheeks. "I was numb. And then you came along and now I feel...everything. It's exhilarating, but it's terrifying, too. I'm not nearly as brave as you think I am. I'm scared, Alex. I'm scared of you. I've never felt as vulnerable as I do when I'm with you. You have so much power over me, and I don't think you even know it. You could break me. But I think I'm ready to trust that you won't."

I stop talking and the silence between us grows deafening. Alex is wide eyed with shock. But after a moment, he blinks, and then a dazzling smile spreads across his face as he cups my cheeks between his palms and wipes my tears away. "I think I just fell even more in love with you."

"You did?" Another fat tear streaks my cheek.

"I did." He wipes it away.

"Alex, I'm yours, completely." I clasp my hands against his cheeks and stare into his eyes as I ask, "Will you be mine?"

"Ariana, I've been yours since the night we met." He gives me a gentle kiss then rolls me onto my back again. "I also haven't had sex since the night we met, and I'm about to explode."

I chuckle and then gasp and nearly come out of my skin when he stirs inside me again. With that wolf's grin and a waggle of his devil's brow, he informs me, "Wait's over, Little Hare."

Acknowledgements

To the readers, thank you from the bottom of my heart. This is just the beginning. Stay tuned for Jake's story, and Greg's too.

I can't give enough thanks to my incredibly supportive and creative family. Mom Berry, Dad Berry, little sis Karen and brother-in-law Jonty, you all inspire me constantly, and I count my lucky stars to have been born into this Berry Patch. To my husband, Errek, your support lifts mountains and your silly songs are the soundtrack to a pretty amazing life.

Byron Reese, you've been a true mentor and a friend. Thank you for every opportunity and every word of encouragement and support. Monica Landers, you've been a great mentor, also, and your encouragement to put this manuscript out there is the reason it's getting published. Reagan Rothe and everyone at Black Rose Writing who've helped make this dream a reality, thank you.

To my Camparet and Casa family, you are the wind beneath my wings. Y'all share your love and hugs and humor without hesitation. The friendship and community we've built is pure magic. All my love forever! Valli, you've always been there with me; let's go somewhere where no one knows us and giggle in the corner like old times. Josh, you're an amazing person, and I'm lucky I had you in my life when I did. Michelle, your feedback and edits helped shape this ball of clay into what it is now,

I couldn't have done this without you. Carjack, you're the one who came up with the "Lost in Austin" name; dude, you're a poet. Nikki, I love you; your hugs and smiles and laughter give me life. And Heather, the third in our "Shit or Get Off the Pot" club, I shat! xxx

Lastly, I would be remiss if I didn't acknowledge the city which I love so much that I made it a character in the book. Austin, you're a hot mess sometimes, but I love you like crazy. There is so much creative energy coursing through the veins of this little college town turned metropolis. So, I give my most sincere thanks to every service industry professional and regular at my favorite dive bars and venues; Casino El Camino, The Jackalope, Mugshots, The Side Bar, Elysium, old Beerland, and old Emo's all played roles in the book, but add to the list The Lost Well and Violet Crown Social Club for further imbibed inspiration. Additionally, I'd like to acknowledge the local groups and individuals who do what they do to make Austin something special; to name just a few: Flipside and Flipizens (my Camparet, Dive Bar, and Tiny Anus family especially), the Lunch Ladies and Grampage, Fat Bottom Cabaret, Bed Post Confessions, both the flat- and banked-track Roller Derby leagues, Austin Facial Hair Club, the early morning Barton Springs regulars, the local bands who bring the crowds to Red River, the Satan's Cheerleaders, the burlesque performers and aerialists, the magicians and comedians, Mr. Lifto, Scotty Body Wotty, Peelander Yellow, the Sixth Street Cowboy, and, the one and only, Leslie Cochran, may you rest in peace.

About the Author

Born in Tulsa, Oklahoma, Christina Berry has spent most of her life in Austin, Texas where she works in online publishing. A student of history and a citizen of the Cherokee Nation, Christina created the All Things Cherokee website where she publishes Cherokee genealogy, art, and cultural content. In her free time, she helps her husband with their never-ending home-remodeling project and chronicles the adventure in a dramedy blog. Keep up with her latest at https://christinaberry.com

Note from the Author

Word-of-mouth is crucial for any author to succeed. If you enjoyed *Up for Air*, please leave a review online—anywhere you are able. Even if it's just a sentence or two. It would make all the difference and would be very much appreciated.

Thanks!
Christina

Thank you so much for reading one of our **Women's Fiction** novels.

If you enjoyed the experience, please check out our recommendation for your next great read!

The Apple of My Eye by Mary Ellen Bramwell

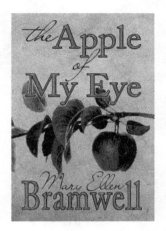

"A mature love story with an intense plot.

This book has something important to say."

–William O. Shakespeare, Professor of English,

Brigham Young University

View other Black Rose Writing titles at
www.blackrosewriting.com/books and use promo code
PRINT to receive a **20% discount** when purchasing.

CPSIA information can be obtained
at www.ICGtesting.com
Printed in the USA
LVHW090256020221
678100LV00006B/48